ZOMBIE LOVE

ZOMBIE LOVE

This is a work of fiction. All characters, organizations and events in this novel are products of the author's imagination and are not to be construed as real. Any resemblance to persons, living or dead, is entirely coincidental.

Published by Angry Sheep Publishing LLC
Findlay, Ohio

ISBN-13: 978-1-938745-24-9

Cover Design by For the Muse Design
Interior Design by JW Manus

BLOODLINES #2

SUZAN HARDEN

More Books by Suzan Harden
(Each series is in suggested reading order)

Bloodlines

Blood Magick
Zombie Love
Zombie Confidential
Zombie Wedding
Amish, Vamps & Thieves
Blood Sacrifice
Love, War & a Bulldog
Zombie Goddess
Ravaged
Sacrificed
Reality Bites
Ghouls in the Grocery Store
Resurrected
Bloodlines Shorts Anthology
Bloodlines: The First Boxed Set

Justice

Sword and Sorceress 28
("Justice")
Sword and Sorceress 30
("Diplomacy in the Dark")
Justice: The Beginning
A Question of Balance
A Modicum of Truth
A Matter of Death
A Touch of Mother
A Twist of Love
A Virtue of Child
A Hand of Father
A Measure of Knowledge
A Hint of Thief
A Cup of Conflict

Seasons of Magick

Spring
Summer
Autumn
Winter
The Seasons of Magick Anthology

The Justice Thalia Stories

Snowfall
Murder Most Fowl
The Sweetest Poison
A Granddaughter of Mine
Too Many Fish in the Sea

Tales of the Twelve

The Trickster Priestess and the Demon

Crossover Worlds

Invasion!

888-555-HERO

Hero De Facto

Hero Ad Hoc

Hero De Novo

A Very Hero Christmas

Hero De Jure

Hero In Camera

Hero Amicus Curiae

A Very Hero Wedding

A Very Hero New Year

Hero Ad Litem

Queer Eye for the Super Guy

Solar System Services, Inc.

Alone Is Not Lonely

Halloween Harvest

("A Place at the Table")

A Place at the Table

Millersburg Magick Mysteries

Spells and Sleuths

Fae and Felonies

Magick and Murder

Feline Navidad

Soccer Moms of the Apocalypse

Pestilence in Pumpkin Spice

Famine in French Vanilla

War in White Chocolate

Death in Double Mocha

Demons Run at Halloween

Miscellaneous

Sword and Sorceress 31

("Pig-Headed")

Sword and Sorceress 32

("Unexpected")

Practical Witches

Revenge Served Hot

The Yule Switch

Chocolate for Dinner

Silver Shoes and Pigs' Ears

Snipe Hunt

For updates, news, and giveaways, join Suzan's mailing list at suzanharden.blogspot.com/p/contact-me.html, or visit her website at www.suzanharden.com. You can also check her out on Facebook @SuzanHardenWriter.

To DH. You'll always be my hero.

Chapter 1

My transformation into the undead started with a pregnancy test stick.

A used pregnancy test stick.

Not mine, thank you very much.

I slammed the plastic zippered baggie, used pregnancy test stick enclosed, down on my boss's desk. "Here's your proof. Jessie Alton is knocked up. Her housekeeper confirmed it."

Ralph O'Malley recoiled in disgust. His blue eyes narrowed, and he snarled, "Jesus, Ridgeway, get that thing off my desk!" He poked at it with his pencil, pushing it away from him, until I snatched it up.

I didn't blame him. I wasn't thrilled about dumpster diving for the proof just because a major TV star peed on the damn thing, but I also didn't want my editor destroying valuable evidence. Legal would want the little stick for DNA testing in case Alton sued.

The A/C kicked on, but the weak circulation did nothing more than stir the lingering cigarette smoke in Ralph's tiny windowless office. Despite the ban on indoor smoking in Los Angeles, the publisher of *The National Scoop* ignored Ralph's predilection for cancer sticks.

"Have the copy on my desk in an hour." He eyed my grime-laden clothes. "Make that two. Get a shower first."

I hesitated a moment.

Ralph guessed at my question. He shook his head and said, "When I told you and Bill I'd have my decision on the assistant editor position on Friday, I meant on Friday." He snatched up the cigarette smoldering in the overflowing ashtray and took a puff before he added, "You've got one hour and fifty-nine minutes."

That wasn't the question I was going to ask, but a cheap thrill filtered through my aching muscles. Bill hadn't bested me out of the job.

Yet.

I focused on my pitch. "I want to do a follow up story on the private investigator—" With the baggie still in one hand, my fingers made awkward bunny ears. I suspected the man was a mercenary, not a P.I. "—Brent Poole hired to rescue his girlfriend—"

"No."

My watering eyes blinked under the double assault of his smoke and my clothes. "What?"

"I said no." Ralph's bulging orbs and quivering jowls resembled his bulldog, Emerson. At least, Ralph didn't drool all over my leg when he visited my desk.

My boss could have knocked me over with the test stick. Alton and Poole sold more issues in an hour than any other celebrity could in a week. I glared back. "This guy rescues the highest paid, most popular actress in television history who's knocked up by the highest paid, most popular movie actor—"

"You got garbage in your ears, Ridgeway? I said no." Pink crawled up Ralph's neck and invaded his cheeks. "Now, have you and Agnes discovered what rehab center Sierra Mallory's holed up—"

I ignored his blatant change of topic. "She's kidnapped by some doomsday cult and saved—"

Ralph rose to his feet, teeth chewing on the butt of the cigarette.

I ignored the warning. "—by someone Poole hired, and you don't want a follow-up?"

A growl filled the room. My editor was actually growling at me. I couldn't ignore that fact. I took a careful step away from the desk.

Twin columns of smoke blew from his flared nostrils. "I said no, and I meant no."

The gray haze quivered as we matched glares. Then air seemed to whoosh out of him, and he collapsed back into the ancient leather chair. Glancing at his watch, he muttered, "You've got one hour and fifty-five minutes if you want the fucking cover for this week."

He knew how to push my buttons. Sheer pride kicked in.

"Fine, boss." I pivoted and charged out the door, careful not to slam it on the way. What the hell was going on? Ralph never nixed one of my ideas. Okay, that wasn't true.

He had.

Once.

Two years ago, I'd snapped the Sabretooths' power forward and the lead singer of a certain boy band having a very good time in a hot tub. Even though Ralph ran my initial story, he refused to let me pursue the rumor of a stalker threatening the outed basketball player. His negation now made about as much sense as it did then.

A smile stretched my lips. Good thing I'd already started on the story, or maybe I would've walked away like I had the last time. I may be a slow learner, but I did learn.

I strode through the bullpen, ignoring the gagging and retching sounds in my wake. Everyone backed away from my aroma, except for . . .

Damn. No way could I dodge the lanky woman headed straight for me. Agnes Durley, AKA Agnes of God, because the rest of the staff agreed only the Almighty could love the crazy bitch.

"Samantha, I need to talk to you." Agnes's idea of a whisper carried through the huge room. The snickers started close to us and quickly spread. At least, she wasn't wearing her tin foil hat today.

"I'm kind of in a hurry." I tried to slide past her, only to be nailed by Agnes's claw-like grip and the pungent scent of garlic. I swallowed my impatience and a little nausea as the garlic aroma mixed with the cigarette smoke and garbage wafting from my clothes and hair. She may be missing a few screws, but no one could match the woman's research skills. And she had saved my ass on more than one occasion. Besides, Ralph needed someone to write the Elvis/alien baby stories.

"This is serious, Samantha." Agnes lowered her voice only a couple of decibels. "You need to be careful. The streets are dangerous."

"So's Ridgeway's smell," someone muttered from behind a cubical wall.

Tell me something about Los Angeles I don't know. Too many disappearances and murders had been happening lately, way too many for even Los Angeles, and no one knew what prompted the new round of turf wars. Two of the more notorious gangs had actually called a truce through a network affiliate in order to proclaim their innocence.

I breathed through my mouth since the combination of smells overwhelmed even my junk-food-hardened stomach. "Agnes, please, can't this wait? Ralph wants my story now." I patted the hand digging into my upper arm and tried not to wince. The woman had a grip that rivaled the Governator's. "I promise I'll come talk to you in two hours."

Agnes leaned closer. "People are vanishing. Kidnapped by bad vampires."

Great. Another one of her conspiracy stories. The last one involved the FBI covering up the fact the former vice-president had been possessed by doves. "Agnes," I began while prying her fingers off my bicep. "Vampires don't kidnap people. They eat them."

Agnes shook her head, the greasy, graying strands whipping wildly. It was hard to believe she'd once been a beauty queen contestant. The porcelain skin over gorgeous cheekbones didn't counter the wild-eyed look she gave me.

"The good ones don't eat us." She yanked a strand of garlic bulbs out of her safari jacket pocket and thrust the aromatic veggies at my head. "Wear this. It will protect you."

"Ridgeway doesn't need those. Her reek would drive away any self-respecting vampire." Bill Morton, my office nemesis, hung over his cubicle wall, smirking at us. A noticeable silence fell over the bullpen.

Eyeing the forty-something definition of kiss-ass, I mustered a bored look. If the rest of the guys saw me getting pissed, their jibes wouldn't stop. I didn't have time to deal with their crap. Not with a deadline in less than two hours. "Geez, Morton, just because you didn't get laid last night doesn't mean you have to take it out on the rest of us." Gales of laughter followed my comeback, and Bill slunk back down in his chair, his lips pursed in a sour grimace.

I turned back to Agnes and tried to give her a reassuring I'm taking-you-seriously smile. Otherwise, Agnes would hound me the rest of the afternoon, and I wasn't about to miss my deadline. Not with the cover bonus. I needed that cover bonus. "If I wear my grandmother's silver cross, I'll be okay, won't I?"

She eyed me suspiciously for a couple of seconds, her gaze boring into my skull. I tried not to flinch. Maybe Agnes really could pick up thought waves without the damn foil hat on and knew I was lying.

Finally, she nodded and said, "Silver should be sufficient." She grabbed my arm again. "Just be careful on the streets at night. They have Normal help." With her bizarre statement, she released me and marched back to the closet that served as her office. It was sadder than her hat. She'd requested the damn closet and had lined the walls with foil too.

Then her words registered. Normal? As opposed to what? Zombies?

I sighed and shook my head. It wasn't worth the effort to figure out what the heck Agnes was blathering about. Not to mention I had to plan a way to convince Ralph to print the follow-up on Poole's hired gun.

I headed for the ladies' room amid another round of chuckles and snickers.

Selene Antonius strode down the antiseptic hallway of Mallory Labs toward the section converted into an ICU. The staccato clicks of her heels echoed against bare tile. The vampire guard at the door bowed slightly, but she ignored him in favor of the man standing vigil at the observation window. The set of Tyrone Mallory's shoulders was one she recognized.

One she remembered all too well despite the passing of the last two millennia.

A death watch.

"How'd the trials go?" he asked as she halted by his side. He didn't look at her.

She folded her arms and stared into the room at the still figure on the bed. The girl's pale neck blended into the white blanket covering her. It might as well have been a funeral shroud. Despite the airlock, Selene's sensitive hearing could pick up the soft beeps of the EKG unit and the muffled hiss of oxygen. "When did they put her on the ventilator?"

"An hour ago." The despair in his voice nearly drowned the last remnants of his hope.

She could feel Mallory turn his piercing grey eyes away from his only child. "You didn't answer my question."

"The results with the chimpanzees look promising." The last thing she wanted was to lose the gifts the vampire virus had granted her. Unlike her asinine brother, she wasn't throwing her immortality away on a cure. Someday, he'd learn his lesson the hard way when his little witch whore staked him in the back. And if Selene found a way to let Duncan walk in daylight again, maybe he'd forgive her.

"'Promising'?" Mallory stepped closer to her. "My daughter has days, maybe hours, and all you can say is 'promising'? This research is the only chance she has."

She turned to face Mallory. The guard flicked a questioning look. A slight shake of her head deterred him. A Normal could hardly be considered a threat to her. Mallory's lack of fear where she was concerned was one of the appealing things about him.

"Do you want to use Sierra as the human test subject?"

The stubborn set of his jaw gave her his answer. His gaze shifted back to the dying girl. "You could—"

Her sigh whispered through the air. It always came down to that request, didn't it? "Is that what you really want for her?" She waved her hand between her and the guard. "To be one of us?" She shook her head. Pain stabbed through her heart. The girl couldn't even give permission. Another lesson learned the hard way. "There's no guarantee she'd survive the Turn, Tyrone." *There's no guarantee she'd still love either of us if she survived.* But there was no gain in burdening him with that knowledge. She knew from bitter experience he wouldn't listen to reason at this stage. No grieving family member ever did. "It's been two years since we started the V-Prime Project. Give the team a few more days."

"Fine." His attention returned to the girl struggling to hang onto life. "But if Sierra dies before they're ready, I'm feeding the entire science team to the prisoners."

Chapter 2

I whipped my little Civic from its parked position into an illegal U-turn. The bag of stale B-B-Q chips I'd been munching slid across the passenger seat and crashed into the car door, sending a shower of crumbs to join the empty wrappers on the floor. The chips were nothing compared to the midnight Suburban barreling down the street after exiting the private garage. I was not losing Duncan St. James tonight.

My resolution had nothing to do with my growing personal interest in Mr. Tall, Dark and Yummy. This was about a story. Not about the six-two, raven-haired, broad-chested hunk who was the subject of said story. No siree, not at all.

God, I needed to get laid.

His driver nearly sideswiped a Mercedes, resulting in an obscene gesture from the other motorist. A slim, black-nailed hand shot out of the SUV's window and returned the bird.

I slid through a yellow light to keep up with St. James. The facts I'd discovered about my suspected mercenary were sparse. The gaping holes in the man's history ignited my curiosity. To top it off, what kind of alpha male hires a teenage goth to drive him around the city at night?

Agnes's eerie warning echoed through my brain despite the reassuring streetlights. What could possibly happen if I stayed in my car with the doors locked?

The theme of *COPS* chirped from my cell phone. Finally.

I smacked the speaker button before I swerved around a braking city bus. "You'd better have something good for me, Fred."

"You're price just went up, Blondie." Anger crackled in the voice of my source in the LAPD.

"What? No way! We agreed to center court, two home games." In the years I'd known Fred Nguyen, he'd never reneged on one of our bargains.

"I just got my ass suspended!"

Dividing my attention between my irate friend and the SUV, I pressed the accelerator. "Suspended? Why?"

"For leaking sensitive information to the press!"

"Wow." I pondered the implications for a moment. What the hell was going on? Fred had mentioned St. James met with the police commissioner after rescuing Jessie Alton and escorting her to Cedar Sinai. The police hierarchy couldn't possibly know about Fred's extra-curricular hacking. Fred was too careful to be discovered. So what could possibly set the brass off over a meeting with a P.I.?

On the other hand, it was kind of cool Fred's boss treated me as a legitimate reporter. "Do you think you could have your captain call my mom?" She considered my job with the *Scoop* a step above prostitution. Barely.

"This isn't funny, Sam!"

I sighed. Despite a nagging sense of guilt, I couldn't make this too easy for him. "The best I can do is a couple more Sabretooth games." Only because Dad took Mom to Europe, and he let me have the tickets while he was away.

"And beer money." The edge eased from Fred's voice.

"And beer money," I agreed. "Now spill."

"The picture you sent me is of one Tiffany Stephens. Nineteen. Graduated from high school two years ago. 'C' student though her school psych profile indicates she's a genius. No college record I could find. Half a dozen speeding and reckless driving tickets. Nothing criminal."

The genius Goth Girl missed a Mustang by millimeters as she changed lanes again.

"Her parents were murdered when she was a baby, and the court made St. James her legal guardian. Sam—"

The last time I'd heard that same quiver in Fred's voice was the night we'd met. The night a beat cop saved a foolish twelve-year-old girl who thought she'd beat her brother to the Pulitzer by snapping the riots in South Central. The night he shot a kid my age saving my ass.

He'd had desk jobs with the LAPD since that night.

Fred's exhalation whistled through the speaker. "You need to back off this one. St. James has connections."

"No shit if he managed to get you suspended."

"Like Poole couldn't put enough pressure on?"

Thank God, I had both hands on the steering wheel and no vehicles were next to me. Some idiot in a Miata decided against turning in front of the charging Suburban at the last second and swerved into my lane. "Fuck!"

"Sam! You okay?" Panic filtered the speaker.

A bead of sweat trickled down my neck despite the winter air. "I'm fine, but I'm wondering how little Miss Stephens passed her driver's test." I took a deep breath and tried to relax my fingers' death grip on the wheel. "What makes you think Poole had anything to do with your suspension?"

"He's got the resources, and no one in City Hall would ignore someone making those kinds of charity donations."

Fred had a point. Brent and Jessie dumped a huge chunk of change into the city coffers after last year's quake. My gut said Fred was also deliberately sidetracking me.

"You said St. James had connections. What kind of connections?"

Fred's silence drug out for a second or two before he cleared his throat. "The kind of connections that can get you killed. Let's just say he belongs to a certain Family."

Family? "Oh my god, are you saying Poole has mob contacts?" The wheels in my head churned. Frank and the Rat Pack were one thing when it came to organized crime. America's super couple were another. My heart palpitated. Breaking this story was going to make my career.

"Not Mafia." I could hear him take a deep breath. "Sam, there are worse people to mess with than organized crime. You need to drop this. Now. Before someone gets hurt."

"Fred—"

"I've got more than just Internal Affairs breathing down my neck." His voice shook. "This isn't South Central, kid. I won't be able to pull your ass out of trouble on this one. You need to let go of this story."

An annoying ping followed Fred's plea. I glanced at the readout. One bar left on the power.

"Fred, I'm going to have to call you back later. I'm about to lose power."

He got as far as "Damn it, Sam!" before I hit the "Off" button.

I managed to keep an eye on the SUV while plugging in the car adaptor. A reassuring beep sounded as my little lifeline began recharging. Quiet unease filtered through my overloaded brain when I realized where they were headed.

What kind of business did Mr. Yummy and Goth Girl have in the warehouse district? After Fred's hints, good, old self-preservation kicked into gear. I no longer had additional traffic to cover me.

The SUV slid to a stop next to a typical, non-descript storage facility. I had no choice but to drive past them. They didn't even look in my direction as I rolled by.

Which made it a hell of a lot easier to swallow my heart.

I turned at the river to circle back and stifled a nervous giggle. The Los Angeles River was a misnomer. It's more like a gigantic drainage ditch. I found a parking spot on the cross street behind them. Not that it was hard to find one at this time of night.

I climbed out of my car and paused. The night was strangely quiet for the second largest city in the U.S. Agnes's warning flittered through my mind, but I smacked the disconcerting thought away. There was no such thing as vampires.

Slipping my camera into my shoulder bag, I eased down to the corner and peered around the pre-fabbed concrete. Nothing. The SUV was still there, but the pair had disappeared.

Damn. I sauntered down the street as casually as one could this close to midnight when an area's deserted. At the end of the block, there was no sign of anyone down the side streets.

I frowned. Something was definitely wrong. Not even one of the city's ever-present homeless shambled down the street or hid in one of the doorways.

Doubling back, I eyed the dumpster across the street. It was about half a block behind St. James's vehicle. Not the best vantage point, but I didn't want to throw in the towel yet. I spent too much time on St. James to give up that easily.

But I didn't relish spending another night in someone's garbage either. I swallowed hard before forcing a decision. Maybe I'd get lucky and just share the space with cockroaches and flies. Rats were another story ever since a junior high sleepover. Crossing the street, I headed for the only potential hiding place.

A shudder trailed up my spine and nestled in the hairs on my neck. Dark, empty doorways stared at the street like eye sockets on a skull. I couldn't shake the feeling of being watched. I raced for the dumpster.

The last thing I expected was to run into someone's chest. I hugged my bag to protect the camera, so my ass took the brunt of the impact on the sidewalk. It took me a split second to catch a tiny wisp of the air that had been knocked out of me. When I looked up, I found the deepest, greenest eyes staring down at me. They practically glowed in the dark.

Before I could think about screaming, Mr. Yummy pulled me to my feet. Before I could thank him, he spun me around, wrenching my right arm behind my back and pulling me snug against his chest. My bag landed on the pavement with a disheartening crack as his other arm snaked around my throat and choked out any oxygen I'd retrieved.

"Who are you and whom are you working for?" The man gave a whole new meaning to growling. He twisted my arm for emphasis.

I didn't fake the whimpers of pain as fire rippled from wrist to shoulder. "I don't know what you're talking about." The words came more as a gasp than real speech.

He shoved me against the warehouse wall, knocking the last little bit of gas out of my lungs. Sharp bits of concrete ground into my cheek. Struggling against his grip sent excruciating waves of pain through elbow and shoulder. Any fear was forgotten when my lungs burned in protest at their deprivation. I settled for trying to gulp air past the forearm across my throat. Despite my desperate gasps, I couldn't miss the subtle scent of sandalwood.

When I didn't answer, his low voice rumbled in my ear. "Only one more chance, my dear. Who are you?" He twisted. I whimpered. "Whom are you working for?"

I squirmed, trying to find any kind of leverage to get him off me. I only succeeded in having more concrete shoved against my face. Damn, this guy was strong.

Despite my predicament, I realized something else. Threats delivered with a British accent still sound sexy. I've always been a sucker for English guys.

Struggling against him wasn't getting me anywhere. "Sam. Sam Ridgeway," I said, answering his first question.

He must have understood the choking sounds I made. The agonizing pressure on my shoulder eased, and the arm encircling my throat disappeared. Something brushed my waist and hips, then the unmistakable feeling of fingers against my left breast sent shivers through me.

Irritation at his audacity warred with the trickle of warmth in my pelvis. What was wrong with me? The man had just slammed me into a wall for chrissakes. The weird attraction only served to escalate my annoyance. "There are more comfortable positions if you want to cop a feel."

St. James chuckled, and his warm breath tickled my ear. He jerked me away from the concrete wall. "Darling, this is 'copping a feel.'" His hand slid to cup me fully, the feeling surprisingly soft and sensual. Totally at odds with the face full of wall he gave me a second ago.

Maybe it'd been too long since Jake and I broke up. The fact a total stranger toyed with my sex-deprived body on a deserted street didn't faze me. I should have been scared witless. Instead, I leaned into St. James' touch, enjoying the wave of heat through my body.

"When you're finished frisking her, let me know."

He whirled us both around to face Goth Girl, who stood on the sidewalk four yards away, tapping a shiny black boot against the concrete. Her rigid arms crossed her perky, teen chest, and she favored me with an ugly scowl.

I glared at Goth Girl. Talk about a mood killer.

"She's not armed." St. James' smug voice indicated he didn't think I was dangerous either. He kicked something over to Goth Girl. "Take care of this."

It took precious seconds for me to slap hormone-addled thoughts into shape. By then, Goth Girl had pulled the camera out of the bag, yanked out the memory card, dropped it on the sidewalk and smashed it with her size-two spiked heel.

"You bitch!" I lunged at the girl, but the firm and painful grip on my arm brought me up short.

"Can you believe she cut me out of nearly every shot she took of us?" Goth Girl rolled her eyes. "And, yes, I took care of the other cameras."

My heart plummeted to my stomach. My extra digital and the 35mm had been hidden in the Civic's spare tire well. What had the little bitch done?

"God, Duncan, you would not believe what a pig she is." Goth Girl continued her rant. "Her car's filled with enough junk food bag—"

"That is enough." St. James's voice held a touch of humor.

Irritation flared even higher that he found the destruction of my personal property so amusing. Oh, he was so going to pay for this. I struggled again, with the same lame results.

"Now, Miss Ridgeway, whom do you work for?" he said.

I fumed at the loss of the pictures. No way was I telling this jerk anything.

"Miss Ridgeway . . ." The menacing edge returned in his tone.

If I could see his face, I could determine how serious he was, but he held me tight against his chest. His very solid, very masculine chest. I was calculating the return on a dislocated shoulder when the pressure on said right joint escalated.

Yep, he was serious.

"I work for *The National Scoop.*" A tear trickled down my face, more from the humiliation at getting caught than the pain. I hadn't broken this easily when cornered by Mel Gibson's Dobermans.

"What the bloody hell?" Confused annoyance filled his voice.

Goth Girl smirked at me. "Well, well, well. You've picked up a tabloid reporter, Duncan."

The cocky grin on the girl's too-purple lips added to my mounting irritation. "That's investigative journalist to you. And isn't it past your bedtime?"

A nasty look covered Goth Girl's face. "Shouldn't you be wiretapping Nicole Kidman?"

Before I could come up with an appropriate rejoinder, the grip on my wrist disappeared so suddenly I stumbled.

"Go home, Miss Ridgeway." St. James' voice almost sounded weary. His suggestion sounded good, real good, but his story sang its siren's song.

I turned to find St. James stalking towards his SUV, Goth Girl hot on his heels. Mobsters didn't just walk away from a potential problem. Or maybe I'd watched *The Sopranos* one too many times.

Despite the numbness running down my arm, I couldn't give up that easily. Not to mention they trashed some expensive equipment. I snatched up my bag and camera, awkward with only one functioning arm.

"Wait!" They turned in unison as I ran to them, matching impatient expressions on their faces. "What about my photo cards?"

He crossed his arms over his fabulously broad chest. "What about them?"

"You destroyed my property," I huffed out around my panting. Damn, I really needed to work out more.

"You have been stalking me. Consider us even." He rounded the vehicle and reached for the door handle.

Dammit! This little encounter had been a set-up. Well, I knew how to play rough too.

I followed and laid a hand on his. Electricity shot through my nerves at the sensation of his cool skin beneath my palm. "Give me the story on the kidnapping by the Sunshine Believers, then we'll be even."

His scowl deepened. "What are you talking about?"

"Jessie Alton." I resisted the urge to slap the arrogant look off his face. "You know, the pregnant star of *Buddies* you rescued two weeks ago."

"I do not know what you are talking about." Madonna's publicist couldn't have said that with a straighter face.

"Look, St. James, give me the interview and I'll stop following you."

"Or?"

I gave him my most convincing smile. "I'll keep following you until you do."

He snorted and climbed into the SUV. Goth Girl had the engine running before he slammed the door shut. I banged a fist on his window. The impact had the unmistakable feel of bulletproof glass.

The passenger window slid down to reveal a still scowling St. James. "Go home, Miss Ridgeway," he repeated. "You have had a very long day, and you are very tired.

Again, the desire to burrow under the covers rushed through my system. What the hell was wrong with me? I shook my head to clear the cobwebs clogging the neural pathways and matched his annoyed look. "Answer my question first."

An exasperated look replaced his scowl. "Go home."

"And if I don't?"

A wicked smile spread across his face. "My 'copping a feel' will be the least of your problems."

Why did St. James' threat sound more like a promise? The desire to push him to see if he'd carry through overwhelmed me.

Tires squealed as Goth Girl tore away from the curb. I jumped back to keep my toes intact.

Before their taillights disappeared, I raced back to the Honda. Four smashed spark plugs laid next to the shattered spare photo cards on the pavement. The only saving grace was I'd pulled the 35mm roll out last night to develop it.

I sighed. So much for locking the damn car doors in this freakin' city.

Chapter 3

Dawn threatened to peek into the bedroom window as I shed my clothes and climbed beneath the white eyelet sheets. The brass bed was one of the few indulgences in an otherwise industrial beige and bare apartment. The parents were constantly on my case about getting furniture. Okay, Mom was on my case. She'd lost on the name change issue, so she'd taken up harassing me about the lack of furniture. It's not like Mom and Dad ever came over or I entertained on a regular basis.

Or even a semi-regular basis. Not since Jake and I broke up a year ago.

And spending my money on Lasik surgery was the better bargain in my line of work.

I tossed my cell on the nightstand and collapsed on the pillows, but I was too tired to think and too wired to sleep. What the hell was going on? Old guilt swirled through my volatile emotions.

I didn't care about Poole or Alton. They played the celebrity card, which made them fair game. What I didn't like was the resurrection of feelings I'd thought had died when I walked away from Jake's marriage proposal. And then there was my unintended fallout landing on top of Fred once again.

Trying to clear the ancient hash from my brain, I watched the hypnotic pattern of passing headlights from rush hour worker bees on the bedroom ceiling and focused on the current situation. The bribe to get a tow truck out to the warehouse district in predawn hours swallowed what was left of my stash of mad money. I could expense the tow with the *Scoop*, but the extra cost wasn't what bothered me. Without wheels, it was nearly impossible to tail anyone in this city. Despite Fred's freaky warning, I wasn't about to let this go.

Duncan St. James intrigued me. What kind of man leaves so little trace of his life? What kind of guy doesn't have his driver's license in the 21st century? Better yet, what kind of James Bond alpha male has a teenage car burglar as a sidekick?

I stretched, a slight twinge in my right shoulder the only physical reminder of the evening. That and the scratches on my cheek, but those could be covered with a little make-up. I had to give St. James credit. He knew how to inflict the maximum amount of discomfort with the least amount of damage.

I frowned at the last disturbing thought. Maybe I'd been in this business too long if I was starting to enjoy the pain.

Rolling over, I smiled at the twenty-four by thirty-six photo pinned to the bedroom wall, the other reason my stash was so low in the first place. Dim pre-dawn light illuminated powerful shoulders and raven hair. Goth Girl hadn't destroyed all my pictures of him.

I had taken this one three nights ago through the massive front window of an antique shop. Part of me wished his warm smile aimed at the beautiful brunette behind the counter could be turned my way. I sat up to examine it a little closer as the first rays of the sun flooded the room, and I grinned as something else dawned on me.

Goth Girl was right. I had cut the annoying little bitch out of this picture, too.

Duncan rocked back on his heels, trying not to let fury override common sense. "I fail to understand why you thought not informing me of these rumors concerning rogue vampires was prudent."

Caesar Augustine, Master of the Western United States Vampire Coven, relaxed in his office chair, fingers steepled, as he returned Duncan's glare with a cool, measured look. "Because I need you looking for our missing people, not settling a vendetta with my sister."

Red filmed Duncan's vision. "How can you even say—"

"I'm not arguing with you about this." Despite the calmness of Caesar's voice, his hazel eyes flared gold in warning.

Duncan sucked in a deep breath, forced down his anger, and resorted to formality. "I am not arguing with you, Master Augustine. I am merely pointing out the rogue—" He'd be damned to the ninth level of Hell before he'd say the bitch's name. "—has used similar distraction tactics in the past. As your Chief Enforcer, I should have been informed. The two situations might be linked."

Pink tinged Caesar's face at the not-so-subtle reminder of the deaths and chaos his twin had caused.

"Duncan." The gentle voice of Dr. Bebe Zachary drew his attention. She rose from the black leather couch, where she'd been sitting next to Tiffany, and crossed the office to face him. "If I had concrete information on Selene, you'd be the second one I'd tell." A small smile curved her lips at her joke. Without a doubt, she'd tell Caesar first, and she had.

Duncan's anger drained away at her words. Caesar and Bebe had suffered as much as his own family had at Selene's hands.

"Right now, all I've got is rumors from patients hoping to curry favor with both Silver Bear and Augustine Covens. These disappearances have all the supernaturals on edge," Bebe said.

"Your grandmother—"

Bebe shook her head, and a few more of her haphazard curls slipped from their pins. "No luck tracking any of the missing. Granny E. has all of Silver Bear on alert." She sighed. "There haven't been anymore coven disappearances since the high school girl snatched in December. That doesn't account for any eclectics who might be passing through Los Angeles."

Duncan's fists clenched at the unspoken worry in her voice, one he shared. Without help from a coven to watch his or her back, any solitary witch would be a prime target. He turned back to Caesar. "Has John heard from the San Antonio Packmaster?"

Caesar gave a solemn nod. "He has concerns their requests to aid the search are a prelude to a takeover. Of course, having a rival Packmaster's pup disappear in John's territory . . ."

Breath hissed between Duncan's teeth at the implied political problems. Los Angeles was one of the few cities in the world where the vampire, witch and were leaders not only cooperated, but actually liked and respected each other. It normally made his job as Caesar's chief enforcer a hell of a lot easier.

And normally, his right hand, Alex Stanton, would be here to assist him. Except Alex had been missing for nearly four months now, along with Logan Polk, the son of the San Antonio alphas. The two friends had gone to a bar one night and never came home. The waitresses remembered the two fellow Texans flirting and dancing with the ladies, but the men had left alone.

Duncan ground his teeth in frustration. This was exactly the sort of game Selene would play. Create suspicion among allies in order to set pack against pack and coven against coven. In any other circumstance, Alex and Logan could take care of themselves, but she wouldn't have allowed a fair fight. He swallowed the accusation. No good would come of rehashing the argument.

"What about Anne? Have we received any word from her?"

Caesar shook his head. "She refused to take a cell phone out of respect for her brother. We'll have to wait for her letter." He rubbed his jaw. "I wish she'd taken the jet."

Duncan paced across the thick carpet. Anne was the only Enforcer who resided in the master's Brentwood mansion full-time. While he would have preferred she remain in Los Angeles during the current crisis, he understood her desire to assist the last living member of her immediate family. It didn't mean he had to like it.

Bebe chuckled. "If I could prescribe an anti-anxiety medication that worked on vampires, I would have to get Anne on the jet."

The byplay snapped Duncan's last reserve of patience. "Instead of worrying about Anne's fear of flying, we need to focus on our immediate problem. What about the International Council?"

Caesar's hand slashed down, the motion as sharp as his tone. "We have no solid evidence of who's responsible."

Duncan took a step forward. Why did his master have such a blind spot for procedure? "We have fifteen known supernaturals missing."

"Before you two totally freak out, let's look at the evidence we've got," Tiffany said.

Duncan looked down at his niece, who sat cross-legged on the couch, boots discarded on the carpet. Thoughtful brown eyes stared up at him.

"Every solid lead we've followed so far points to Tyrone Mallory, a Normal with no known Family connections, not some major league supernatural conspiracy, so we'll need the I.C.'s blessing to go after him. Let's eliminate him as a suspect before we start whittling stakes for Selene. If this is really a good old-fashioned Normal witch hunt—"

"Hey!" Bebe glared at Tiffany.

"Sorry, Doc." As usual, his niece did not look the least bit sorry. "But you guys know what I mean."

Unfortunately, the child was correct. The International Council had been formed to keep cross-species aggression to a minimum, which meant Normals were included, even if the majority of them didn't know it.

Bebe's musical laughter filled the room. "The universe is surely messed up when she's the logical one."

Tiffany scowled at the grin on Bebe's face. "Gee, thanks for the vote of confidence."

Duncan couldn't help smiling at Tiffany as well. Maybe there was hope for the brash girl after all. He raked a hand through his hair and focused on the immediate task. "I need to get inside of Mallory's lab. Surveillance has not produced any results." But then there hadn't been any reports of missing supernaturals in the last three nights either. He eyed Bebe. "Do you have a spell that can breach a wall and still hide the hole if I need to bring anyone out?" He trusted his own skills, but he didn't want to impale a kidnap victim accidentally during the rescue. Steel spikes reinforced the concrete blockade of Mallory's facility, rivaling any defensive works he remembered from his childhood in England.

Bebe nodded. "I can have something to dissolve the wall ready by tonight, but if it's the size you're describing, it'll need forty-eight hours to work or someone will notice it." She tapped her chin and her eyes focused elsewhere as she ran through a mental list. "You're going to need a blurring spell to hide from any electronic surveillance inside the compound, but I can't mix that potion until just before you head out."

His lips tightened in a grim smile. "I can wait. The labs will have the fewest personnel on Sunday evening anyway. Thank you." He turned to leave, only to be stopped by Tiffany's blatant cough.

Caesar's eyebrow rose as his gaze flicked between them. "Was there something else?"

Tiffany leaned forward on the couch and fixed a pointed look at Duncan. "Aren't you going to tell him?"

Confusion filled Duncan, along with the sense of a chasm opening beneath his feet. "Tell him what?"

"Your fan club?"

Irritation returned at Tiffany's comment, but his groin tightened at the thought of the firebrand he'd caught last night. Maybe his self-imposed celibacy was cracking under the stress of the last two years, but she'd felt so warm, so right when he held her.

Quelling the wayward thought, he shot Tiffany a stern look. "That problem has been dealt with." Granted, Miss Ridgeway seemed to resist his telepathic suggestions last night. He'd looked up the woman's information on his laptop as Tiffany drove to Mallory Labs. A personal visit to the pretty, little reporter may be necessary.

"What problem?" Caesar cast a suspicious look at both of them.

Tiffany chuckled. "Duncan has a tabloid reporter stalking him."

"I do not." He'd never struck Tiffany in all the years she'd lived with him, but now he understood why some parents advocated corporal punishment.

A grim expression filled Caesar's face. "Who is it and which magazine?"

"Her name's Ridgeway. She works for the *Scoop*," Tiffany chimed.

"I have already taken care of the situation." Duncan crossed his arms and faced Caesar, his irritation back in full force at the insult to his competency.

Caesar nodded in acknowledgement. "I'm sure you have. However, a call reminding O'Malley to keep a leash on his people will be additional insurance you are no longer bothered. I believe we've had a problem with her in the past."

Even though Duncan would have recommended the same action under any other circumstances, the thought Caesar had to babysit him grated. Granted he had been distracted by the investigation of the recent disappearances, but his preoccupation didn't mean he couldn't handle one little girl.

Except the curves he caressed last night were hardly girlish.

Some of his emotions must have leaked because Caesar added, "This has nothing to do with my opinion of your abilities, Duncan. As Family, O'Malley has responsibilities to our coven. Setting one of his reporters on my chief enforcer hardly fulfills his obligations."

While Duncan was sure Caesar's words were meant to be reassuring, they still left an acid bite in the air. He didn't envy Ralph O'Malley the tongue-lashing Caesar was about to deliver the editor.

Bebe clapped her hands together. "In the meantime, while I whip up the spell, why don't you two go upstairs get some rest? Miko's already laid out fresh bedding."

Tiffany's yawn reminded him his niece was still Normal, despite how hard she pushed herself to keep up with the supernaturals. And common sense told him they both needed to be fresh to deal with the espionage they planned for the next few nights.

He nodded his thanks to Bebe before he and Tiffany left Caesar's office and climbed the stairs to the mansion's second floor.

"What time do you want to head out tonight?" Tiffany's words were garbled by another yawn, but his scan of her surface thoughts caught the question.

"Shortly after sunset, but we need to perform a small errand before we set out for the labs."

Tiffany's thin, black brows drew together in her confusion. "Errand? What errand?"

"A personal visit to Miss Ridgeway's abode. I want to make sure she has no more information concerning me or any member of the supernatural community."

A grin lit Tiffany's face. "Sure you're not really planning a panty raid?"

"No, I am not." The tightening in his groin belied his stern words. Because he'd very much like to see Samantha Ridgeway in her undergarments.

Chapter 4

"I need to ask a favor." I propped the cell phone between my shoulder and ear as I opened the third pack of sugar for my daily dose of java. The aromatic steam caressed my face like a long-lost lover.

"Can't you ever say hello like a normal person?"

"Hello, Max. I need to borrow your car tonight." Catching the phone as it started to slide off my shoulder, I grabbed the steaming cup from the counter. A quick glance around the coffee shop showed I had my pick of seats.

My brother's deep, exasperated huff blasted through the cell receiver. "Jack Nicholson get yours towed again?"

"No." I bit back the usual sarcastic reply. I wasn't the most pleasant person after four hours of sleep, but today I had to try extra hard. I really needed Max's help. "It's in the shop."

"Uh-huh," Max drawled. "Seriously, who had your car towed this time? Brent Poole still pissed at you about the pregnancy test thing?"

"*I* had it towed last night. I had some problems with the spark plugs, and it wouldn't start." Which was part of the truth. I'd never been able to lie to Max. Mr. Pulitzer Prize can sniff a fabrication faster than the Beagle Brigade could detect an unauthorized apple in customs. His lie detection abilities didn't mean I had to tell him the whole truth. I slid into a seat and managed not to spill my desperately needed caffeine.

"Sure you did." His drawl scraped over my sleep-deprived nerves. "George Clooney?"

"Don't you read the papers? He's living in Italy these days. And I really did have car problems!" I winced at the desperation in my voice. It wasn't pretty. I counted to ten, but Max gave in first.

"Sorry, Sam. You can borrow it, but I can't get to your place until six."

I expelled a sigh in relief. I wouldn't need Max's car until dark anyway. With no mad money left and the credit card maxed out for the car repairs, I was up a creek until payday. Goth Girl had sabotaged more than the spark plugs. Someone needs to tell dear, sweet, little Tiffany paybacks are a bitch. The sugar in the gas tank really burned me. Thank God, my mechanic had discovered it before he started the car, or I'd be looking at a whole new engine. With replacing the tank, pump and gas line, I couldn't pick up my car until Tuesday morning at the earliest, and it's damn near impossible to trail someone using public transportation.

I hated to say it, but I didn't have any friends to call. At least none who would trust me with their cars without wanting to horn in on my story.

God, I really needed to find some friends outside of the business.

A soft beep warned the battery was low. New annoyance added to my general irritation. I'd forgotten to plug the phone into the recharger before I'd crawled into bed. Time to end this conversation before it totally died.

"Thanks, big bro. I owe you one." I flipped my phone closed and tapped my fingers on the black laminate table. This morning, the coffee shop was quiet. The rush hour crowd was long gone, which would suit Fred, assuming he arrived soon.

When I had called him earlier about delivering the Sabretooth tickets, he insisted on meeting me here. His voice sounded weird. Not like he was still mad at me for getting him suspended, not like his anxiety-ridden warning last night, but something else. I was too damn tired to figure it out though.

I glared at the few jots in my notebook, wishing more information on St. James would appear. I tapped my pen against the table, earning ugly looks from the elderly chess players two tables down. I smiled in apology, and they returned to their game. Jerry Springer on the overhead T.V. was slightly more interesting than the chess match.

Swallowing the bitter dregs of my triple espresso did nothing to ease my exhaustion. The expected jolt wasn't much more than a love peck. I glanced at my wrist again. An hour late. Something else unusual for my favorite police geek.

I seriously contemplated leaving when a strange character outside the window caught my eye. He had a baseball cap pulled low over Poison-era hair and mirrored shades. The wig and glasses did nothing to enhance the portly man in the trench coat. I just prayed he wasn't planning to rob the place. He'd shoot me for spending my last five dollars on the caffeine. Then his sleeve slid up as he reached for the door, and I caught a glimpse of a red watchband.

Fred's vintage Disney Pooh timepiece was the only recognizable thing about him when he sat down across from me.

"Fred—"

"Don't use my real name. I'm George. George Carver."

Great, just great. My favorite police informant included a racial identity crisis in his nervous breakdown.

"Okay, 'George.' What's going on? Is this about our friend and his family?" If Fred didn't want me using his own name, I wasn't about to send him over the edge saying St. James's.

"Sam, I can't—" He licked his lips, the mirrored shades swinging across the room. I followed his sweep of the place. Other than the kid behind the counter and the two men intent on their game in the corner, we were alone.

"You can't what?" This quivering wreck wasn't the man I knew. The man who had fled Vietnam as a child, shepherding his younger sisters to safety against all odds. The cop who pulled me to cover during the South Central riots. The man who killed to save my life.

"Other people are asking questions."

"What people? What are you blabbering about?"

"Don't ask!" he hissed. A bead of sweat trickled from under his wig and down his cheek. "I don't want to see you get hurt."

"You said that last night." I laid a hand on his wrist. "Fred—"

He shot out of his seat. "I-I-I'm sorry, Sam. For your own sake, don't call me ever again." He scurried out the door, trench coat flying behind him.

And the Sabretooth tickets still sat in my purse.

Shit! Worry won out over anger at Fred's erratic behavior. I snatched my bag and charged out the door. Spotting Fred as he headed for the crosswalk, I jogged to catch up and yelled his name.

Fred was road pizza before I even noticed the van scream through the red light. I froze, unreality penetrating my bones as Fred flew through the air to land with a sickening smack on the pavement. The van never slowed as it spun around the corner and disappeared from sight.

Something clattered at my feet and I looked down. Pooh stared at me through shattered crystal.

"Sam?"

I pried apart sleep-gummed eyes to find Max leaning over me.

"You've got drool running down your face."

Brothers are so good for the ego.

Leveraging myself upright, I looked down and swiped one jacket sleeve across the wet spot on the hospital's avocado vinyl couch and the other across my cheek. Max nudged me over so he could sit on the drier side.

"You okay?"

"No." I never would be again. Not after the ride in the ambulance with a mangled Fred.

Dragging my thoughts into some form of coherence, I focused on the blue eyes examining me through black frames. The memory snapped into place. I had called Max a couple of hours ago to meet me at the hospital instead of my place. "Thought you wouldn't be here until after work."

I really did need to get more friends. I couldn't rely on my big brother to fish me out of jams. Heaven knew Fred never would again.

He leaned back, raked a hand through what was left of his receding blond hair and grinned. "Business. I'm here to interview a witness to a hit-and-run."

Anger boiled away the threatening tears before I could stop it. "Fuck you!"

He spread his hands. "Hey, I was just teasing."

"Fred Nguyen didn't deserve to be murdered."

His frown looked sincere despite the crappy fluorescent lighting. "Murder? That's not the official word."

I leaned back, the scene playing in slo-mo across my closed lids as I returned to my previous misery. "You weren't there."

"So tell me."

My eyes popped back open. "And let you scoop me? Not!" One of Max's eyebrows rose above his Clark Kent frames. So much for my fake bravado.

None of this made sense. I pursued a guy who rescued pregnant sit-com actresses from apocalyptic cults. Who went out of his way to cover his tracks. Enough to stage an accident to kill an innocent cop?

This story had taken a whole new context. I owed Fred far too much to let his death slide into oblivion. I stood up and held out my hand. Max dug into his jeans and pulled out his Bugs Bunny key ring. He paused just short of my waiting palm.

"Let me buy you dinner first."

Damn. He knew I couldn't pass up free food.

By mutual, unspoken agreement, Little Sicily was neutral territory in our sibling rivalry. The cheap pine and red vinyl gave the place a tacky appeal, but the food was excellent. Waving to the hostess, we claimed our usual corner booth.

Heading off Max's inevitable interrogation, I started with the small talk. "So, have you heard from Mom and Dad?" I pretended to examine the menu. My parents' noveau riche status didn't bother me as much as the fact they never called me on their trips. Ever.

"They phoned from their hotel in Venice." Max closed his own menu. "They're staying an extra week."

"Mr. Cuddles is going to love that."

He grimaced at the reminder of his dog-sitting duties for Mom. "You know you could watch him next week in return for borrowing my car. We'll trade when you drop it off."

"Let's not. You know he hates my guts. And you don't want to be responsible when a certain toy poodle takes a suicidal leap from my bedroom window."

No comment from Max. Not even a slight smile at my snarky comment. He stared at the plastic-coated cardboard. I didn't want to bring up his own depressing situation, but I couldn't stop my mouth.

"Heard anything from Anne?" A homeless girl Max kept an eye out for, she had disappeared a couple of weeks ago. Max had dragged me along at first, searching the shelters and local teen hangouts. I wasn't sure why he cared so much. The kid was overly pale, too thin, never smiled and always wore dark, long-sleeved shirts with long, dark skirts in sunny Los Angeles. All the signs of someone trying to hide her heroin tracks.

Then again, maybe she was one of Agnes' imaginary vampires since the couple of times I'd encountered her were at night.

My brother had almost decked me when I pointed out the evidence to him. I hoped for his sake she had moved on to San Francisco. Or Seattle. Or anywhere. I tried not to think about the other possibility.

"No, I haven't heard anything." He yanked the menu out of my hands. "You always order the same thing, so quit stalling."

Over lasagna, I spilled my guts, starting with the possibility of Brent Poole's mob connections and ended with the bizarre incident at the coffee shop, including how Fred went into cardiac arrest and died on the ambulance ride to the hospital. Somehow, I managed to edit the story so Mr. Yummy didn't make an appearance. A girl can only take honesty so far with her big brother when it comes to members of the opposite sex. Or scooping my story on a murderer.

And I had to face the possibility Mr. Yummy may have ordered Fred's "accident."

I handed Max the remains of Fred's watch. "Do you know anyone who could repair this?" I should have given it to Fred's sisters at the hospital, but some bizarro feeling of sentimentality made me want to get it fixed before I gave it back to them.

This caring about others could indicate a serious problem. Maybe I should make an appointment with Mom's shrink.

He looked over the smashed crystal and dented casing, then cocked an eyebrow as he glanced back at me. "You're kidding, right?"

"Never mind," I muttered. "You wouldn't understand." I held out my hand.

Instead of giving it back, he slid the broken timepiece into the breast pocket of his blue oxford shirt. "Let me see what I can do. Consider it your birthday present for this year."

"You didn't give me a present last year so you still owe me."

He ignored my comment and flagged our waiter for coffee. When he turned back, he wore his "serious investigator" face. I should have run but I wanted the coffee too much to move. Maybe there's an AA group for the caffeine-addicted.

"Did Fred have any enemies?"

An image of the blood-splattered man lying on the ambulance gurney rose, threatening to bring my lasagna back up.

I swallowed hard and held up my hand. The waiter misunderstood and started to take away the coffee tray. "Stop right there." The waiter froze. "You," I said, waving him towards the table, "bring that back." I glared at Max as the waiter poured. "Fred didn't have a mean bone in his body."

"He was suspended," Max pointed out.

"For spilling info to me the commissioner tried to squelch."

"This wasn't the first time."

"The other time was normal procedure when investigating a police shooting. And you know damn well that reason." I concentrated on dumping two huge spoonfuls of sugar into my liquid love. It beat meeting Max's eyes.

Max waited until the waiter cleared the rest of our dishes and we were alone before he continued. "Could he have been involved in something dirty?"

"No. Not Fred." I blew on my after-dinner coffee to cool it. "He made Mother Theresa look like Darth Vader." I took a sip and still managed to burn off the top layer of my tongue.

"Sam, I hate to tell you this, but there's been some unusual activity in Fred's bank account."

I didn't like the way he was watching me. "What do you mean 'unusual activity'?"

"Some large sums passed through his checking account. Way too large for an IT guy with the LAPD," Max tapped his fingers to the theme of "The Lone Ranger." Not a good sign. Heaven help whoever he was tracking down.

"Where's it coming from? Are you sure it's not one of his sisters loaning him money or paying him back?" I took another sip, willing myself to stay calm. It was bad enough Max insulted my friend, but Fred couldn't even defend himself anymore.

"What about his sisters? Any idea why they'd be paying him?"

I shook my head and took another painful sip. Tranh, the youngest, had threatened to serve me at her restaurant if I showed up at Fred's funeral. And she didn't mean as an honored guest.

Other than Tranh's penchant for threats when it came to me, the two sisters were good people. I couldn't fault them for blaming me for Fred's death. Hell, I blamed me too. Fred had raised them, educated them—

My head jerked up. "Wait a minute here. Tranh and Mary could be paying him back. He put them both through college," I said. "And he helped Tranh open her restaurant."

He shrugged. "Assuming you're right about the money, what makes you think Fred was murdered?"

I opened my mouth, then clamped it shut. I wasn't about to spill the beans about Duncan St. James and his "Family." It wasn't worth the hassle from Max. And my very dark suspicions were growing faster than the mold in my fridge.

Max gave me a knowing look. "If you're right and the money's clean, you've got nothing but a police nerd under suspension and a van driver who can't use his brakes." He spooned ice from his water glass into his java. "I hate to say it, Sam, but this kind of thing happens all the time."

I eyed Max over the rim of my cup. "You didn't see him. He was scared out of his mind. And why would he warn me not to contact him?"

Max laid down his spoon but didn't take a drink. He leaned on folded elbows, his stare intense, coffee forgotten. "What aren't you telling me?"

I blinked. "What are you talking about?"

"Sam, it's me, and you're involved in something over your head." We both had practiced stare downs with our Siamese cat, DC the First, so it was a long time before he broke and took a sip. "You're lying."

"Am not!"

"Your left eye's twitching."

I rubbed the betraying orb. "Something's in my contact."

"You got Lasik two months ago."

I cursed him under my breath. "Either Alton's or Poole's connections got Fred suspended when I asked him a few questions about Alton's rescue from a cult." Technically, St. James was Poole's connection.

"God, are you still going on about that alleged kidnapping?"

It wasn't alleged, but I wasn't going to argue about it with Max again. "The only other possibility I can come up with is someone with a vendetta in IA."

Max huffed at my lame-ass theory. "Are you sure?"

No, but I wasn't about to admit it aloud. Besides, why would IA kill a police officer for giving me copies of St. James's files? Which brought me back to St. James and his "Family" connections.

Max took my silence as permission to press on. "What about the van?"

I rolled my eyes. "What about it?"

He held up his index finger. "The make and model were so generic the description matches ten thousand vans in the metro area."

I opened my mouth. Max zipped his free hand across his lips.

Another finger joined the first. "By your own admission, the windows were tinted to the point you and the rest of the bystanders couldn't see the driver." A third finger joined the other two. "And the license plate was missing."

Max grunted, lowered his hand and leaned back in the booth.

Damn, he could be exasperating. He wasn't going to let this go, so I went on the offensive. "Why would Malibu Barbie or Malibu Ken go to the trouble of knocking off a police computer analyst, who, by the way, could tell me squat?"

Max stared at me.

I threw my napkin at him.

Instead of tossing it back in my face, he folded the red and white checked cloth. His voice was so soft I could barely catch his next words. "I think you're right about what happened to Fred. There's more to this than a pissed-off Hollywood power couple."

My brother? Believing me?

Hell had just frozen over.

Chapter 5

Duncan stood before the front door and extended his senses into the apartment. Nothing but the dull silence of empty space. He shook his head, and Tiffany went to work on the lock. In less than two seconds, she had the deadbolt picked and the door open.

The idea had been to give the child some practical experience, but now he wondered how much she already knew. During his pause, her expression melted from pleased to a scowl.

"Don't thank me all at once." She stomped past him and into the apartment. Light flared inside.

Swallowing his exasperation, he followed her into Samantha Ridgeway's living room. Stunned, he looked around.

Samantha Ridgeway's totally bare living room.

The only thing between the four beige walls was a sad, broken cobweb fluttering from the ceiling. He closed the door.

"Oka-a-ay." Tiffany pivoted. "Am I the only one getting creeped out by this?"

"Let us check the rest of the rooms."

The kitchen wasn't quite as pathetic as the living room. The counter held a coffee maker, a toaster oven and an open package of biscuits. He checked the refrigerator. The appliance gave the mold colony in a Chinese take-out box a home, a partially consumed six-pack of diet soda its only company.

He swung the door shut in time to catch Tiffany reaching for an Oreo on the counter. Smacking her hand away, he said, "Do not touch the biscuits. In fact, do not touch anything unless you must."

"They're called cookies, Duncan. You've been living in the U.S. over a century. Learn the language."

A grunt expressed his opinion of how Americans mangled the Queen's English.

She grinned at him. "Here I thought you may have been concerned for my health."

"That too." He surveyed the spartan cooking area. What a sad life Miss Ridgeway must have. Was the emptiness of her home indicative of an emptiness in her life? He gestured for Tiffany to follow him.

And stopped short at the bedroom door.

"Holy shit. Someone's been here before us."

"No." His eyes registered the papers scattered across the floor. A computer desk was tucked in the corner. Empty mugs and CD cases littered the space between a flat screen monitor and the phone on top. Piles of clothing didn't make it into the open closet or the various open dresser drawers. Somewhere in the chaos, a pattern existed, but he couldn't think past the rumpled bed sheets holding her apple-sweet scent. Pushing aside the wave of desire, he surveyed the room with a critical eye. "No, I believe this is the room's natural state."

"Ugh." Tiffany brushed by him and stepped into the room. A foil wrapper crinkled under her boot. "This is worse than her car. Uh, Duncan—"

He spotted the poster-sized photograph pinned to the right wall the same moment as Tiffany. Under other circumstances and with other subjects, he'd have offered to buy the piece. It showed an excellent eye for detail and naturalism of the subjects. The window of Phillippa Mann's antique shop framed the shot, an aesthetic black and white print that captured the humor shared by him and the proprietress.

Stepping closer, he examined the clothing they both wore in the photo. "Bloody hell!"

"Yeah, this was taken Monday night." Tiffany's eyes narrowed. "Bitch cut me out of this shot, too." She shook her head before grinning. "You seriously have a stalker problem here."

Through gritted teeth, he growled his niece's name.

Sobering, Tiffany shifted into enforcer mode. "This confirms she's been tailing us at least four days." Maybe there was hope for the girl. She slid into the desk chair, hit the tower's power button and started rifling through the files in the little two-drawer cabinet while she waited for the computer to boot.

Dumbfounded, he returned his attention back to the photo. How the bloody hell had he not noticed Ridgeway had been following him? If it weren't for Tiffany spotting Ridgeway's vehicle, Duncan would have blindly exposed himself, not to mention the entire coven.

"Because you've been a little preoccupied with Alex and Logan, along with the other missing folks," Tiffany said.

He turned to her, surprise at her perception interrupting the shock of Ridgeway's game. Tiffany shrugged her thin shoulders before she said, "You're leaking."

Hands clenched into fists. Damn! He needed to get himself under control. He hadn't accidentally transmitted his thoughts since his seventy-fifth birthday party.

Tiffany gave him a little reassuring smile. "It's okay. I'm worried about them too. Here." She handed him four files. "Nothing about supernaturals. Looks like she's working on a story about Jessie's kidnapping."

"How the devil did she find out? Davis kept it—"

A sly smile lit Tiffany's face. "Look at Ridgeway's file. Remember, Jess said there was a witness in the alley when those nutcases grabbed her. And Commissioner Davis had to cover up an anonymous 9-1-1 call."

"Ridgeway," he muttered as he started looking at the reporter's notes.

"Ridgeway." Tiffany nodded in confirmation. "According to her notes, she was trying to get a shot of Jess coming out the back door of the maternity shop when our dear cousin was nabbed by those fucking idiots."

"Language, child."

He ignored whatever obscene hand gesture Tiffany not so subtly aimed in his direction. How did a simple search-and-rescue operation get so screwed up? He flipped another page of the file concerning him. Ridgeway thought he was "yummy"? Blood started flowing south. *Spanish Inquisition. Remember the Spanish Inquisition.* "Anything on the computer?"

"More of the same. Doesn't look like we're in trouble." She snickered.

"She's aiming to make you the *Scoop*'s 'Hunkiest Man Alive.' I'm down-loading Kensai's virus now."

He couldn't help a smile at the little piece of revenge on Ridgeway. The Japanese-born enforcer's program would corrupt anything on her hard drive. Of course, she might recover the information.

If she coughed up a year's salary for a data retrieval expert. From her bank account records, she'd be lucky to produce next month's rent.

They both froze when the phone rang. On the heels of the second ring, the answering device on the set beeped and Ridgeway's recording said, "You know the drill."

"Sam. Ralph." A severe bout of coughing interrupted the man's voice. When he spoke again, the hoarseness almost obscured his words. "I just talked to Max. I'm sorry to hear about Fred. Let me know the funeral arrangements, and I'll have Agnes send flowers." Another bout of coughing echoed through the speaker. "Max's worried about you and this mystery project of yours. He'd better not be talking about the Jessie Alton follow-up. Call me."

Tiffany's breath released with a hiss. She shot Duncan a look. "Be glad she doesn't use the phone company's voice mail."

"O'Malley." His fists clenched. "Caesar was supposed to speak with him."

She nodded, a thoughtful expression on her face. "You know he has. Sounds like Mr. O'Malley had already nixed her story on you."

So what was Ridgeway up to? "Let us finish before she returns." He crossed the room. On top of the dresser lay more digital photo cards and three packages of conventional 35mm photos. Air froze in his chest as he examined them. Every single one featured his image. When he found the negatives in each of the envelopes of prints, he released the pent-up breath in a small prayer of relief and shoved the entire mess into the huge pockets of his coat.

Something caught on a sleeve button as he turned. He lifted the flimsy material to find a pair of black lace panties. His breath didn't catch but turned into a solid lump in his chest.

"Okay, done."

Somehow he managed to shove the lingerie back into the drawer while Tiffany swept the CDs on top of the desk into her messenger bag, shut off the computer and wiped down any surface area she touched. He thanked every saint he could name she hadn't noticed the undergarment.

Careful to turn off lights and lock the door again, they exited Ridgeway's apartment. As they headed for the SUV, he paused.

Tiffany stopped, her hand reaching for her favorite weapon. "What's wrong?"

Something crawled along his spine. He tasted the night air, but no particular scent aroused suspicion. No stray thoughts. Nothing.

He shook his head. "I had the sensation of being watched."

She brandished the standard yellow No. 2 pencil. "Can you be any more vague?"

He shook his head at his discomfiture. No doubt Ridgeway's lucky success at following him on top of his failure to find their missing people played with his mind. The first problem was rectified. The second problem could be solved in the next forty-eight hours.

"It's nothing. Come." Long strides brought him to the vehicle's door and forced Tiffany to run to keep up with him. "We have an appointment at Mallory Labs."

The plastic casing of Selene's cell phone creaked under the strain of her tense grip. "Are you sure?"

"I think I can recognize my former boss." Marcus's sardonic reply filtered through the tiny receiver. "His snot-nosed little whelp is with him."

Fury iced the blood in her veins. She rose and began pacing in front of her office window. Two years ago, Marcus would never have dared to speak to her in such a disrespectful tone. "Do you regret following me into exile, my grandson?"

"No, Your Majesty. I am merely following up on the woman seen with Nguyen this morning as my queen requested." The younger vampire's voice held the proper contrition.

Maybe she depended on Marcus's loyalty too much. Most of those who followed her into banishment were opportunists, but she counted on the real family bond between her and Marcus to keep the rest in line.

She couldn't worry about Marcus's discipline now. Her suspicions concerning Nguyen's behavior were justified. "Have they discovered your presence?"

A soft snort, one not audible to Normal hearing, came through the speaker. "Of course not. I'm on a rooftop, downwind and nearly a block away."

She let his sarcasm slide. There was too much to be accomplished in the next few hours to allow any complications. "Search the apartment and question the reporter. I want to know what Nguyen leaked and if she's spoken to any of her superiors."

"Shall I dispose of the reporter as well, my queen?"

"Yes." She pressed the "End Call" button. A manicured fingernail tapped against the cracked plastic as she stared across the Los Angeles skyline and considered her options. Nguyen obviously tried to reach Caesar through a subsidiary company under the Augustine Conglomerate. At first blush, Nguyen's choice of the *Scoop* seemed suicidal until one considered the editor was a supernatural. No doubt, O'Malley would have reported an employee's findings to Caesar by now. She and Mallory would need to move up their timetable if her take-over of the Augustine Coven was going to succeed.

And the only way to accomplish her goal would be to prove the V-Prime project worked.

Crossing back to her desk, she punched the number for security.

"Adams here."

"Mr. Adams, we need a candidate for human testing. Tonight."

Chapter 6

I wiggled my butt deeper into the soft leather seat of Max's car and sighed in pleasure. Definitely worth the crap he gave me at dinner. He had finally backed off when I told him he wasn't coming with me tonight for the umpteenth time. Then he piled on the dire predictions of what he'd do to me if I so much as scratched the clear coat on his car. I smiled sweetly before peeling rubber out of his driveway and speeding into the brightly lit Los Angeles night.

Yummy and Goth Girl already knew what I looked like so I wasn't taking any more chances. I may not be the chick from *Alias*, but I can hold my own in the disguise department, not to mention driving a different vehicle. A quick stop at my apartment before tonight's fun and games would be sufficient.

My fingers drummed a rhythm on the steering wheel as I headed home. What was Fred's connection to the Jessie Alton story? It was definitely something more than me asking him to run a couple of illegal background checks. I rolled it over and over but came up with nothing. Nothing but me, which sent another round of guilt-ridden acid to join the lasagna sitting in my stomach.

I had to be missing something, a major piece of the puzzle. Fred's death less than twelve hours after St. James threatened me made no sense. Guilt gnawed at my conscience. What little conscience I had left any way. Why not come after me?

In my brain fog, I nearly rear-ended the Saab ahead of me when he slammed on his brakes. The two other drivers in front of him had also slammed on their brakes to avoid a black SUV roaring out of the driveway to my apartment building.

A very familiar black SUV.

My heart lodged in my throat, but Goth Girl didn't spare the Camry a glance, much less the other drivers giving her friendly one-fingered waves. The gas-guzzler sped down the street, my suspects intent on their own destination. Had they been waiting for me all day and had finally given up for the night?

Annoyed honking erupted behind me and I tapped the accelerator. A smile tugged my lips. Two could play the follow-and-wait game. And I tried very hard to shove the thought they'd been waiting at my apartment to kill me into a deep, deep hole.

I hung back, not making the overeager mistakes I had last night. Goth Girl also wasn't driving in the same erratic pattern, which made me want to kick myself for falling into her set-up. This time they headed for a different section of the city.

Pre-fab office buildings rose from the overly landscaped terrain of a city park on my right. On the left, the blue and white neon of the Mallory Laboratories, Inc. sign glowed under the halogen streetlights. They passed the biotech campus and pulled into the overflow parking lot between the labs and another set of office buildings.

Damn, no way I could get closer without revealing myself.

Glancing up the street, I headed for the parking garage serving the next huddle of offices. A few cars were still scattered on each level. I breathed a sigh of relief that the top deck was deserted. I parked and climbed out of the car. Snatching my equipment, I crossed to the concrete barrier edging the deck. A nearly full moon and the lack of Los Angeles's usual smog gave me an unobstructed view of both the bio-research complex and St. James's SUV.

I couldn't resist a smirk when I peered through the telephoto lens. Goth Girl's profile edged the driver's window, but no large shadow sat next to her. Where was St. James?

I frowned and pulled out the nightscope I'd picked up on eBay. Maybe St. James thought the damage to my Civic and the photo cards would discourage me. Maybe he believed he had scared me off between his threats and Fred's death. I nibbled my lower lip as I considered the events at the warehouse district. If he wanted me out of the way, why not kill me when he had the chance? No witnesses and a handy dumpster would have been much easier than mowing down Fred in broad daylight.

A lot of this wasn't making sense. Okay, most of it wasn't making any sense whatsoever. Like the one security camera on the Mallory complex's outer wall that seemed to stare at me for a couple of minutes before it continued to scan the grounds.

I was getting paranoid in my old age. And I still had nearly four years until the dreaded three-oh.

A slight movement a hundred yards from the SUV caught my attention as I peered through the night scope. From the ground, St. James would be invisible to the rent-a-cops in their go-carts. Heck, he was nearly invisible to me even with the nightscope. Only his movement crossing the grounds gave him away. He seemed to flow in and out of the shadows faster than humanly possible as he approached the campus wall.

Mallory Labs had spent some serious dollars on the landscape surrounding the main complex. Instead of one gigantic concrete slab, the area was broken up into smaller parking lots with contoured hills, shrubs and trees giving the illusion of the wild. Probably some idiot exec's idea to mimic the forest around his retreat in Colorado. I hated to think about the water bill for this place. But the foolish expenditure definitely gave St. James an advantage.

Timing his moves with the rhythmic sweep of the cameras, St. James froze next to a tree when a pair of guards passed before he proceeded to the next shrub for cover. My appreciation for him leveled up a notch when he shinnied up the brick wall encircling the main buildings. His gloves and boots must have climbing hooks on them, but the similarity to Spider-man was eerie. Except . . .

I blinked a few times before I peered through the lens again. He wasn't wearing gloves.

Deadly looking steel spikes embedded in mortar ringed the top of the wall. They were spaced too closely for even an anorexic like Goth Girl to slide through. Anyone insane enough to try to climb over them would impale himself. And as much as St. James annoyed me, I didn't want him eviscerated. Otherwise, I couldn't watch his sexy ass squirm in jail.

St. James reached the top of the wall and stretched out. Lying on his side despite his bulk and the spikes, he pulled a small object from his clothing and tied it to the spike above his head. Curiosity drove me crazy, but I couldn't make out what he held.

He pulled something else from a pocket and tied the second object to the spike closest to his waist before he crawled back down the wall. St. James retraced his steps and climbed back into the SUV. Goth Girl departed the parking area at a sedate speed. Whatever they were up to, they weren't worried about being caught.

I noted the position of St. James' objects before gathering my equipment. His acrobatics had to have been the weirdest thing I'd seen since I started with the *Scoop*. Running through possibilities, I settled into Max's car, switched on the ignition and headed for the exit. The auto attendant had its wooden arm raised for the night so I didn't have to climb out to dismantle the thing.

I considered heading for Mallory Labs, but I didn't have the equipment or the fingernails to climb the wall like St. James. Daylight would give me a better opportunity to discover what he tied to the wall spikes.

Spy cameras were a feasible prospect. Somehow, I didn't think it was a bomb. Taking out a small section of brick wall didn't make sense if he wanted to damage Mallory's operation. I'd have to check with Agnes to see if she'd found where the billionaire's celebutante daughter was taking her "vacation." Maybe a little bargaining was in order to find out if any new projects of the biotech firm had pissed off someone like PETA.

A giant yawn reminded me how little sleep I was working on. After a full eight, I could come back in the daylight, check out what St. James left behind and still be in position when he and Goth Girl came back tomorrow evening. Whatever they were planning wasn't happening tonight. A shudder reminded me they had been at my apartment earlier. Maybe I could talk Max into letting me stay at his place. Just for tonight.

The tension wringing my neck and shoulders eased as I regarded my game plan. I left the car window down, trying to stave off my sleepiness. The chill breeze helped as I turned onto the little two-lane road cutting through the northwest side of the recreation park parallel to the main thoroughfare and headed for home.

What was up with the Deranged Duo? There wasn't a link between Mallory and St. James that I had found unless St. James had added industrial espionage to his resumé. What would interest him in a squeaky-clean biotech corporation?

I frowned while I considered St. James's path each time I had followed him. The visit to the antique store in one of the older neighborhoods of the city. Talking to a bunch of homeless kids in an abandoned building downtown. A visit to Reno's, a notorious biker bar in an ugly section of Los Angeles. Last night's escapade by the river. Tonight's visit to Mallory Labs. And then losing them near Brentwood the first three nights. What was the connection between the disparate destinations?

A droning sound behind me caught my attention. The flash of moonlight on metal in the side mirror warned me a split-second before the van rammed into the back of Max's car. *What the hell?* The jolt nearly ripped the steering wheel from my death grip.

The idiot didn't have any headlights on. High-pitched whining warned me, and I wrenched the wheel hard to the left, avoiding the van's second try at me. All moisture disappeared from my mouth. The driver gunned his engine to bring the van even with the Camry. A quick glance sent my heart into overdrive. It looked just like the van that mowed down Fred.

Thank god, I had metal and plastic around me. That didn't mean I was safe. I sucked in a harsh breath through dry lips and stomped the gas pedal. The van careened as the attempted sideswipe launched it into the narrow, grassy berm between the road and the duck pond.

I risked a quick look back. The van was an inky spot against the moonlit vegetation. Still no headlights glared from the rearview mirror. The spot grew to a blob as the van sped towards me.

Fear and anger chased each other through my brain. Anger won the race. This bastard was not making me pay for any more damage to Max's car. Bracing myself, I yanked the emergency brake and a hard left on the wheel at the same moment. I would definitely send a thank you gift to Jake, ex-boyfriend and stuntman extraordinaire, for the driving lessons.

If I survived the night.

The bumper screeched a mournful protest as the van caught and ripped it from the backend as I whipped around. With any luck, the jagged plastic would poke a hole in the van's radiator. The one-eighty complete, I punched Max's six-cylinder forward and flipped off the headlights. Two could play this game. Aiming for the picnic area, I prayed I could find a hidey-hole in one of the spots long enough to call the police for help.

No one ever told me how hard it was to drive at night without lights. Moonlight turned everything either into pale imitations or gigantic shadows, potentially hiding the bogeymen chasing me. I slowed to avoid dunking myself in the duck pond. There was no hint of the van's telltale drone between the whistling wind and my own pounding heartbeat. I really wanted to believe it wasn't the same vehicle that mowed down Fred.

Taking the curves among the barbeque pits as fast as possible under the pitch-black grove, I headed for a picnic pavilion with a lean-to. Glimmers of moonlight between the trees guided the way. Pulling up short behind the slanted sunshade, I switched off the ignition. With all the screeching tires and crunching metal on plastic, the park wildlife had fallen silent. As the rasp of my own breathing slowed, the chirps and whispers started again.

The lean-to would cover an infrared signature from the Camry's engine from the main road. The metal shade didn't quite meet the concrete pad so the tires would be obvious if the bad guys had a nightscope. A familiar engine hummed louder as the other driver wound down the main lane through the middle of the park. My breath caught, lungs refusing to work.

Please go past. Please go past.

The sound of the van's engine remained steady as it continued past my hiding place. I waited until it faded completely before I gulped some air and flipped the ignition. Not daring to turn the headlights back on, I eased the car back towards the park's west road while I dug for my cell phone in the bottom of my purse.

Panic dropkicked my heart at the blinking low battery light. I'd forgotten to recharge it at the apartment earlier. I hadn't been home since Fred's death. And my car adaptor was sitting in my Honda.

Please God, all I need is a few seconds of airtime. Just let me get through.

Time dragged on forever. In the corner of my eye, the phone's icon blinked faster.

"9-1-1. Please state your city and state."

Yes! I was definitely going to church on Sunday.

My voice was shaking so bad it took three tries to rattle off my location to the cell company's 911 operator before she could patch me through to the local emergency line.

The second operator clicked on. "9-1-1. Please state the nature of your emergency."

"I'm being chased by a van. It's trying to run me off the road, but—"

A soft click and both the display and the line died along with any possibility of help. I drew in a deep breath and released it, counting to ten in Spanish. *Think, girl!*

Okay, I'm on my own with these guys. I nodded to myself. No problem. I've gotten out of worse scrapes. Except I've never had someone actually try to kill me. Russell Crowe and a hotel phone not withstanding.

Up ahead, the lights of the tennis courts winked a friendly greeting. I was almost to the park's west entrance. The next instant my last little twinge of hope I had died a fast, painful death. A dark van sat waiting in the driveway to the courts' parking lot.

Damn! How could they have swung around me so fast?

My blood froze in my veins as two and two finally made four in my sleep-deprived head. There was more than one van after me.

I eased up on the gas. My pulse beat an erratic rhythm in my ears. If I hit the brakes, the driver would see the taillights. Just a few yards between the van and the park exit. Freedom was close enough to taste.

Fingers clenched around the leather steering wheel cover. No choice then. Coast as close as possible, then hit the gas and pray I'd make it to the street before the van's driver reacted. If this worked, then it would be a race to the closest police substation.

Quarter of a mile. 300 yards. 200.

I jammed the accelerator hard. The Camry's injectors whined in protest. Lights blinded me the instant I was past the park billboard. A sickening crunch sent me and the Camry spinning like a toy top.

For the couple of seconds I could think clearly, I wished vertigo made me see two vans. Then the guy who had been hiding behind the park's announcement billboard revved his engine, aiming to broadside me again. My heart clambered up my throat in its own desperation to get out of the car.

I stomped the accelerator. The Camry roared but went nowhere. Flinging the gearshift into reverse, I pumped the gas again to no avail. All I could do was watch as the huge shadow charged.

The van nailed the driver's side, sending me sliding down the embankment towards the retaining pond. A lurch as something caught the car, a deeper dip on the right side. Then the car started to roll, the ground rushing up to smash the passenger windows.

My last coherent thought was Max would kill me for wrecking his car.

Chapter 7

Consciousness came back with painful reality. My head throbbed in time to the beeps next to me. I eased my right eye open, then pressed it closed as the fluorescent bulb spiked new agony in counterpoint to my headache. Maybe drowning in the retaining pond was a better idea after all.

If I was lying in a hospital, someone must've found me. Maybe a patrol car passed through as the Camry and I were rolling down the embankment.

I started to reach for my head. Nothing moved. I tried again. Okay, right arm not responding. The left hand couldn't lift any further than the right. Neither leg so much as twitched.

Shit! I'm paralyzed!

Panic eased when I realized I could still feel the nubby texture of a blanket underneath my immobile fingers. Despite my brain's best efforts to shut off, I raised my head and opened my eyes. The wave of nausea left me choking, but I registered the straps holding me down. The accident must have been worse than I thought if the hospital staff had to tie me down.

A round of dry heaves left me gasping for breath. Damn! If the idiot hospital staff were going to anchor me to the bed, they should have left someone to watch me. I really needed some water to drown the sandpaper and acid exfoliating my throat. Not to mention the probable concussion beating its way through my gray matter. I didn't see a call button, not that I could reach it if I found one. I would have to wait. And patience was never my strong suit.

I must have drifted off because the sound of the door swooshing open woke me from a dream about Daniel Craig leaving his wife for me. I considered looking at who had entered the room but refused to surrender to another round of heaves.

"No faking, honey. I know you're awake," a saccharine-loaded voice said.

God, I hate cheery nurses.

I peeled one lid open. Except I never saw nurses before who could pass for goodfellas. The two ladies in the center dressed in traditional puke green scrubs. A couple of blinks revealed only one nurse, but she had the broad build of a Rams defensive lineman though she lacked the height. The muscle with her wore the proverbial black t-shirt, black sports jacket, and black slacks. The color did nothing to slim their bodies or hide the guns they both carried under their coats. The double-vision returned with a vengeance, threatening another bout of dry heaves.

Wonderful. So much for my sweetly imagined, last-minute rescue.

I groaned and closed the one eye. "Water." The raspy noise from my throat was not recognizable as my voice, and it burned to make the sounds, but Nurse Ratchett must have comprehended. Fingers slid under my skull and raised my head up so I could sip from the cup held to my lips. She took away the blessed coolness too soon. "More," I croaked, a little more coherently this time.

"Sorry, honey. We need to ask you some questions first."

"Head hurts."

Acid fire shot through my left hand, and I screamed. Both eyes shot open.

"Oh, I know, honey. Unset bones can be so painful."

Through tears, I saw the bitch smile at me as she pointed an index finger at my swollen left hand, something I hadn't noticed earlier with the overwhelming headache. Nerves screamed along with me as she deliberately jarred the broken appendage again. Bones scraped against each other under my skin.

"Now we've taken your mind off your headache, let's talk, shall we? Girl to girl?" Nurse Ratchett pulled a chair close to the bed and plunked her fat ass down.

The combined pain brought the threatened dry heaves close to the surface. I swallowed hard and gripped the nubby blanket with my right hand. The insane part of me rejoiced my writing hand wasn't hurt, which meant I was damn close to shock. And I needed what brains I had left to figure a way out of this.

"Now, dear," she started, laying a motherly hand on my arm, "what's your affiliation with Duncan St. James?"

My "huh" ended with a scream when she jabbed my injured hand.

Anger mixed with pain so I saw red either way. It took a couple of minutes before I could think coherently enough to talk. "What the fuck are you talking about?"

"He was seen leaving your apartment tonight."

My thoughts could have been ice cubes in Dad's martini shaker. I had more people than St. James watching me? "What?"

She poked me again, waiting patiently for my howling to stop.

"You fucking bitch—" I started, but my words dissolved into another hacking round of dry heaves. The aches in my throat and stomach were closing in on the ones in my head and hand.

"Now, now, now. I get after the boys for that kind of language." She wagged her torture instrument at me. "Let's try again, shall we? What's your affiliation with Duncan St. James?"

"I don't know what you're talking about."

She raised the finger.

"I'm serious! I don't work for him or anything!"

She poked anyway.

I must have passed out because the next thing I knew she was spraying icy water in my face. Heckyll and Jeckyll were in the corner of the room, trying not to piss their pants from laughing. Tears dripped down my cheeks to join the freezing mist. Now I understood why cats hated getting spritzed in the face so much. I was ready to claw Nurse Ratchett myself.

I settled for the hissing and spitting part of feline behavior.

"You can torture me all f—" At Ratchett's warning look, I changed my word choice. "—freakin' day. You can have Heckyll and Jeckyll start cutting off fingers." I nodded toward the duo in the corner before returning her look glare for glare. "It doesn't change the fact I can't tell you jack."

I could rat out his business address and his PI license number, but the basics obviously wasn't the information Nurse Ratchett wanted. And what was he doing at my apartment? From the grin on her face, Ratchett enjoyed the torture way too much to stop while I puzzled everything out.

She aimed the finger. I squeezed my eyes shut, gritted my teeth, counted each breath, and waited for the shifting bones to set fire to my nerves.

When I got to fifty, I dared to peek at Ratchett. She was still poised, but her lips pursed as if she actually considered my words. I wasn't sure how long she stared at me, but finally she lowered her hand and stood.

"Keep an eye on her," she ordered her two goons. She favored me with a frown before she marched out the door.

Once the door stopped swinging, my jaw muscles relaxed. Until I noticed that Heckyll eyeballed my lowly little B-cups. A brand-new queasiness developed in my tummy. My concussion and broken hand wasn't going to deter a gangbang if Ratchett gave them the go-ahead. Probably wasn't going to even if she didn't, but I still found myself praying for her quick return.

Someone must have been listening to me because the door whipped open. A tall, thin man in a lab coat strode in, Ratchett on his heels. Peering at his clipboard through coke-bottle glasses, he hummed to himself like my pediatrician used to, but I definitely wasn't getting a lollipop at the end of this visit.

He looked down at me and smiled, his face reminiscent of someone who enjoyed his job. From what I read in history class, so did Mengele.

I was screwed.

His attention flicked from me to the chart then back to me. "She's baseline. If she can't tell us anything about St. James, then we should find a better use for our patient."

"The pit?" asked Ratchett.

He nodded.

"Aw, man!" Heckyll whined. "What a waste!"

What could possibly be worse than rape and a bullet through the head? Not wanting to find out, I made a pathetic attempt at struggling with Heckyll and Jeckyll as they unstrapped me. So pathetic they held me over a waste can while I puked up the miniscule sip of water in my stomach.

Waves of dizziness prevented me from memorizing the layout of the place as they dragged me to "the pit." Anger kept me from passing out. Anger at these bozos for not realizing I wasn't worth the effort of kidnapping. Anger that Max would blame me for his demolished car. Anger my end would be in some crappy pit.

Maybe it was the concussion, but I giggled. *Garbage made my living, garbage would be my ending.* Maybe shock was finally setting in, but I was laughing hysterically by the time my escort dragged me into some room with a metal grate floor.

Ratchett crossed to the middle and bent to pull up a trap door. She motioned to Heckyll and Jeckyll, who hauled me over and lifted me off the floor. Survival instinct butted aside the insane laughter. I flailed, screamed and kicked. Ratchett grabbed my face and squeezed hard.

"If the boys drop you in head first, you won't survive the fall." She pressed a vicious smile against my face. "If you land feet first, you might have a fighting chance."

Once again, blood froze in my veins. Whatever was about to happen wasn't going to be quick. Or painless. Her words startled me long enough for Ratchett's boys to shove me through the opening.

I landed hard, remembering at the last instant to roll right, not left. Even so, the impact flashed searing pain through my broken and cracked parts.

Soft whimpering filled the space, and it took a minute to realize I was making the noise. Boots on metal echoed as the quartet tromped out of the room above. I caught a glimpse of concrete walls and a sawdust-covered floor before they shut the door behind them. A small splash of light fell through the tiny window in the door upstairs, then filtered past the grate to land in the middle of the wood chips. So the sick bastards weren't even going to watch.

I sighed. For all I knew, microscopic web cams lined the wall, and Ratchett and her boys didn't want to chance my blood splashing up through the grate and staining their clothes.

Hugging my broken hand to my chest, I rose to my knees, dizziness tracking every move I made. I carefully tilted my head up and gauged the grate to be ten feet above the floor. I was damn lucky not to break anything else in the fall.

Rising to my feet, I stumbled and waited for the nausea to lessen before examining my cell. The couple of inches of sawdust on the floor wasn't enough to pile, even if the stuff was remotely stable. The walls appeared smooth except for some darker areas at the rear of the room. No way was I going to climb out of here.

I crossed the cell and ran my good hand over the wall. No, just one dark area. Not concrete as I first thought but matte steel. I frowned as foreboding flooded through my tattered nerves. Not wall at all but a door to who knew where. Or what.

The hinges were on the other side—not that I had any tools to pry the pins out. I swallowed hard then cursed my captors. They couldn't come up with anything better than some "B" horror flick ending for me. I checked what the bad guys had left me with.

Not much, I discovered. T-shirt, jeans, bra and panties. Nothing in my pockets and no socks or shoes. Damn. If I had something to cut with, maybe I could make a rope of my clothes. Then I remembered Heckyll's leer and decided I'd rather meet the monster behind the door clothed than Heckyll while I was naked.

I ran my good hand through my hair, desperate to think. How the heck was I getting out of this?

My fingers brushed the goose egg behind my left ear. The tender flesh ached but didn't give to the slight pressure. It seemed my skull was intact under the knot. I sucked in a deep breath and concentrated. Injuries were the least of my problems.

I shuffled through the sawdust, hoping to find a piece of wood bigger than a Frosted Flake. Any weapon was better than no weapon, but all I accomplished was to stir up enough dust to set off a round of sneezing. My head pounded harder than ever.

I sat down in the middle of the pool of light and let loose the tears of despair. Giving up was not in my vocabulary but I figured I might as well add it before I died.

The bad guys didn't let me wallow in self-pity long. I had sniffed twice when the metal door swung upon on silent hinges. I rose to my feet. I had more of a chance than Fred had against the stupid van. Ratchett and her boys were probably stuffing their faces with popcorn while they watched me, hoping for a good show. Then dammit, I'd give them one.

An awful reek flooded through the black opening. I took two steps toward it when something dark, filthy and incredibly thin slunk through the doorway. My first guess of a rabid dog crashed when it seemed to alternate between all fours and its hind legs. I heard a snuffling sound as it slid along the perimeter, like it was testing my smell. No, not a dog. More like a starved baboon with mange.

I tensed every muscle and backed slowly, circling toward the gap in the wall as well to keep as much distance as I could between us. I didn't dare move too fast and provoke the creature, but my effort was for nothing. The door swung shut, dashing any hope I'd get out before the thing attacked. My attention shifted to the thing trapped in the pit with me.

What I assumed was thin fur at first appeared to be a thick layer of dirt embedded in sparse body hair and possibly ragged cloth. I couldn't be sure without a closer look, and its atrocious body odor and my own fear didn't make checking a desirable option. I wasn't sure how the thing could distinguish my smell from its own. I sure as hell couldn't.

I matched its pacing around the room until I was once again on the side farthest from the steel. When the creature reached the door again, it sank to the floor on its rear haunches and stared at me. I bit my tongue to keep from screaming. Large eyes regarded me through matted, dank locks. I'd never seen anything like the neon blue orbs glowing softly in the dim cell. Worst of all were the two-inch fangs protruding from the sunken, almost human face.

Raw fear gripped me. My pain receded to a dim throb in the face of my panic. Why was the thing just looking at me instead of attacking?

"You know they expect me to eat you, don't you?"

I jumped at the hoarse sound coming from the creature. It was right on that count, but a monster with a Texas accent was the last thing I anticipated.

"Well, actually they expect me to drink your blood," it continued. Or was that he? The voice sounded masculine. He gave me a grotesque grin. The skin on his skull resembled a facelift gone horribly wrong.

"What are you?" I tried to project confidence. The quiver in my voice didn't help.

"Don't worry, darlin'. I'm not doing the sons of bitches' dirty work. Hear me!" His voice rose to a bellow though how he got volume out of his emaciated chest I'll never know. "I'm not doing your goddamn dirty work!" He seemed to collapse upon himself after his outburst, like he used the last of his life in his show of defiance.

He looked so pathetic I took a tentative step towards him, but he gave a small shake of his head.

"Don't come any nearer, darlin'. The bastards've been starving me, hoping I'd lose all reason." He favored me with another hideous smile. "I can't guarantee my gentlemanly behavior will continue if you get too close."

I nodded and eased back to the wall opposite from him. Once seated in the sawdust, the throbbing pain returned full force now that my adrenaline charge was shot. We watched each other for a few minutes before he spoke again.

"To answer your question, I'm a vampire."

I couldn't help the laughter burbling from my throat. "I'm sorry," I said, attempting in vain to smother the giggles. Yep, definitely going into shock. Either that, or this guy needed one of Agnes's tin foil hats.

He just watched me, like a predator who finds an unknown animal curious and isn't sure if he wants to take a bite.

Finally controlling the laughter, I cleared my throat and tried again. "I think they've held you here too long. You're delusional. There's no such thing as vampires."

"Used to think the same thing until I met one a little over a century ago." He shrugged. "Doesn't matter if you believe me or not." Another grin. "Wouldn't happen to have a stake on you? Or some silver?"

"What do you mean? What for?"

He sobered, sending a skitter of fear down my spine. "They're planning to leave us in here until you die of thirst or I kill you." He shrugged again. "You killin' me would prevent option number two."

"I'm not killing you any more than you're killing me. Got it?"

He smiled again. Maybe I was getting used to him, but the fanged grin didn't quite scare the beejeezus out of me this time.

"You got spunk, girl. What's your name?"

"Sam." No sense giving whoever might be spying on us any more information than I had to. Oh, who was I kidding? They'd probably retrieved my ID from the wrecked Camry.

"Short for Samantha, I bet." At my nod, the glowing eyes seemed to leave me for another place and time. "I knew a saloon girl by that name once. Pretty thing." His eyes returned to me. "Not as pretty as you though."

His comment didn't have the same vulgar quality as Heckyll's. I laughed and began to relax. Maybe I wasn't going to have to battle for my life after all. Not that I relished dying of dehydration.

"Are you always this charming in challenging situations?"

"Charm enough to make up for my looks and smell."

I laughed again, wondering what he'd look like after a full hot-water heater and a bottle of soap. Not as good as Yummy. Not even Brent Poole cleaned up as good as Yummy.

"I don't clean up half bad, darlin'."

The skitter reversed course back up my spine. Was he reading my mind?

At my pause, he gave me another toothy smile. "I can't stand the smell of myself, so I sure as hell don't know how you can stand me."

I grinned. "I don't usually comment on strangers' hygiene."

He laughed at the easy camaraderie. "So what'd you do to piss off the bastards upstairs?"

I frowned, not sure how much or what to tell this man. Sorry, vampire. The possibility of Ratchett and her boys spying on us remained. "If we're going to exchange life stories, how about you tell me your name?"

"Alex."

I couldn't help another grin. "Short for Alexander? I knew an Alexander once. I beat the daylights out of him in fourth grade after he dropped a rat down my shirt at his sister's sleepover. You're definitely uglier than him."

Alex's laughter turned into a coughing fit that left him prone on the floor, panting.

I started crawling toward him, but he waved me off. "You may not believe my story, but it's not worth risking your life over," he said, his voice gruffer than ever. If he wasn't starving and filthy, he was the type of man every woman in the room would swoon from his personality alone.

"So where in Texas are you from originally, Alex?"

"Born in Baltimore actually. Father moved us west when I was three 'cause of Mama's health. He was mortified I picked up the local accent."

I laughed softly. The story was all too familiar. "It's not hard to disappoint parents, is it?"

"What'd you do to yours?"

Hot blood rush through my cheeks. I don't know why I was embarrassed telling Alex about my job. I sure as hell wasn't last night with St. James. Assuming it was last night when I'd had my run-in with St. James in the warehouse district. I'd lost all track of time since the van clobbered me and the Camry.

Still, my reticence had nothing to do with potential spies. I swallowed hard before I said, "I work for a tabloid."

"Not fond of the yellow press, are they?" He grunted. "So you got too close to Tyrone Mallory and his kidnap and torture club?"

I gulped. "Is that where we are? Mallory Labs?"

He cocked his head. "Where did you think you were?"

"I wasn't sure." I sighed and rubbed my temple, trying to ease the obscene headache. "I was driving through the park on my way home last night—" I frowned and shrugged with one shoulder, not wanting to aggravate the broken bones. "At least, I think it was last night. This van rammed my car and ran me off the road." I gave Alex a wry grin. "Actually, it was—" I couldn't take the chance of mentioning Max. "—a colleague's car. I guess I don't have to worry about him killing me now."

Alex's chuckles dissolved into another coughing and choking fit. I couldn't stand seeing him suffer. The frustrating part was not being able to do a damn thing to help the man. I didn't try to approach him again, but the reporter in me kicked in once he caught his breath.

"What do you mean about Tyrone Mallory's kidnap and torture club?"

He shook his head. "You don't believe in vampires, remember?"

"Indulge me."

"He snatches supernaturals—"

"Supernaturals?"

A chuckle escaped from Alex. "You really are a journalist, aren't ya, darlin'?"

Funny. Alex calling me "darling" didn't send my heart racing the way St. James had. Or maybe it had been the way he'd touched me when he said it.

An odd look came over Alex's face, but his voice retained some humor as he continued. "A supernatural is someone who isn't Normal. Witches, weres, and vampires fall into that category."

His emphasis made "normal" sound like a proper name. Almost the way Agnes said it when she warned me about bad vampires. I rolled it over a couple of times in my head before I asked, "Upstairs, they said I was baseline. That means a normal human, right? Why the hell would they grab me?"

"Good question."

Well, wasn't he just the font of information. My gray cells may have been damaged, but there was an unspoken statement in his story. "So you're saying there are other races?"

He chuckled again. "The fairies are another tale."

Fairies, huh? Maybe the poor guy had lost it down here in the dark.

If Alex believed he was a vampire, I wasn't going to correct him about the non-existence of the rest. Then I frowned as I remembered the mad scientist's opinion of me. What the heck was going on here?

Before I could formulate another question for my compadre, the steel door swung open again. Three men in full combat gear marched into the room. Two had giant guns at the ready. Alex had no chance to react before the assholes pulled the triggers. No crack of bullets, but the double electric shock of the tasers left him screaming in pain.

I scrambled to my feet as Thug Number Three strode towards me. I aimed a kick at his shin. Bad move because he only grunted when I connected. Before I could aim higher, he grabbed me in a headlock and dragged me towards the door.

Alex yelled, "Leave her alone!" But the reward for his attempted chivalry was another round of electric shocks. If he wasn't starved to near undeath, I'm sure he would've taken all three bastards.

Maybe my concussion was worse than I thought if I was beginning to believe his insane story.

My eyesight started to go fuzzy, but I wasn't sure if it was the head injury or lack of air. The door slammed behind us, but I could still hear Alex's hoarse cries behind the steel. Tears of rage and pain leaked down my face as I clawed at the arm encircling my throat.

The thug half-dragged, half-carried me through a couple of more doors. When we stopped, the thug tossed me on linoleum tile. Without thinking, I tried to catch my fall with my broken hand. I collapsed at the excruciating pain. Through my moans, I heard him march away and another door slam shut.

Uncurling from the fetal position on the floor, I raised my head. A utility folding table rose in the middle of the stark, white room, flanked by two equally utilitarian metal chairs. Two more goons stood in opposite corners with stun guns ready.

The only color in the room was a scarlet tie. It took a few minutes for enough oxygen to reach my brain to register the tie was connected to a man. A man I recognized from the Mallory Labs website.

Like most CEOs, Tyrone Mallory had the well-preserved look of someone who works out without actually working and the hard eyes of someone who sold his soul decades ago. His immaculate black helmet hair held the right touch of gray at the temples, looking distinguished and powerful instead of ancient and weak. The artful dye job would have made Mom's stylist proud. Manicured fingers strummed next to a stack of papers on the tabletop. He examined me with the same distaste displayed by the head of a soft drink distributor after finding a mouse in a can of his product.

"I expected better of both Maxwell Howell and Duncan St. James."

I frowned, but the best comeback in my pained state was "Huh?" I was really slipping in the smartass department. And what did my brother have to do with this? I'd been careful not to mention him to Alex.

"Don't play coy with me, Ms. Ridgeway. I know you spied on my research facility. My people mistook who you were working for." The smile on Mallory's face would have given Jaws the shivers. "Howell and St. James have joined forces, haven't they?"

"I don't know what you're talking about." The sad part was I really didn't know. Even without the recent brain rattling, I'd have a hard time connecting my nerdy brother with Mr. Yummy. But if I wasn't any use to Mallory, I wouldn't survive long either. I had too many puzzle pieces, even if I had no clue of how they fit.

Mallory frowned and stared at me. "Sitting on the floor is uncivilized, Ms. Ridgeway." When I failed to move, both goons crossed the room, jerked me up and slammed me down in the other chair, hard enough to rattle my teeth. Stars swam in my vision as my brain protested the additional shaking.

Fear flooded my body. What the hell had I gotten myself into? This sounded less like some Hollywood-Mafia deal and more like one of Agnes's conspiracy theories every minute.

"The games aren't necessary, Ms. Ridgeway. I'm aware of Howell's investigation as well as St. James's."

I swallowed the hard lump of nausea collecting at the back of my throat. Time. I needed time. "I don't know what investigation you're referring to. I'm working on a story about Jessie Alton. You know, the TV sitcom *Buddies*?"

Mallory's right eyebrow twitched. He didn't believe me.

My neurons struggled to work past the pain. How was Max involved in this? He didn't mention anything about working on a story at dinner. He'd been more worried about his street snitch, Anne . . .

Oh God! My stomach lurched as four and four jumped to eight. Agnes had mentioned folks disappearing off the streets. Alex said he'd been kidnapped as well. Was the Jessie Alton incident related to the other missing folks? Had Mallory's goons fed homeless teens to their monsters in the basement? Had Max and St. James both followed leads to Mallory Labs?

And Fred? Fred had paid for my stupid curiosity with his life.

The fear contorted my insides. My body curled as dry heaves racked it. I expected to hit the floor, but one of the goons held me in the chair. When the retching stopped, he held a cup of water to my lips. The blessed coolness disappeared after a few greedy sips.

The shark smile returned to Mallory's face. "Isn't that better?" He checked the manicure on one hand. "Now then, Ms. Ridgeway, what do Howell and St. James know and what do they expect to discover?"

I blinked the tears out of my eyes, trying to make the spinning stop. "Max doesn't have anything to do with this. I borrowed his car because mine's in the shop." If Mallory didn't hesitate in killing Fred, kidnapping me or torturing Alex, then he'd do worse to my family. I needed to stall long enough to find a way to warn Max and my parents.

"You haven't illuminated me as to why St. James was at your apartment earlier."

I licked my cracked lips. "I didn't know he came by."

"So you don't deny your association with the Augustine Coven?"

The man was obviously missing more than one screw. "Coven? What coven? Do I look like a witch to you?"

"Just because you're not a coven member doesn't mean you're not Family."

Family again. My vision blurred as I connected the dots. Fred had said there were things worse than the Mafia. I blinked until the two Mallorys melded into one once again. "You might want to get your accusations straight. Am I supposed to be a witch or a mobster?"

Ice gray eyes bore into the core of my soul, and I shivered in response. "We've already recovered Mr. Howell's car. The only question is whether you'll be in it and conscious when I have it destroyed. I suggest you answer me."

I had no doubts about his sincerity, so I launched a little of my own. I returned his gaze, but it took all my willpower not to flinch. "Max doesn't know jack. Nurse Ratchett was closer to the truth than you. I borrowed the car to tail Duncan St. James for a story I'm working on."

Forefinger and thumb framed Mallory's face as he leaned an elbow on the table.

I needed to talk fast. But how the hell to spin it to keep me alive long enough to call for help? Would Alex live long enough for assistance to arrive? He was already in pretty bad shape. First, I needed to give Mallory a reason to keep me alive.

I sucked in a deep breath. "This isn't Max's story. I'm writing a follow-up on St. James's rescue of Jessie Alton from the Sunshine Believers a few weeks ago."

"Waitaminute! You're Sam Ridgeway? From *The National Scoop*? I read your stuff all the time. I thought you were a guy." The goon behind Mallory grinned in pleasure until the death glare from his boss shut him down. Despite the situation, I felt a little thrill. I would have offered him my autograph if the guy wasn't under orders to kill me.

When Mallory turned back to me, his grimace of distaste was reminiscent of my mother's. I couldn't help the smug look I knew was spreading across my face. "Guess your people aren't crack investigators after all?"

"I find it hard to believe a Pulitzer Prize-winning journalist would let a tabloid reporter borrow his car." He drew out the last few words like it pained him to force them from his throat.

In that moment, I knew Mallory had no idea of the real connection between Max and me, so keeping the smart-ass look on my face wasn't hard. I had legally changed my name to Grandma Neel's maiden name as soon as I turned eighteen, more to piss off Mom as much to sever any connection professors and potential employers might make between my brother and me.

Now, I had to make sure Mallory didn't have a reason to dig deeper. Mom and I had our differences, but I didn't want her dead along with Max and Dad.

"Then where did Max work in high school?" At Mallory's suspicious look, I added, "Long before he joined the *Times*?" An annoyed edge came with my words. Not smart in my situation, but no sleep and a concussion will seriously mess with your head.

His attention flicked to the papers in front of him, and an eyebrow rose in surprise. Narrowed eyes returned to me, and I shrugged. It wasn't my fault he didn't bother to read Max's full résumé. "My editor used to be Max's, and Max owed him a favor. Everyone at the *Scoop* already knows you're behind the disappearance of a bunch of people, and we've already connected you to the Sunshine Believers. Anything happens to me, and they'll run the story."

I held my breath, waiting for him to call my bluff.

Dark red suffused Mallory's neck and face. "Have Howell's home and office searched again to be sure," he snapped. "And have someone search the *Scoop*'s offices." Static crackled behind me as Goon Two relayed the order on his mike. "Has anything been recovered off Ridgeway's hard drive?"

"No, sir. The hard drive's been corrupted with a virus. The techs are still working on pulling the residual data."

Crap. They'd already searched my place and found St. James on my wall. No wonder they thought I was an obsessed employee. Had they found my backups stashed in the crawlspace behind my tub too? No, they couldn't have if they were messing with my hard drive. And what virus were they talking about? I was meticulous about my virus protection. Is that why Yummy and Goth Girl had been at my apartment? To search it and fuck with my computer?

Another worry poked my damaged brain. Neither Max or I were big on photos. Okay, photos of each other or family members. My conceited brother only had framed pictures of him with the rich, the powerful, or the popular on his walls. I was fairly certain they wouldn't find anything at his place connecting us other than the birthday card I sent him last month, the one signed "To Snotface, From PITA."

But if Max really was working an angle on Mallory or they decided to search Mom and Dad's . . .

And Mallory's people had already visited Max. Now, I knew the real reason he had talked our parents into staying in Europe for an extra week. Oh God, what if they ignored him and came home? I tried to shut off the ugly train of thought, but it chugged right along through my consciousness, amping up the fear and nausea.

Mallory's holier-than-thou demeanor didn't lessen. "The question becomes what do I do with you, Ms. Ridgeway."

"How about sending me to a hospital so I can get my hand set?"

Instead of answering, he motioned to Goon One. "Please have Dr. Able and Dr. Kane join us." Goon One hesitated for a moment before turning smartly on his heel and marching from the room.

This wasn't good. "No offense, but I think I'd like my own doctor."

"I assure you, Ms. Ridgeway, we have the finest medical facility in the city." The smile he flashed me was not reassuring at all.

"Murdering me isn't going to hide what you're doing here. If you let me go, I can kill the story. We can go our separate ways. No harm, no foul. Right?"

"I don't plan on killing you." My shoulders didn't have the chance to relax before he added, "At least, not yet."

Which meant I was about to become someone's play toy, or worse, food. *Think, girl!* Shoving the looming hysteria aside, I analyzed the situation. I'd never make it to the door. Not with Goon Two's stun gun leveled at me. It would take a distraction of some kind, maybe the next time they moved me.

I managed to keep my mouth shut until Goon One returned with the so-called doctors. Ever the fake gentleman, Mallory introduced them. Dr. Able turned out to be the asshole who ordered me thrown into the pit with Alex. Kane was Hardy to Able's Laurel, a rotund little man with a cheesy Adolph moustache.

"Dr. Able, please explain why you choose to put Ms. Ridgeway into the pit."

Able's sadistic bravado from earlier disappeared, and his Adam's apple bobbed at his audible gulp. "She's baseline, sir. We didn't need her for research." He swallowed again. "Her usefulness seemed limited to breaking Stanton."

Alex's last name? The information would be useful if I managed to escape. Maybe even notify his family. Poor folks were probably worried sick. Focusing on Alex and his family kept thoughts of my own fate at bay.

"I see," Mallory murmured, though his tone clearly indicated he didn't. "And your opinion, Dr. Kane?"

Able's partner visibly shook, but his voice remained steady. "As I told my associate earlier, Ms. Antonius ordered testing of the V-Prime project. We shouldn't waste a viable human candidate." He shot a withering look at his partner who turned white.

V-Prime project? Candidate? Oh God, they weren't using me as a guinea pig?

Mallory watched them both like a cat deciding which mouse to eat first. "If we're ready for testing, I see no reason to wait." He rose from the table but paused next to Able. Without looking at the scientist, he said, "Next time, remember to clear any disposals with me." Then he strode from the room.

As if Mallory's words hadn't told me what was coming next, the goons started towards me. I jumped from the chair, shoved Kane into Able with my good arm, and dodged to keep them between me and the goons. There was a crash behind me as I charged for the door.

The first electric jolt slammed through my body as I wrenched the door open. Unlike Alex, I didn't have the luxury of screaming. White-hot bolts exploded in front of my eyeballs as every nerve short-circuited. I collapsed to the linoleum, writhing uncontrollably. By the time my five senses returned, the goons had carried me to another room.

I bucked and clawed against the straps holding me to the gurney, broken bones grinding in my desperation. The mad scientists busied themselves at the counter and ignored my cries and curses.

Nurse Ratchett appeared above me, syringe and needle ready. "Now, sweetie, I'll take good care of you."

I renewed my futile attempts to escape. Her elbow, sharp for the amount of flesh surrounding it, jammed into my chest and knocked the breath out of me. As I struggled to get air, her fingers tied the rubber tourniquet to my right arm and jabbed the needle into the vein.

The weight disappeared from my chest, followed immediately by a floaty feeling from whatever she injected into me. Ratchett reappeared with a pair scissors and went to work on my clothes.

"Bitch! Those are my favorite jeans!" My words sounded slurred even to my ears. I wanted to fight but couldn't muster the coordination to blink, much less spit at her. My mouth felt like it was full of marbles. Ratchett must have understood me because she chuckled and said, "I don't think you'll need these again."

The disassociated sensation became worse. I couldn't wiggle my bare toes. And the panic-induced tears trickling into my hair and ears didn't even tickle. The waft of air from the A/C raised goose bumps on someone else's naked flesh.

Soft voices murmured around me, but I couldn't understand the words. Then Kane appeared in my blurred vision, gripping a needle that had to have been a foot long.

I started screaming before he touched me and continued long after the fire he injected burned its way through my veins.

Chapter 8

The nightmare jolted me upright. The hospital-issue gown I wore was soaked with sweat. I ran a hand through my damp hair, trying to remember the dream. Something about a group of Frankensteins turning me into their monster.

I took a deep breath and looked around. Soft blue walls reflected the fluorescent tube above the bed. Electronic beeps timed my heart's rhythm. The wire from the EKG machine dived down the sleeve of the gown. Solution dripped through the IV tube taped to my right wrist. I read the bag hanging next to the bed.

I frowned, squinted, blinked, then read the bag again. Damn, I could actually see the microscopic print of the Cleveland manufacturer at the bottom. My ophthalmologist said it could take up to three months for my eyes to settle from the Lasik, but dang! I needed to call and congratulate him for the terrific job.

I relaxed a little at seeing the clear liquid was standard glucose. I plumped the pillow. Or I tried to. I have the firm opinion powdered cement filled hospital pillows.

Focusing on the tiny spider weaving away in a corner of the room, I leaned back against my cement pillow and tried to remember why I was in a hospital. Fuzzy thoughts twirled inside. Closing my eyes, I breathed yoga-style until something materialized.

Fred!

I bolted upright again. Fred had been hit by a van. I had been following him from the coffee shop, and he had been plowed over.

Lying back down against the bed, I battled through the confusing images clogging my neurons. Fred died. No, he'd been hit by a van first and his Pooh watch broke. Max picked me up at the hospital. I had dinner with someone. Was it Fred or Max? I had been tailing St. James until someone named Alex said he was supposed to eat me. More vans chased me or was it the one that hit Fred? A really bad Elvira impersonator licked her fangs. The rest fell apart in the fog.

I rubbed my left hand over my face, trying to clear the cobwebs. If Fred was killed by a hit-and-run, the emotional trauma would explain the nightmares about vans, weird doctors, and secret labs. Had the same van clipped me when it hit Fred?

No, I was in Max's Camry when the van crashed into the side. The car rolled with me in it.

Or had it? I held out my left hand and stared at it. The distinct memory of broken bones and agony haunted me. I flexed the fingers and rotated my wrist. No discomfort and everything bent and stretched like it was supposed to. I never had a dream so . . . vivid before.

I was searching for the nurse call button when the room door swung open.

Nurse Ratchett!

Everything poured back into my brain in an instant. The look on Ratchett's face said it all. I wasn't supposed to be awake.

Raw fury drove me. I leapt from the bed and crossed the room before Ratchett could grab the door handle. The electrodes ripped off layers of skin as I moved, and the EKG screamed a warning. The IV needle tore from my hand, but the adrenaline rush must have overridden any pain I might have felt. Slamming Ratchett against the door, my fingers dug into the wattle of flesh below her chin and squeezed.

Her eyes bulged as her nails clawed at my hand. I heard frantic thumping and looked down to see her feet kicking the door a good six inches off the ground. So, the stories about extreme strength in extreme stress were true. I set her down and eased the pressure from her neck but still kept a firm grip on her.

"Where am I?" My voice sounded alien, a demonic growl.

Naked fear shone in her eyes. She didn't like the tables turned. I tightened my grip and released to encourage some cooperation.

"Where am I?" I repeated.

"You're in Mallory Labs." *Damn, I was still here?*

"Show me where to get some street clothes." The idea of trying to escape from a bunch of mad scientists and their armed thugs with my ass hanging out the back of a hospital gown sucked the big one.

"Down the hall." Ratchett choked the words out.

Survival instinct made everything so clear. Ratchett smelled of fresh apples covered in ash. I could count the beads of sweat on her pasty face. If I wasn't so focused on escape, I'd question my own sanity.

I yanked her away from the door and peered through the tiny, vertical window. No one out there. Good.

I looked at the woman whose neck I had my fingers wrapped around. I had a good four inches on her, but she probably outweighed me by seventy or eighty pounds. From her quivering flesh, she was scared shitless right now. I should have been scared shitless, but I felt good. Better than good. Like I could take on Mallory's entire fucking army.

Eventually this fabulous adrenaline rush would wear off, and she'd try to take me or escape. I frowned at her, deciding to deal with that when it happened. Ratchett shook harder.

Easing the door open, I took a longer look up and down the hallway. Still no one. Considering my luck lately, it wouldn't be empty for long.

I jerked her in front of me. "Which way?" I snarled. Might as well make the most of my advantage.

She pointed right so I marched her in that direction. Four doors down, she pointed right again. "H-h-here. Th-th-this is the employee locker room."

What the hell was wrong with her? She was shaking so bad I could barely keep a grip on her. She acted like I was the sadistic bitch who tortured her.

Then again, helping me escape would probably land her ass in the pit. With something a lot worse than Alex.

I yanked the door open and shoved her inside. Cream ceramic tile flooring reflected industrial green walls. A small kitchenette flanked the left side of the room while rows of lockers and benches dominated the right. The overwhelming smell of disinfectant and soap indicated a bathroom somewhere close. I pushed Ratchett toward the lockers before I grabbed a chair from the kitchenette and wedged it against the closed door. The flimsy plastic and aluminum wouldn't stop Mallory's goon squad, but it might buy me a few precious seconds.

Ratchett had edged further away from me as I dealt with the door. I turned in time to see her hit a bench with the back of her knees and thud down ass-first.

"W-what are you going to do with me?"

I couldn't believe it. She and her cronies had kidnapped me, tortured me, experimented on me, and she was worried about what I would to *her*?

"I need a size twelve. Both pants and shirt." I swallowed because I really hated admitting the next thing to anyone. "And size ten shoes."

Ratchett blinked. "Locker seven. Shelly's a fourteen. I-I-I don't know about the shoes."

I took a step towards her, and her face went from pasty to blotchy. Good grief, the woman was going to give herself a heart attack before I could escape. "C-C-Charlie wears eight in men's. Locker sixteen!" Her voice had risen to a shriek, and she threw up hands as if to ward me off.

My head shook with disgust. The bitch was super brave as long as I was tied down or she had backup.

I popped open the first locker she pointed to while keeping an eye on her. She quivered in place, all her joints locked by her fear. My own worry and panic disappeared at the sight of the shopping bag from my favorite lingerie store. I poked a finger in and pulled it open. Tags still hung from the aqua bra and panty set. I smiled, flung the hospital gown at Ratchett's face, and wiggled into the smooth satin. I wasn't about to don someone's used undies. Mallory and his people owed me. Big time. My boobs swam in the C cups, but I didn't care.

I pulled on the denim next. Shelly was not a fourteen. The three-sizes-too-big jeans started sliding down my hips. Not good if I needed to run during my escape. Rummaging through the locker, I found a gaudy scarf serviceable as a belt. The rose-colored ruffled shirt wasn't my taste, but it was better than the hospital gown. I grabbed socks and athletic shoes from Charlie's locker and pulled them on. I stood up and wiggled my toes. A little roomy, but I could run in them.

Ratchett hadn't moved from the spot where she landed. I crossed to stand over her. Whites completely surrounded her pupils.

I crouched next to her. If I tried to find Alex, the odds of me getting caught were pretty high. If I were caught, I'd die, no one would warn Max that Mallory was onto him, and Alex would starve to death. Choosing between a stranger I barely knew and my family tore at my gut.

But if I made it out, I could report Alex's whereabouts to the authorities.

Okay, Max could report Alex's whereabouts. My cachet with the LAPD still sucked from the Alton kidnapping.

I glared at Ratchett. "How do I get out of the complex?"

She shook her head. "Y-you can't." She wetted her lips. "T-t-too much security."

I reached for her, and she flinched, sliding away from me along the bench until she hit the floor. I stood and stalked after her, and she crab-crawled until she slammed into the row of lockers against the wall behind her.

"You can tell me how to get out of here, or I can give you the same treatment you gave me." I prayed she wouldn't call my bluff.

"He'll kill me!" she wailed.

"You think I won't?" Not that I would, but she didn't need to know that little tidbit.

The door rattled against the chair. I whipped my head around, searching. There was no place to hide. My only chance would be to take the person at the door by surprise. I raced for the entrance. Part of me wondered if I'd totally lost my mind.

A sharp blow to the door sent the chair skidding across the tile.

"Charlie!"

Before Ratchett's scream died, I reached Charlie, jerked the stun gun away and rammed the butt into his groin. As he collapsed to his knees, I brought the stock down on his head. Hard. Both his helmet and the gun shattered with a sickening crunch.

I stepped back in shock. It was the goon who stood behind me during Mallory's interrogation. Who gave me water. Who wasn't breathing, his chest way too still. I couldn't have hit him that hard.

My own gasps were harsh in the silence. The fragments of metal and plastic fell from my nerveless fingers, and I took a step back. *This is not happening to me.*

Ratchett didn't give me time to contemplate my new career in assault and manslaughter. She landed on my back, screaming and hitting. I staggered under her weight and the force of her leap but managed to stay upright. I backpedaled into a steel locker. She didn't loosen her grip. Nails raked across my lids. I rammed her into the bank of lockers again and again until she sank to the floor.

Gulping for air, I turned. The corner of the first locker had caved in. My view slid down to the floor. Ratchett's eyes stared blankly at the ceiling.

Oh God, this isn't happening! It's just a nightmare. Drugs from the accident.

Blood seeped from the back of Ratchett's head and oozed across the tile. Backing away, I whirled and raced for the bathroom on the other side of the lockers. Bending over a toilet, I hurled. Instead of normal vomit or the expected dry heaves, a dark, curdled liquid flew from my lips. When I was done, I just stared at the reddish stuff in the john. Something was terribly wrong. The normal, post-puking ache in my gut turned into something worse. Vicious cramping drove me to the tile. Every breath stretched my limit for pain. Curling into a ball, my body spasmed in agony. I needed a real doctor, and I didn't know how I would crawl to the bathroom door, much less get out of the complex.

After a few minutes, the agony eased enough for me to drag my shaking body upright. Not looking at the toilet, I flushed and stumbled to the sink. My hands shook so bad it took me three tries to turn on the water. I couldn't bear to look at myself in the sink-to-ceiling mirror. I rinsed and grabbed a towel from the basket sitting on the counter. It came away from my face stained pink. I dropped it and fled the bathroom.

Only to face the bodies of the two people I had killed.

Self-defense, the rational part of me told the horrified part. *They were going to kill you.* It didn't change the fact I had murdered two people. Tears welled, but I brushed them away. *No time for this*, the rational part ordered. I needed a way out, or I'd be joining Ratchett and Charlie.

I stepped over the corpses, trying to avoid the blood pooling underneath Ratchett's head and spreading across the tile. Easing the door open, I peered up and down the hallway. No one had come to investigate the commotion.

Not sure which way to go, Eenie-Meenie-Mienie-Mo seemed my best option. On Mo, I turned left and jogged back up the hallway, trying not to think of the dead man whose shoes I wore.

Knowledge tickled the back of my gray matter. Somehow, I knew I was underground. I also knew it was after sundown. The certainty I felt of those facts scared me.

At the first intersection, a bank of elevators appeared on my left. I glanced at the single control panel. No option but up, so I punched the button. The chrome doors slid open, and I jumped aboard, afraid another goon would come around the corner of the hallway any second. The buttons were sequential so I had no clue how many underground levels there were. I pressed "7", and the doors coasted shut. I figured worst-case scenario, climbing down stairs was a lot easier than climbing up.

"Please enter your security card."

I jumped a foot at the computer-generated voice. Once my heartbeat returned to normal, I prayed the damn machine would let me back out. As the doors opened, I breathed a small sigh of relief, then swallowed the acidic taste of nausea and guilt and headed back down the hallway to the employee lounge.

Once I grabbed the badge clipped to Charlie's belt, I ran back for the elevators. My imagination worked overtime. I would have sworn I heard screams echoing faintly down the corridor.

Just don't let the damn thing ask for more than the badge. If the elevator required retinal scans or fingerprints, I was screwed. I was not chopping off anyone's hand or head to make the damn thing work. I inserted the badge into the key slot.

"Identification: Charles Adams. Please select destination."

Damn, now "The Addams Family" theme ran through my head. I hit "7" and released the breath I hadn't realized I'd been holding. As the machine rose, my muscles tensed the closer each number blinked to "7", scared the elevator would stop and I'd have company. Finally, the doors parted. I took a tentative step out.

This must be an executive floor. The plush burgundy carpet offset the silver and gray striped walls. Recessed lighting gave the hallway a relaxed atmosphere, totally opposite of the sterile nightmare below. I glanced right. Out the window at the end of the corridor, I spotted the parking garage from which I had watched St. James, not sure if the incident had been last night or several nights ago.

The lawn was a good thirty or forty feet down.

Okay, I went a couple of floors too high.

The elevator doors had already closed, so I punched the button.

Instead of the elevator opening, claxons howled and the subdued golden light turned a flashing red. Damn it! They must have found Ratchett and Charlie's bodies. I jabbed at the button again, but the doors weren't opening this time. I spotted a glowing exit sign and dived for the door to the stairwell.

I whipped it open to come face-to-face with one of Mallory's armed squads. Slamming the door shut, I raced back up the hallway. *Please let there be another set of stairs!*

Bullets ripped through the metal door and shattered drywall as security unloaded their weapons in their blind attempt to nail me. So much for the stun guns. Mallory must have decided I was now a liability.

The bang of metal on plaster and men shouting echoed up the corridor as I rounded the far corner. Just visible through glass and plants, open space appeared ahead. An atrium. The reception area and the front doors would be close by. If I could make it to the street, I could flag down a driver.

Yeah, right, Sam. This is fucking L.A.

I glanced back at my pursuers. They weren't behind me. Yet.

I turned back in time to run nose first into someone's chest. I bounced off, both of us landing in a tangle on the floor.

"You!" St. James' green eyes glared at me from between my legs. A black turtleneck and tight black pants emphasized the planes and angles of his body.

He picked tonight to break into the labs?

Approaching boots stamped a rhythm. Fear-induced adrenaline ripped through me. Survival overrode lust. I scrambled to my feet. "I've got to get out of here!"

St. James yanked my wrist. Hard. Hormones and fear spurred a reaction the opposite of my usual fast-talking solution. A roundhouse left connected with his jaw. My left fist. He flew backwards. His head slammed into the drywall, sending out a spider-web of cracks.

No pain. I must not have broken my hand after all. St. James wouldn't be so gentle if he got a hold of me this time. Mallory would be worse.

Whirling, I circled the landing and raced for the atrium's decorative staircase. If St. James had any sense, he'd follow my lead. Another squad shot out of an intersecting corridor and spotted me. There was nowhere to go. For a long, slow, horrible instant, I watched the leader raise his gun and aim it at me. In the back corridors of my mind, I heard St. James yell a warning.

Something hit me in the chest. I fell into gray and red mist.

An instant later, St. James held me in his arms. There were sounds of firecrackers all around us. Something stung my face, but the pain seemed so far away. I looked up and his eyes were no longer just green but glowed neon like Alex's had. His lips were drawn back in a snarl. Fangs protruded from his mouth.

I wanted to scream but couldn't find the breath. No. Alex was wrong. Vampires didn't exist.

Still carrying me, St. James leapt on top of the planter ringing the landing. I caught a glimpse of the main floor, three stories down. Then he jumped. I gladly landed in the blackness rushing up to meet me.

Chapter 9

Fine cracks rippled across the marble from the impact of Duncan's boots. The girl hung from his arms, literal dead weight. Brilliant crimson streamed out of her flesh and soaked his clothing. No breath, no heartbeat and his mission blown to bloody hell.

He couldn't help her, but he couldn't just drop her either. He didn't wait for the Normals to recover their wits. Another leap covered the lobby. The glass may have been shatterproof, but a kick sheared the metal bolts locking the front doors. Wind rushed across his face as he ran. Behind him, the crackle of radios called for reinforcements. No time to head for the gap in the wall Bebe's potion had created before he was intercepted.

Tiffany, meet me at the front gates.

No coherent answer, just a stream of vomit green disgust flowed through the mental link. The spicy scent of sandalwood interrupted his partially formed rebuke.

Supernatu—

Sharp reports echoed across the campus, swallowing the remainder of his warning. Panic hammered at his heart. *Tiffany!*

Brick-red anger replaced his niece's disgust. *Nailed three of the bastards. Hurry!*

Another crack of gunfire, this time from the building, not the parking areas. Gathering his strength and clutching the dead girl to his chest, he launched his body straight up and over the front gate. Concrete crunched beneath his feet when he landed.

The putrid smell of rotten meat mixed with burning rubber as the SUV slid to a stop in front of him. He wrenched the rear door open and threw himself and his load on the seat. "Go!"

Acceleration slammed the door shut as Tiffany executed a tire-squealing J-turn. "Holy crap! All I can smell is dead vamps. Were you hit?"

"No." He brushed blond hair from the girl's oval face. Skin, translucent from the lack of blood, seemed to glow pale silver. The only thing marring her visage was a small cut above her right eye. His fingers sought a pulse in her neck. Nothing.

"Who is it? Who'd you find?"

He glanced up to find wide brown eyes reflected in the rearview mirror. "Samantha Ridgeway."

"What! You rescued a Normal? What the fuck was she doing there? Did she blow this whole operation?"

He let Tiffany's tirade continue as the SUV zig-zagged through the streets. He twisted to face the rear window, scanning for anyone following them. After a few minutes with no sign of pursuit, he relaxed enough to consider Tiffany's questions. What was Miss Ridgeway doing at Mallory Labs? Guilt stabbed at his heart. Had his mental suggestion to drop interest in him not taken effect? Had she shaken the compulsion by reviewing her files at her apartment?

Or had she really been working for Mallory all along? No, the security team had definitely been chasing her, not him. He glanced down at the still form. Curiosity may not have killed the cat, but it certainly had snuffed the life of the reporter lying in his arms.

Now that the immediate danger had passed, something odd struck him. Miss Ridgeway's scent wasn't right. No longer crisp Granny Smith with citrus overtones, her scent was more like, like . . . steel. He inhaled deeply, letting the odor sit on his tongue. No, the hint of apple and grapefruit was still under the omni-present metal.

"Is she dead?"

Tiffany's soft question drew his attention. "Yes. The guards shot her."

His niece slammed a palm against the steering wheel. "Great. That's just fucking great."

But there should have been a touch of decay in Ridgeway's scent already as the individual cells collapsed and died. The bullet had hit her point-blank. Her mind was the empty slate of the deceased. He peered closer at the obscene hole in her ribcage.

A horrible squelching came from the cavity in the girl's chest.

"What the hell was that?" A note of panic edged Tiffany's voice.

Miss Ridgeway's lips parted. A wet moan filled the passenger compartment. Another squelching sound, and her chest rose ever so slightly. His fingers rose to her neck. A soft thrum pulsed beneath his touch. Was her body tricking him into believing she was alive? One last firing of neurons?

Again, the veins jumped beneath his fingers. The spongy sucking as her chest rose. Then the ephemeral sensation of *presence*.

"Duncan?" Tiffany's panic no longer edged just her voice. The emotion filled the passenger compartment, clogging everything with ashes.

Miss Ridgeway struggled with another breath, the sound of lungs expanding in the wound no longer as horrifying. The beat in her throat grew stronger, less erratic.

"She is alive."

"You just said she was dead."

As Tiffany spoke, the small cut on Samantha Ridgeway's forehead sealed and faded.

He frowned. "Apparently, I was incorrect." The same steel scent flavored another deep inhalation, not a vampire's distinctive sandalwood. He hadn't spotted her since their encounter Thursday evening, had assumed his suggestion had worked. "Three days" rang through his mind, but she hadn't been Turned.

He should detect musk if she were part were. A witch couldn't heal with this speed, and a fae wouldn't smell like an iron blend. No, something else was going on.

Tiffany made a hard left.

He braced a leg against the frame to keep him and Miss Ridgeway from slamming into the opposing door. "Where are you going?"

"Nearest hospital's Cedars. We're too far from Good Sam."

"No."

Tiffany glared at him from the rearview mirror. "She's a Normal. She needs a Normal hospital. If you're worried about the ER reporting the GSW, we can buzz Commissioner Davis and have him meet us there."

Protectiveness curled through his chest. Whatever was happening in his city, Samantha Ridgeway was in the middle of it. "Our townhouse is closer."

"Are you fucking insane!" Tiffany flicked a harried glance over her shoulder before turning her attention back to the traffic. "We don't have the equipment to take care of her."

"I do not believe supplementary medical assistance will be necessary."

"What do you mean?"

No, additional aid definitely would not be necessary. The obscene squishing sound Miss Ridgeway's chest made grew quieter, approximating normal breathing. He held a palm over the wound. It no longer extended past his spread fingers. She was healing with the speed of a vampire, but why? And what did it have to do with the missing supernaturals?

He looked up to find Tiffany staring at him from the rearview mirror. "I mean you will drive us to our townhouse. Now."

"Fine," Tiffany muttered, zooming through a yellow traffic light. "But I still think this is a really bad idea."

An icy finger of unease poked the back of his skull. Samantha Ridgeway was the key to this whole situation. So why did it seem she was about to do more than turn his world upside down?

Chapter 10

I woke to the sharp smell of alcohol. My brain took a few minutes to focus. An alien picture snapped in place, and I jumped out of the strange bed I was lying in.

Duncan St. James stood in front of me with an open first aid kit and a mass of bloody towels in his hands. His aristocratic eyebrows knitted in a puzzled frown as he stared at my chest. "I really think you should lie back down."

Ri-i-ight. I'm going to do what the nice vampire tells me.

Like hell.

Part of my brain chanted, *Vampires aren't real.* The rest screamed, *Get out now!*

Putting on my best charming smile, I edged along the bed. "Thanks for all your help back at Mallory Labs." I estimated about eight feet between me and the door. "I promise your name won't be mentioned in any story I write."

Six feet. "Or your ward's."

He just stood there watching me. I had a sinking feeling he was playing with me. Just like Mallory had.

"Where do you think you are going?"

"Home."

"You will not make it very far in your current condition."

I reached for my neck, checking both sides for bite marks.

Again, an arrogant smirk covered his face. "Do not worry Miss Ridgeway, I have not bitten you. You are not exactly my taste."

It's always amazed me how polite a British accent makes an insult.

"Then where did all the blood come from?" I pointed to the towels in his hands. I can't say I was courageous by asking an alleged vampire the source of all the blood. I'm pretty sure the drugs the mad scientists at Mallory Labs had given me were damn wicked. Maybe that's why I saw glowing eyes and fangs. But the blood had to come from somewhere, and I couldn't deal with anymore dead bodies today.

He ignored my question and continued to stare at my breasts. Granted, my little B cups were nothing to write home about. Besides, weren't vampires supposed to be neck men? I looked down to see what he found so damn fascinating.

Then I realized St. James wasn't staring at my breasts but at the bloody, fist-sized hole between them.

A nightmare of memories flashed. The armed squad facing me on the balcony. The leader raising his weapon. The thud of something hitting me.

I wanted to scream. The rational part of my brain, the part I wished would shut up, pointed out with a hole of that size, both lungs were probably punctured from breast bone shrapnel and had collapsed. Therefore, I couldn't scream even if I wanted to. The rest of my brain voted to pass out and try waking up again.

St. James dropped the towels and kit, caught me before my ass hit the floor, and carried me back to the bed. After everything that had happened, his arms felt oddly comforting.

Not that I'd tell him.

"She's awake." Goth Girl stood in the doorway, carrying another armful of towels. "You still need these?"

"I do not think so. The bleeding seems to have stopped." Sitting next to me on the edge of the bed, he reached for my chest.

My sanity returned, and I slapped his hand away. "No touching without permission."

"May I?" he said with an ironic twist of his lips.

My stomach roiled at the thought of what had been done to my body. Getting shot was simply the icing on the freaking wedding cake. I tried to breathe deeply and evenly to control the nausea. Nothing's worse than the dry heaves, and I'd had quite enough of those the last couple of days.

Then it dawned on me I was still breathing. I looked down at the gaping wound, which didn't appear quite so gaping.

"She's healing almost as fast as you," Tiffany offered.

"I noticed," St. James replied dryly. He raised a questioning eyebrow, and I nodded. I must have been in shock to let him touch me in such an intimate manner. As he probed the rapidly healing wound, I marveled at the gentleness of his fingertips. Too bad this wasn't one of my recent fantasies involving him. It would've been a lot more fun.

He frowned again. "Am I hurting you?"

I shook my head. All three of us watched as my skin sealed itself without even a scar. After a few minutes, the only evidence of my close encounter with a bullet was the bloody hole in the ugly ruffled shirt and the gory towels on the hardwood floor.

"Tiffany, take the towels downstairs. There are new test strips and solution in the bottom drawer next to the dishwasher. There should be enough of Miss Ridgeway's blood in the towels to sample. Then package them for destruction."

Tiffany made a disgusted face at St. James but scooped the gross linens off the floor and stomped out of the room. Then it registered with my overwrought brain she wore rubber gloves.

"Turn around," he ordered.

I didn't want to, but something about his voice made me. Maybe Bram Stoker was right about the hypnotic powers of vampires after all. It would explain the weird desire to go home when he told me to the other night in the warehouse district.

I felt a sharp tugging, and then he tossed a blood-soaked pillow onto the bed in front of me. My teeth worried the inside of my right cheek at the sight. I hadn't even felt the pillow stuck to my back. Bile swam in the back of my throat at the crusty, reddish-brown bits flaking the lime cotton. Back meant exit wound. At least I wouldn't have a bullet taking a joyride around my guts.

Once again, strong but gentle fingertips probed my skin, sliding the borrowed, and now ruined, bra out of the way. I shivered in response, but St. James didn't seem to be paying attention to my current state. How the hell could I be turned on after Mallory's mad scientists had done who knew what to me? After I'd killed two people? After I'd been shot point-blank in the freaking chest?

Warmth pooled in my belly. The familiar and much-missed heat spread through my limbs. A delicious musk filled the air. I wanted to bury my face in the smell. What was wrong with me? I'd nearly been killed tonight. No, not nearly.

She's healing almost as fast as you. Tiffany's words finally sunk through my poor overloaded brain, along with those final moments in the hallway of the lab. Those *were* my final moments.

I flung myself across the king-sized bed, trying to get as far away from St. James as I could. "You changed me, didn't you?" I accused once I had my back against the opposing wall.

A farmer could have planted a garden in the deep furrows on his forehead.

"Changed you into what?"

"I saw you. Right after I got shot. Y-y-your eyes were glowing and you had fangs." I sucked in a painful breath. "You changed me into a vampire."

"You are not a vampire. And I did not Turn you even if you were one." He actually sounded offended. It was more of a response than he gave me Thursday night at the warehouse.

"B-b-but . . ."

We both looked at my chest. When I glanced back up, I noticed he seemed to take a little more interest in my boobs this time.

"We do not know what you are. Tiffany is testing your blood to confirm my . . . suspicions." St. James tore his gaze from my partially exposed breasts and rose from the bed to shuffle through his closet. After pulling out an ebony v-neck sweater and a matching pair of drawstring cotton pants, he held them out to me and pointed to another door. God, didn't the man wear any colors?

"You can clean up in there." He smirked again, bringing out the cutest dimple in his cheek. Not that I'd tell him that either.

I scooted as close to him as I could to snatch his clothes. I jumped back into my corner as soon as I had them.

Irritation replaced the smirk on his face. "I believe there are a couple of my towels left on the linen shelf you have not ruined. Join us in the kitchen when you are finished." With his imperious proclamation, he grabbed the blood-soaked pillow and stalked out of his bedroom, slamming the door behind him.

I looked at the remains of his beautiful paisley comforter. Crossing back to the huge bed, I flipped blue and lime fabric down. The matching solid-color sheets underneath it were soaked as well. But then again, maybe blood in bed to a vampire was the equivalent of cracker crumbs for us humans.

I sobered quickly. Except I wasn't human. Not anymore. A normal human couldn't have done the things to Charlie and Nurse Ratchett I had. A normal human couldn't heal from a point-blank gunshot wound within minutes.

What the hell had I become? What had those assholes done to me?

Trying to focus on practical matters, I sucked in a breath and headed for the door Duncan had indicated. Behind it, his bathroom was some dream out of *Architectural Digest*. Marble tiles covered the floor and the steps up to a whirlpool tub that could easily fit the entire Rams cheerleading squad. Golden fixtures accented the white, cream and beige tones.

While I longed to go for a spin in his tub, I opted for a quick shower. I needed answers more than I needed a luxurious bubble bath. But even the shower was extravagant. Double shower heads with a ledge wide enough to shave comfortably. Or do other fun things.

I tossed the ruined clothes into the trashcan under his sink. Thankfully, the can had a plastic garbage bag lining it. Duncan and Tiffany must have been concerned about some kind of contamination, given the precautions they took. I climbed into the shower stall and set the water as hot as I could stand it before I leaned into the flow.

The steaming spray did nothing to halt the instant replay that wound through my brain. Too much death. Fred. Charlie the Goon. Nurse

Ratchett. And I caused it all out of my stupid pride. By not letting this stupid story go. And now my stupid family was in danger. I sank down to the ledge and sobbed, my tears mixing with Los Angeles tap water.

I've been chased, hit, bitten and almost run over in my career. In my line of work, you expect the rough and tough stuff. But not having psycho scientists experiment on you. And turning into the living dead was definitely not part of the bargain. There was no way I could be alive. Was this my punishment for getting Fred squashed in the street?

By the time my skin turned pink, a proper heat-related pink not bloody-water pink, the tears had stopped. Numb, I turned off the water and dried with the one remaining fluffy white towel. Poking through the drawers of Duncan's bathroom, I found a wide-toothed comb, a hair dryer, and some extra toothbrushes.

Maybe the stress was getting to me, but I had a fit of giggles at the sight of the toothbrushes. A vampire who had toothbrushes. His bathroom looked so normal.

He looked so normal. At least until the fangs came out. I thought the fangs came out. Oh hell, I wasn't sure of anything at this point.

When I headed for the stairs to join Duncan and Tiffany, I almost felt normal myself. Normal enough to take quick peeks in the rest of the upstairs rooms. Besides the master bed and bath, there were a guest bedroom and a study. The last room, a black-walled cave plastered with Sandman and Dark Hunter posters, had to be Tiffany's. I followed the stairs down to the light at the end.

The kitchen they sat in held the same understated elegance as the rest of the townhouse. Duncan's soft murmur stopped when I appeared in the doorway. Rather than saying anything with her mouth full, Tiffany just shoved the bag of Doritos across the granite bar to me. I sat on the stool opposite of them and popped a chip in my mouth. Bless her for having my favorite junk food.

My stomach gave a gurgle of delight, and suddenly I was ravenous, shoveling chips into my mouth as fast as I could chew. I stopped when I realized Duncan and Tiffany were staring at me.

"Sorry," I mumbled. I scooted the empty bag away from me. A loud rumble filled the kitchen. Hunger clawed at my insides, making itself known rather rudely. It made sense in a warped way. I wasn't sure how many days it'd been since I'd eaten.

Tiffany grinned. "It's okay. Given your speed healing, I figured this might happen." The ringing doorbell interrupted her. "That should be our pizzas."

When she returned with eight extra-large pies with the works and a couple of 2-liter bottles of soda, I wondered who she planned to eat all of it. Turned out, it was me.

Tiffany only ate two slices, not even the whole pieces, since she had a thing against crusts. I scarfed those as well as the rest of the pizzas. Duncan settled for a glass of red wine. That's what it looked like, and I wasn't about to ask. Definitely too much information.

After eating the pizzas, a humongous belch escaped before I could slap a hand over my mouth. Duncan glared at me. Tiffany giggled at my lack of manners while I muttered an apology.

"Ignore him. If he had his way, we'd still be wearing corsets," she said.

I eyed the empty boxes and bottles and shook my head. "I've never eaten so much in my life."

"Really? I would not have guessed considering the amount of debris Tiffany described in your vehicle." Duncan's dry comment should have irritated me, but I was feeling too drowsy to care.

Tiffany leaned across the counter. "Don't let him needle you, Sam. If one of his werewolf buddies is hurt, they can go through ten pizzas in five minutes." Tiffany snapped her fingers to emphasize her point. "He can drink a gallon of blood—"

"We do not need to discuss everyone's eating habits," Duncan said. He turned his gaze back to me. "Though it is good to see you're eating like a human."

"As opposed to?"

"You can relax. You're not a vamp." Tiffany sipped her soda as she watched me.

"So if I'm not a vampire, what did they make me?"

"We don't know." She shrugged. "We just know you don't have the V-virus."

"The V-virus?"

"The virus that causes vampirism." She hopped down from the stool. "You like mint chocolate chip ice cream?"

I frowned at the abrupt change of subject. My gut burbled, but I confirmed the answer to her question anyway. "Love it."

She yanked open the freezer door on the side-by-side. Pulling out a pint carton, she yelled, "Catch!"

She would have made any Major League pitcher proud. I barely snagged the ice cream before it beaned me on the forehead.

She pulled out another carton. "She definitely has vamp reflexes though," she pointed out to Duncan as she grabbed two spoons from a drawer.

Duncan rolled his eyes. "Tiffany, please do not throw any more objects at our guest."

The man who had shoved my face into a wall coming to my defense? I had to admit he did rescue me from the mad scientists.

Tiffany shrugged and bumped the drawer closed with a black leather-clad hip. "Just testing her. I still can't believe you came out with her instead of Alex." She shoveled a huge spoonful of ice cream straight from the carton into her mouth.

He shook his head. "I have no reason to believe he is still alive. There were several were bodies—"

"Alex?" My head jerked up from my carton. "Alex Stanton?" They both stared at me with their mouths hanging open. A dribble of melted ice cream slid down Tiffany's chin.

"He's alive. At least, he was." I frowned as the thought hit me. "What day is it anyway?"

Fury flashed across Duncan's face. He reached across the bar, grabbed my arms and shook me. "Where is he?"

I yanked out of his grip. "In the goddamn labs, you idiot." I couldn't look at them. I jammed the spoon into the carton, trying desperately to ignore the guilt crowding into my soul. I had completely forgotten about the poor guy between my futile efforts to evade the firing squads and waking up here.

I twirled the spoon, making a soupy mess. "At least he was alive between Friday and Saturday, I think. Mallory's men grabbed me late Friday night." I grimaced at the memory. "Then they tried to make Alex eat me."

A very odd look flashed across Duncan's face. Almost like jealousy.

With a clatter, Tiffany's carton and spoon landed in the sink. "We've got to go back!"

"Tiffany . . ." Duncan's warning stopped the girl from diving through the back door she had wrenched open. Lights bounced off the familiar SUV in the garage behind her.

"Duncan!"

"I will go but not without a plan."

She snorted but closed the door. "I'm going with you."

"No, you are not. The stakes in this venture are unknown."

Tiffany jammed a thumb toward her chest. "I'm a full enforcer now, remember?"

"And we do not know how many of Mallory's security forces have been altered as Miss Ridgeway has been. I will not risk your life."

Her anger and defiance melted into whiny teen-ness. "I've been your backup all along in this investigation. You've got to let me come."

"I said no." He left the impression this wasn't the first time they've had this type of conversation and his answer wasn't changing any time soon.

"In case you haven't noticed, Duncan," Tiffany bit out sharply, "I'm nineteen."

"And all of your ancestors thought they knew everything at nineteen as well, which is the reason so many of them died at such an early age."

Real affection lay behind their banter. I wondered if my family would be as accepting of my new status. No. Dad would ignore the situation, Max would turn me into his next Pulitzer, and Mom? Mom would rant about how I'd never find a man and get married now because what live man would want a dead bride. And I wasn't even sure what I was. Undead?

Tiffany crossed the room and laid a hand on Duncan's arm. Pain and determination filled her huge brown eyes. "We have to get him out of there."

I couldn't think about Alex trapped in Mallory's dungeon. Not naked and filthy and starving. "Not that I'm unsympathetic or anything," I interjected, "but you still haven't told me what day it is, much less what I am now."

My smart mouth. My best defense against uncomfortable thoughts instead of vodka. God, I was becoming my mother with an alternate addiction.

"It is Sunday evening. How—" Duncan cleared his throat. "What were they doing to him?" The guilty look on his face mirrored my own feelings.

Damn, he was going to drag me into the abyss anyway. I sucked in a deep breath and twirled the spoon in the ice cream some more. They needed to know what was happening to plan a rescue, but the image of the pathetic creature Alex had become turned all eight pizzas in my stomach into a putrid mess. "They were starving him, trying to break him. That's why they threw me in the pit with him at first. When Mallory's boys dragged me out, they were shocking him with stun guns." My jaw muscles jumped at the memory and my own frustration. "For the fun of it, too."

Duncan's hands clenched into fists on the counter. If he hit the granite, I had no doubt it would crack in two.

I raised my head to meet Duncan's frustrated gaze. "Is there anyway we can contact his family?" My voice squeaked as I tried to avoid the tears threatening to spill.

Tiffany shook her head and waved a hand between herself and Duncan. "We're pretty much it."

I didn't want to know the answer to my next question, but the reporter in me asked anyway. "How long can a vampire last without—" I gulped hard. "—blood?"

"Years. The real danger is insanity after four or five months." Green eyes bore into mine. "And Alex has been missing for four months today. How did he seem?"

"Other than the atrocious b.o. and the starved dog look, he seemed okay. He's very charming."

Again, the weird jealous look appeared on Duncan's face. "Really?"

My eyes dropped to the now melted ice cream. "He wanted me to stake him before he lost control and hurt me," I whispered.

I raised my head at Duncan's sigh.

He gave me a rueful smile. "That would be Alex. Always the hero."

Tiffany's scowl remained in place. "We need to get him out of there before it's too late."

Duncan's face went sober. "We will. However, I used all the charms I set getting Miss Ridgeway out tonight."

I blinked. He didn't just say what I thought he said. "Charms? Like magic charms or Lucky Charms?"

"Magick charms," he said.

Tiffany rolled her eyes at his faraway tone and grinned at me. It was nice to know someone got my really bad joke. "He means 'magick' with a 'k,'" she said. "As in the real deal, not Vegas showman crap."

Duncan rubbed a hand across his jaw before he returned his gaze to me. "And first, we need to find out what was done to Miss Ridgeway. The information may give us an edge over Mallory."

"What do you mean?" I really didn't like the gleam in his eyes.

"We know you're not a vampire, a were or a witch," Tiffany proclaimed, ticking each item off on her black-nailed fingers.

My head bobbed back and forth, looking at each of them. "Are you sure? I may not have this V-virus, but the full moon was three nights ago. What if I sprout hair and start licking myself next month?"

Tiffany chuckled. "I tested for both were and witch too. There's a particular blood enzyme each one has, and neither showed up"

"The vampire skills do concern me." Again, Duncan watched me with a thoughtful look on his face. "Especially, your recovery from being shot. You did not have a pulse for nearly five minutes."

"Yeah, but If I died, then . . ." My voice trailed off as the horror engulfed me. "Oh my God, I'm a zombie!"

"Zombies are a myth, Miss Ridgeway." Duncan rose to refill his glass from a green bottle in the fridge. He took this awful revelation way too calmly. "And I certainly have not seen you take any orders."

"Or eating any brains," Tiffany chimed in cheerily.

"Okay, smarty-pants," I shot back. "Then how come vampires are real?"

He sighed wearily, sitting back down. The rich acidic odor of wine mixed with sandalwood. "Samantha, if we fully explain the other races to you, you must promise not to repeat this to anyone."

"I promise nothing until I hear the whole story."

Duncan and Tiffany exchanged looks, obviously coming to some silent understanding between them. He took a deep drink before he started. "Weres and witches are mutated branches of humanoid evolution."

"You mean, like the X-Men?"

He gave me a confused frown.

"No," Tiffany said, waving her hand at me. "Forget all the comic book jazz." Leaning close, she continued. "Their abilities are based in scientific fact, using parts of the brain and DNA normal humans don't. Since they are close enough species-wise, they can interbreed with and pass for regular-old humans."

"And vampires?"

Duncan stared at the empty pizza boxes for a long time. While my anxiety over my condition demanded answers, I had learned long ago silence brought out far more information than pestering my interviewees.

"Vampires are, or were, human."

"Oh geez, lighten up!" Tiffany's patience had left the building. She turned to me. "Like I said before, vampirism is caused by a virus. It's a disease, except you live pretty much forever, are allergic to UV radiation, and are on a liquid diet for the rest of your life."

"It is not that simple, Tiffany." A peeved expression filled Duncan's handsome features.

An expression I wanted to kiss away. I really needed to stop treating him like Chippendales eye-candy. I was dead. Wasn't I? It's not like we could do the mattress mambo. Could dead chicks have sex?

Tiffany spread her fingers in a defensive gesture. "I'm not saying I want your germs."

I got the impression Duncan suppressed a groan when he turned back to me. "The V-virus was the AIDS of 10,000 years ago. It can only be passed through the exchange of bodily fluids. It also leaves you sterile," he said.

The bitterness in his voice made me want to wrap my arms around him and sooth his pain. Geez, dying must have permanently killed some brain cells for mushy sentimentality to cross my mind. And understanding the cost of such a disease crossed out any desire for hanky-panky. But if I was dead, could I still get sick?

Distraction. Yeah, distraction is good. "But if you're talking about immortality, I'd think everyone would want to be infected."

"Dammit, Samantha!" He smacked the granite countertop hard enough to make Tiffany and me jump. "You are not listening to me. We may not age but we can still die. If everyone has the disease, we are talking about the extinction of the human race."

I sat back. Part of my mind was screaming, *Too much information!* But I had to ask the questions. "Someone must have figured out what was going on back then. What did they do to contain the disease?"

"The old rulers segregated the populations. At first, anyway." He grimaced and tried to rub the tension from the back of his neck. Could vampires get headaches? "Then human nature took over."

His pronouncement was so matter of fact it took a second for the horror and tragedy of the situation to dawn on me. "They were ostracized and then treated as second class citizens," I whispered. Were we doomed to make the same stupid mistakes over and over again?

He nodded. "They eventually became a nation unto themselves. The dying would approach them for relief. Others would kill them for sport. Tensions hit a boiling point and war broke out."

A holocaust. And it's always the winners who paint the picture of the losers. "That's where the stories about drinking human blood came from, isn't it?" I would have done anything to wipe the sadness from his eyes.

"Yes," he whispered. "There were those who used it as an instrument of war."

"So you really drink human blood?"

His fingers stopped their play with the goblet stem as his eyes met mine. "No, I do not." He actually sounded offended.

I couldn't let the unspoken remainder rest. "But other vampires did or still do?"

"Once in a while, we'll have a problem with a rogue, but we deal with it immediately." And permanently from the tone of his voice.

"If you're a vampire, how'd you end up as Tiffany's guardian?" I turned to her. "You are human, aren't you?"

"How did you discover Tiffany is my ward?" Duncan's frigid voice drew my attention back to him.

I shrugged. "Court records."

"Those dealing with minors are sealed." He glared at me.

I glared back at him. "What matters is if I can find this out, so can Mallory. He had his people snatch me because he thought I was working for you." Another ugly thought popped into my head. "I need to call my brother and warn him. Mallory thinks the two of you are working together to investigate him."

"Your brother?"

"He's a reporter for the *Times*. Look, I'm not sure how this all fits together, but I'm not going to let Mallory's goon squad kill him." *Too.* We all ignored that unspoken word.

Duncan snatched the portable phone off the base tucked at the wall end of the bar and handed it to me. "Be careful what you tell him."

I shot him a dirty look. "Well, duh." I punched Max's home number. The phone rang six times before I clicked it off and tried his cell number. I didn't want to think about why Max's home phone didn't roll over to voice mail. His voice on his cell's outgoing message made me close my eyes in token relief.

"Max, I don't know what you're working on, but Tyrone Mallory knows about it. Duck and cover. I'll call you when I can." I sighed in disappointment as I hit the "Off" button. I would have felt better talking to him in person. Then again, maybe not. Mallory had probably already disposed of Max's beloved Camry. Now, if only my big brother would check his messages . . .

"Why is your brother investigating Mallory?" Duncan crossed to the refrigerator and pulled out a different bottle of red stuff. He unscrewed the top, and the coppery scent confirmed my suspicion this wasn't wine.

The pizza rumbled in my stomach at the thought of having to drink it. I would suck as a vampire. *Ha-ha.* Right now, I needed an ally, and I couldn't afford to insult the one person who seemed to be on my side. Something about Duncan made me want to trust him too. I prayed he wasn't using some vamp mojo to engender that trust.

I toyed with the condensation on my glass of cola and took the plunge of faith. "One of his street sources disappeared a few weeks ago. Also, one of my co-workers mentioned something about an increase in missing persons over the last few months. Both situations sound awfully similar to your friend Alex. I'm assuming he isn't the only one of your people missing." Maybe Agnes wasn't crazy after all. Maybe she'd been mind-fucked by vampires one too many times. Maybe I was drawing the line between two wrong dots. But I really didn't think so.

Duncan said nothing for a long time. He poured the blood into a mug he'd retrieved from the cupboard and set it into the microwave. Turning back to me as his dinner heated, he crossed his arms across that broad chest. "What kind of experiments were Mallory's people performing?"

His non-answer spoke volumes. I shook my head, the frustration welling through the contents of my stomach. "How the hell should I know? You can't even tell me what they did to me."

The microwave beeped and he pulled out the mug. "If I knew, I would tell you, Samantha."

So. I was no longer "Miss Ridgeway." Maybe there was a heart beating in his undead chest.

"I do not appreciate being referred to as dead." His face expressed his irritation more clearly than his snappish tone. Something must have shown on my face because the annoyed look immediately softened.

"Yes, we can read minds, but if I may be frank, you just transmitted your thoughts."

"No, I didn't."

"Yeah, you did, Sam." Tiffany's face scrunched into a scowl. "I heard you too. Accidental broadcasting is pretty common in new vampires."

"But-but-but—" *Oh god! This is not happening to me.* "You said I wasn't a vampire!"

"No, you are not." Duncan took a sip from his mug before adding, "I do not know what Mallory is up to, but before this is over, I will find out what he did to you." His eyes gleamed brighter than the overheads. "And he will pay."

Chapter 11

A full-blown Tiffany-tantrum jerked me from another nightmare. This one had Zombie Charlie scooping brains from his cracked skull and forcing me to eat them. The bedroom was still dark, even though my funky awareness said the sun was up. I glanced at the LCD clock on the nightstand through grainy eyelashes as more high-pitched shouting filtered through the air. Dealing with the teen terror seemed a great deal more palatable at eight in the morning than more godawful dreams of the two people I had killed. Even better, the siren call of coffee floated in the air.

I straightened the replacement covers on Duncan's bed. The king-sized monstrosity turned out to be a heated, self-supporting waterbed, so the plastic mattress wasn't soaked with my blood. I had to grin. No crypt, no coffin, no sleeping in native dirt. He'd shot me a dirty look when I pointed out those myths last night. The man had no sense of humor at all. It was a wonder Goth Girl hadn't committed suicide in high school.

Ugly thoughts intruded as I tucked the corners. Maybe I should have taken the couch after all. Nightmares of Nurse Ratchett and Charlie, with their heads caved in and wanting my brains to replace theirs, had interrupted my sleep every hour or so. Those alternated with the emaciated Alex apologizing as he ripped open my throat and drank me dry. At one point, I woke to Duncan rocking me and stroking my hair. I wanted him to stay.

Instead, I had punched his chest and told him to get the hell out of the room. He grunted, rose, and warned me if I ripped open his bed with my thrashing, he would drown me in it. Maybe neither of us would have been so grouchy if we weren't exhausted and I wore jammies instead of my birthday suit.

I snagged the shirt and pants Duncan had given me the night before and pulled them on. In retrospect, I should've kept them on while I had slept.

Another whiff of fresh java enticed me out of the bedroom and down the hallway. I wiped gunk out of my eyes and sighed. Unfortunately, the coffee was in the same direction as the shrieking.

Something was wrong, and not just with Tiffany. Unlike the total darkness enveloping the bedroom, sunlight streamed into the downstairs rooms. And my insides twinged like they had in Mallory Labs after I'd thrown up and before I ended in a fetal position on the staff bathroom floor. Such intense pain wasn't something I wanted to experience again. I needed food and caffeine, not necessarily in that order, then I'd be coherent enough to piece everything together.

Tiffany didn't notice me entering the kitchen. Her flushed skin offset the usual stark black and white of her appearance. Duncan leaned against the sink and watched her scene with arms crossed over his fabulous chest until he saw me. Then he rolled his eyes as if to say, *Teenagers.*

Tiffany's voice had gone hypersonic, so only every other word was comprehensible. And most of those were obscenities. "...and I don't need a fucking babysitter. I can take care of myself against a Normal asshole."

When she paused for a breath, I said, "Duncan's right."

They both stared at me in shock. I shrugged. "Mallory's playing for keeps, and he admitted he knows Duncan's gunning for him." I crossed to the fridge, thirst and hunger twisting my insides to the point my caffeine addiction was an afterthought. I ignored the red bottles of what could only be blood and grabbed the milk. Thank God, this was a vampire who took care of his mortal guests.

I chugged the liquid heaven, the coolness taming the beast in my gut. It took a second or two to realize I'd demolished the entire gallon. Swiping my mouth with the back of my hand, I noticed their stares, Tiffany's of disbelief and Duncan's faintly of disgust. I glanced at the empty jug in my hand, then slammed the fridge shut. "I'll pay you back for the frickin' food," I muttered.

"You're probably still healing," Tiffany stated, crossing to join me. Tantrum totally forgotten, she yanked open the freezer door, pulled out two boxes of waffles, and shoved them into my arms. "There's butter if you want it. Syrup's in the pantry." She pointed to the tiny door in the wall next to the fridge.

She turned to pull a toaster and plates out of another set of cupboards. I dumped the boxes on the counter next to her and retrieved the rest of her list as well as a jug of orange juice.

For the next five minutes, we worked like a well-oiled assembly line. Tiffany would pop the waffles into the toaster and pour juice while I pulled them out and slathered them with butter, in between gulps of steaming coffee from the mug she'd shoved into my hand. When we sat down at the bar to eat, she had two waffles on her plate. I had the other eighteen plus my third cup of coffee.

As I dumped half a bottle of syrup on my pile, I noticed Duncan, still leaning against the sink, watching me with a bemused smile. Sunlight glinted off his dark hair, leaving reddish highlights in its wake.

Sunlight. God! I can be so stupid sometimes. All of his "woe is me, I'm a vampire" speech was bullshit.

New anger worked its way through my blood. Usually I can smell BS a mile away. Why was this time an exception? Because torture and death were such beautiful new experiences, that's why.

"Feeding me breakfast is the least you can do for lying to me," I snarled. I didn't bother with the knife and fork. Rolling up the first waffle, I shoved it whole into my mouth and chomped, taking my fury out on innocent breakfast food.

He frowned as he reached for his own cup still sitting on the counter next to him. The same heavenly aroma drifted from the ceramic in his hand as the mug by my side, which should have been clue number two.

"I find your thought processes very hard to track, Samantha." He eyed me while sipping his coffee.

"You lied to me about the whole damn vampire thing, you son of a bitch."

Tiffany blinked in surprise. "What are you talking about?"

This time I used the knife, jabbing it in his direction to emphasize my point. "You're standing in daylight."

That damn eyebrow of his cocked upwards in confusion. "I beg your pardon?"

Realizing he couldn't understand me with the second waffle in my mouth, I washed it down with a swig of juice before trying again. "You're standing there in freakin' daylight, drinking coffee."

He smirked, then turned and rapped on the window behind him. "It is called UV film, darling. Keeps the dangerous rays out. And I can drink other fluids. I simply cannot eat solid foods."

I shivered despite the sarcastic inflection he put on "darling." "Sorry," I muttered, though part of me didn't believe him.

He turned back to Tiffany. "Get your things."

She threw her fork down so hard the ceramic plate cracked. "I'm not going to hide like a baby! Besides—" She waved a hand at me. "You don't know if the zombie chick here can handle sunlight any better than you."

"Hey!" Only I could give people obnoxious nicknames.

"Sorry, Sam." She whipped back to Duncan. "You're going to need me—"

Her tirade stopped in midstream as Duncan strode over to me and yanked me to my feet. "Let us find out Samantha's limitations." He hustled me to the back door and shoved me through before slamming the door. The garage didn't even have an LCD clock to break the blackness. I swallowed hard to get the remains of the fourth waffle down my tightened esophagus.

Turning round, I shook the knob and banged on the door, but it didn't budge. "Dammit! Let me back in!" What the hell was he trying to do? I pounded on the door again. "I want the rest of my waffles!"

I frowned as my eyes adjusted to the dim light, so faint I shouldn't be able to see anything at all. Small dents from my brand-new, super-human strikes shadowed the door. Reinforced steel. I'd bet my next check the townhouse windows were bulletproof just like the SUV.

With a click and a hum, the garage door inched its way upward.

Oh God! He wasn't really going to do this, was he?

Why was everyone determined to turn me into his guinea pig? The bright sliver between concrete slab and garage door widened, and new fear jittered the waffles in my stomach. What if I really was a zombie now? What if I melted in sunlight just like the shambling undead on those late, late movies? Bright yellow crawled across the floor, seeking my bare toes. Total panic ensued. I turned and grabbed for the door handle to the SUV, but the damn thing was locked. In desperation, I shook the handle, which only rocked the SUV.

Then it was too late. Sunshine blinded me, and I screamed.

"Oh for cryin' out loud. I'm cleaning it up."

I blinked sun-induced tears from my eyes. An elderly woman glared at me from the sidewalk, pooper-scooper in one hand and the leash for her poodle in the other.

The dog could have been Mr. Cuddles' twin brother. He bared his teeth and growled despite his awkward crouch. Yep, complete with the same psycho attitude.

I gave the lady and the dog a half-hearted smile. "Sorry. I locked my keys in the car," I said, waving at the SUV. "Running a little late this morning."

There was a click and whoosh behind me. I turned to find Tiffany, all teen earnestness.

"Hey, Mom, you forgot your keys." She stomped over and held out the key ring. I was so stunned I was still alive and not melting goo, I let her drop them in my palm. Glancing down, she added, "You forgot your shoes again, too." Then she flounced back through the door.

Oooooo! Goth Girl was going to pay for the "Mom" crack. Right after I decapitated St. James for his little experiment.

With a jolt and a hum, the garage door began its downward track, shutting out Old Lady with Poodle. This time when I twisted the knob, the back door opened easily.

"You two are so dead meat!"

Tiffany sat at the kitchen table, laughing so hard tears streamed down her face. The serene look on Duncan's face was even more infuriating.

He looked at the girl. "I think my experiment answers your question."

Tiffany still protested loudly from the back seat when I pulled into the garage where Duncan had directed me. He had given me the keys to his SUV before man-handling Goth Girl into the backseat and engaging the childproof locks. She finally gave up the physical fight when he threatened to chain her. The possibility of being clapped in irons hadn't stopped the steady stream of cursing from the backseat as I drove.

On the way, I had dodged a caravan of carnies beginning to unload their trucks. Street fairs were non-existent in Beverly Hills when I was growing up. Okay, they still were non-existent, and I envied Tiffany having the opportunity to hang out here today.

The attached garage and apartment sat behind an antiques store. The same antiques store I had followed them to last Monday. I'd googled the owner, Phillippa Mann, but I hadn't turned up a whole lot on her. At least, she had a California driver's license. After the shocks of the last couple of days, what else was I getting into? Who or what would a vampire trust with his living charge?

Okay, maybe not the best turn of phrase since it seemed I was already dead. With my luck and Mann's supermodel looks, she was probably a nymph or something.

"I still don't see why I can't stay at the townhouse," Tiffany whined while we waited for the garage door to close. Her pinched face pouted in the rearview mirror.

Duncan turned in the passenger seat to glare at her. Like it really made a difference with the kid's tantrum.

"As I said before, the same reason Samantha cannot."

I really wished he'd stop repeating that. It was bad enough I couldn't get any of my own clothes and I was wearing a pair of flip-flops one of Tiffany's ex-boyfriends had abandoned at Duncan's place. It was only a matter of time before Mallory and his goons put two and two together. Then Max and my parents were goners. With the parents God knew where in Europe, I had left two more messages to call me on Max's cell voice-mail and another three at the Times, all with St. James's cell number. I still hadn't heard from him, and I didn't want to admit how much his silence worried me. Especially since his home phone just rang and rang.

And I didn't dare call Ralph and let him know where I was. No doubt, Mallory's goons had bugged the *Scoop* offices when they searched them. The less I involved my editor, the safer he would be. So I tried to blame my roiling stomach on the eighteen waffles, half pound of butter, pint of syrup, quart of juice and gallon of milk.

God, Goth Girl was right. I was a pig.

The door between the apartment and garage swung open. The tall, elegantly coiffed brunette who appeared in the opening could have passed for Tiffany's older sister. You know, the one who does everything perfectly for Mom and Dad.

I just didn't remember her glowing when I took pictures of her last week. Now, a faint sheen covered her from head to toe. And it wasn't glitter lotion.

I climbed down from the SUV, and she stuck out a hand, gold brace-lets chiming.

"I'm Phillippa, Samantha. Why don't you come in?"

I changed my mind. At least one member of this insane assembly had some class. My third impression vanished as I gripped her hand. She had the handshake of a Rams linebacker.

And yes, I still rooted for them even though the traitors moved to St. Louis.

A rueful smile curved her rose-painted lips when I tried to shake the feeling back into my fingers. "Sorry, I'm so used to dealing with super-naturals I forget my own strength."

Duncan joined us with Tiffany's elbow firmly in his grasp. "As I said when I rang you, I need you to look after Tiffany."

"I don't need a fucking babysitter!"

He shook his head and shared a look with Phillippa.

She laughed and linked her arm through mine, and we followed the Deranged Duo inside. I blinked in surprise at her kitchen. If Duncan's was understated, rich-jerk elegance, Phillippa's was . . . homey. A bowl of daisies anchored the blue gingham cloth covering the table. Matching curtains framed the windows, which must have had the requisite UV film. The butcher-block pine chairs gave off the same warm glow as the cabinets. Rag rugs protected the hardwood floor next to the stove and sink. And that smell! Could it be?

Saliva filled my mouth at the delicious aroma.

"You think you can bribe me with apple pie?" Tiffany snarled. Duncan had released her, but her boot tapped out a furious rhythm.

"Phil can bribe me with homemade pie anytime!" My stomach gurgled its agreement loud enough for everyone to hear.

One homemade apple pie and a half-gallon of vanilla ice cream later, I sighed in contentment. The tantalizing scent of the second pie was tempting, but I had wolfed enough food for this hour. Teasing on the edge of the aroma of pie though was the sharp tang of ocean. I don't know why Phil bothered with the room deodorizer when her wonderful baking did the job.

Tiffany still toyed with the fruit and ice cream sludge on her plate. Phil eyed me, curiosity etched on her face.

"May I ask you a question?"

"Only if I can ask you some questions in return."

She smiled. "Fair enough. Did you eat like this before you died?"

My warm fuzzies evaporated at the reminder of my new status, but before I could answer, Tiffany chimed in.

"Oh God, Phil! You should see her car! She's got—"

"Thanks. Tiff." The look I shot her would have withered an ordinary person. Instead, she just shrugged and glared in return.

I turned back to Phil. "I admit my eating habits weren't the greatest, but I didn't eat as much as I have in the last twenty-four hours."

Tiffany opened her mouth.

"Bring up the brains, and you'll join me," I growled.

She shut her mouth and returned to poking at her pie.

The rest of what Phil said sank into my sugar-loaded brain, and I looked at her again. "What makes you think I'm dead?"

Her lips pressed into a thin line before she answered. "You don't look right." Her attention shifted to Duncan. "Have you called—"

He nodded. The way their faces twitched some kind of communication was going on.

It confirmed my suspicion that she wasn't human, so I interrupted what was obviously a rude conversation about me. I couldn't say it was behind my back. "My turn. What are you? You're not a vamp, so how'd you get hooked up with these two?"

Her eyebrow flicked upward and a faint smile tilted the corners of her mouth. "My. You're even more direct and to the point than Tiffany, aren't you?" She took a sip of her tea. "To answer your question, I would be considered a demigoddess."

Okay, that's not something I heard every day. My brain took a couple of seconds to process the new tidbit.

"But she was raised by Amazons," Tiffany piped in.

Ignoring Goth Girl, I tried to puzzle out Phil's real meaning. "So what you're saying is . . ."

She sighed, and said, "An Olympian was the sperm donor. Let's leave it at that."

"But—" I started.

Duncan's expression turned from irritated to downright pissy. "I did not bring you here to interrogate my friend."

"Really?" I shot him a nasty smile. "Friend? Or girlfriend?"

The comment was catty even for me. Vampires may not be able to turn red in the face, but his skin climbed towards a satisfying pink.

Phil, on the other hand, smirked behind her cup of black pekoe. "Amazing. Finally, someone has been born who can perturb the imperturbable Duncan St. James."

"So how long have you been seeing jerk-off here?" I aimed a thumb in his direction.

"You can relax, Sam. We're not dating, and I wouldn't dream of poaching on your territory."

"I knew you had better taste tha—" Her words smacked me in the head. "Hey, wait a minute!"

"Sam and Duncan sitting in the tree," Tiffany sang.

I raised my fork in a stabbing motion, and she stopped. I turned back to Phil. "Sorry, it's just when you were looking at him the other night . . ."

Amusement flashed in her eyes. "So you're the one," she said, then chuckled.

"What do you mean, I'm 'the one'?"

"The one who's been running background checks on us lately." A manicured finger stroked her cheek as she contemplated me.

"She was checking out Duncan because of the whole thing with Jessie's kidnapping," Tiffany chimed in.

A fine, perfectly sculpted eyebrow lifted on Phil's forehead. "You're a reporter?"

"Tabloid," Tiffany and Duncan said at the same time.

Their condescension irked me. "You say that like it's a bad thing. Do you know how many stories we beat the conventional press to?" I turned back to Phil and jerked a thumb in Duncan's general direction. "Seriously, how did you get mixed up with these two?"

Phil regarded me for a long time. So long I didn't think she'd offer anything else until she gave Tiffany a fond look. "After Tiffany's parents died, Duncan needed a daylight assistant so I volunteered to help raise her." She laughed again. "It was hard for him to attend parent-teacher conferences. And there were a lot."

I propped my elbows on the table, rested my chin in the palms, and regarded Duncan. "So she's not just your ward, is she?"

"Our relationship is none of your business," he bit out, fists clenched at his sides.

A horrible suspicion rolled out of my mouth before I could stop it. "Oh God, you didn't kill her parents and steal her, did you?"

Duncan's jaw dropped and his gorgeous eyes bulged. He looked on the verge of stroking out.

"Actually, she is his niece." Chestnut wisps artfully floated as Phil nodded her head. "She would be Duncan's—" Her eyes rolled toward the ceiling and her index finger tapped her cheek as she silently count-ed. "Is it fifteen or sixteen generations?"

"Sixteen," Tiffany mumbled around a mouthful of pie cream mush.

Green eyes flared with anger as Duncan fumed silently and jammed his fists into his coat pockets.

I, on the other hand, was impressed and gazed at Tiffany. "You can trace your ancestry back that far?"

Tiffany swallowed and shrugged. "Duncan's sister, Margaret, was my fourteenth great-grandmother on my mom's side."

His eyes went neon. "She doesn't need to know our family history."

"You didn't have a problem spilling history last night," Tiffany mut-tered.

He shot a furious look at her. She ignored him and shoveled more mush into her mouth.

Phil laid a hand on mine. "Never mind him. He's very touchy about family since Tiffany is the last survivor of Margaret's descendants."

Pain warred with irritation in Duncan's deep green eyes. I understood now why he was so protective of Goth Girl.

Before either Phil or Tiffany could say more, Duncan wrapped a huge palm around my wrist and yanked me from my chair. "I will ring you when I know more," he barked over his shoulder, and he shoved me into a garage for the second time that morning.

I yanked out of his grip. "What the hell is your problem!"

"I don't appreciate you invading my family's privacy," he shot back.

"You didn't have to bring me here!"

"No, I should have left you at the labs instead of saving your arse!"

Under the faint overhead garage light, I could see the muscle in his jaw tic.

He was right. As much as it galled me, I needed him more than he needed me right now. I swallowed the bile in my throat along with a huge helping of pride.

"You're right. I didn't say 'thank you' last night." I stuck out my hand. "So, thanks."

He stared at my outstretched hand like it was a rattler. After a couple of tense seconds, he reached for it. But instead of returning my shake, he drew my hand to his lips. The gesture was so old-fashioned and so . . . intimate I couldn't breathe. The brush of his lips across the back of my hand sent tingles through my body.

"My apologies as well, Samantha. I should not expect you to act contrary to your nature."

My system was so electrified it took a moment for his comment to register.

"What do you mean by my 'nature'?"

He didn't answer. Instead he chuckled then crossed to the passenger side of the SUV and climbed in.

Irritated, I fished the keys out of my pocket and jerked open the driver's door. "By the way, St. James, join the twenty-first century! It's 'ass,' not 'arse'!"

Chapter 12

Duncan's directions fed us to the underground parking garage of Good Samaritan Hospital, his only words the entire trip. He wouldn't tell me why we drove here. I didn't think the argument in Phillippa Mann's garage was such a big deal despite his Neanderthal attitude. Maybe he liked being the strong, silent jerk. Maybe he was dragging this out to torture me. Maybe he was pissed about babysitting me.

He was out of the passenger seat before I shifted into "Park." I jumped out of the SUV and slammed the door shut. The eerie echo sent a shiver up my spine. I raced to keep up with him as he headed for the elevator. Other than his crack at my expense at Phil's, his foul mood permeated the ride over and spoiled my sugar-induced high.

"Wait a minute. Where are we going?" I wasn't puffing as I had when I chased after him a few nights ago. What the hell had Mallory's people done to me? Not that I was complaining.

"You have an appointment with Dr. Zachary this morning." Once inside, he jabbed the buttons for the private offices on the tenth floor. I resisted the urge to whistle. His Dr. Zachary must be damn successful to afford the rent here.

"What's a regular MD going to tell me?" I peered up at his face, but his stoic façade remained fixed on the elevator doors.

"Dr. Zachary specializes in treating supernaturals."

Interesting. His malpractice probably consisted of "don't screw up, and we won't eat you."

It didn't help I'd rather go another round with Mel Gibson's Dobermans than endure an exam. My gaze dropped back to my reflection in the hyper-polished stainless steel doors. I didn't look any different.

Well, maybe a little scared. Then I got pissed at the wussy woman looking back at me, someone who needed to hold her mommy's hand while getting a shot. The mom who worried I'd somehow damage her nail polish if she held me.

No, damn it! I've been taking care of myself for a long time. I could handle this too. The determined look of my reflection made me feel marginally better.

As we rose upward, Duncan's fists clenched and released in a rhythm, like he considered throttling someone. Probably me. He would have rescued his friend last night if the alarm hadn't been triggered over my escape. I couldn't stand the silent treatment any longer.

"Why don't you just get it over with?"

He started at the sound of my voice, as if he had forgotten I was there. "I beg your pardon?"

"Just kill me and get it over with."

"What the devil are you talking about?"

Fine. Pretend to be shocked, you pretentious SOB.

I turned to face him, itching for some throttle-action of my own. "That's why we're here isn't it? So you can figure out what they did to me? So why don't you just kill me and do the autopsy, and then neither of us will feel guilty about leaving Alex behind?" My voice ended with a quiver, but I didn't take my eyes from his face.

Neither of us breathed at the ugly truth shimmering in the air. His eyes turned to liquid emeralds, his pain a tangible thing sucking the oxygen out of the tiny space.

The elevator doors slid open, and I could breathe again.

"We're here," he mumbled, his eyes turning from mine. For once, he guided me with a gentle hand at the small of my back instead of yanking me by the arm. "Suite 1050."

Great. A man over four hundred who still couldn't deal with his feelings.

I blinked away furious tears as we went into the office, not sure why I expected him to be different. Maybe I harbored secret Cinderella fantasies since he did rescue me. Not that I would admit it to him. There's something inherently sexy in a man who can carry you. Especially if you're not Emmanuel Lewis or one of the Olsen twins.

Inside, I decided I'd have to reassess Dr. Zachary's net worth. Crappy, industrial mauve dominated the front office with a darker version of the color pretending to be the carpet. Holiday Inn starving-artist-sale land-scapes decorated the walls.

One other person sat in the waiting room, an average-looking man who lounged on the couch. Lank brown hair fell across his face while he flipped through a magazine.

Average except the overabundance of musky aftershave smacking me from fifteen paces. I bit my tongue. One of my New Year's resolutions had been to refrain from commenting on other people's hygiene.

I'd already broken the other eleven resolutions.

I followed Duncan to the receptionist's window. As he spoke with the woman behind the counter, the hairs on the back of my neck rose. I eased a look over my shoulder. Mr. Average stared back with a confused look on his face. And then, I would have sworn, he sniffed me.

Right. Like he could talk. How could he possibly smell me over his aftershave? And I'd taken another shower this morning.

Duncan wrapped a large hand around my bicep and tugged me to where the receptionist held a different door open. A glimpse revealed a hallway, which probably led to exam rooms and offices. I glanced back. Mr. Average still stared at me with nostrils flared. As if I didn't have enough problems with creepazoids over the last few days. Though I had to admit, he seemed more curious, and slightly less threatening than Heckyll and Jeckyll.

The receptionist ushered us into an exam room. "Dr. Zachary will be with you in a moment, Mr. St. James." I knew the door only clicked shut, but to me, it sounded like a massive slam of doom.

Panic flared in the pit of my stomach as I took in the table and instru-ments. I backed into Duncan's chest. He murmured incomprehensible words in my ear. His voice disappeared along with all oxygen in the room. My heart thudded a terrible rhythm. Any second, the little pump would explode in my chest.

"I can't do this," I whispered. Images flew past my eyes, blood roared in my ears, and remembered pain bloomed in the rest of my body. Then mercifully, everything went black.

A god-awful smell interrupted my fluffy, warm grayness. I swiped at the offending aroma near my nose and connected with someone's skin. Regular human temperature skin, not Duncan's coolness.

"She's coming around."

I didn't recognize the voice, but once the ammonia odor disappeared, I inhaled the comforting scent of sandalwood and decided to risk a peek.

The woman kneeling next to me had an exotic look about her. Olive skin complemented her warm brown eyes and luxurious black hair swept into a loose bun on her head. She held my wrist in a loose grip.

I snatched my arm back at the sight of her white lab coat. Inching away from her failed because of Duncan's tight hold on me.

"Relax, darling. Let Bebe make sure you are all right."

Instead of reaching for me again, the woman held out her hand, a look of compassion and patience on her face. The kind of doctor who was great with screaming kids. "I just want to check your pulse. That's all, Samantha."

If Duncan trusted her, she couldn't be one of the bad guys. Since when had my opinion of him changed?

Since he dragged my bullet-riddled ass out of Mallory Labs. After a moment, I laid my hand in hers.

"Her pulse is fifty but strong." She graced me with a smile that, if I were a guy, would have made my toes curl. "Her aura is another matter."

"Huh?" I knew I was a little foggy, but did she actually say "aura"?

She shook her head in puzzlement. "I want to do a full work-up."

Duncan stood and, with no effort, lifted me to the exam table. I stiffened, every cell in my body screaming to fight.

The woman pulled a sachet out of her pocket and held it out to me. Another soft smile. "Inhale this."

Wariness prevented me from taking it. I'd had more than enough of doctors in the last few days, even if she was a friend of Duncan's. And why were all of his friends women? Gorgeous women. Didn't he have any guy friends? Oh god, was he gay? Had I been making a fool of myself over someone who would never take the slightest interest in my gender, much less me?

The doctor's voice dragged me back to my current dilemma. "It contains lavender and eucalyptus leaves, natural relaxants. Nothing more, Samantha." When I didn't take the cloth bag, she laid it next to me. "If you change your mind." Again, she graced me with a smile meant to calm children and crazy people.

"Samantha, this is Dr. Bebe Zachary." Mr. Impeccable Manners decided to speak up.

"You didn't bother to tell me she was a 'she.'" I couldn't stop my cattiness from spitting out a hairball.

"I thought you were a, what is the term?" His arrogant smirk covered his face again. "Ah, yes. 'Liberated woman.'"

"Oh, fuck off!"

Dr. Zachary tried to smother her own grin as she wrapped a blood pressure cuff around my arm. "Don't let Duncan egg you, Samantha."

"It's Sam." I couldn't stop the automatic correction, but somehow I felt a little more at ease with the good doctor. She relaxed noticeably as well.

"From what Duncan's told me, you're probably suffering from post-traumatic stress. I believe that's why you fainted."

"Oh, really. What else did he tell you?" Sarcasm laced my voice.

She laid a gentle hand on my arm. "Sam, I'm here to help you, but you're free to leave if you want."

Embarrassment hit me. I hated going to my own doctor. And I needed this lady's help. I couldn't exactly go to Dr. Brown and say, "Hey, I think I died last night. Can you explain why I'm still running around?" I nodded my consent.

Dr. Zachary bustled through the rest of her exam, checking temperature, heart, lungs, ears, eyes, nose, throat, and even reflexes. Like any other physician, she kept making "hmmmm" sounds until I was about to go batty.

"Well?" I jumped when Duncan said it at the same time as me.

"Sam, I'd like to take a blood sample." Her gaze flicked to Duncan before returning to mine.

Unease crawled up my spine. "Why?"

"You already suspect what I'm about to tell you." She took a deep breath and exhaled slowly before continuing. "By all rights, you should be dead. Your pulse is too slow, your blood pressure too low. And your aura—"

"Why the hell do you keep bringing up my aura? What the hell are you? A witchdoctor?"

She pursed her lips but amusement lit up her eyes. "Actually, I am a witch as well as a licensed physician."

"Oh." Why not? I've already run into mad scientists, vampires, and a goddess in the last three days. "I suppose the guy in your waiting room is a werewolf."

Surprise registered on her face. "Yes, he is." Her expression morphed into confusion. "How did you know?"

I had to give her credit for not lying to me. "His smell. At first I thought it was too much aftershave, but it reminded me of Mr. Cuddles before a trip to the groomers."

"Mr. Cuddles?" No mistaking the humor in Duncan's voice.

I glared at him. "My mom's toy poodle."

"And you normally sniff your mother's dog?"

I so wasn't going there. Ignoring him, I returned my attention to Dr. Zachary. "So what about my aura?"

For the first time, she truly looked uncomfortable. Her face held the expression all doctors get when they don't want to tell you the really bad news.

"It's black."

"And black means?" Was she fidgeting?

Her eyes couldn't meet mine any longer. "Ultimate evil."

"Or?" I prompted.

"Death."

It was relief to hear someone else say it out loud. Well, whisper it out loud anyway. "Okay, I think we can all agree I'm not Darth Vader."

She sagged as she realized I wasn't going to spaz out on her. "No, I don't think so either."

"I would have to disagree."

We both turned to glare at Duncan.

I returned my attention to the sane person in the room. "So we know I can't be cured," I said, deciding to ignore the vampire standing next to me again. I can deal with this. "What's the best course of action, Doc?"

"I'm still not sure what's going on. As I said, I'd like to take a blood sample, and—" She paused again, the supremely uncomfortable look plastered on her face.

She was getting on my last undead nerve. "Come on, Doc, spit it out."

"I'd also like to cast a spell to detect any magickal residue."

Maybe I'd been playing in "freaky" world a little too long. Dr. Zachary's words didn't even faze me. Instead, I nodded. "Sure. Whatever you need to do."

My courage didn't last though. I flinched at the sight of the needle she pulled out, anxiety setting my nerves on end. It was all I could do not to jump down from the table and run screaming for the Hollywood hills.

"Hold my hand, Samantha."

I screwed my eyes shut and clung to Duncan's words, and his hand, like a baby. If it had been anyone else, I would have crushed his bones to powder in the time it took her to extract five vials of blood.

Then I remembered whose hand held mine. More like what held my hand. I looked up at Duncan when she was done. "This isn't making you hungry, is it?"

"Unlike you, I had a sufficiently satisfying breakfast," he said, but he gave me a reassuring squeeze.

Dr. Zachary's spell was a lot easier to deal with than the blood samples she took. She prodded Duncan out the door. His protest at leaving sent a tremor of warmth through me. I just wished it had more to do with me than the fact I was his enemy's science project.

The doc flipped off the lights. Somehow, despite the darkness, I could still see the doctor. A faint yellow glow seemed to light her from within, not as bright as Phil's glitter, but obvious without the fluorescents.

A fruity smell tinged with flowers and spice filled the room and teased my memory. The doc's perfume or lotion was a hell of a lot more tolerable than the werewolf in the lobby. Maybe the heavy musk was a turn-on for lady werewolves.

She muttered a few words under her breath, and the glow flared. The thick, acrid smell of ozone filled the exam room. Tendrils of energy flowed from Bebe to wrap around and embrace my body. It tingled but didn't hurt.

The eerie part was I could see the doc's golden yellow light dance, meld, and then get swallowed by the nothingness surrounding me. The scene reminded me of a documentary I saw on the Discovery Channel, where the black hole ate a neighboring star.

Finally the remaining tendrils pulled back into her. She walked over to flick the lights back on. Her hand trembled as she held herself against the wall momentarily. Then she seemed to collect herself and called Duncan back in.

"Well?"

Geez, could this man do anything besides growl? When he wasn't making fun of me, that was.

"Let's go into my office." She gave us both a shaky smile. "I could use a drink."

Chapter 13

Dr. Zachary disappeared for a good fifteen minutes after she escorted us to her personal office. Duncan paced, but I sat hypnotized by the clown fish dancing inside the doc's aquarium. I didn't know why he was so worried. Okay, so he had an incurable disease. I was . . .

Oh hell. I didn't think the good doctor knew any more than I did.

She strode back into the office, closed and locked the door. A quick rummage through her desk produced shot glasses and a bottle of whiskey. After she handed Duncan and me a full glass each, she downed her own in one gulp, refilled it, then plunked the bottle of Jack Daniels on her desk within easy reach. Sensible shoes flew across the room before her stocking feet plopped on top of the desk beside Jack.

"It's nanites keeping you alive."

"Huh?" I blurted. It's a bad day when I can't even think of a follow-up question. I set my untouched glass on the desk before I dropped it in my addled state.

She sighed and sipped her drink. "If you can call it that. What I don't know is if the nanites are responsible for your death or are keeping your body functioning after you were shot." Duncan must have filled her in on the details of our little adventure last night.

"What the bloody hell is a 'nanite'?" At least Duncan looked as confused as I felt.

"It's a microscopic machine. In theory, they're meant for repair work on the cellular level."

The skin around my eyes tightened. "What do you mean, 'in theory'?"

She took another sip of whiskey before she answered. "Until today, I thought such a level of robotics and medicine were only that. A theory."

"You mean, there's little robots running around inside of me? That's why I'm alive?"

She winced and rubbed her temple like a bad migraine had started. "Something to that effect. I've sent your blood down for DNA sequencing."

"Huh?" God, I never liked science classes as it was, but she was talking way over my head.

"So you believe these machines are repairing Sam's body, not magick or the V-virus," Duncan said.

She nodded.

I was glad someone else was there to carry the conversation. The thought of things crawling around inside of me made my skin, well, crawl.

"But I'm dead, right?"

She leveled a no-nonsense look at me. And it wasn't as supportive as the pantyhose by the same name. "You saw what happened in the exam room when I cast the spell, Sam. If you were still Normal, you wouldn't have been able to see what I did."

I could hear the capital "N" in her words. Normal. As in an average, everyday normal human being. "How d-did you know I could—"

"The touching of our auras created a low level empathic bond. I felt what you knew, and you knew your aura was swallowing mine."

My throat convulsed in a painful motion. "I didn't mean to."

"I know." She smiled, the wry one of someone faced with an impossibility that had reared up and slapped her in the face. "But by magickal standards, you are dead."

"B-b-but I feel fine!"

"Except?" I didn't like the look on her face.

"Except what?" Then my stomach gurgled. Rather loudly.

"You told Phil you do not normally eat the amount you have in the last twelve hours," Duncan prompted.

Having a gorgeous guy notice my eating habits was not improving my day.

"Yeah, but I've been doing other things I don't normally do," I retorted. "Like, oh, I don't know, getting kidnapped, tortured, starved, experimented on, and shot!"

"Duncan told me about your gunshot wound. With your permission, I'd like to run some more tests, Sam. I'm not sure what the nanites are doing to you. Definitely accelerating your body's ability to heal, but I believe they may also be rewriting your genetic code."

"Huh?" I definitely needed better dialogue for this insane B-movie I was trapped in.

She set her glass down. Her elbows traded places with her toes as she leaned over the desk to regard me.

"You're not human any more, Sam. The problem is I don't know what you're becoming."

"Other than a zombie, you mean."

"You're not a zombie, Sam."

I waved my hand to shoo away her lame attempt to console me. "I know, I know." I rolled my eyes. "Duncan already told me they aren't real."

She shrugged. "According to my grandmothers, zombies were just stories used to scare children. It may be possible in theory, but a zombie would just be a magickally animated corpse. It wouldn't have a will of its own, much less a personality."

"Yeah, and you just told me nanites were only a 'theory.'" My fingers made quotation marks in the air. I clenched my eyes shut as a new *Fear Factor* stunt passed through my head—eat the zombie before it eats you.

"Oh, she has plenty of will and personality, all right," Duncan muttered next to me.

My eyes popped open, and I rammed a fist into his shoulder.

"Stop hitting me, woman."

"What? Your damn sixteenth century manners make you too good to hit a girl?" I really needed to hit something. Anything. I also knew I couldn't really hurt Duncan.

Unlike Nurse Ratchett and Charlie.

I shoved that thought back into its deep, dark hole.

I must have pushed Duncan too far. An evil grin spread across his face. "I would not strike a human girl."

He was teasing, but his comment was the camel's last straw. Next thing I knew, heavy sobs racked my chest. And like most guys, Super Vampire didn't know what to do with a crying chick. Even a dead one.

Dr. Zachary came around her desk with a box of tissues. She wrapped an arm around my shoulders and brushed damp hair out of my face as my sobs turned to hiccups. "It's a lot to deal with, I know, Sam. I'll do what I can to help."

She turned to Duncan while I awkwardly blew my nose one-handed. "I'll notify Caesar. The Council needs to know what Mallory's up to now that we have evidence. It would be best if you take Tiffany with you. Do you have a safehouse in mind?"

He nodded. I noticed why I had trouble holding the kleenex. His fingers were wrapped around the ones not clinging to the soggy tissue.

"Who's Caesar?" I asked.

"My, um, boyfriend." Dr. Zachary gave me a very big grin. "I guess it would be the best way to describe him."

"I will call him once we are settled," Duncan stated, as if his decision were the only one.

They both rose. Since he still had my hand, I had no choice but to follow.

Dr. Zachary hugged me, then gave Duncan a kiss on the cheek. "Be careful."

"Wait a sec." I yanked on Duncan's hand to stop him. Despite the madness, I had finally recognized the doc's perfume. "I've got to ask. Where did you get your secret stash of Peach Hyacinth?"

"I beg your pardon?"

"Victoria's Secret Peach Hyacinth. Where'd you find it? I love that lotion, and I was royally pissed when they discontinued it."

She shook her head. "I'm not wearing any lotion from Vicky's."

"Oh." I shrugged. "Sorry. My bad." Maybe the fruit, flower and spice scent she had was her normal odor, similar to the werewolf in her waiting room. Giving up on figuring out my over-sensitized nose, I let Duncan drag me out of her office.

We were in the elevator before I realized I had no more answers than before we came. If the doc was right and I was turning into something else, what the hell was I turning into? I shivered at the thought.

Duncan wrapped a large arm around me and pulled me close. I snuggled into his hard chest covered by a soft, gray sweater, hanging on to what comfort I had.

My stomach growled like crazy and my head ached by the time we reached his SUV. I pulled his keys out and handed them to him. "Would you mind driving? I just don't think I can deal right now."

As he stared at the keys, pink flared on his neck and ears. He handed them back. "I am sorry. I cannot."

"Cannot? Look I know you didn't bother to get a freakin' driver's license in the U.S. But c'mon! Stay within the speed limit and no one will be the wiser."

His face glowed neon bright compared to the dank concrete around us. "I mean, I do not know how."

"How can you be over four hundred and not know how to drive a freakin' car!"

His brow furrowed. "How do you know my age?"

"Quit changing the subject!"

"I am quite serious."

I took a very deep breath and ticked off one to ten, first in Latin, then in Japanese. "Because I can count, you moron. If Tiffany's the sixteenth generation from your sister, and there's roughly twenty-five years per generation, that's about four centuries. Let me guess. They didn't teach girls math in your day?"

That smile of his would be my undoing. It made me tingle all the way down to my toes.

"There were other things for women to learn in my day."

"Like cooking and cleaning?" I sneered.

He took a step closer, his thighs pressing against mine. He bent, his lips brushing my ear. "Serving their men," he whispered.

His voice felt like the best café mocha flowing across my body. Deep, dark, and oh, so rich. Maybe I wasn't quite so dead after all if I could feel this want. That was it. I wanted Duncan St. James. And I could never have him.

He stepped back, and regret dulled his eyes. He knew it too.

My stomach protested its emptiness. So loudly, the noise echoed off the low ceiling and support pillars.

Our shared laughter broke the tension. I gave him a playful shove.

"I need food. And clothes. If I'm driving, you're buying."

We headed for Arco Plaza. Well, City National Plaza, but I still had a hard time thinking of it by its new name. It wasn't the Beverly Center, but the underground shopping center in the middle of downtown was the safest place I could think of for both of us. I didn't relish a Mallory goon squad finding us in broad daylight, and I had to assume his people were looking for me. Billionaires don't become billionaires by letting their investments walk away. I hated to admit Duncan was right, but Mallory's goons probably watched or had wiretaps on all of our contacts. Odds were Mallory and his people thought I was stupid enough to be holed up somewhere, not cruising the Food Court with worker bees and the handful of kids skipping school.

After five Big Macs, two Mexican pizzas, and a 44-ounce root beer float, I felt satiated enough to shop. Late afternoon on a Monday meant we had most of the stores to ourselves. I figured I might be on the lam for a while so I kept to the practical—jeans, t-shirts, and pajamas. I did splurge on lingerie. Somehow, I resisted the urge to model those purchases for Duncan.

Once I had shoes and some cotton ankle-hi's, we headed back for the garage by unspoken agreement. Like last night, I knew it was close to sunset, and I had a feeling he knew too. But then, night came earlier in January. I sighed in comfort as I wriggled my toes in the clean socks and new Nikes. I slurped my extra-large chocolate shake while we walked back to the garage.

Duncan had paid for everything since my purse was long gone, and he had carried shopping bags without protest. When I asked him why, he shrugged. "You needed something to wear. Besides—" The evil grin was back. "I do not think I can resist last night's sleeping attire again."

Tingles skittered across my skin at his look. "You didn't have to come in and check on me." I had been naked and in his bed last night. It would have been so easy . . .

No, I needed distance from him before the naughty thought train continued. Except its absence left room for the uglier images I'd been trying to suppress all day. No, dammit! I was not letting Ratchett and Charlie back into my head.

I pressed the key fob and was awarded with an obnoxious beep that echoed between the forest of concrete pillars. Trying not to look at Duncan, I yanked the door open and pulled myself into the driver's seat.

His smile faded, replaced by a sober look. He tossed my bags in the back before rounding the SUV to climb into the seat next to me. He laid his hand on mine before I could turn the key.

"Sam—" He stared out the windshield, suddenly lost in another time and place, before he turned back to me. Bleakness seared its way into my soul at his gaze. "Killing someone is never an easy thing to live with, even if it was in self-defense."

I had managed not to think about last night for the last three seconds, but the bozo had to shatter my self-imposed blindness. Apparently, he wasn't as blind as I pretended to be. Tears welled in my eyes, visions of a sightless Nurse Ratchett swimming in the blurriness. "You didn't see them," I whispered, then shook my head in a vain attempt to erase the memory.

"They would have destroyed you." His thumb stroked my skin.

Anguish, guilt, desire, and regret mixed a strange concoction in me. I wanted to fall weeping into Duncan's arms. I wanted to erase the weekend from history. I wanted to kill the assholes who had turned my life, or death, upside down. I wanted a chance to be with a cute guy I had known less than twenty-four hours.

Except I wasn't getting any wishes fulfilled in this Rod Serling fairy tale.

"We need to get back to Tiffany and Phil." I pulled my hand from his, wiped away the couple of tears trickling down my cheek and started the SUV. Ignoring my feelings for the immediate danger of Mallory seemed the better option than pretending there could be something between Duncan and me.

Purple and pink clouds trailed between downtown high rises as I pulled out of the parking garage. We merged with rush hour traffic, folks on their way home to their regular lives. It was a beautiful sight, showing just how much my undead life sucked.

Chapter 14

Both night and the street fair were in full swing when we reached Phil's eclectic neighborhood. Between the street closures and the copious crowd, I had to park twelve blocks from her shop. Tiny white Christmas lights cocooned the trunks of palm trees while strands of larger, multi-colored bulbs swayed over the crowds. Hopped up on cotton candy and soda, kids ran screaming up and down the brightly lit streets, their parents trailing behind. Definitely not your typical LA scene-and-be-seen.

The delicious smell of popcorn wafted by on the chilly evening air. My stomach grumbled in answer.

Duncan chuckled and bought three corn dogs for me at the closest stand before we continued. We could have been like any other couple strolling up and down the carnival. I sighed as I sucked the last bit of bread off my last stick. This could have been a great first date.

Except for the zombie thing.

Teens across the way showed off for their girlfriends, trying to knock over milk bottles with softballs while the barker mocked them. Duncan grabbed my hand, tugging me through the crowd towards the game, one of many lining the street. Out of sheer curiosity, I let him. He shelled out the bucks for an entire bucket of balls and made a show of shoving up his sweater sleeves, playing to the crowd around us.

Maybe one of us was having a brain aneurysm. Yeah, he'd been affectionate with Tiffany, and to some extent Phillippa. Except for the flirtation in the shopping center parking garage, the rest of the time he'd been alternately angry or brooding. I stood watching him, trying desperately to figure out what was going on with the brand new show-off in Duncan's form-fitting sweater. Though I did notice his smile wasn't so wide as to give away his extra-sharp canines.

His first wild pitch almost took off the head of the barker. The kids broke out in hysterics while the barker glared at him.

"Turn around slowly and check out the crowd behind us."

Duncan's voice was pitched so low I knew I was the only person around us to hear him. Maybe there were advantages to these nanite things after all. I never would have been able to understand him in the controlled chaos of the midway otherwise.

His second pitch missed the milk bottles and bounced off the back canvas.

I did as he commanded, though it rankled me. I've never been good at the "obey" thing. I played the bored girlfriend and scanned the crowd. Maybe it was their designer clothing in the middle class neighborhood. Maybe it was their peculiar attention to our game from so far away. Or maybe it was strong thread of sandalwood not coming from Duncan's direction.

"The blonde and two brunettes at the sno-cone stand?" I whispered as I continued my pivot so our stalkers wouldn't notice. His vampire hearing would pick up my words despite the crowd.

He gave an imperceptible nod as he whipped a third pitch. I heard the distinctive crack of glass and bit my lip to keep from laughing. He must have taken out one of the colored light bulbs illuminating the booth. The barker swore as fragments tinkled to the concrete.

I had seen the women Duncan indicated on the sidewalk after we had parked. Damn! I had been expecting Mallory to send linebackers after us, not supermodels. I couldn't underestimate the bastard again. Assuming we got away from these gals. With my luck, they'd be some kind of super-ninja supermodels. The blonde looked familiar, but I couldn't catch the memory of where I might have seen her. Not someone I shot, but I'd seen her in someone else's work. I sauntered to Duncan's left so I could keep an eye on both him and our trio of possible assailants.

"Recognize them?"

He gave a slight shake of his head as his fourth pitch nailed the middle stack dead center and bottles crashed to the floor. The boys around us whistled and cheered. He shot me a cocky grin as he made short work of the other two stacks.

Grumbling, the barker handed Duncan the three-foot-high neon pink teddy bear my escort had chosen. Before I could make a sarcastic comment, he presented the prize to me with a flourish accompanied by catcalls from the teens.

I'd never had anyone win a prize for me, much less an obnoxiously bright stuffed animal. I was so surprised I didn't resist when he wrapped my free hand around his arm and guided me in the direction of the antique shop.

"If we've got a tail, how do you know Mallory doesn't have someone watching the shop?" I whispered.

"He probably does. Come on. We need to warn them."

He tugged my arm and picked up speed. I caught the reflection of Mallory's Angels in the shiny aluminum of a funnel cake stand. They were a block back and trying discreetly to catch up with us.

Duncan made a sharp left and yanked me into a picture booth just as another couple exited, folks dressed very similar to us. The bear disappeared from my arm and appeared in the other woman's as the flap closed behind me. I heard him tell the couple to keep it.

"Hey, I liked that bear." My harsh whisper didn't get his attention because he was already speed dialing his cell phone. He told Phil to get out of the place through the emergency exit—whatever the hell that was—and meet us where we had parked. She must not have questioned his orders because he snapped the phone shut and peered out.

"Let's go." He pulled me out and headed back the way we came.

After thirty yards, a familiar figure rose above the crowd. Heckyll might as well be wearing a sign saying, "Sadistic muscle for hire."

Panicking, I yanked Duncan between two tents, pulled his head down, and kissed him. His response was immediate. He pulled me closer and deepened the kiss, demanding and gentle at the same time.

The roar of the crowd disappeared under the thunder of blood in my head. Our tongues tangled and explored while his hands roamed my back and hips.

As much as I'd rather do some exploring of my own, I forced my hands between us and shoved. My breathing was as ragged as his as we stumbled apart. Something dangerous, alluring and very neon flared in his eyes, but I ignored the invitation and placed a finger against his lips even as I stepped closer to him.

"Behind me, next to the peanut stand. Jean jacket and black tee."

Duncan pulled his gaze from me, then nodded and frowned.

"Has he spotted us?" It felt like my heart would jump through my throat any minute.

He kept his eyes fixed on a spot behind me. "No. One of Mallory's?"

"Yeah."

We wouldn't make it back to the SUV. Jeckyll had to be nearby as well and God knew how many others were tracking us.

He grabbed my hand in a firm grip. "We will head for Phillippa's shop."

The sight of Heckyll shook me more than I wanted to admit. I didn't question Duncan's command. We rejoined the crowd meandering down the street and headed back towards the shop.

"Phil may be able to defend herself, but what about Tiffany? She's just a kid." For the first time in my life, er, death, I didn't have a problem talking and speed walking at the same time.

We dived around parents comforting a toddler screaming over a lost balloon. "They should be out of the shop by now." He smiled at me. "And Tiffany would surprise you."

"Knives tucked in her boots would not surprise me at all," I muttered.

He chuckled. "We will go out the basement same as them. Otherwise, we can make a stand there."

I glanced over my left shoulder. "Looks like we'll be making a stand. Mallory's Angels at seven o'clock. And the bitches have spotted us."

"Oh bloody hell!"

He picked up his pace, nearly bowling over the twenty-something quartet in front of us. The men shouted a few choice words in Spanish, but Duncan ignored them, intent on our destination. Sounds of the carnival faded as we turned the block. He had keys out and unlocked the door before I realized we were in front of the store.

I automatically reached for the wall, but he stopped my hand as I found the switch.

"They will see," he whispered. So I wasn't the brightest person while I was being followed. I was usually on the other end of the food chain.

Despite my enhanced vision, I stumbled over furniture as he pulled me through the dark store. We both turned as we heard the door rattle. Glass and splintered wood exploded inward. We dived for the floor.

Debris rained over me, pinging or clattering against the surrounding furniture. I didn't have time to check for injuries. Glowing yellow eyes hovered over my prone body. Brunette Number One flashed her fangs at me before seizing me by the throat and throwing me across the room. I crashed headfirst into some very heavy wood. Proverbial stars flared in my vision.

I blinked the stars away along with the birds chasing after them. A shadow stalked toward me, and I threw the first thing I grabbed. The ceramic shattered on the head of the shadow, which mumbled an unladylike curse. I just prayed I hadn't destroyed a Ming vase or something equally expensive.

I scrambled for the front of the store and yelled "Switch!" as I hit the lever. The sudden light startled the brunettes on top of Duncan. He tossed Brunette Number Two across the room before Number One hit him with a nasty uppercut.

I couldn't pay any more attention to his plight because Blondie was aiming a fist at my head. I dived and rolled as plaster crumbled above me. She pulled out her fist and a good chunk of drywall with it.

"Stake her!"

I could only spare Duncan a glance as I screamed back, "With what!"

"With wood! Oof! You bloody git!"

I wasn't sure if he meant I was the bloody git or the brunette he fought. Not that it really mattered at the moment. I avoided another punch, but Blondie's spinning kick caught me in the gut. Her second kick, aimed at my head, barely missed as I fell back. My nanite fortified lungs fought for a breath, any breath. A brass spittoon dived for my head. I rolled, and the spittoon cracked the one bit of concrete slab not covered by Persian rugs, the blow so close slivers of concrete and spittoon must have flown up my nose. The scent of metal was that strong.

My vision raked the room, but all the wood was connected to what I was sure were very valuable pieces of furniture. If it were Mom's expensive crap, I wouldn't have hesitated. Payback for all the lectures about dirt on her precious collector's items.

But Phil was a nice lady. For an Amazonian demigoddess.

I'd feel obligated to pay her back for the rest of my unnatural life, which was probably how long it would take. And I seriously doubted she'd make me any more of her wonderful pie if I trashed her store.

On the other hand, I had become attached to my own undead existence.

Scrambling to my feet, I snatched up a chair and brought it down on Blondie's head. It splintered on impact, and suddenly I had a usable stake-like leg in my hand. Without thinking twice, I jabbed the jagged end at Blondie's chest.

She knocked it out of my hand and threw another right cross at my head. This time the stars chased the little birdies when I landed on my ass with a distinct *thump*. Instinct made me roll, and a steamer trunk splintered as it crashed down where I had been.

Blondie snatched a fireplace poker, a determined look on her sculpted face. With some internal organ in my throat, I crab-crawled backwards. Her first blow missed me but shattered the glass case containing estate jewelry. Shards rained down on me, but a few cuts were the least of my problems. I scrambled to my feet and dived through the beaded curtain separating the store from the apartment.

The short hallway ended in a door. I grabbed the knob and twisted. In the bare instant my brain registered it was locked, I felt someone behind me. I jumped to the side to avoid the poker thrust at my chest. Her momentum drove the steel rod through the door. I turned to run, but the bitch grabbed me by my ponytail and yanked.

Not wanting to lose a hunk of hair, I threw myself backwards. We both crashed through the damaged door, landing in a heap of limbs and splinters on Phil's kitchen floor.

Knives! The cutlery next to the sink gave me some hope. I struggled upright, despite Blondie's kicking and scratching, and lunged for the counter.

Cold metal across my throat brought me up short. Blackness swam across my eyes and fingers clawed at the constricting steel. Blondie pressed the poker harder. My heart pounded and my lungs cried for oxygen. A miniscule crunch said my trachea wanted to give up the battle. Desperate, I racked my head back. From her muffled screech, I must have nailed her nose. Her grip loosened slightly, and I dived for the knives. She only hesitated for an instant before she tightened her hold.

My vision blurred as my air was cut off again. A wooden handle brushed my fingertips. I had no idea what I grabbed. Red and black dots flared, warning signs I was about to pass out.

I stamped down hard on Blondie's instep and was rewarded with a shriek of pain. The metal across my throat disappeared. I whirled and plunged the object I held into Blondie's chest.

Instead of a knife, the handle of a wooden spoon stuck out from between her ribs. Unlike the vamps on *Buffy*, she didn't explode into dust like I half-expected. She staggered back against the stove, her eyes wide and her mouth a perfect "O". In slow motion, the rag rug slid from beneath her and she landed in a sitting position, back propped up by the oven door.

I sighed with relief when her chest stilled and she didn't get up. Lids slid down over her glazed eyes. Thank God, I didn't have to deal with a dead person looking at me. Okay, a dead vamp. The nightmares from the two humans were bad enough.

Except she didn't have the distinctive spicy wood scent I was coming to associate with vampires. She smelled more like . . . a steak knife. I took another deep whiff. The leftover apple pie made my stomach rumble.

A grunt followed by a triumphant shout from a female voice sounded from the store area. Worried, I raced back to the front.

Not that Duncan needed the help.

Unlike Blondie's quiet expiration, Brunette Number One screamed in fury as Duncan plunged half of a broken coat rack through her chest. At her partner's demise, Brunette Number Two ran for the gaping hole where the front door had been. Snatching up the other half of the coat rack, he threw it javelin-style. The force of the flying wood caught her in the back, shoved her through the doorway, and slammed her face-first into the sidewalk. Leaping over a dining table, Duncan grabbed her by the ankles and dragged her back into the store. Then he pushed an armoire, the same one I think dented my skull, across the entry.

With the shades down and the doorway blocked, no one could see the massacre from the street. I prayed the fight had been quick enough we hadn't attracted any other attention and the three dead vamps hadn't contacted any other members of the goon squad.

The godawful smell of rotten meat hit my nose. I gagged, searching for the source, and looked down next to me. Brunette Number One was melting. Literally.

Flesh and goo dripped from her bones, landing in a congealed mass on the Persian rug where she lay. I stepped away as dry heaves threatened.

"It's all right," Duncan murmured. He pulled me against him, and strong arms wrapped around me, holding me tight. I buried my head in his chest. Only to block the smell, I told myself, but I started shaking in earnest as the adrenaline from the fight phased out.

A second rush of rotten meat odor told me Brunette Number Two's body performed the same melting act. I stiffened as my stomach rebelled at the odor.

"Do you all turn to sludge when you die?" His sweater muffled my voice, but he must have heard from his rueful chuckle.

"I am afraid so. Let us go to the back," he said, steering me in the direction of the beaded curtain.

Then I remembered and muttered, "Shit."

"What's wrong?" Concern etched his face.

I gulped. "Blondie's still back there."

One of his eyebrow's rose. "You did kill her, did you not?"

I punched him in the arm. "Yes, damn it!"

He glared at me. "What have I said about hitting me, woman? Besides—" His scowl shifted to a reassuring smile that made my insides almost as gooey as the dead vamps. "If she is dead, you have nothing to concern yourself about."

"But she'll be all gross and yucky, too." I shuddered.

"Gross and yucky? This from the woman who drank an entire gallon of milk straight from the jug this morning." He rolled his eyes.

"It's not funny!" Tears threatened. I never thought myself capable of killing anyone, much less three people in twenty-four hours. Okay, two people and one vampire. Considering Blondie was just as strong as I was in my undead state, I had no doubt she was dissolving even as we spoke. My relief melted into more guilt, adding to the huge lake of it sitting in the pit of my stomach.

Duncan stroked my neck, and I had to admit it was comforting. "We must pass through the kitchen. Access to the exit is in there." His fingers drew my head up to meet his earnest gaze. "I will protect you, darling."

Ire pierced my self-disgust, and I knocked his hand away from me. "Why do you do that?"

Confusion replaced the concerned look on his face. "Do what?"

"Call me 'darling.'"

The amused glint in his eye did not amuse me one bit. "I did not realize I offended you, Samantha." I shivered at the way he drew out my name. God, I hated the way he made me feel. And I loved it too. I stomped towards the kitchen, wishing he couldn't read my mind.

He can still read your body, a little voice whispered inside me.

Not that we can do anything about that, I reminded my damned little voice.

Blondie was still intact and propped against the stove when I entered the kitchen. Something was definitely wrong.

"Why hasn't she—"

Blondie blinked. Blue eyes wide open, she looked down at the spoon sticking out of her chest. Then she and I both started screaming.

Chapter 15

"What?"

"She's not dead! Why isn't she dead!" I couldn't stop shrieking the same phrases over and over. I'd practically shoved the entire long-handled utensil through her chest. Why the hell was she still moving!

Duncan tried to fend off my attempts to climb his back in my effort to get away from the not-quite-dead undead chick.

Blondie stopped screaming long enough to pull the spoon out of her. It came free with a stomach-turning *squish* and a gush of noxious-looking liquid down her silk blouse. Lucky for her, the shirt was also a noxious red. She sobbed as Duncan held the poker he had snatched off the floor in a threatening position. I stayed behind him, satisfied to peer over his shoulder as I clung to his back. He was better equipped to deal with her anyway.

"Who are you?"

She flinched at the menace in his voice.

He took a step forward. "I will not ask twice, and this—" He waved the poker at her. "—will hurt a hell of a lot more than a wooden spoon."

"S-s-sierra Mallory."

Holy shit! No wonder she seemed familiar. While researching Mallory, I had seen a picture of her with her father from six months ago at one of the many charity functions he sponsored. Even with the hole in her chest, she looked healthier now than she had in that picture. The gossip circuit held her disappearance from the blueblood social scene was due to a stint in rehab, but neither Agnes or I had found out which one.

I peered at her chest. The tiny hole from the spoon had already sealed itself. Just like the gaping wound in my chest had last night.

I gasped as the realization hit me. I had heard screaming in the lab last night. Hers.

With the chance to calm my own roiling panic, I analyzed Sierra's scent. Definitely not the sandalwood of a vamp. More like a frying pan. A just-washed, rinsed-clean Revereware frying pan. I poked Duncan's shoulder. "Does she smell like me?"

He didn't spare a glance over his shoulder, his attention on the weeping heiress. "What do you mean?"

"Metallic."

This time he looked at me. "Yes."

No wonder we couldn't confirm a rehab facility.

Sierra cried harder, spasms racking her body. Compassion waved through me along with a healthy amount of curiosity. What lunacy would possess Mallory to experiment on his own daughter? I eased around Duncan and knelt next to her.

"Samantha, are you insane?" he hissed. "She just tried to kill you."

Sympathy overrode my preservation instinct. I wrapped an arm around her, and she buried her head in my shoulder. I rocked her as Duncan stared at me in disbelief.

After a couple of minutes, Sierra's words became comprehensible. Her pleading mascara-streaked face looked up at me. "What did he do to me? Daddy said I'd be okay."

The childlike voice was not a good sign. Sierra was close to some kind of breakdown. After what the mad scientists had done to both of us, I couldn't blame her. I was pretty close myself after the last four days.

"The same thing he did to me." My whispered words didn't ease her distraught expression. I honestly didn't know what would.

She clutched my sleeves. "Help me, please," she begged. "He said I wouldn't be a monster."

"You're not," I murmured, stroking her hair. "It'll be okay." An eerie sense of deja vu hovered over me. I had mimicked exactly what Duncan had said and done after one of my many nightmares last night.

I looked up at Duncan. "We've got to help her."

Disbelief etched itself across his features. "She is the enemy."

"Not if her father did this to her," I mouthed back. Sierra's hearing would be just as good as mine, even in her state of shock. Her teeth rattled as she began shivering uncontrollably. "Duncan, would you please get us a blanket?" I said out loud.

He stalked out of the kitchen and down a side hall. I could hear muttering about New World women and lack of common sense, but he returned with a ratty patchwork quilt that saw its best days in the nineteenth century. I couldn't blame him considering the blood that stained Sierra's shirt even though the wound had healed.

I took the proffered quilt and wrapped up Sierra, then surprised myself by lifting her in my arms. Her shivering abated, but her eyes still held a glazed look as tears trickled down her cheeks.

"Where to?" I asked.

"You cannot be serious!" Duncan's eyes bulged, not to the extent of Jim Carrey's character in *The Mask*, but they bulged nonetheless.

"We can't leave her here." Some perverse need in me to help reared its head. The same one that drove me to ride in the ambulance and hold Fred's hand as he died.

"She just tried to shove a spittoon through your skull out there." He waved the poker towards the showroom before he shook it in my face.

"She goes with us, or we both stay." I prayed all my experience playing poker with Max and his buddies would pay off in this bluff. I didn't think Duncan's Elizabethan code of chivalry would allow him to abandon two helpless women, but he was pretty pissed. I wouldn't last two seconds against Mallory's people. I knew it and I knew he knew it too. Also, if I could get Sierra out of shock and away from her father, she may provide the answers I needed about our condition.

He tossed the poker across the kitchen in exasperation, smashing the bowl of daisies. Water ran off the table to splash on the floor. I clucked my tongue but refrained from saying anything further due to the murderous look in his eye. He opened the pantry and fiddled with the second shelf. The rear wall of the pantry swung backward on silent hinges.

He gestured at the opening. I eased through with my load but looked back at Duncan.

"Would you grab the other pie for the ride?"

My stomach gurgled loudly. Despite watching the street as I drove, I saw Duncan turn to glare at me out of the corner of my eye.

"I told you to bring the pie."

Tiffany snickered from the backseat where Sierra sat propped up between her and Phil. The heiress had passed out during our trek through the tunnel.

Phil and Tiffany had been waiting with the SUV at the tunnel's exit, which was fifteen blocks from the store in the opposite direction from where I originally parked. How they got to the vehicle and drove it back through the mob without getting caught freaked me out in itself, but given the proximity of Mallory's goons, I didn't ask any questions. Somehow, I got nominated to drive, and we rode in silence except for Duncan's terse directions.

The theme from *Buddies* jingled from behind me. In the rearview mirror's reflection Tiffany whipped out her phone. "What's up?"

Her eyes darted to Duncan, who glared over his shoulder at her.

"I dunno if I can go shopping tomorrow." A long pause while someone who sounded suspiciously like Jessie Alton prattled on about baby accessories. "Chill, cuz. Your hormones are out of control."

My attention alternated between the traffic and Tiffany's conversation. This super hearing could be invaluable to my job. I bit my bottom lip as Tiffany's caller burst into tears.

Tiffany sighed. "I know you're not supposed to go out without a special security escort, but I'm working on a case right now." Her gaze met Duncan's. "I've got to go." Another protest. "I'll tell him." A tiny click as she shut off the phone. "She wants to talk to you when you have the chance."

Duncan ignored his niece in favor of more orders. "Turn left up here."

Around the corner, I spotted a Mallory Mystery Machine facing the intersection with Jeckyll in the driver's seat, and I whipped from the turn lane back into main traffic. My brand-spanking-new zombie eyesight was barely keeping us one step ahead of the bad guys. Thankfully, I didn't cut off any vehicles by diving back into traffic, but Duncan's head hit the doorpost with a resounding *thunk* at my evasive maneuver.

"Bloody hell, woman!"

"Mallory's got your safehouse staked out, asshole."

His eyes widened, and all of us, except Sierra, looked back. No nondescript van followed, but we couldn't remain out in public much longer.

"How could they know?" Phil asked.

"The bitches read my mind," I muttered. How the hell was I ever going to hide from a bunch of freakin' vampires?

"No," Duncan drawled.

"Isn't that how Phil knew to meet us? Vampire telepathy?" I shot him a look before I flipped off the Mercedes who cut in front of us. Duncan proceeded to fill the girls in on Sierra's vampire friends who attacked us. I also noticed he didn't answer my question.

"Ahem."

He returned his attention back to me. "What?"

"Unless you want me to pull over and call Mallory myself, answer my freakin' question."

"The two we battled were dead before I told you of this condo," he said.

"What about others? What if Mallory had more than the Bitch Squad and Heckyll following us at the carnival?"

"I didn't sense anyone else, but . . ." Duncan shrugged. I wanted to smack him. How could he be that nonchalant about our continued survival?

From the reflection in the rearview mirror, Phil's brunette curls whipped as she shook her head. "Why would any rogue work for a Normal in the first place? It doesn't make sense."

"I thought a rogue was a vampire who drank human blood."

Tiffany took a little sympathy on my ignorance. "Technically, it's vamp not associated with a coven." She snorted. "And there's usually a good reason they were kicked out." There was a slight pause before she added, "A vamp might work for a Normal if he's offering a cure."

Duncan leaned over to look into the back seat. I gripped the steering wheel until my knuckles turned white when his hair brushed my cheek. "What are you talking about?" he asked.

"Think about it. From what I've seen, Sam's got all your abilities, but none of your weaknesses. What if he's offering the vamps who work for him a cure? You get to keep the cool stuff, but you can eat solids and walk in the sun again."

"Then why kidnap Alex or any of the other folks?" I piped in. I really didn't like the implications. I knew what happened to lab rats after experiments, and as far as Mallory was concerned Alex and I were his lab rats.

Duncan leaned back in his seat. "Unless the ones who are missing are folks who didn't accept his offer or are his research subjects." He reached into his pocket and muttered an oath. "My phone's missing."

"The shop during our fight?" I asked.

"Probably."

"Here's mine." Tiffany reached forward and dropped her silver box into his lap.

While he jabbed the number in, I glanced at the fuel gauge. An eighth of a tank. The way this behemoth drank gas, we would have to stop soon. And stopping meant we'd be sitting ducks.

He muttered another oath. "Caesar, call me on Tiffany's cell phone." He rattled off the number, then tried Dr. Zachary with the same result.

"Maybe they're busy getting busy." I peeked at Duncan. In the oncoming traffic's headlights, I could see face muscles twitch. "Come on, don't you have any other friends?"

"None that I would trust at this moment or would be close enough to aid us."

"You think someone on the inside of your organization is a snitch for Mallory?"

No one responded, which only confirmed my suspicions.

So Super Vamp was out of options. Now, I knew how Princess Leia felt after she made the crack about hoping to be around when Han Solo was wrong, and the Imperials were closing in on the *Falcon*. "Okay, then it's up to me to save our asses." I made a sharp right and headed west.

"Where the devil are you going?" he snapped.

I shot him a grin. "Apt description. We're heading for the Gates of Hell."

It was a serious gamble on my part, I admitted to myself as I headed towards Mom and Dad's place in Beverly Hills. Mallory knew I was with Duncan now. I hoped his obsession with capturing us blinded him from following up on Max.

Fifteen minutes later and with no tail following us, we rolled down Mom and Dad's deserted street and into the driveway. I thanked my guardian angel for the favor and punched in the six-digit code. The ornate steel gate swung open. White stone glowed in the wash of security lights as we cruised up the concrete. Much better was the fact the windows remained dark.

Thank God they stayed their extra week in Italy. I released air I didn't realize I had been holding. I wasn't sure how I'd explain things to them if they were home. I parked in the covered area behind the garage, so the SUV couldn't be seen from the gates.

We climbed out with Phil carrying the still unconscious Sierra. I was beginning to worry. Maybe the spoon to the chest did more damage to her than the bullet did to me. At least she hadn't turned into rotten meat goo in the backseat.

No one said anything as the group trailed me to the back door. A quick check of the ceramic frog in the neighboring flowerbed produced the key. I smiled at Dad's predictability. All this security and anybody could still get into the house.

A familiar beep sounded when I popped open the door. "Follow me. I'll get the alarm, and then we'll take her up to one of the guest bedrooms." The house was too quiet without Mr. Cuddles' hostile greeting. If Max really was in trouble, I hope he had sense to take the nasty little canine with him. I'd lay odds on the poodle over Mallory any day of the week.

I entered, crossed the kitchen and headed straight for the security pad in the front hallway, Phil hot on my heels with her load. I turned off the system, but something raised the hairs on the back of my neck.

Like I was being watched.

I whirled to see Max perched on the loveseat in the living room. My beloved older brother had Mom's .45 aimed at my head.

Chapter 16

This wasn't my big brother. Max would never aim a gun at someone. Anyone. But the ugly expression on his face scared the hell out of me. "Put that thing down before someone gets hurt."

Max gave a sharp shake of his head. "Sorry, Sam, I can't."

I planted my fists on my hips, trying not to show my fear. "I get kidnapped Friday night, I try to warn you Mallory knows about your investigation, and this is how you greet me." Pale yellow from the security lights outside reflected off the ugly metal in his hand. The barrel didn't waver from its focus on my forehead.

Static electricity pricked along my skin. Phil's harsh breathing contrasted with the slow, even intake by the still unconscious Sierra. *Oh god.* The last thing I needed was a demigoddess throwing lightning bolts at Max in the middle of Mom and Dad's living room.

He didn't answer for a long time, his attention flicking between me and the other two women. The switch in his attitude freaked me out. He's the one who tried to talk Mom out of buying the firearm years ago, citing endless statistics on how often handguns at home were used to kill occupants. And I was about to become one of his statistics, assuming I could be killed again. I really didn't want to test my survival capabilities from having my brains blown out.

"Well, I never thought you'd pull a Patty Hearst." His short bark of laughter sounded rough, so unlike the person I thought I knew. "You know, I was worried sick when you disappeared."

"Gee, thanks. I can tell. Now put the gun down." An ill feeling crawled through my gut. Any other time I'd have said Max was the analyzer, not a violent bone in his body. I half expected Rod Serling to step out of the shadows.

"Tell your other friend to get in here."

I didn't really want to get shot for the second time in twenty-four hours, but I wasn't about to put Tiffany in the line of fire. Maybe Goth Girl was beginning to grow on me.

Yeah, like a fungus.

"Now!" Max roared.

"I heard you the first time." The clipped British accent sounded right next to me, but I didn't dare look. "This woman needs medical attention."

Max's hand shifted so Mom's gun pointed at Duncan. "Like I'm going to believe one of Tyrone Mallory's lackeys." Max snorted to emphasize his point.

"Duncan's been investigating Mallory, too. He already thinks you two are working together." I raised both hands to where he could see them with his Normal vision. Damn. Less than a day and I was thinking like a supernatural. "You need to pool your information."

Max's attention never wavered from Duncan. "Let my sister go."

"Do you really believe your toy will work?" Duncan taunted.

"Long enough," Max countered.

Something clicked in my overstressed brain, but I was too concerned about Tiffany or Max getting hurt to analyze it.

Instead, I focused on the immediate problem. "Get. A. Clue. Snot-face." I took a step forward with each word, and as I planned, the gun swung back towards me. Maybe not such a great plan after all. I clamped down on the fear spinning in my belly.

"Mallory kidnapped me because he thought I was spying on him for you." I took another step forward. "After he originally assumed I worked for Duncan." I jabbed a thumb in the general direction of the vampire behind me. "I'm not working for anybody but Ralph, so I'm getting really tired of people slamming me into walls and pointing guns at me for a story I'm not even writing."

The great thing about my new enhanced vision was I could see the doubt cross his face. Otherwise, the shadow from the partially opened drapes would have obscured my view of his ugly mug.

A familiar voice moaned behind me.

I kept my eye on the gun. "Now, Phil's going to take Sierra upstairs. She's had a very bad night." I really didn't want her to wake up with the .45 pointed at her. There was no telling what the nanite-enhanced heiress would do in her disorientation.

"Sierra?" The gun wavered. "Mallory? Here?" Nervous perspiration sparked along Max's forehead. He rose from the cushions. "What the hell did you do, Sam?"

"It's a long story. She tried to bean me with a fireplace poke—"

"Can I please put her down somewhere before you two continue your argument?" Phil asked. "She isn't exactly a featherweight."

Tiffany chose that moment to saunter through the entry to the dining room. "Hey, Sam, all I could find was cookies 'n' cream in your mom's freez—"

Startled by her appearance, Max spun to his left, his finger squeezing the trigger. Zombie speed saved Tiffany's brains from splattering across the imported hardwood floor. The shot went wild, shattering the Mikasa vase on the dining room table, as I slammed him back into the loveseat.

Awakened by the gunshot, Sierra started another round of her ear-splitting shrieks.

The living room lamps flared on, and I blinked at the sudden shock to my optic nerves. At least the same shock shut up Sierra. Thank God for Dad's kooky auto-timers.

"Give me that before someone does get shot!" I grabbed the gun away from Max and accidentally crushed the barrel in the process.

"Sam?" Raw fear shone in Max's watery gaze as his eyes flipped from me to the steel Silly Putty in my hand. "What the hell is going on?"

"Ouch! Get off of me!" Tiffany's muffled voice came from somewhere next to the china cabinet. Max and I peered over the arm of the loveseat to see Tiffany punch and kick her way free of Duncan's protective embrace from where they lay on the floor. Ice cream and chocolate cookie crumbles slid down the floral wallpaper behind them to puddle on the living room's very expensive Berber carpet.

"Mom is going to kill you," Max muttered in my ear.

After we calmed Sierra down, Tiffany and Phil cleaned up the ice cream mess the best they could, I stole a couple hundred from Mom's mad money stash to order pizza, and Max raided Dad's liquor cabinet.

I didn't question the cooler Duncan brought in from the SUV, and I sure didn't want to look in it either. He disappeared into the bathroom with it. I was thankful he didn't eat, or is that drink, in front of the rest of us. Okay, in front of me. This morning had left me a little sick as it was.

The cooler represented the one disgusting habit of your otherwise perfect boyfriend you ignore. Except I never could ignore the disgusting habits, which was probably why I didn't have a boyfriend.

And since when did Duncan graduate to possible boyfriend status? I decided to shove that thought into a deep dark hole and cover it with quick-drying cement. The whole subject of food was bad enough.

And I didn't have anything to brag about in the disgusting food habit department, considering the way I had been eating everything in sight for the last twenty-four hours. By the time the delivery girl rang the gate buzzer, Sierra's stomach had joined mine in a rousing chorus of rumbles.

After giving the delivery girl a hefty tip, I walked into the kitchen with two carriers full of pizza boxes. Taking a good look around me, I realized why I hated Duncan's kitchen. It must have been put together by the same designer Mom hired. The same stainless steel and black appliances with the same butt-ugly Italian tile on the floor. I really needed to re-evaluate my attraction to the man.

Max looked up from the virgin sex-on-the-beach he was mixing for Tiffany. "Geez, Sam! Who the hell is going to eat 20 pizzas?"

Duncan stuck his nose in his glass of wine—I was sure it wasn't blood since I had poured the damn bottle—to hide his chuckle. I shot him a dirty look.

Turning back to Max, I tried to change the subject. "You didn't leave Mr. Cuddles at your apartment, did you?"

He shook his head. "The break-in traumatized the poor guy. He's at the vet, enjoying some doggie tranquilizers."

Wonderful. Something else Mom will blame me for.

Max gave me a quizzical look. "You still haven't told me why we need 20 pizzas."

I swallowed hard, and my stomach warbled at the scent of pepperoni and cheese. "There's a few things I need to tell you."

The guys had grabbed the stools next to the kitchen island, so I joined the girls at the table in the breakfast nook. I'd much rather sit next to Duncan, but now was definitely not the time for lust.

Instead, I poured out the events of the last few days to Max between slices of nine pepperoni and mushroom pizzas. Well, I edited the story quite a bit. I wasn't going to spill Duncan's secrets without his permission, and I wasn't sure how Max would react to the whole vampire thing.

He did seem to take the whole nanite scenario rather well, though he'd probably hold it over my head later. While he chewed his slice of sausage and black olive, I could almost see the little wheels turning in his brain. "So which side is she on?" He nodded towards Sierra who was finishing her sixth veggie pizza.

She flushed a bright crimson against her dark roots. I frowned. Her hair didn't look that bad a couple of hours ago, but then I wasn't paying much attention to her 'do as she tried to bash in my skull and strangle me. Did the nanites consider hair color a problem to correct? If so, any highlights were in serious danger.

"I know you have no reason to trust me. Especially after..." She waved vaguely in my direction.

"You mean trying to brain me with a spittoon and skewer me with a poker?" I couldn't help the sarcasm dripping from my words.

"You're the one who wanted to bring her with us," Duncan said, an innocent look on his face.

I gave him another dirty look before turning back to Sierra.

She stared at her licked-clean plate. It took me a minute to realize she was crying again.

"Sierra, come on . . ."

"No." She sniffed and raised her head to meet my gaze. "You have every right to hate me. I listened to my father. I knew the things he was doing were wrong, and, and—" She gulped air to keep from totally breaking down. "I was sick, and I wanted to live so bad, I didn't care who he was hurting." She sniffed again. "Or who I was hurting. I'm so sorry, Sam."

She looked around the room, meeting each person's eyes squarely. "I'll help you stop him. He won't do this to anybody else." Maybe the spoon stabbing in Phil's kitchen had scared her straight.

Tiffany rose to grab another slice from the box she and Max were splitting. "So why were you checking out Mallory?" she said around a mouthful of pizza, using the rest of the slice to point at Max.

Max surprised me by turning beet red himself. The last time he looked that embarrassed, I had caught him in our bathroom fifteen years ago with one of Dad's *Playboy*s and his pants down. The incident netted me an extra allowance for six months. It also taught my brother to lock the freakin' bathroom door.

"Come on, Max," I said. "Spill."

"I linked Anne's disappearance to Mallory."

"Who?" Tiffany mumbled around another full mouth.

"She's a runaway Max keeps an eye on," I answered. I turned back to Max. "That doesn't make sense. Why the hell would Mallory be interested in a street kid?"

He took a large gulp of his rum and coke. "This is difficult to explain."

"What? He's some kind of child perv?"

"Hey!" Sierra objected.

I glared at her. "Remind me to talk to you about your dad's basement." Sierra took a sudden interest in her seventh pizza.

Max plucked a sausage chunk off his slice. "I don't want to violate any confidences." The weird thing was the way he watched Duncan, trying so hard not to be obvious.

"Now you're the one stalling. Protecting your sources is one thing, but Anne's life and a lot of other people's are at stake!"

"You're not going to believe me." Max gaze shifted to an imaginary spot on the floor. "She's a vampire." He looked up. "Go ahead and laugh."

"Anne?" Phil held up her hand. "Anne Levy? About this high? Mousy brown hair down to here?" Phil gestured at the middle of her back.

"Uh-huh." Max looked thoroughly confused. "You know her?"

"Bloody hell!" Duncan swore.

My gaze flip-flopped between Duncan and Phil. "She's one of yours?"

Phil's hand clenched around the knife she was using on her pizza, and Mom's stainless bent like soft wax. Duncan nodded in confirmation. "She left to visit her living family in Ohio almost three weeks ago," he said.

"And no one called to check on her?" I shouted in disbelief. "With all the freakin' disappearances, you were too lazy to phone?"

"It is not that simple, Samantha," Duncan said.

"What do you mean 'it is not that simple?' You dial the freakin' number, you moron!"

"Her living family is Amish."

"Oh."

An Amish vampire. Who'd have thought? Not me, that's for sure.

"Sam knows what you are, right?" Max inclined his head in my direction.

Duncan gave one of his long-suffering sighs. He really needs to trademark those. "Unfortunately."

"Wait a minute." I glared at Max. "You knew what he was."

Max nodded. "The room temperature feel when I shook his hand. It's a dead giveaway." Then his expression shifted, and he launched a perplexed look at Tiffany and Phil.

"Hey, I'm just related to them," Tiffany said. She gave him a devilish grin. "And my sister's not a zombie."

Max's eyes shot to me. I shrugged.

"We're still waiting for her to eat her first brains," Tiffany volunteered.

"What?" Sierra shrieked.

"She's just teasing Sam." Phil laid a consoling hand on Sierra's arm.

"It's not funny," the heiress grumbled back.

"What does she mean you're a zombie?" Max looked thoroughly confused.

"I died last night. Got shot by one of Mallory's goons, but I'm still walking around. The nanites fixed me." I shrugged again when Max gave me a horrified look. "It's about the best explanation I can give you because I don't understand how it works myself."

Max's horrified expression melted into his super skeptical reporter face. "Zombies aren't real, Sam."

"So says the brother who's friends with a vampire," I retorted. "Do you have a better explanation of what I am with these damn robots inside of me?"

"Frankenstein?"

A wadded paper napkin launched itself from my hand and hit his forehead. "Snotface."

Max grabbed the napkin and tossed it into the waste can. "I had no clue what Mallory was really up to. I only figured out he was connected to Anne's disappearance because I got lucky. A couple of the homeless kids Anne watches over recognized the MLI insignia on the money clip of someone who was asking a lot of questions about her. They didn't believe his story he was her dad, so they didn't tell him anything."

Duncan set his goblet down. "But they told you."

Max shrugged. "I help Anne deliver food to them."

"Crap," Tiffany muttered. "All he needed was a vampire close enough to read their minds. When he questioned them, they couldn't help thinking about the truth."

Another puzzle piece fell into place in my shaken, not stirred, brain. "That's how you knew about Mallory?"

She nodded. "A few people recognized the pictures of some of the missing folks. Duncan could pull the memories. Employees of MLI or one of its subsidiaries were spotted by the witnesses shortly before or after about three-quarters of the disappearances. We just didn't have any solid evidence against Mallory until you."

Max's attention returned to Sierra. "You said you were sick. What was wrong with you?"

Sierra wouldn't meet anyone's eyes. Her voice barely rose above a whisper. "A rare form of leukemia. The doctors thought I was in remission, but it showed up again. They gave me six months, and that was six and a half months ago. When I woke up this morning, I felt normal for the first time in ages."

I whistled. "These things are a cure for cancer?" The implications hit harder than one of her punches.

Tiffany bit off the last of her slice that had sauce on it and handed me the crust. After nine pizzas, I was still a little peckish. Apparently, my appetite was not altered in the face of world-shattering events. Max stared at me, his look even more horrified than when Tiffany announced my zombie status. He hated people eating off his plate and refused to eat off other people's. But devouring something another had bitten into was the absolute worst.

Tiffany noticed him staring at the crust I bit into. "I'm sorry. Did you want my crust?"

"No, thanks," he mumbled.

The teen crossed the kitchen and tossed her paper plate in the trash before continuing. "If Mallory's looking for a cure for cancer and not for the V-virus, then how's he keeping his vamps in line?"

"He is looking for a cure for the vampires too." Sierra wiped her mouth. "According to Dr. Abel, the virus has similar properties to cancer cells."

"But why test it on me? I'm not a vamp and I don't have cancer!" The thought hit me like a freight train. "Do I?"

Sierra shook her head. "Not that I know of."

Okay, now I was starting to get pissed. If I had an incurable disease, then I'd probably be the first to volunteer as one of Abel's guinea pigs. But dammit! I'm a healthy twenty-six year old woman. Or at least, I was.

Sierra stared at the grease stain on her plate. "He wanted to make sure I would survive the nanites. They hadn't been tested on humans before."

Phil took a sip of her wine and frowned. "That makes sense. If the nanites are programmed to act similarly to the V-virus, he'd want test trials to confirm his data."

Max grabbed a clean napkin and a pen. "What do you mean?"

I really didn't want Phil to answer my brother's question. My stomach was threatening to heave nine pizzas as it was.

"Not everyone survives the initial infection of the virus," she said. "Otherwise, we'd be neck deep in vampires."

Everyone groaned at her atrocious joke.

"What doesn't make sense is the were and witch kidnappings," Tiffany said.

"It does if Mallory's not really looking for cures." Fury twisted Duncan's face. We all looked at him, waiting for him to finish.

"He's looking for immortality."

Chapter 17

With a sharp crack, the stem on Phil's wine glass split in two. The entire thing fell from her hand. Red liquid splashed across the table. "Gaia," she whispered.

Somehow, the rest of the goblet didn't shatter when it hit the wooden tabletop. Tiffany grabbed a handful of napkins to mop up the spilled liquid.

The implications of Duncan's words sank through my pizza-fogged brain. No, this was way too much for anyone to deal with, much less comprehend. I gulped a couple of times before I could jump on a decent train of thought. "Wait a sec here. You mean there's more than just vamps disappearing off the streets," I said. After everything we'd been through, I couldn't believe Duncan had been holding out on me. Maybe twenty-four hours didn't create a lifetime bond, but geez!

"I am aware of three that are missing. One werewolf and two witches."

"I know there're covenless witches, but don't the wolves keep close tabs on their packs?" Max said. The amount of his knowledge of the real occult world was beginning to scare me.

"Yes, they do." A wry smile crossed Duncan's lips. "Which is why we are looking at a potential invasion since the missing pup is the son of the San Antonio pack's alpha. Also, the two missing witches we know about belong to the Los Angeles coven."

No matter how I twisted the info, the pieces weren't fitting. I held up a hand. "Whoa. What does one set have to do with the other? Cancer and viruses are one thing. Why would Mallory kidnap the werewolves and witches? You guys told me they're just variations of humanity."

"Longevity is the commonality. Their lifespans are twice as long as normal humans. Not on par with vampires, but—" He shrugged, reached for his own wineglass, and took a sip. "They also have specialized abilities which we do not have."

The churning in my stomach grew worse. Dr. Zachary said the nanites were rewriting my DNA, but she wasn't sure exactly what they were doing to me. The bizarre appetite and uncontrollable telepathy were bad enough. Would I need a lawn mower to shave my legs once a month?

I turned back to Sierra, who stared at her plate again.

"How many people is your father holding in his rat hole?" My fingers flexed. I itched to wrap them around her scrawny little Paris Hilton wannabe neck since I couldn't get to her father and his mad scientists.

"Eight," she whispered. "Right now, anyway."

"How many more was he holding?" Duncan's voice held an edge of menace.

"Does it matter? They're dead . . ." She still wouldn't meet anyone's stare.

Phil not-so-subtly shifted her chair away from the heiress. Whether consciously or not, she cleared space for a potential fight.

"You stupid bitch." Tiffany was even less subtle than the demigoddess as she crossed to the island to throw away the broken goblet and soggy napkins. "People are dead because of you. Don't you care?"

"Yes." The word was almost lost in her sob. "Yes, I do."

"How many?" Phil rose from the table, her empty hand raised to strike. Instead of the calm, cool, collected Lauren Bacall look-alike I was used to, she resembled an avenging Fury.

Sierra flinched.

"Phil, no!" Tiffany leapt and grabbed her wrist. Not that she could stop an enraged demigoddess, but I had to give the kid credit for balls.

Tiffany's interference seemed to rattle some sense into Phil. She stalked across the kitchen to retrieve another goblet and poured more wine into the new one. She chugged it down before refilling the glass.

Sierra glanced up at Tiffany and whispered, "Thanks."

Tiffany glared at the huddled Sierra. "Don't go thanking me yet. Spill, rich bitch, or I let Sam and Phil rip you apart."

"I don't know exactly."

"Then give us an estimate." Duncan's voice could have dripped icicles. "I saw two dead weres in the facility last night."

"Maybe twenty, twenty-five." A sliver of defiance appeared on her face when she raised her head. "I was in a coma for the last week. My father was trying to save my life."

"And neither of you cared who you hurt in the process," Max said in disgust.

"I already said I was sorry. I can't change what happened," she said, pleading obvious in her voice.

I can't help rhetorical questions, and I knew we needed a quick change of subject before things got ugly. "So what do we do about Mallory?"

"We rest until we hear from Caesar," Duncan said.

"Who the hell made you boss?" I was so getting tired of him ordering me around.

He ignored my grumbling. "I'll take the first watch." His green eyes had the faintest of glows under the kitchen fluorescents. "The rest of you get some sleep."

Something pressed against my head, an unseen force. I shook my head, more in disagreement than discomfort, and the pressure disappeared. "When Mallory figures out Max and I are related, this house won't be safe."

"You said Mallory knew we were related," Max said.

I shot him a nasty look. "Get your ears cleaned, big bro. I said Mallory thought I was spying on him for you. He didn't know we're related, and I didn't tell during his little torture session. I pushed the Ralph connection, but it doesn't mean someone with his resources won't eventually check court records and find out we're brother and sister."

Max climbed to his feet and started clearing empty boxes. "Well, they haven't tossed Mom and Dad's place yet. Let's wait until Duncan hears from his boss."

I frowned. "But Mallory ordered his goons to search your place and your office."

"He did." Max smirked. "They didn't find my research. He even had them search the *Scoop* and Ralph's place too."

"Did they hurt anyone?"

Max shook his head. "Ralph was pissed as hell though and worried sick about you. We need to let him know you're okay."

"It's not safe—" I started.

"I know, I know. I wasn't going to call." He rubbed a hand across his face, the last few days obviously catching up with him. "I figure Mallory's got wiretaps on everyone, but it sounds like he's got his people working the Duncan angle to find you. We have a little time."

"Your files aren't here, are they?" I whispered. God, I hoped Max wasn't that stupid.

"Don't worry. There're in a safe place." He didn't clarify and the rest of us didn't ask.

Max and I went upstairs to scrounge blankets and pillows for everyone. I really hated staying here. It wasn't safe, but as my brother pointed out, our options were pretty limited at the moment. Especially if Mallory already knew about one of the vampire safe houses.

"I saw his picture in your bedroom," Max whispered in my ear as I pulled an extra comforter out of the linen closet.

I should have known Max's smirk earlier had nothing to do with his apartment getting searched and trashed. "You were in my place?" He was the only one with a key. Oh God, what if he'd been there when Mallory's goons had arrived?

"I was trying to figure out where the hell you had disappeared to. When my car vanished off the face of the earth, I got worried."

My evil glare didn't faze him. I shoved the comforter into his chest, knocking him back a step. "It's so nice you were more worried about your damn car than me." I turned back to the closet and yanked out a couple of pillows.

"Sam, from reading your notes—"

"How did you —"

He shot me a 'duh' look. "The plumbing access behind the tub? That is so amateurish, little girl."

My eyes narrowed. "Were you the one who messed with my computer? Mallory didn't find my notes, and he complained about a virus wiping out my hard drive."

Max shook his head, a confused look on his face. "You sure it wasn't something Fred planted? You said he'd been acting freaky before the accident. Maybe something he remotely activated?"

I shook my head. "Don't think so."

"Sure it wasn't your crush?" Of course. If my brother had been in the apartment, he'd seen the photo on my bedroom wall. Max's teasing look turned sober before I could whack him. "I was afraid St. James worked for Mallory, and you were in danger."

I held out the pillows, refusing to look at him. "He's not, okay." I wasn't sure why I was so pissed Max had seen the poster-sized photo of Duncan.

"I know that now. Sam . . ."

I looked at him, the concern on his face highly unusual for him.

"It won't work."

I frowned. "What won't work?"

"You and St. James."

"I don't know what the hell you're blathering about," I snapped, turning back to the closet.

He tugged on my shoulder with his free hand. "Sam, I'm not being a jerk. He's got what, a couple of centuries on you?"

"Four," I whispered.

"And Anne's got over a half century on me."

Confessions weren't an everyday occurrence between us. His crush on Anne must have been bad for him to spill.

"When did she tell you?"

A wistful smile crossed his face. "Fifteen years ago."

I gasped in shock. Max used to sneak out nearly every night during his junior year in high school. Anne explained a lot of his weird behavior during that time. "You've known vampires really existed all along and never told me?"

"Honestly, Sam, would you have believed me?" He shook his head. "I wasn't sure I believed myself, but as the years went by . . ." His self-deprecating laugh indicated his own amazement at the situation. His gaze met mine. "The point being, a relationship between a vampire and a human can't work. The age difference is bad enough. It's amazing the change in perspective a few years can make, much less a few centuries. Even so, would you be willing to give up sunlight, ice cream, your family, your life to be with him?"

I snorted. "In case you missed the memo, I don't have a life."

"You can still eat and go out in sunlight, right?" Max shook his head. "There's no guarantee the nanites can cure the V-virus or prevent you from being infected despite what Sierra says. Because that's what it comes down to. Most vampires won't have a human because of the guilt of cursing someone they love with an incurable disease. It's either that or watching the person you love wither and die from old age, never being able to touch them, to love them."

Fury raised its ugly head. Max spoke the thoughts racing silently in my mind since Duncan told me the truth. God, was that only twenty-four hours ago?

To hide my anger, I turned back toward the closet. "You don't have the right to lecture me just because things didn't work out between you and your high school crush," I hissed.

"I admit to my crush, but your copious files on this guy make you a psychotic stalker."

"Pictures of what guy?"

I jumped a foot at Duncan's soft baritone at the head of the stairs. "Geez! Can you just not sneak around for two seconds?"

"I'll take these downstairs." Max slid past Duncan and took the steps two at a time. I ignored both my brother and the hunky vamp standing next to me by grabbing a couple of light blankets.

"What guy?" Duncan repeated.

"It's a story I'm working on."

"Ahhh." He folded his strong arms over that fabulous chest and leaned against the wall beside me. "This wouldn't have anything to do with the black and white glossy of me on your bedroom wall, would it? Or the multitude of other photographs you've taken?"

I felt my face flush. Of course he heard every single word Max said. The only person in the house who didn't have super hearing besides Max was Tiffany.

Again, I turned back to the closet, praying there was another pillow I could smother myself with. "Max doesn't know what he's talking about." Then I realized Max hadn't mentioned any photos, and Mallory said Duncan had been seen at my place. Hell, *I'd* witnessed him and Tiffany leaving my apartment complex.

I whirled back to face him. "What the hell were you doing in my apartment?" I liked my privacy, and I really didn't appreciate everyone traipsing through my place like it was Walmart.

"Deducing why you were following me."

"I told you why Thursday night. I'm writing a follow-up on your rescue—"

"—of Ms. Alton from the Sunshine Believers." He pursed his lips. I couldn't take my eyes from them. Tingles ran up and down my spine at the memory of his kiss when I yanked him between the carnival tents earlier this evening. "At the time, I had no reason to believe you. And as I pointed out Thursday night by the river, you were stalking me."

I dragged my attention away from his lips. "Oh, really? And that gives you carte blanche to commit B&E?"

He shrugged. "While Tiffany believed you were harmless, I was not as confident you were not employed by Mallory."

"For crying out loud! Why does everyone think I'm working for someone else? Doesn't it occur to you people umf—" His mouth covered mine with a possessiveness that literally took my breath away. The blankets fell to the floor, and my fingers wound through his hair.

All of my indignation disappeared in the onslaught of his kiss. His hands wrapped around my waist to pull me even closer, his body against mine overloading my senses. Maybe it was the adrenaline rush from the last few days. Maybe it was something else. I wasn't sure what, but I didn't want the kiss to end.

Tongues and lips tangled and explored. Extra-sharp teeth nipped my lower lip, not hard enough to break the delicate skin, but a thrill of dangerous pleasure rippled through me at the risk. The rich scent of sandalwood rose, enveloping me in its embrace as Duncan's hands roamed over the sensitized skin under my t-shirt.

When he drew away, I almost keeled over. So this is the feeling all those sappy romances Mom read were talking about. He rested his forehead against mine, his breathing loud in the silence of the hallway. Dimly, I heard the other four downstairs, talking.

"I am sorry, Samantha. I should not have done that."

"Says who?" Why was he talking now? I pulled his head down for another taste.

Gently, he extricated my arms from around his neck. "Your brother is right." He brushed his fingertips lightly across my cheek, the sadness in his eyes overwhelming. "A relationship between us would never work."

"Like Max knows what he's talking about?" Anger replaced desire. I placed my hands on his chest and shoved. Hard. "So you were just leading me on? Is that it?" Silence reigned in the kitchen, which meant Phil and Sierra were listening to us. Fine. They wanted a show? I'd give them one.

"That is not true, Samantha, and you know it."

"You kissed me first, buster." I stepped forward and poked a finger at his chest. I was furious, at him for kissing me, at myself for wanting to believe I had a chance with him.

Irritation flared in his face. "No, you kissed me first. At the fair. After I told you what I was. So if anyone was acting dangerously, it was you."

"Excuse me? I figured out what you were at Mallory Labs. You did not tell me a damn thing! And that so-called kiss at the fair was to avoid the goon squad, not because I wanted to kiss you. You, you pervert!"

"So what is your excuse for kissing me back just now?"

God, I so wanted to smack the smirk off his arrogant mug. Mainly, because I know he was right.

I whirled on the heel of my brand new tennis shoes, trying not to remember Duncan had bought them for me, and marched to my old bedroom. I slammed the pastel pink door behind me, but instead of the usual satisfying bang, there was a screech as the wood splintered down the middle. The side with the knob teetered for a second before it landed with a *whoomph* in the middle of the obnoxious pink shag covering the bedroom floor. The other section creaked on the bent and warped hinges.

This damn zombie strength would be my downfall.

Through the broken door, I saw Duncan still standing at the other end of the hall. He smiled, winked at me, picked up the blankets from the floor, and headed back downstairs.

I stared at the half door lying in the carpet. A broken hunk of it would make a very good stake.

Chapter 18

Tiffany's cell phone woke all the supernaturals but one at four a.m. I used to be able to sleep through mine when it sat on my nightstand six inches from my head, but with my new hearing, Tiffany's sounded like a grenade going off outside the house. It didn't wake Duncan because it sat in his pocket as he circled the grounds on lookout.

These new abilities were starting to be a bitch.

The good news in this insane situation? Duncan's friend, Caesar, had another safehouse for us. We had barely enough time to beat both the sunrise and L.A.'s morning rush hour.

The mysterious Caesar Augustine and Dr. Zachary met us at the canyon house he had directed us to. He seemed vaguely familiar, but I couldn't place him. Dark hair accented his olive skin. His deep brown eyes were warm and charming as was his old world personality, but for a split-second, they flashed gold when Duncan introduced me. Like I couldn't figure out what he was from his handshake. The unusually chill hands were a dead giveaway. Pun intended.

He also made it clear he wanted to speak with Duncan and Phil privately. Complaints, loud ones, from the rest of our little group convinced him otherwise.

Actually, Duncan's slight nod convinced him. Max, Tiffany, and Sierra didn't notice the byplay.

Dr. Zachary, on the other hand, did notice. I had the impression she didn't miss much. Still, she played the gracious hostess and escorted us to the family room.

A gray stone fireplace dominated one wall. Opposite of the fireplace, a wet bar with wooden shutters separated the family area from what was probably the kitchen. Heavy navy drapes covered the wall between the bar and the fireplace, giving the place a sepulcher feel. If this was the typical canyon home, behind the cloth were the sliding glass doors leading to the back deck and pool. Even though they probably were covered with UV film, and Caesar definitely seemed the careful type, I didn't try opening them. I didn't think the vampire contingent would appreciate being fried if the glass wasn't protected.

Seated in a wing-backed chair next to the fireplace, Caesar looked like a medieval king holding court, if medieval kings wore polos and chinos instead of silk and chain mail. The rest of us scattered on the couches and floor, except Duncan. He paced in front of the drapes, a feral jungle cat blending into his surroundings.

Caesar glared at Max, then Sierra, before turning his death ray eyes on me. "Anything said in this house will stay in this house. Am I understood?"

No threats, which meant something pretty bad would happen if we tattled. Caesar Augustine was one of those people my instincts knew wouldn't waste his time on threats. All three of us gave meek nods. Seeing Max intimidated would have thrilled me if our benefactor didn't cow me as well.

Before Duncan started into the events of the last thirty-six hours, Caesar held up his hand. "The Council has authorized us to rescue those we can and destroy Mallory's labs."

"Wait a minute! Who asked us to do what?" My little outburst escaped before I could stop it. Tiffany and Duncan shot me horrified looks. Dr. Zachary hid a smile behind her hand, but Phil openly smirked at my brashness.

Caesar's chin rested on steepled fingers as he regarded me. The look he gave me could have frozen Lake Tahoe solid for the entire year. "I tolerate your presence, Ms. Ridgeway, at my chief enforcer's request. Do not push my tolerance further."

Chief enforcer? Duncan? Was he a vampire police officer or more like head muscle? Instead of asking though, I murmured, "Sorry."

Part of me wanted to kick my own butt for such a rookie mistake. Getting info from someone like Caesar would take finesse and probably a butt-load of flattery, not me acting like the Grand Inquisitor. I chalked my slip up to dying a couple of days ago.

At least Caesar wasn't king of the vampires if he was taking orders from someone else. And I didn't want to meet the guy who was giving them because this vampire seriously gave me the willies.

"So they are finally taking our concerns seriously?" With his arms crossed and his stance wide, Duncan appeared likely to kick this unknown council's collective ass if Caesar said no.

"The Council needed proof, Duncan, not speculation." Caesar waved in my direction. "Ms. Ridgeway has provided that proof, albeit indirectly."

He turned his unblinking attention to Sierra, who paled noticeably. "You have a choice to make, Ms. Mallory."

Despite the tremor in her hands, she nodded firmly. "I'll do whatever you want, but—" She licked her lips and straightened. "I want your promise, no matter what happens, you won't hurt my father."

"She should not be involved in this," Duncan said. His defiant tone speared me. Was he still questioning my decision to bring her along?

I kept my tone logical. "Why not? She knows the compound better than anyone here."

Duncan's cool green stare turned from his boss to me. "You should not be involved either. You barely have any self-control at the moment. Or do I have to remind you of the basement?" he said. "Or that you cannot help broadcasting your thoughts?"

"Those were accidents." My protest sounded feeble, even to me. "And I only killed in self-defense."

Duncan arched a black eyebrow. "And you accidentally crushed your brother's gun."

"Technically, it's Mom's gun," Max offered.

I so didn't need his help right now.

Satisfaction flickered across Duncan's face, and he turned back to Caesar. "None of them should be involved in any rescue attempt. I'd prefer the Gryffudds or the Osakas—"

Caesar shook his head. "We don't have the time to fly in any other enforcers, and I want our daytime guard at the mansion."

Duncan opened his mouth, but a strange buzz cluttered my brain. Voices speaking so rapidly it sounded like multiple tracks of the guy from the old FedEx commercials playing at the same time. Except no one's mouth moved until Duncan's teeth clicked shut at the same instant the voices stopped.

Caesar turned to Max, Sierra and me, fixing us each with a pointed look. I felt more like a rat under a microscope than I did with Doctors Kane and Abel.

"You may be right," Caesar said, his comment aimed at Duncan even as his gaze drilled holes through my eye sockets.

Before I could throw a scathing retort, Sierra said, "After what my father did to your friends . . ." She gulped hard. Not that I blamed her. Her own guilt, the realization of what her father had turned her into, plus the whole Caesar intimidation factor must have weighed heavily on those debutante shoulders. "And Sam and me, my father needs to be stopped."

"How are we getting in?" Tiffany spoke up for the first time. "After Sam and Duncan's escape, they'll have doubled security."

Sierra seemed to gather her courage. "I can get you in."

Duncan took a menacing step toward her. "Why should we trust you?"

"You shouldn't." She met Duncan's measured stare, digging her fingers into her thighs probably to keep them from shaking. "You can't. But I'm the only hope the survivors have right now. She's right." She inclined her fake blondness toward Tiffany. "Daddy's already tightened security, but the guards will let me in."

I rose to my feet before I realized it and glared at the heiress. My support didn't lend itself to absolute trust. "Why should they? You're missing as far as they're concerned. Won't they be suspicious if you show up a day later with no communication?"

Sierra lifted one shoulder, her nonchalant manner at odds with the nails burrowing into her legs. "I tell them the truth, or as much as I can anyway. St. James killed my backup and captured me. I escaped but encountered difficulties with Augustine's people, which was why I couldn't take the chance of contacting them." She turned her puppy dog eyes toward Bebe. "Maybe jinx me so I can't use a phone?"

Voices buzzed around and through me again, even more this time. The sensation was akin to having my iPod playing every file at once, but I couldn't focus on any one voice. The weird thing was no one's lips were moving though eye contact between the supernaturals made it feel like a conversation was happening. Even worse, Tiffany had been included in the high-speed conversation from the way her eyes twitched. The entire incident happened within a second or two.

God, I really hated being left out of the loop and was about to make my displeasure known when Caesar nodded.

"Your assistance is accepted on the condition your father's life is forfeit for any betrayal on your part," he said.

Sierra gave a sharp nod in return. "Give me a pen and paper. I'll map out everything."

I've relied on insiders in the past for story tips. They want the money, the revenge, or the publicity. Generally though, the motive's revenge. The maid at the luxury hotel who saw the two married film stars (and not to each other) together and was stiffed on her tip. The bathroom attendant who saw and heard interesting things in the stalls—and was stiffed on his tip. I'd bet a year's salary Duncan and his friends were very good tippers.

While Sierra was adamant about her dad not being harmed, I'd bet another year's salary her motive was revenge. If anyone asked how I knew what she felt, I wouldn't be able to tell them. It was something in my gut, like the weird knowledge of sunrise and sunset without physically viewing the environment.

Just as I could tell by the look in Duncan and Caesar's eyes their guarantees concerning Mallory's safety were to placate Sierra in return for her information. If push came to shove, they'd take Mallory out in a heartbeat. I hoped the vampires could handle her when they did. Hell, I barely survived when she was stone cold lucid.

Since Sierra and Max had more knowledge concerning the compound than my scant memories of the basement, my contributions were largely ignored as were Tiffany's. The only redeeming point was Duncan's attitude was slightly less condescending to me than to his niece.

"Screw 'em," Tiffany whispered in my ear. She inclined her head towards the kitchen.

Best idea I'd heard since we got here. My stomach started the most tentative of rumbles as I sauntered after her.

I was surprised to find the good doctor already by the stove. She had slipped out of the great debate so quietly I never saw her leave. She stirred a large pot of—well, it sure wasn't spaghetti. The strange odor from the stove tickled my nostrils, sending me into sneezing spasms.

In countertime to my nose, my stomach started another round of gurgles, which sent Tiffany into gales of laughter. Even Dr. Zachary smiled as she stirred.

"Whatcha makin'?" the teen asked as she poked her own snout over the pot. The doctor rewarded her by smacking the tip with the handle of the wooden spoon she used.

"Sleeping potion for this little rescue mission." She reached into one of the bowls next to her and sprinkled a yellowish powder into the mix.

I glanced around. The kitchen had similar expensive stainless steel appliances as Duncan's. I don't know what was worse—vampires with gourmet accessories or that they all had the same decorating tastes as my mother.

The corners of my mouth quirk in amusement. Other than the fridge and maybe a microwave, what use would be the other stuff to them? I doubted too many of the vampires were in the position of serving home-made dinners. Well, except to their girlfriends and nieces.

I grabbed the fridge handle, praying to find a snack because the hunger pangs were becoming damn uncomfortable. What I saw would have made me barf if it wasn't for my zombie appetite. Blood bags packed two whole shelves of the side-by-side at eye level. I slammed the door shut.

"Don't you have anything not red to eat, Doc?" I wasn't normally a rude guest, but the gnawing hunger made me irritable.

Dr. Zachary smiled instead of firing back. Nothing rattled this woman. "There's a dozen chicken cordon bleu breasts in the freezer," she said.

"I can't wait for those to cook." My stomach seconded the motion.

She laughed outright. "Cherry tomatoes are in the veggie bin at the bottom, if you can tolerate the red. Carrots and celery if not. They should tide you over until the chicken bakes. That's all we have right now. I'll make a grocery run after I finish this potion."

Relief tinged with worry spread through my uncomfortable abdomen. What would happen to me if I stopped eating every five seconds? Even worse, what would happen to the people around me if I couldn't control my appetite? I didn't have the excuse of an Andes plane crash in the dead of winter.

My stomach grumbled again. Tiffany scrounged a box of crackers for us, forcing aside my worries about the future. While munching the stale saltines, I arranged the prepared poultry on a baking sheet, popped it in the oven and set the timer. She had to retrieve the salad dressing and vegetables. I couldn't handle seeing the vampires' dietary requirements again. Not when the crackers only blunted the slightly nauseous hunger feeling in my belly.

"Want a tomato?" Tiffany scooted the bowl of washed veggies toward me.

I grimaced. "No, thanks. The small ones remind me too much of eyeballs."

"Consider it practice for later." Tiffany popped one into her mouth and bit down. She rolled her eyes and made a spectacle of rubbing her stomach with accompanying yum-yum noises.

The urge to smack her arose, but after what I did to my old bedroom door, ignoring her seemed the safer option. But her jokes brought an ugly thought to the front of my consciousness. "Doctor?"

"You can call me Bebe," she said. "We don't stand on a lot of ceremony when it's just Family." She flashed a brief smile before returning her attention to her pot.

"Um, okay. Bebe." I tested the name on my tongue. It seemed weird not to address her formally, but she couldn't be more than five years older than me. Then I remembered what Duncan said last night about witches living longer than Normals. For all I knew she could be Grandma Neel's age.

"What's wrong, Sam?" Bebe's face carried a patience I didn't know if I'd ever master.

I swallowed the suddenly dry bits of cracker. "Did you check Sierra's aura?"

Again, discomfort flickered across her patrician features, and she took a sudden interest in her potion. "Yes."

"It was black, too." When she didn't answer, I added, "Wasn't it?"

"Yes."

Tiffany's attention whipped between Bebe and me. "Really?"

The doctor shrugged and sprinkled a greenish-gray herb into her pot. "I'm still trying to figure that out. Serious injuries were inflicted on both women before I could examine them. I don't know if the nanites killed them or—"

My hand automatically rubbed the spot between my breasts where the bullet had ripped through me. I might have killed Sierra. I might not have. Either way, my rising body count bothered what was left of my conscience. Almost as much as Bebe's inability to figure out what I was becoming.

I opted for a change in conversation. "So what all goes into this sleeping potion?"

"You are a curious one, aren't you?" Her brow furrowed in concentration as she tossed a handful of aromatic herbs from another bowl into the mixture. "A little bit of this and a little bit of that."

Vague answers irritated me. If someone doesn't want to answer my social chat question, they just need to say so. Those types of answers also increase my smart-ass quotient by tenfold. "Eye of newt and all that shit, huh?"

She looked up from the pan. "Well, if I'm out of newt eyes, I can always use cherry tomatoes."

Chewed orange bits exploded out of Tiffany's mouth as she choked on her laughter and a large piece of carrot. A few zombie pats on the back dislodged the hunk in her throat.

We munched on the carrot and celery sticks as the doctor stirred, bubbles in her brew popping in countertime to the conversation in the next room. The voices of the vampires and Phil sounded like Allied generals planning D-Day. I guess they were, in some supernatural equivalent.

At the ding of the oven timer, everyone from the living room swarmed in for food. Unabashed, Duncan poured a couple of mugs of blood and shoved them into the microwave. Tiffany and Bebe split a chicken cordon bleu while my brother and Phil scarfed a half-pound breast each.

I couldn't talk. Sierra and I wolfed down the other nine. The chicken, crackers and vegetables took the edge off, but I'd need to eat again—soon. Worry chewed on the back of my mind. What would happen if I didn't have access to food while we were on the run? Would my friends turn into dancing steaks to me, like in those old Warner Brothers cartoons? All zombie jokes aside, turning into a George Romero extra terrified me.

It dawned on me that Caesar hadn't come in with the rest of the troops. Duncan had slipped out while I ate. It's pretty bad when I pay more attention to a piece of chicken instead of the hot guy.

Okay, make that a couple of pounds of chicken.

I eased out of the kitchen, but the family room was empty. The boys had succeeded in having their little testosterone tête-à-tête while the rest of us were eating. Forget their little fight-against-world-domination plots. If they didn't want my help, then fine.

Except it was the Dr. Frankensteins who created me the vampires were going after, and I wanted in on the destruction of my mad scientists.

Crossing the room, I felt between the drapes until I found the lock to the glass doors. Flipping it, I slid the door open and walked into some glorious California sunshine. The cold front plaguing the area last week had moved west, letting warm air caress my face. Blue ripples reflected off the white-washed pool bottom. I really wished I had a suit. If it weren't for the house party inside, I'd consider skinny-dipping.

The few steps to the deck railing yielded a spectacular view of the canyon. In the distance, some bird of prey glided on the thermals. Even my enhanced vision couldn't see more than dark feathers. It was the kind of beautiful day made for playing hooky from work.

The soft murmur of voices rose from below the house. I strained to catch the words when Caesar's unmistakable tenor said, "You might as well come down instead of eavesdropping."

In the time it would take me to go back inside and climb the stairs down to the garage, they could find somewhere else to hide from me. I looked over the railing. Only a one story drop to the concrete parking pad below. If I had Jaime Sommers' strength and hearing thanks to the nanites, I probably had the rest of her skills. Hiking my legs over the redwood, I glanced down once more, uttered a quick prayer and jumped.

Heck, my landing was even semi-graceful. At least I didn't fall on my ass in front of Duncan.

Well under the shade created by the pool deck, the missing vampires reclined on lawn chaises, each with a can of beer in hand, looking for all the world like a couple of suburbanites discussing their lawns.

"So how is your grass doing this season, Duncan?" Caesar said.

That damn vampire mind-reading was really starting to piss me off.

Caesar grinned, gracing me with a full display of very sharp canines. Gone was the eerie mystique he'd affected earlier. He looked, well, normal. Apparently, he heard those thoughts also because he broke out into a hearty belly laugh.

"You know, eavesdropping on people's thoughts is rude." Heat seeped through the soles of my Nikes from the concrete. I strode into the shade to stand in front of the two vampires. I crossed my arms and glared at Caesar.

He tossed his beer can into the garbage bin in a behind-the-back shot that would have made any Sabretooth proud. *Eavesdropping in any form is rude, yet you have no problem indulging.*

I tried not to let the weirdness of his voice in my head get to me. If the jerk would tell me what was going on, I wouldn't have to eavesdrop. This craziness concerned me as much as it did his people.

True. But I won't risk my people's safety on guesswork where you're concerned.

What a load of sanctimonious bullshit. "I'm not the one who's a threat to you! And I don't get how you can be that concerned when you can read minds."

Confusion spread across Duncan's face. "What are you talking about?" He turned to Caesar. "You heard her?"

Caesar's eyebrow quirked up. "How can you not? She's transmitting louder than Tiffany's MP3 on full volume."

Maybe I was picking up on Duncan's confusion because Caesar's comment made no sense. "B-but I heard you in my head."

"You entered my mind, Sam. Not vice versa."

Interesting new trick, even if I hadn't meant to wing my thoughts in Caesar's direction or grab his. I stuck my tongue out at Duncan. In a way, it was a relief to know he hadn't read my thoughts. Especially the ones I'd been having about him.

He scowled. I couldn't blame him. I hate being the one person who's not in on the joke, too.

I scooted his feet over to sit next to him. "Told you Mallory's bitches read my mind."

His scowl deepened. "Or you told them."

I locked eyes with him. "I did not."

"Beer?" When I nodded at Caesar's obvious effort to change the subject, he dug into the cooler next to him and tossed me a can.

I popped open the top and, for a split-second, hesitated. I had no clue of what alcohol would do to me now so I hadn't indulged in Mom and Dad's stash last night. *Oh, screw it!* I gulped down half the can and waited for a few seconds. Nope, I didn't explode, melt, or keel over. The beer tasted the same as all the others I'd had before I died.

Unfortunately, Duncan wasn't about to let the telepathy thing go. "Maybe you accidentally told someone else. You did not know the whereabouts of the other safehouse when we encountered those women. It's likely there were other vampires scouting the area."

"And if Sam didn't accidently transmit the address, we have a different problem," Caesar said.

Duncan turned to Caesar, cocked an eyebrow and frowned. "A traitor."

Caesar shrugged at the statement. "Perhaps. Given what you've told me of your assailants, we may not have discovered all of the plants."

Reporter instincts took over. "Plants? As in vampire spies?"

Duncan ignored my questions in favor of his boss. "If you truly believe my security team is so incompetent—"

"This isn't only about you." Caesar's cool look would have had me shaking in my boots. Okay, my Nikes. "In case you haven't noticed, my own sister plotted against me for decades. I will not be that blind to any and all possibilities ever again."

I just love interesting dirt. There was history between Duncan and Caesar's sister from the dark look on Duncan's face.

Then an abashed expression spread over Duncan's planed features. "Yes, sir."

Caesar's posture eased a fraction. "It's equally probable Mallory could have recruited someone within the coven. There's been sufficient mutterings of dissent over the last two years between not executing Selene and my relationship with Bebe."

Interesting that the men's relationship was still intact. It made me wonder what this Selene had done to betray Duncan as well as her brother.

"To answer your question, Sam, yes, we do have internal problems from time to time." Caesar fixed me with his golden gaze, and I was very glad to feel the reassuring pressure of Duncan's legs against my lower back.

Not wanting to get deeper into vampire politics than I already was, I took a sip from the can to gather my courage, but I didn't have a chance to ask Caesar my question.

"Yes, you may," he said.

"No!" Duncan bellowed. If I hadn't transmitted to Duncan, then Caesar must have.

"She was well on her way to breaking out when you found her. Her assistance will be invaluable." The corners of Caesar's mouth crinkled in a wry smile.

"That does not mean we have a right to put her back in danger."

"Hey, I'm volunteering here!" I could yell right back. I turned to Caesar, lowering the volume first. "So, what am I volunteering for?"

"Sierra will escort you back to the complex as her prisoner in my vehicle," Caesar said. "Bebe's spells will cover the rest of us in the back."

"Oh." Helpless captive was not what I had in mind. I was thinking more of Linda Hamilton in *T2* or Sigourney Weaver in *Aliens*.

"Helpless, you are not," Caesar said.

"Wise vampire, you are," I said, mimicking his Yoda voice.

"Mallory's people will be prepared for us after my break-in from the other night." Leave it to Duncan to poop on the party. "And we now know we will not be dealing with only Normals."

"Yes, they will be ready for us," Caesar replied. "Which is why both Sierra and Sam will be the keys for our success. Once the captives are freed, we will have additional allies if it becomes necessary to fight our way out."

I lowered my voice to a whisper. "You're not using Sierra as a hostage, are you?" No point in taking chances that she'd overhear us, and I wasn't about to trust any telepathic talent I'd received from the nanites.

Caesar shook his head. "That's not our intention." A strange expression flitted across his face. "However, I don't believe Mallory will endanger his daughter, given the extremes he's gone through to save her life."

Duncan mumbled something under his breath I couldn't decipher. I didn't really try either since I was sure it wasn't complimentary. I ignored him and focused on Caesar's words while he relayed his plan. I just hoped our vampire Yoda's plan wasn't as disastrous as the little green Jedi master's in the last Star Wars movie.

Chapter 19

I rolled my wrists, trying to ease the bite of the manacles on my skin. While the quick-release catch was reassuring, Caesar insisted they appear as real as possible. I tried not to think about why he had them at the safehouse. There are things about other people's lives you just don't want to know.

The duck pond rolled past the passenger window of Caesar's Hummer, the last vestiges of sunlight bouncing off the surface. I couldn't repress the shudder at the memories of my last ride through this park.

"Cold?" Sierra asked from the driver's seat.

"No," I said, unsure whether she was deliberately mistaking my reaction. If she wanted to play the naïve heiress, that was fine with me. But I'd lay odds she knew exactly how I'd been caught by her dad's goons.

"I'm not either," Bebe hollered from the cargo area. "It's stifling back here. Wanna turn the A/C up?"

We had pulled out the back seats of Caesar's Hummer. Somehow Caesar, Duncan, Bebe and Phil managed to cram themselves on the floor. Gray tulle netting covered them, and with Bebe's illusion spell, it made the cargo bed appear empty. I knew the back wasn't empty, and I still had trouble seeing the folks, even with my super vision.

Max and Tiffany had stayed behind at the safehouse over the kid's very loud and very obscene protests. My brother, ever the voice of reason, talked her into common sense, not that she had a whole lot to begin with, but I wasn't sure about the speculative eye Goth Girl was giving him when we left. The thought of someone her age interested in my over-thirty brother was just—

Icky.

A hint of brakes forced my mind off that track. Thank God.

"This is it, folks," Sierra said. She turned down the back driveway towards the security gate for the delivery entrance. I slumped in the passenger seat, pretending unconsciousness but with my eyes open a slit. Just in case. I may have been the idiot to talk everyone else into trusting her, but part of me still had doubts.

Butterflies in the stomach were nothing compared to the roll of nausea filling my gut as we approached the guards. Semi-automatic weapons gleamed under exterior lighting that clicked on as the sun faded behind the horizon. One of the guards sauntered to the driver's side as we rolled to a stop. He ducked to take a good look at us as the driver's window slid down. His cocky smirk disappeared the instant he recognized Sierra.

"Ms. Mallory, what are you—"

"Doing your job." Gone was the sweet, shy girl who apologized for trying to kill me after I had skewered her with a spoon. The superbitch was back. Not a reassuring transformation.

As the guard stammered, she snapped, "Are you going to let me in or do I have to talk to my father, Irving?"

"N-n-no, ma'am." Irving stumbled back from the vehicle, signaling the guard inside the gatehouse to open the gates. Steel bars retracted smoothly along recessed tracks in the concrete.

Sierra floored the Hummer as soon as the opening widened enough for us to fit through. A relieved sigh emanated from her. She shot me a grin. "We're in."

"Not inside the building, we're not," I mumbled.

"Piece of cake," she said, as we approached a ramp that dipped into the complex. Two more guards flanked the closed rolled-steel door at the bottom. "Everyone in the back needs to keep quiet."

A whispered, "Well, duh," came from behind me, made funnier by the British clip. I stifled a smirk. Tiffany's lack of manners was wearing off on her uncle.

The new guard approached us as we coasted to a halt. He didn't look half as dumb as Irving did. I held my breath as he poked his head to get a good view of us and the interior. Bebe's cover spell better hold because this guy would shoot. My gut had no doubts on that score.

He nodded. "Ms. Mallory. You've been missing for a day."

Super cool, she inclined her head towards me. "She took a while to catch. Nailed Val and Chee. I lost contact with the rest of the retrieval team, but I knew how bad Daddy wanted her back."

Shit. She was changing the cover story. This whole scheme was going bad before we were inside the building.

The guard frowned. Damn, he wasn't buying it. My index finger poised a hair above the release catch. He took a long look at the interior again, stepped back, and motioned. His buddy didn't move, so someone had to be watching us on the monitors. Great, just great. Sierra had better be right about disabling the cameras inside the garage.

With a jerk, the door started its rise. She eased the Hummer forward. A small squad waited for us in the garage.

How many?

I nearly jumped out of my seat at Caesar's telepathic words. Even though I expected it, the feeling of someone else in my head was disconcerting despite the practice he and Bebe put me through before we left the safehouse. I bit my tongue to keep from answering aloud.

Six. Two more came through a side door to join their compadres. *No, eight.* Maybe I should be flattered that I required this many men to control little old me. I clenched my hand around the tiny PVC tube in my fist.

Sierra braked. The team swarmed to the passenger side to get me. I leaned against the door so when one of the goons yanked it open I fell partially out of the Hummer.

I looked up at six pairs of eyes and said, "Nighty-night, boys." Raising the tube in my hand to my mouth, I blew. Golden dust exploded across their faces, and one by one, they collapsed to the floor. Still holding my breath, I swung up and unlatched the manacles, then the seatbelt.

A few yards away, Sierra dusted the seventh guard. But one guard had stayed out of range of the sleep spell I'd blown. I panicked when Number Eight swung his gun towards her.

"Yo, bud!" Startled by my voice, he twisted in my direction but too late. I leapt. My right cross sent him reeling into the wall. It wasn't as satisfying as smacking the shit out of Alexander Radcliff when he put that rat down my shirt in fourth grade, but still . . .

I knelt and placed two fingers on his neck.

"Well." Duncan looked down at me. I smiled back.

"He'll have a nasty headache when he wakes up, but he's alive."

He gave a brusque nod. "I am relieved you did not kill this one."

I rose, brushed golden dust off my shirt, and sucked in a welcome breath. "Told you I'd get the hang of this super-strength stuff."

"You are not Lynda Carter," he replied.

"Oooo, two pop culture references in one shot. You sure American TV isn't turning your stuffy British brain to mush?"

"I don't think your brain is what he's interested in." Bebe popped up beside us, a wicked grin on her face. "Speaking of which, here's a Snickers. I heard your stomach growling on the way in." She handed me the candy bar. Leave it to the doctor to monitor my less-than-desirable body functions in the middle of a rescue.

Duncan waved at her to hush while Sierra made some excuse that her nanites were interfering with the garage's video signal over the intercom. She told them the security team here would assist her in escorting me down to the lab. Either the folks Mallory hired were that stupid or she carried a lot of credibility as the boss's daughter. Either way, only Kane, Able and their fellow science geeks should be waiting for us downstairs.

Once she flipped the intercom off, Bebe threw a Snickers bar at her. She snagged it as neatly as an outfielder with a pop-up fly. While Sierra and I snacked on chocolate and peanuts, Phil and the boys stacked the unconscious security team in the back of another truck in the docking bay. If Bebe was right, her fairy dust would keep them out for eight hours.

We trooped through the inner dock doors and down the hall. Sierra waved towards the cargo elevator. She entered first and yanked out the wires on the security camera before waving us on. The butterflies circling in my stomach turned into Indy race cars. I prayed the Snickers wouldn't come back up. Going down into the rat hole where I was tortured? What the hell was I thinking?

Duncan and Caesar took stances next to the elevator doors, like SEALs with fangs, and motioned everyone behind them. I didn't argue. Getting shot once had been bad enough. I tucked Bebe behind me. She was the only person who came close to Normal in the group, and I wanted to keep her that way. I expected her to protest, but she kept silent.

Tiffany would have protested. Loudly.

The elevator took so long to move I figured I'd die of terminal boredom instead of anxiety before we hit the basement.

My stomach rumbled again. Duncan glared at me.

"I can't help it—"

Duncan laid a finger over my lips. I would have gotten the message if he had put his damn finger over his own damn lips. It was all I could do not to pull his finger into my mouth and start sucking. Which led to thinking about sucking on other parts. Which led to . . .

I clenched my fist against my thigh in an effort to clear the erotic thoughts from my brain. I should have asked Bebe if my super metabolism meant everything increased. Even worse, we were in a life-and-death situation. And from the grin on Duncan's face, he understood and enjoyed my internal struggle without the telepathic assist.

I reached behind and pinched him on the ass. His jump had everyone staring at us. Caesar appeared ready to reprimand both of us, but the elevator ground to a halt, and the doors slid open.

Tyrone Mallory stood in the hallway, behind a goon squad with very big guns pointed at us.

Chapter 20

There was a click to our left. "Elevator's locked, sir."

"Daddy!" Before anyone could stop Sierra, she plunged off the elevator and threw her arms around Mallory. "I knew you'd figure out my message."

Despite nearly getting knocked on his ass, Mallory hugged her back. "Are you all right, baby? They didn't do anything to you, did they?"

"I'm fine, Daddy." She waved at me and smiled. "I told you I'd get her back."

"When we found the bodies in the antique shop, I was so worried about you." He gave his daughter another fierce hug. "Let's have Kane double-check."

"Just a damn minute!" I stepped from behind Duncan, only to have all ten semi-automatics follow my movements. I should have been scared, but I was so pissed about Sierra's double-cross the possibility of turning into Swiss cheese only dimly registered. Duncan hissed at me to get back. I ignored him and marched out of the elevator.

"Mr. Mallory?" The lead goon stepped between us.

"Don't shoot, Bob," Mallory said.

"Yes, Bob," Sierra purred. "Sam has been sooo helpful. See, Daddy? Aren't you glad you didn't activate her self-destruct?"

Now, I really was going to puke up the Snickers bar. "What self-destruct?" I bit out.

"Ah, Miss Ridgeway, you didn't think I'd let my proto-type run all over Los Angeles without a fail-safe, did you?" Mallory actually had the nerve to smile. I wanted to grind the asshole to a pulp. My fists clenched while I fought the urge.

"Can we keep Sam? Please, Daddy?" Sierra stroked her father's cheek.

The way she clung to her father triggered a different kind of nausea. I didn't want to think about the possibilities there.

"No, baby, it's not safe to keep her or the others. Now I know you're all right, we need to get rid of them."

From the look on Sierra's face, this was the first time she'd ever been told no. "Daddy, I know you love me." She played with his tie. "Please? I've never had a sister."

Despite Bob standing between us, I glared at Sierra. "After what your dad did to us, to you, you're just going to kiss and make up?"

"Well, you know, Sam . . ." One hand rested on Mallory's shoulder as Sierra slithered behind him. She peered past him as she placed her other hand on his opposing shoulder. "Sometimes a girl's gotta do what a girl's gotta do."

Her hands whipped up, and with a sickening crack, she snapped her father's neck. A surprised look was the only thing Mallory had time for in the split-second before he died. She dropped the body, which landed with a thud. My mouth fell open. Even Bob's face turned green.

"Well, Mr. Augustine, I guess you and your people no longer have to worry about my father." Sierra wiped her hands on her thighs.

I didn't dare look behind me. The vampires' one bargaining chip had just evaporated.

"Now, gentlemen," she purred as she stepped over the body. Bob backed away from her, only to run into my shoulder. "Unless you want the same thing to happen to you, you will follow my orders. Is that understood?" She smiled sweetly at each man in turn.

Then she looked at me. Her eyes carried her insanity. There was no other word for it. I didn't know if it happened when they injected the nanites in her, when I stabbed her with the spoon, or a long time before either, but Sierra Mallory was definitely psychotic.

"You'll always have a place here, Sam." She held her hand out to me. "We're two of a kind, you know. The only two in the universe."

I couldn't help looking down at her father's body behind her. I may have killed since becoming a zombie, but in self-defense. Not like this. Not in cold-blood. Suddenly, I couldn't breathe.

She clucked her tongue. "Really, it's for the best, Sam. You don't want him experimenting on more people anymore than I do."

My eyes rose back up to meet hers. She must have seen something in my face. She dropped her hand and shook her head. "Don't give me that look. I want you to stay here." She smiled again. "With me." She sighed, the kind you make when the kid you're baby-sitting gets on that last nerve. "To show you my good faith." She snapped her fingers, and the ten guards looked like they'd nearly pissed themselves.

"Bob, take your men and release the prisoners."

"Ma'am." Bob's gulp would have been audible from Nevada even without my super hearing. "Are you sure?"

Leave it to the goon squad to tick her off. The expression of distaste crossing her features left no doubt as to Bob's fate if he questioned her again.

"Ma'am, yes, ma'am!" he barked. He and his men trotted down the hallway and disappeared around the corner.

Keep her talking, Sam.

Gee, thanks. And how do I make conversation with Hannah Lechter here? I thought back at Caesar.

String her along. You need to buy enough time for her men to bring the prisoners back.

Do I look like Kevin Spacey in The Negotiator? *And what if she tells her bozos to open fire while we're trying to get the victims out of here? Not to mention the damn elevator's locked and she could blow me up at any time.*

I was starting to get really mad. Get in, get the goods, get out. That's my style. Not playing Jodi Foster to little Miss Patricide. I guess I should have been thankful she hadn't started eating him.

You can do this, Sam. You're the only one who can. Sierra Mallory's developed an attachment to you—

Oh, I so didn't need to hear that.

"What's your problem?" Sierra snapped.

I blinked in confusion. "What do you mean?"

"Your face keeps twitching." She stepped closer and stared me in the eyes.

Pretend she's Matt Damon. Pretend she's Matt Damon, I chanted to myself. Damon was a much harder target to nail than Affleck. But I got Damon's bare tush once before. I could do this.

Pretend she's who?

Shut up, Caesar! Yelling telepathically at the man, who in all probability was some kind of prince, even if he wasn't king of the vampires, wasn't my wisest move. But I needed to concentrate on my acting skills.

"I was just considering your offer, Sierra," I said. Waving nonchalantly, I added, "I tend to have conversations in my head when I'm trying to make a decision. Max would tell you."

A skeptical expression filled her face. "I'll be sure to ask him."

"You know, I don't know if I can get used to all the money," I said as airily as I could.

Sierra laughed without any humor. She made Margaret Hamilton sound positively benign. "I've seen your parents' place, silly."

Oh, crap. I should not have brought my family up. She knew where they lived. Panic formed a physical lump in my throat I could barely talk around.

"Well, you know teenagers. Gotta rebel. If the 'rents have the dough, I gotta be poor." I shrugged, praying I acted and sounded casual.

"Oh, Samantha." My full name never boded well for me. "This isn't about money." I tried really hard not to cringe when she grabbed my hand and began stroking it. "It's about power," she whispered. She leaned away from my ear, her voice rising. "Absolute power. We can control life and death."

Footsteps coming down the hall interrupted her evil-takes-over-the-world monologue. Slung between each pair of squad members were five supernaturals: three vamps, a werewolf, and a witch. I was starting to figure out the signature scent of each species. The fact humans and witches smelled delicious didn't help my worry over controlling my appetite.

I knew for sure they were alive. I could hear their hearts beating. But I've seen pictures of African famine victims looking healthier than these five. My heart rose as I recognized Alex as the second person. The guards carried Anne behind him.

"Where's the other three, Bob?" Sierra's tone promised pain to the poor security guard.

Bob paled underneath his eye protection. "They died while you were gone, ma'am."

She let out a dramatic sigh. "Oh well, I guess five is better than none."

Each pair of guards handed me a prisoner. I passed them to Duncan and Caesar behind me in the elevator. As I handed Alex back, he tried to wink at me. The garbled words from him sounded vaguely like, "Damn time the cavalry showed up." But I couldn't be sure.

Once the last person was on the elevator, I turned to board when Sierra grabbed my hand again. She squeezed and tugged, nodding towards the hallway. "Come on, Sam. I'll show you the rest of the compound."

"I haven't said yes yet, Sierra."

The National Weather Service should issue severe storm warnings about Sierra Mallory's moods.

Matt Damon. Matt Damon.

I smiled and said, "I haven't said no either. Why don't you give me a couple of days to think about it?"

The smile she gave me could have frozen liquid nitrogen. "All right then. You can have seventy-two hours." She leaned close to my ear and whispered, "Then Sammy goes boom." She stepped back, and in a normal tone, said, "Let them go, Bob."

Bob twisted the key, and the elevator doors slid closed. Ten people in the elevator, even if it was a cargo elevator, made for a tight squeeze, especially since five of them were prone on the floor. Everyone who was conscious held their breath as the car started to move. Bebe knelt next to the former prisoners, checking vitals.

The vamp I didn't know sniffed at her ankles. It was so starved and filthy I couldn't be sure of its gender. She rapped it on the nose. "Just wait a few more minutes. We have blood in our vehicle."

The vamp muttered something that sounded like, "Thirsty now," but it managed to stop treating her like a scrumptious doggy treat. If I were starved for three months, I don't think I would have any kind of self-control. Heck, I was already worried about my self-control after three hours with nothing but a candy bar.

The elevator finally jerked to a halt. For an agonizing minute, I didn't think it would open. Would Sierra order the cable cut? Or was this another sadistic game and she'd trigger the nanites' self-destruct anyway, taking care of me and everybody in the tiny space? Everyone outside of Mallory Labs who knew what she really was besides Max and Tiffany.

And blowing my nanites would turn the two Normals into sitting ducks.

Then Phil was through the sliding doors and pulling Alex upright before they fully parted. In a flurry of motion, the healthy folks carried, or in Bebe's case dragged, the injured and starved towards the Hummer. We all were waiting for Sierra to sic the security guards on us, but no one showed a hair in the docking bay.

We piled in, trying to make Alex and the rest of the former prisoners as comfortable as possible. It wasn't easy. Caesar jogged over to the garage door controls.

I climbed into the driver's seat, only to realize Sierra still had the keys. Duncan slid into the passenger seat, the witch cradled in his arms. I took a good look at her for the first time. Underneath the haggard appearance, she couldn't have been out of high school. Bile rose in my throat. Tiffany's age.

He held out his fist to me. "You did not think we would let her keep them, did you?" I raised my hand, and he dropped the keys into my palm.

Gotta love a sexy British pickpocket. I looked from the keys back to his grinning face. *Eat you heart out, Artful Dodger.*

"We're not out of the woods yet," I said, but my lips spread in a matching smile.

The engine roared to life, and I eased the massive vehicle into reverse. Once through the garage door, I slowed long enough for Caesar to jump in through the passenger door Phil held open. The two guards at the garage door stood by and watched as I executed a J-turn and sped down the driveway. I shared a glance with Duncan, then gunned the engine.

With my questionable control, we may not be able to hear each other telepathically, but I was definitely learning his expressions. I had already figured out Caesar's Hummer wasn't the civilian issue version, despite the paint job. I just hoped the custom reinforcements would be able to knock down the security gate.

Sierra must have called ahead because the gates were wide open as we approached. Again, the guards just watched as we raced past them and into the night. A deep-felt sigh filtered past my lips at the temporary reprieve. Now, I could only pray we made it to safety before any more of the prisoners died.

Chapter 21

Selene eyed Sierra over the goblet she held and took a sip. "That wasn't necessary." Not that she hadn't planned to eliminate Tyrone anyway, but his premature death altered her timetable once again.

The petulant girl flung herself on the brown suede couch, a pout tugging her lips. "Father would have kept us apart. You know it."

Setting the glass of blood on the bar, Selene schooled her expression. This situation was no different than the maneuverings she'd done in Rome or with her own kin over the centuries. She only had to keep her focus on her goal.

She crossed what had been, until an hour ago, Tyrone's office and settled on the couch. Sierra automatically shifted until her head rested on Selene's lap.

"In my time, we believed the killing of a family member unleashed the Erinyes."

"Well, you're still here, aren't you? You haven't been dragged off by any Fury."

The whine in Sierra's voice joined with her words and sent a wave of cold through Selene's soul. Ptolemy's death had been an accident. It didn't negate her real intent, killing Caesar and his whore.

Sierra pulled her cell phone out of her pocket. "Maybe I should go ahead and kill her now."

Selene wrapped her hand around the hot pink device and tugged it from the girl's hand. "No."

"But—" Sierra rolled into a sitting position.

"Let Caesar and his boys play hero. They'll be too involved saving the reporter to give us any trouble over the next two days." She wanted to give Caesar and Duncan time to call in other Augustine enforcers. The more she could take out in one blast, the easier it would be to force the other vampires into compliance. She stroked Sierra's hair. "And we need to be ready for the shareholders meeting."

A sly smile filled Sierra's features. She trailed fingertips across Selene's silk clad arm. "I can think of other things to do in the mean time."

Selene wrapped her hand around the girl's and brought it to her lips for a kiss. "I have some last minute details to handle. Why don't you find one of the guards to play with?"

A loud, disappointed sigh filled the air. "You know what they say about all work and no play."

Letting a smile cross her lips, Selene leaned back. "You play enough for both of us. Record it and I'll watch with you later."

Sierra's delighted grin was her only answer before she flounced out of the office.

The fake flirtation faded as Selene's muscles relaxed. A slight headache twinged behind her eyes. The charade would have to hold until the end of the week. She didn't want to eliminate the girl until the board signed the paperwork giving her full control of the Mallory businesses in the event of Sierra's death. There would be fewer questions and fewer disappearances to deal with.

Rising from the couch and retrieving her dinner, Selene stood at the window and watched the evening traffic. It hurt that Sierra had become a liability. Mallory shouldn't have rushed into using the nanites. Now, the girl's mental instability could destroy everything she'd worked toward over the last two years.

She sighed. Maybe she truly was doomed to repeat Mother's mistakes and destroy everything she loved.

"We need to strike, and we need to strike now!" The sound of a body part hitting a solid object punctuated Duncan's statement. Despite the thick brick walls of Caesar Augustine's real house, everyone in the formal living room jumped, including the Normals. The argument in the study continued, but the voices dropped to the point I couldn't hear them anymore.

Apparently, you had to reach the century mark to earn Caesar Augustine's trust. Only Duncan, Alex, and Anne were allowed in on his little strategy session.

I stomped in a circle around the room, not knowing what else to do. The navy and gold upholstery and cherry paneling on the walls made the freakin' place feel like a funeral parlor. Not what I expected in the Mediterranean-style Brentwood mansion when we first pulled up to the steel gates.

The good news was Alex and Anne weren't rotten meat mush. A few gallons of blood, showers, and in Alex's case a shave, and the vamps were almost as good as new. Alex turned out to be better looking after he was fed and clean than I would have guessed.

Not that he had anything on Duncan.

I never did find out the name of the third guy. He took off while I whacked off the rats' nest Anne's hair had become after her weeks of imprisonment. I didn't have a choice. Now, her waist-length tresses gone, she sported a short, spiky 'do that rivaled Sharon Stone's. She didn't seem very pleased even though it set off her elfin features perfectly.

While I flaunted my ability with a pair of scissors, Bebe had called the teen witch's family. They collected little Sabrina, and the dad stated they were going into hiding. Alex's buddy, Logan, went with them as a bodyguard. When Duncan protested, the tall, hunky werewolf flashed a grin that raised the hairs on the back of my neck and said the assholes wouldn't catch him sleeping again. I pitied anyone who crossed this guy after everything Mallory's goons had done to him.

After contacting Los Angeles's head witch, Bebe had left for her medical lab. She had taken blood and tissue samples from all the former prisoners, including another round from me and the ones Tiffany had taken from Sierra while the heiress had been unconscious in the back seat of Duncan's SUV.

Phil had disappeared as well, muttering something about calling her insurance agent concerning the damage to her shop. I noticed she waited long enough to make sure Alex was all right, but as soon as he tried to talk to her, she got bitchy on him. There was a story behind the two of them, but my curiosity would have to wait.

Max and Tiffany had driven Bebe's car to the mansion, or vamp HQ as I called it. He phoned Mom and Dad and told them to stay in London for yet another week. When Dad questioned him, Max finally relented, keeping his story to the break-ins at his place and the Times. He added we were fine, but he was concerned about their safety if they returned to Los Angeles. Despite Max not spilling my new status, Mom still got on the phone and claimed his problems had to be my fault somehow.

Receiver still glued to his ear, Max had caught my grimace and rolled his eyes. I can't say I was fond of my new abilities at that moment. Suspecting Mom trashed me behind my back on a regular basis was one thing. Hearing confirmation of said suspicions was another.

"When are they coming out of there?" I muttered, more to myself than anyone else, and glared at the wall. Why couldn't the mad scientists have given me x-ray vision along with the super hearing?

"Whenever they're done, Sam."

I turned to find Max looking up from the couch, irritation on his face. I had tried to ignore him and Tiffany making googly eyes and whispering for the last hour. And here I was worried about Tiffany pulling a Lolita.

Duncan hadn't seemed to mind my thirty-one-year-old brother making the moves on his nineteen-year-old niece. Or maybe he had been ignoring them as well.

I don't know why it bothered me so much. Tiffany was an adult. Sort of. Or maybe I didn't like being reminded of the age difference between me and Duncan.

Another bang made the three of us jump, but this time the noise came from another area of the humungous house. I could hear Bebe shouting for everyone as she headed in the direction of the study.

"We're in here!" Tiffany yelled back.

Breathless, the good doctor paused in the doorway of the living room long enough to wave us to follow her before charging down the hall to where Anne and the boys held their strategy session. Despite her excitement, huge, dark circles had surrounded her eyeballs and taken them prisoner. She must have been up all night. Curiosity overwhelmed my wariness of Caesar, and I followed. Max and Tiffany trailed in our wake.

Bebe shoved the study door open without knocking.

Caesar's head jerked in our direction, annoyance plain on his face.

"You can have your snit fit later, sweetie. Everyone needs to hear this. Especially Sam."

Okay, she didn't say "Samantha". Full name equaled bad. The news couldn't be that terrible. Right? So why did my stomach fill with acid?

Duncan edged closer to me, his presence comforting in the insanity my world had become. He wrapped an arm around my shoulders and whispered, "It will be all right." I nodded at his words, but numbness spread throughout my body.

Bebe addressed her words to everyone. "All the prisoners' tests came back negative for alterations. The only problem is Sam." She kept eye contact with me as she continued. "As we suspected, your nanites are programmed to rewrite a person's DNA. Similar to the V-virus, but without most of the nastier side effects. Since cancer is your own cells gone wild, Sierra was cured by the nanites fixing them."

"What do you mean 'most of the nastier side effects'?" I already knew I wouldn't become meat mush under a small dose of UV. I steeled myself for the worst.

Bebe took a deep breath and launched into her lecture. "Ultraviolet radiation, silver and garlic are not detrimental to your cell structure. You have a lot of the positive attributes, such as increased strength and stamina, accelerated healing, and enhanced senses."

"What about my increased appetite?"

She shrugged. "You're consuming a Normal diet, which to me is a good sign. If you were a vampire or a were, the consumption would be expected with the changes in your body and your recent injuries. My guess is your appetite should taper off in a few days."

"And you're rehashing what I already know." My eyes narrowed as I regarded the doctor. "What bad stuff are you leaving out, Bebe?"

Her face blanked. "Maybe we should discuss the rest privately, Sam. There's—"

"No, dammit! We're talking about this here and now." My fists clenched at my sides, nails digging into my palms. Marginalization and patronizing attitudes didn't sit well with me.

Bebe paused for so long I didn't think she was going to speak, but she finally gave a slow nod. "You won't be able to have children, Sam." Tears pooled in her brown eyes, but she tried to blink them away. "It's the one component of the virus they couldn't eliminate. Other than that you're totally healthy."

I was fine. The relief sank as the import of the rest of her words registered.

No kids.

Nada.

Never going to happen.

I really hadn't thought about having babies. I just assumed when I met the right guy, it would happen. Like deciding to move to Beverly Hills or O.C. for the better school districts.

I never thought the choice would just be taken from me. Anger flared and died. I couldn't even smack around Tyrone Mallory now. He was as dead as me and my non-existent children.

Sympathy swam in Bebe's unshed tears. She understood part of how I felt. She loved a man who was in the same position I was. But dammit! She could still conceive and carry a baby.

If she walked away from the man she loved. Or if he consented to another man donating sperm.

Would someone be willing to make those kind of sacrifices for me?

I had to drag my attention from my pity party to concentrate on the conversation.

"What about the V-virus?" Max asked. "Could the nanites be a cure for the vampires?"

Bebe shook her head, disappointment etched in her face. Damn, no wonder she was so intent on discovering how the nanites worked. A possible cure for her sweetie would mean everything to her.

"The virus completely rewrites a vampire's genetic code, too," Bebe said. "The nanites aren't sophisticated enough to distinguish between what's original and what's been added. Maybe someday, but not yet." She turned back to me. "The irony is anyone with nanites can't become infected with the V-virus."

I didn't care for the knowing look she shot me. Infection of a potentially fatal disease was enough to keep my lust at bay when it came to Duncan. Was I that obvious to everyone around me?

Yes. Caesar's grin matched Bebe's.

I hate it when someone else figures out my feelings before I do. I didn't bother giving him the satisfaction of a reply.

"So basically Sam will have super strength, super speed, and live forever," Max said.

Bebe nodded. "There's no reason why she can't lead a normal life." She turned back to me. "You can't go to your regular doctor though. We can't let news of your real condition get out, to either the Normal or the supernatural communities."

"No, she can't pretend to be Normal."

I stared at Caesar. The look on his face was a mixture of pity and steel.

"I'm sorry, Sam, but if you don't age, someone will figure out there's something different about you," he said.

I shrugged out of Duncan's comforting hold. I couldn't accept Caesar's inevitable truth. "So I move every few years."

"What about your family?"

I waved in Max's direction. "My brother already knows about the supernatural community."

"And your parents?"

The desire rose to shove Caesar's relentless logic back down his immortal throat. I couldn't answer his question because frankly I wasn't sure they could accept the truth. But he wasn't the only one with logic as a weapon. "The point will be moot if Sierra activates the self-destruct."

Full-blown sympathy filled his eyes. "Which leads to our original problem with Mallory Labs." He drummed his fingers on his desk, the only outward indication of his worry. "We still need to destroy it."

"Why? If they are on the right track to finding a vampire cure—" Tiffany started.

"A cure potentially worse than the original disease," Duncan responded, more gentle with her than I would have been. "They obviously have not found a way to prevent the sterilization of the patient. And if they restore such functions, there is the possibility the robots might miss a snippet of RNA that will result in a future child becoming a vampire."

"It doesn't mean they won't find a way to solve those problems." Tiffany's eyes flitted from face to face, seeking an ally.

I hated to burst her bubble when her gaze met mine. "Tyrone's dead, and Sierra has no interest whatsoever in altruism."

"Think she'll sell to the highest bidder?" Alex said.

"Not necessarily," I ventured, a little surprised the vampires were now taking my opinions seriously. "She's more concerned with power. She'd exchange the nanites for personal favors, people she can control." I frowned and shivered. "She'd put a self-destruct in them in case someone gets out of line."

"Isn't that a little James Bond?" Max asked.

"You think it's fiction?" I raised an eyebrow and waved a hand at the assemblage in Caesar's office. "You're kidding, right?"

A scowl creased Duncan's face. "How can we be certain there truly is a self-destruct in your nanites? Sierra Mallory's claim could be a bluff."

"We aren't," I said. I could barely get my voice above a whisper. Tyrone Mallory was a lot of things, but stupid wasn't one of them. He'd have figured some way to keep tabs on me.

Everything dropped into place, and I smacked a palm on my forehead. "It wasn't telepathy. They've been tracking me through the nanites. But why'd it take them so long to catch up with me?"

"Magick."

Everyone looked at Bebe. She raised her hands and affected a Georgian accent. "I'm a doctor, not a computer geek."

"Seriously, though," she continued in her normal voice. "Between my spells for breaking into and out of the labs and my examination of you yesterday morning, there was probably enough magickal interference to disrupt the homing signal."

"Look," I croaked, throat dry at the thought of an impending, and very permanent, second death. "Sierra gave me seventy-two hours to take her up on her offer. Couldn't we create a computer virus or something to destroy the nanites?"

Caesar shook his head. "We're talking about very sophisticated code. My people could use one of your samples to reverse engineer, but they couldn't do it in less than two days. And we don't know what removing the nanites would do to you."

I felt the empathic wave of concern from him. From the little I'd learned about him, he had to be pretty upset to let that kind of emotion slip. Not that I was happy with his analysis either.

"Too bad we cannot drop a tactical nuclear device on the git's head," Duncan muttered. The flutter of air tattled his approach before both arms wrapped around me and pulled me snug against his chest. "We will figure something out, Sam," he whispered.

Damn, it was bad if he didn't use "Samantha". His hold felt comforting against the thought of dying twice within a week. Even in my limited knowledge, the nanites couldn't act as repair-bots when they were the explosive cause of damage. And there's no fucking way Sierra would let me live if I refused to join her little crusade.

"Too bad Mallory killed Fred. He's the only one I know who could backward engineer these damn robots," I muttered.

"Who's Fred?" Alex asked.

"A friend of mine who was a computer geek for the LAPD. Mallory's goon killed him because he . . ."

My voice trailed off as Max's eyes met mine. I could tell by the flash in his that he had the same thought.

"Oh shit," I whispered.

Max shook his head, his expression bleak. "Mallory's probably already searched his apartment, assuming Fred had anything with him."

"What the hell are you people talking about?" Tiffany's gaze flicked from person to person, totally lost. I could tell from the vamps' faces they had already read our minds. Duncan may not be able to read mine, but he sure as heck could read Max's.

I took sympathy on the kid. "We think my friend Fred may have been working for Mallory. It would explain why he warned me away and why Mallory's people killed him." I shook my head and stared at the floor. "I just wish I knew for sure."

Bebe cleared her throat, drawing everyone's attention. "There is a way we can find out."

"No!" Caesar roared, leaping to his feet. Red suffused his face, and the tidal wave of anger from his mind almost knocked me off my feet despite Duncan's hold.

"It's the only way, sweetie." Bebe's voice was velvet-coated steel. "You know Mallory wouldn't let anything regarding this project out of his control. But by murdering Sam's friend, he's done just that."

"And what if he refuses to leave your body when he's answered our questions," Caesar snapped.

"I'm willing to take that chance." Her chin raised in defiance, a slight tremble in her hands the only outward sign of nervousness.

"What are you talking about?" I asked.

"A séance to speak with Fred."

Damn. I was afraid Bebe was going to say that.

<h1 style="text-align:center">Chapter 22</h1>

Duncan and I closed heavy scarlet drapes against the late afternoon sun drifting through UV film into Caesar's conservatory. That's what he called the room. Sounded like a pretentious way of saying, "This is where Mariah Carey sings during her private performances."

I grabbed a couple of heavy upholstered chairs. "Don't we need to do a séance at midnight? Or at least wait until it's dark?"

Duncan shook his head and hoisted two chairs on each arm. Showoff. "Not with someone as powerful as Bebe."

He explained the danger to Bebe as we moved chairs into the hallway. If the ghost still hung around without crossing to the "other side", a witch could talk to him or her. No muss, no fuss.

But if the ghost had crossed the line, the witch would summon the spirit back to this plane of existence and allow it to possess her physical body for a short while. Most times the ghost would answer questions and then depart, leaving the witch none the worse for wear.

Sometimes though the guest phantom decides to take up permanent residence. If the witch's soul, spirit or whatever you wanted to call it isn't strong enough to fight back, then she is forced out of her physical body and dies. The ghost thinks it's home free in the land of the living, but it's not. The physical body reacts to the soul transplant just like an organ transplant, and there wasn't any way to stop the rejection.

Duncan said the one time he saw such an incident, the ghost lasted less than a week in its new body, and its second death still gave him nightmares. For Mr. Tough-Guy to admit any weakness, the reality had to be pretty bad, and it scared the hell out of me.

We carried the last of the furniture out of the room when Alex and Anne strolled in with armloads of white and black candles and set them in a corner. The four of us started rolling up the intricate red and gold Persian rug dominating the room, now that every other furnishing had been removed.

I wanted to reassure Duncan that Fred wouldn't do anything like trying to keep Bebe's body, but if he had worked for Mallory as Max and I suspected, then all bets were off. My heart felt like it would sink through Caesar's Italian marble floor. I didn't want to believe Fred had stooped so low as to whore his skills out to a sadistic asshole like Tyrone Mallory. If he had, I prayed Fred wasn't too busy burning in Hell to help me.

Underneath the remarkably dirt-free wool rug was an intricate pattern in the floor. We stood to lift the rug, and I looked back. A giant pentacle, done in various shades of white, black, and gray marble and outlined in silver, took up the entire room. I whistled, amazed at the workmanship and detail. The goods and labor had to have set Caesar back seven figures.

Maybe Bebe was a material girl after all.

The vamps and I lugged the rug out into the hallway. As we dropped our load against the far wall, the rest of the gang trooped towards us, Bebe, in the lead, dressed in a gauzy white robe, with Max and Tiffany right behind her. Caesar brought up the rear, a nasty scowl still plastered across his handsome face.

I caught a whiff of herbs emanating from the huge bag Bebe carried as she passed by. I couldn't say what they were, but ghosts probably loved them. They were a sweet counterpoint to the sandalwood pervading the house. We followed her back into the conservatory, and she began ordering everyone where to put equipment and which color of candles went where. Kind of like George C. Scott in *Patton* but without a cute little helmet and whip.

By the time she was satisfied, white candles followed the ring of silver, except each tip of the pentagram had a black one. Bebe sat in the center, surrounded by her bowls of water and herbs, incense burner, a goblet I was certain held wine with a little something extra from the musty odor, a laptop (of all things), and a couple of gross objects I didn't want to think too hard about. In the middle of her pile, Pooh's cracked crystal winked at everyone.

My eyes shot to Max's.

"She needed something personal of Fred's if we had it. I didn't think you would mind," he said with a shrug.

Bebe rose and shooed Tiffany and Max into a corner. "Go sit down. And no matter what you see—" She waggled her index finger. "Do. Not. Move. If you break the circle before I dismiss the ghost—" She lowered her voice. "The consequences would be dire."

Wide-eyed, Tiffany did what she was told for the first time since I'd met her. Max dropped to the floor next to her and wrapped an arm around her scrawny shoulders. I tried not to gag.

Bebe turned and gave me a secret wink. I didn't care if she was bull-shitting the kid, but she wasn't reassuring my nerves one bit. I'd been holding Fred's hand when the doctors pronounced him upon our arrival at the ER. With everything I'd suspected and the wallowing guilt, I sure didn't want to face him, but the alternative was me splattered over Caesar's walls, ceiling and floor.

She flicked the light switch. With the drapes closed, total darkness enveloped the room except for the doorway's rectangle of dim ambient light that managed to penetrate this deep into Caesar's fortress. The illumination was sufficient for me, so I was sure the vamps could see as well. The mortals would be nearly blind.

The mortals. Shit, I was really beginning to accept this undead stuff.

Witches must have excellent vision, too, because Bebe moved unerringly and placed each of the vampires at a star point. She instructed them to sit inside the circle and hold one of the black candles. The vamps did as instructed, but they all were careful not to touch the silver embedded in the floor. Interesting. How many of the other Hollywood stories of vampire deterrents were true?

Before I could ask, Bebe tugged my arm and guided me toward the last one. My feet dragged in my brand-spanking new tennies.

"Uh-huh. I'm going over there," I insisted, pointing at Max and Tiffany's corner.

"Sam, I'll have a much easier time with this if I have five supernaturals."

"So get another vamp." I jerked my arm out of her grip.

"You're the only supernatural who also knew Fred. He'll respond to you much better than anyone else here."

I held up my hands. "Whoa, there. You didn't say a damn thing about me having to actually talk to a dead Fred."

Tiffany giggled behind me. I could feel everyone's eyes boring into me. Okay, everyone who could see me. I couldn't do this. I had watched the man die for Chrissakes!

Bebe's big brown eyes blinked. Twice. Three times. "It's your choice, Samantha. It's your life." Her soft voice wasn't threatening but pronounced my doom all the same.

"What life?" I muttered. I couldn't meet her earthy gaze any longer. I stared at the tips of my shoes and wrapped my arms tight around myself. Here was a woman willing to risk her real life for my undead one, and all I wanted was to run for the Sierras. And I didn't mean my psycho zombie twin either.

If nothing else, I would find out the truth about Fred. Maybe find a way to redeem him if he had been that deep in with Mallory. The scrawny-assed kid in me owed him. Raising my head, I took a deep breath, nodded, and headed for the last candle.

After I sat, Bebe picked up a butane lighter. As she approached me, I said, "Aren't you supposed to be able to light them with your fingertip?"

She rapped my head with the extra-long Bic before igniting the wick of the candle I held and proceeding around the room. Once all the candles glowed, she closed the door. The flickering flames resembled our church at Christmas, all lit up and pretty.

I hadn't thought of church in a long time, had stopped going years ago. Could I even go to a service now? Now that I was dead, did I even have a soul? I'd have to ask Duncan and Bebe when this was over.

Bebe curled up in the middle of the pentagram in some kind of yoga position. The flexibility she displayed as she sat left no doubt in my mind as to the real reason Caesar was enamored with the beautiful witch.

That's none of your business, young lady.

I waggled the fingers on my free hand in apology at the still scowling Caesar across the room. Anne and Alex shared wicked grins. The fact Duncan, sitting to my right, rolled his eyes in confused disgust relieved me to no end. It was bad enough every other vampire in the room knew how sex-obsessed I had become. Maybe my attraction with Duncan did have more to do with my revved up metabolism than him.

Okay, my self-deception didn't extend that far. If I were that horny from the damn robots, I'd be after anything with a penis. My heavy sigh sent my candle's flame darting in every direction.

Ignoring the byplay of the vampires and me, Bebe lit her incense and rose. Starting once again at my point, she circled the outside of the silver ring, waving the burner as she went and muttering something under her breath. Even with my enhanced hearing, I couldn't quite make out her words, almost like the sounds were another language in another dimension. I shivered, as a chill seemed to seep from the floor. My candle flickered again and not from my breath. Drops of melted wax burned my skin, but it was uncomfortable, not painful. The nanites were already doing their job.

She reached me and began a second circle on the inside of the silver ring. Ozone mixed with the earthy incense. Her robes whispered as she strode past me. For the first time, I noticed her eyes were closed as she walked. Yet she avoided each candle.

If I were performing this little ceremony, my clothes and the house would be on fire by now.

The chill grew and was joined by an electric tingle in my fingers and toes. I glanced over at Max and Tiffany. The kid shook violently, and big brother now had both arms wrapped around her.

Part of me rejoiced the freezing temperature wasn't my imagination. Another part was concerned about the attention Max showered on her. Being a Normal surrounded by folks who weren't must be tough for Tiffany. Having Max around must be reassuring for her in some way, but the seeming attraction between them bothered me. Maybe because of my own reservations about the age difference between Duncan and me.

I mean, how do you talk, really talk and not trade wisecracks, to some-one who probably knew Queen Elizabeth I?

Bebe drifted by me again, but this time she returned to the center of the star and raised her arms. She shouted something in her unrecognizable language and golden light flared from the ring surrounding us, arcing upward until the six of us were surrounded in a half bubble of energy. Did the golden sphere extend through the floor to surround us?

With the completion of the half sphere, warmth spread through my body. I placed the flat of my free hand against the marble. Heat now seeped through the floor. Not uncomfortable. More like bed sheets fresh out of the dryer.

Damn, I could write an entire series for the *Scoop* on Bebe's tricks. Not that she'd let me though. What she was doing didn't come close to the crap my Blessed-wannabe roommate did in college.

Soft popping came from the little cast iron cauldron in front of Bebe, but no fire burned under it. She threw some of her herbs in the pot, and the contents hissed and bubbled. Muttering again, she held the silver goblet up in salute then drank deeply. She sat the cup down and picked up the remains of the Pooh watch.

Eyes closed, she rocked to the rhythm of her chanting. The only words I could make out were "Fred Nguyen."

I couldn't tell how long Bebe's ritual went on. My butt began to ache. The marble may have been warm, but the temperature didn't change the fact it was still rock.

The watch hit the floor with a clatter, and my attention jerked from the discomfort in my behind back to our resident witch. Her eyes were open, and a grin spread across her face as she eyed me.

"Hey, kid. Hear you're causing another ruckus."

Despite the warmth in our bubble, my veins turned to ice at the deep voice. Bebe had definitely left the building.

Chapter 23

I recognized the expectant look on Bebe's face from another person. Someone whose face I watched a nurse cover before the ER staff formed a morose line out the swinging doors.

I swallowed hard, but my voice still shook. "Hi yourself, Fred. How's it going?"

The witch's shoulders shrugged, the gesture unmistakably my dead friend's. "I'm okay. All things considered."

"Where were you?" I choked out.

She, or was that he, wagged a finger at me. "I can't answer questions about what happens after you die, Sam, so don't ask." The sound bursting from his lips could only be described as a cackle. "But then, you're as dead as I am."

"Yeah, but I look a hell of a lot better," I shot back.

He sobered and fixed me with a sad stare. "Didn't think I'd die this soon. Or that way. Thanks for staying with me until the end."

"You knew?"

He nodded, then grinned again. "Didn't think you'd join me so soon either." He picked up the cracked Pooh from the floor. "Or that you'd stoop to stealing my watch." He sighed and shook his head. "I really thought you'd be smart enough to drop the whole Alton story after I died."

Anger flared inside me, and I could barely hold my candle in my trembling fingers. "Your fault, asshole. You should have told me what was going on. And I didn't steal your damn watch."

He shrugged again. "Doesn't matter. Can't take it with me and all that jazz."

He noticed the fingers that held the watch for the first time. A look of shock crossed his delicate features and the watch crashed to the marble for a second time.

I wondered if the timepiece could ever be fixed with all the trauma it had suffered the last few days.

Fred yanked the gauzy robe away from his neck and looked down. "Hot damn! I've got boobs."

"Fred." I waved. He ignored me. Wonderful. His breast fetish had taken over.

Caesar growled and made to rise. I wasn't sure what would really happen if one of us broke the circle, but I figured it couldn't be good. I waved the vampire prince back down with my free hand.

"Fred! Fred!" I snapped my fingers to get his attention.

His eyes returned to me.

"Do you understand what's happening now?"

He licked his lips and nodded. "You need to talk to me about Tyrone Mallory." He grinned. "Heard the bastard got whacked by his own daughter. Serves him right."

I nodded, but he was already looking down into the robe again. I wasn't sure if Fred's boob obsession would override his common sense, but I didn't want to take chances with Bebe's life. I snapped my fingers, and his attention returned to me.

"Were you working on the side for Mallory?"

"Yes." His face turned almost mournful. "It was easy money at first, and when he approached me, what he was doing—" He shook his head. "It would have revolutionized medicine, Sam."

Concern tugged at me. "You didn't know what he was really up to?"

His head turned from me.

Realization washed through my conscience. "Oh my god. Fred!"

When he looked back at me, tears shimmered in his eyes. "It's not the first time, Sam. I—" Unreleased sobs choked his voice. "I didn't want you to know. I didn't want my sisters to know. What I am. What I was capable of." He swiped his hand across his face. "All of you thought I was some great hero. It felt good, and I wanted to be that hero, but—"

He turned away again. A cheek muscle clenched on Bebe's face as

Fred fought his emotions. He swallowed, a rough grinding on the witch's delicate throat, and he met my gaze once more. "The only reason *they* let me come to you was to save your life. They said what I do now doesn't tip the scales enough to—" Another choking sound. "I-I couldn't let you get hurt."

Bitter laughter ripped from my throat. "You mean, any more than I am?" I didn't have time to worry about who Fred's mysterious *they* were.

"I'm so sorry, kid. Mallory kept tabs on me. I didn't put him and your mystery PI together until it was too late. I never meant for you—"

"I know." Tears gathered in my own eyes. "I know, Fred. But right now, I need answers. Is there a self-destruct in my nanites?"

He seemed to gather himself and blew out a deep breath. "Yes. I can tell you how to disable it."

"Can it be re-enabled?"

I jumped at the sound of someone else's words. The vampires had faded to my peripheral awareness as Fred and I talked, but Duncan's concern was evident despite the harshness of his voice.

Fred shook his head as he turned to face my guy. "It's all software, not hard-wired. I'll show you how to remove the code and lock out access to Sam. Without me, Mallory's people won't have a chance breaking the encryption."

For the first time in a week, hope glimmered in me. I pointed to the computer sitting next to him. "Can you use that?"

He grinned as he flipped the laptop open and booted it up. "Piece of cake, kid."

"How do you introduce the disable code?" Anger still tinted Caesar's voice.

Fred shot a look over his shoulder. "Wi-fi, same way the destruct works. When the witch brings down her circle, log into your ISP. I'll set it to automatically download to Sam's friends."

"And how can we trust you?" Caesar snarled.

"Don't worry, big guy. I have no intention of staying in your girlfriend's body." A shudder wracked Bebe's petite frame, and he turned back to the laptop. "I definitely don't swing that way."

For the next hour or so, Bebe's slim fingers flew over the keys as Fred typed. Candlelight flickered strange shadows through the magickal shield and across the walls.

The writer in me marveled at the juxtaposition of magick and technology. I had to bite my tongue to suppress a giggle. If someone had told me a week ago all this bullshit was real, I would have said he should be certified. I sighed, sending the candle flame dancing again. Max was right. I wouldn't have believed him.

Above the clicking on the keys, I heard the soft sounds of Tiffany snoring in the corner.

Finally, with a triumphant grunt, Fred set down the laptop and closed the lid. He eyed me with his shit-ass grin. "You'll be right as rain, kid." He patted the computer. "Just remember to download as soon as I'm gone."

"Wait. What about Sierra Mallory? Is there a self-destruct trigger in her nanites?" Duncan asked.

Fred shook his head, long brown curls flying. "No. Sierra was the one person Tyrone trusted. We told his partner there would be one." He shrugged again. "Tyrone was careful to keep her away from me after that."

Mallory's partner had to be a vampire. From the ugly looks on the other vampires' faces, they knew who she was.

Except Duncan. His mind continued barreling down the zombie heiress track. "Could we introduce a virus—"

Fred shook his head more vehemently. "No virus. Anything that would take down Sierra would also kill Sam."

"But—" I started.

A sad smile crossed his lips. "I'm out of time, kid. Just remember your key to Sierra's destruction is in you."

The weird surety the sun was setting filled me as Bebe's body collapsed on the floor. Fred was gone again. This time I knew it was for good.

Chapter 24

"How do you feel?" Duncan's tension sent his eyes into neon overload, a prelude to a full vamp-out I was beginning to discover. Somehow, I took comfort in the fact he was ready to take on the world for me. He scooted closer to me on the living room couch.

"Take a chill pill," I murmured and patted his cheek. Stubble grazed my palm, sending my thoughts to places I really shouldn't go. "I don't feel any different." My stomach gurgled loud enough everyone stared at me, including Caesar from where he sat in an overstuffed chair with Bebe in his lap.

Her energy bubble had dropped the second she passed out, but it took her a few minutes to come around after Fred had left her body. Apparently, sunset is as much a trigger for ghosts as sunrise.

Caesar hadn't let anyone else touch her in the meantime. He cradled the pale, drawn woman in his arms, trying to get her to take a sip of the protein drink he held. I didn't blame her for batting the glass away. I always thought they tasted like crap myself, but right now, I could probably drink Jonestown Kool-Aid with no problem as long it met my caloric requirements.

While his boss carried Bebe into the living room, Duncan had hustled me along behind them, Alex on his heels carrying the laptop. Maybe they were afraid the magick would interfere with the house's wi-fi if we stayed in the conservatory, but I didn't get the chance to ask. Fred's code had been uploaded to the Internet in less than a minute. Alex confirmed the self-destruct had been disabled.

Now, five minutes later, everyone still eyed me like I was the astronaut on *Alien* and they were waiting for my chest to explode. My stomach gurgled again. Louder. Maybe the gut explosion thing wasn't that farfetched.

"I really need to get some food, guys." I stood and stretched, the pain in my butt cheeks finally starting to recede. "What do you feel like, Doc? I make a mean omelet."

"Eggs sound a hell of a lot better than this crap. I can't believe people think this is good for them." Bebe dumped the remains of her glass into the fichus sitting next to the chair. I'd lay odds Caesar would need to replace the plant within the next couple of days.

I followed Bebe to the kitchen, biting my cheek hard to keep any Stevie Nicks wannabe comments from spewing forth. The woman had saved my life. If she wanted to wear floaty white dresses around her house, so be it. Now, if I could get "Rhiannon" to stop playing in my head . . .

Max, Tiffany, and the vamps trooped in behind us. Everyone pitched in on the prep work. Soon veggie and cheese omelets were frying and blood was poured.

I noticed the vamps weren't being as subtle about their eating habits around Max and me anymore, almost like we were now part of the gang. I'd still probably make Duncan brush his teeth after meals. Watching him drink the stuff was one thing. Kissing him afterward was another.

Oh god.

The omelet I flipped landed on the floor with a splat. Tiffany scooped up the mess, but I stared at the frying pan until it started to smoke from the burning butter. Anne gently tugged the handle out of my hand before she pushed me toward the table and into a chair.

What the hell was I doing, thinking about kissing him again?

The doc said it was okay. You won't get sick.

I told the taunting part of my psyche to shut the fuck up, and I dug into the stack of toast Anne plunked in front of me. But I wouldn't be able to avoid the subject forever the way Duncan watched me over the edge of his mug. I pushed any relationship thoughts into a black hole in the back of my brain and reached for a knife.

My second concern, a half hour and six dozen eggs later, was how I was going to afford groceries when I started back to work. Alone, I had eaten five of the six dozen with a pound of cheese and a couple pounds of veggies mixed in, not to mention an entire loaf of bread. Contrary to Tiffany and Bebe's estimates, today was day four of my zombiehood, and my appetite had not slacked off.

While it could be wonderful to eat a whole cheesecake in one sitting without packing it on my ass, what would happen if I didn't have food readily available? What if I go insane from starvation like a vampire? Would I eat people if nothing else was available?

Under the table, Duncan squeezed my thigh. "I will not let you go hungry."

Ire raised its ugly little head. I stared at those mesmerizing green eyes of his, not sure who had betrayed me or if he was lying about not being able to see into my thoughts. The anger lashed out at the most convenient target. "I thought you couldn't read my mind."

He smirked. "I did not have to with the way you were salivating over the remains on Tiffany's plate."

The teen shoved the last half of her one, and only, omelet towards me. "Go ahead and finish it if you're still hungry."

I should have hesitated. I wanted to hesitate. Instead I pulled the plate over and shoveled.

That is, I shoveled until I felt vampire eyes boring into my skull. I looked up to see Caesar contemplating me like, well, like Kane did before he and Able started experimenting on me.

I choked down the last bite I was chewing. The lump began an uncomfortable slide to my stomach. "What?"

He took a sip from his wine glass. "The phantom said the answer to defeating Mallory was inside you."

"And?" The way he eyed me frayed what was left of my nerves. "You think I have some secret knowledge?"

"It could be as simple as reverse engineering your nanites, Sam," Alex drawled. "You can't take ghosts too literally."

"And sometimes they deliberately mislead the living," Duncan snapped back.

"Fred wouldn't hurt me. He came back to help me." Annoyance crept into my voice. "He gave us the way to deactivate my little self-destruct problem, didn't he?"

"He did not have to. And he stated he had little to gain." Something flashed in Duncan's eyes, and not just anger. Shit, was that jealousy?

"He didn't have anything else to lose either," I said, my voice soft at the remembrance of the remorse and guilt Fred exhibited.

"He lied to you, Samantha," Duncan said, his voice low, concerned.

"Mallory probably threatened his family the minute he had an inkling Fred was backing out." I shrugged. "I just got in the way. Besides, Mallory's suspicion of me had as much to do with you and Max as it did Fred."

"I am trying to protect you." Anger colored his words.

I threw down my fork. It bounced and backflipped before landing with a clatter on the tiled floor. "Well, stop it! Your protectiveness got me in this mess to begin with!"

"What is that supposed to mean?" His voice dropped, the tone ice-cold.

"If you had just given me the goddamn interview, instead of playing Mr. Mystery Man, I wouldn't have followed you Friday night. And I wouldn't be dead!" I grabbed the napkin off my lap and threw it on the table before I rose and stomped out of the room. Blood roared in my ears as I headed for the garden. The audacity of that man!

Soft night noises greeted me as I stormed out the French doors. It took every ounce of self-control I had left not to slam them. I would have twisted the metal hinges and shattered the wood frame as well as the delicate glass panes. After everything Caesar and Bebe had done for me, they didn't deserve to have their home smashed up.

The backyard was classic Brentwood. Decorative lighting illuminated the pool, leaving sections of the flowerbeds in shadows. A romantic setting if I didn't want to deck the only person for whom I currently had lustful feelings.

I lay down on one of the decorative concrete benches scattered through the garden. A handful of the brightest stars glimmered through the hazy glow of the city lights. I stared at Orion drifting across the sky. How the hell had I gotten into this mess?

Deep down, a tiny part of me was thrilled by Duncan's attention. God only knew how I would have gotten away from Mallory without him. It wasn't just the knight in shining armor act though. He was a genuinely nice guy. Grandma Neel always said to trust how a man treats the females in his family.

Then again, maybe he needed to be a little harsher to Tiffany after all.

My issues with Goth Girl aside, he was sweet and a great kisser and cared about his friends to the point he risked his life to save them and . . .

He was a total chauvinistic jackass. This is the twenty-first century. I wasn't his freakin' lap dog.

"He knows you're not a dog, Sam."

I fell sideways off the bench at Alex's voice. Crawling back up, I glared at him while brushing off my clothes. "You could warn a girl, you know."

He chuckled and sat down on my bench. "You were too busy with your mad-on to hear me coming."

"So now he can't get the pole out of his English *arse* and sent you out here to suck up to me."

Alex ignored my rant. "Beautiful night, isn't?" He leaned back and gazed up at the few stars filtering through the Los Angeles light pollution.

I snorted. "No fair. I don't know how to read your mind, so just say what you're going to say."

He drew his attention away from the sky and regarded me. "I didn't tell you how I became a vampire when we were in the pit, did I?"

Now thoroughly confused, I shook my head and sat next to him.

"I dropped out of medical school to join the Texas Rangers. My father threw a fit of course. He always said being a Ranger would be the death of me." He laughed softly at the memory he was lost in before turning his attention to me. "I do understand loving what you do and the parents not comprehending." He stared back up at the sky.

Silence seeped into the garden as I waited for him to continue. I'd rather gotten the impression the vampires didn't cough up their personal information often. Alex wouldn't have brought up his transformation without it having something to do with Duncan. And I really wanted to know about my mystery man.

"We were escorting a group of cargo wagons headed west when we were attacked. Bandits." He shrugged and turned to look at me. "By the time they were done, everyone was dead. The drivers. The guards. And my fellow Rangers."

"Everyone but you?" I interjected.

He nodded and rubbed his jaw. "Not sure how many times I was shot. I passed out when they were ransacking the wagons. They must have thought I was dead." He chuckled again. "Which probably saved my life. Anyway, the vultures were circling when I came to. I figured I didn't have much time left. I managed to crawl under the shadow of one of the wagons and kept 'em away as best I could, but I passed out again. A noise woke me up about sundown."

I wished I had my recorder with me. This was a hell of a story.

He grinned at me. "Just can't let go of your journalistic streak, can you?"

"Quit reading my mind and tell me what happened next," I snapped.

"The bottom of the wagon fell out. Our Duncan had himself in a hidden compartment that could only be opened from the inside. Was on his way to California to meet up with Caesar."

His face sobered. "There wasn't anything he could do for me, Sam."

"Except Turn you," I whispered. Oh God. What a decision to make. Watch someone die, or condemn him to a horrible disease.

"He told me what he could do to save me and asked me if it's what I wanted. At that point, I would've said yes to Old Scratch himself. I didn't want to die."

"So Duncan . . ." I couldn't say the words.

"Yep."

My breath caught, waiting for him to finish.

Alex's gaze pierced me through. "You've got to understand, Sam. I'm the only one he's ever Turned. And he's been torturing himself with guilt ever since."

I blinked, all my assumptions flying out the window. "What about Anne?"

He shook his head. "Rogues. We think they may have been working for Selene."

"This Selene is Caesar's sister, right?"

Alex nodded. "And the vampire who Turned Duncan. Against his will, I might add. She thought Turning him would bind him to her, make him grateful for immortality. He was horrified by what she'd done, so she never forgave him for rejecting her."

A wave of jealousy poured through me at his words.

He chuckled. This whole telepathy thing was really beginning to piss me off.

The humor died as he continued. "Over the centuries, she's killed almost all of his living family. The rogues she sent would've slaughtered baby Tiffany too if Duncan hadn't stopped them in time."

"How old was Tiffany when it happened?"

"About six months if I recall."

For once, I had a little sympathy for Goth Girl. "So that's why Duncan raised her," I murmured.

"As best he could. We all chipped in to help." He grinned. "Phil and the day guards handled the sunlight duties, but a houseful of vampires makes the nighttime tasks a little easier."

"I can just see him changing Tiffany's diapers." Humor laced my next comment. "So he was your Tonto, huh?"

Alex roared with laughter. It took him a couple of minutes to catch his breath before he commented, "Trust me, Duncan's not as stupid as the producers made Jay Silverheels act. More James Bond, I would think."

Oh yeah, he'd look great in a tux. I was sure he'd look great without a tux too. "So what happened after he Turned you?"

Alex's grin widened until his fangs glinted from the pool lights. "Three nights later, we went hunting."

I chewed on the information Alex gave me for a good long time after he went inside. It definitely put Duncan in a different light. To face someone who'd deliberately infected him with an incurable disease. To watch your family murdered one by one over the course of centuries. To raise a baby girl without the ability to do real dad things like picnics in the park and afternoon recitals.

This was Tiffany though, so maybe no recitals. I really couldn't see Goth Girl in a pink tutu.

Still, I'd give almost anything to have someone in my life who was that loyal, that concerned about my welfare, that loving. We may have a difference of opinion on what constituted manners and affectionate behavior, but I had to admit he meant well.

I stood up and brushed off my jeans. No more games. It was time to do a little hunting of my own.

When I stalked back inside the mansion, somehow I knew the location of each person in each room. All it took was a little concentration. Maybe I was getting the hang of my new abilities after all. Definitely would come in handy with my job. Since no one was nearby to hear anything, even with super auditory abilities, I removed my bra *Flashdance*-style on my way through the hall.

The sharp smell of whiskey greeted me when I walked into Caesar's library. Duncan sat in one of those large squishy chairs perfect for curling up with a good book. He wasn't curled up though. His boots were firmly planted on the plush carpet, all the better to support the laptop across his knees.

He watched me through hooded eyes but didn't say a word while I grabbed a glass from the wet bar tucked in an alcove next to the door and sauntered over to him. Maybe I didn't need the false courage, but it gave my hands something to do so they didn't shake. I made the most of my braless state as I bent over to grab the bottle sitting on the end table next to him. A whistle escaped my lips as I read the label. These boys didn't skimp on the good stuff. I poured a shot and tossed it back. The phrase "going down smooth" didn't do the whiskey justice.

I wasn't sure if the liquid fortification was to deal with my feelings for Duncan or the thought of him and Alex eating the bandits. Well, drinking their blood anyway. When I had decided the bandits sounded like they tasted better than lizards, which was probably the only other thing the two could find in the West Texas desert, I realized my real problem.

Duncan scared me and thrilled me at the same time. Nothing like the adrenaline rush I'd had with Jake. Deep down, I knew my ex couldn't hurt me. With Duncan . . .

I splashed another round in the glass. With Duncan, there was surety and not so sure at the same time. The physical aspect wasn't half as scary as the emotional. Could I bear to give this man my soul?

I was really glad he couldn't read my mind right now. I'd run. Or he'd run. Besides, some things are better when shown.

I poured the third shot before I could meet his eyes. He held his glass out for a refill, still not saying a word, watching me with those unnerving green eyes.

I sat down on the chair across from him and leaned forward, my tumbler cupped in my hands. "So what are we going to do?"

"Get back into Mallory Labs and destroy the nanite project before Sierra can distribute—"

"No," I interrupted. "I mean us."

"Us?" He raised an eyebrow.

"Yeah. You know, you and me." I waved my glass between us, sloshing whiskey over the side. Rather than waste anymore of the amber liquid, I drank the rest in one swallow.

"There is no 'us,' Samantha." His attention shifted back to the laptop screen.

Ok-a-a-ay. I didn't expect him to throw me on the floor and start doing the nasty, but what happened to all the protection bullshit he spouted earlier? I wasn't going to let him yank my chain anymore.

"Look, I know you're in total denial, pulling the whole 'tortured vampire who can't love anyone because he's cursed' bullshit. But guess what? David Boreanez didn't get an Oscar for his role, and you aren't either."

"Emmy."

"Huh?" I blinked.

His eyes met mine again. "David Boreanez did not receive an Emmy for his role as Angel."

I grinned. "Ah, so you pay attention to the real world after all." And I would have sworn those green irises of his had the faintest of glows.

"No." A wry smile crossed his lips. "Tiffany made me watch the show."

"You poor baby."

"It was torture."

We both fell silent as his words hit way too close to home.

My gaze fell away from his. A change of subject was necessary. The glass clinked when I set it down on one of the stone coasters on the end table. A plan was forming, and I was really, really glad he couldn't read my mind. "So you're telling me you have absolutely no interest in kissing me again?"

"Samantha, we both know it is not a good idea to continue a relationship given the circumstances."

I rose from my chair and faced him. "So you're admitting a relationship exists?"

"I am admitting no such thing." His haughty expression transformed into one of puzzlement when I picked up his laptop and laid it on my chair.

"You didn't answer my first question, Duncan." I plucked the tumbler out of his hand and set it on another coaster. No one can say I'm a rude guest who gets water rings all over other people's furniture.

He blinked as I leaned over him and braced my hands on the armrests.

"Are you telling me you have no interest in kissing me again?" I repeated.

Our faces were inches apart. His breath brushed my cheeks as he fought to control himself. His oh-so-delectable lips firm, he shook his head. "We cannot."

I crawled into the chair and straddled his lap. An undeniable urge spread through me as I pressed against him. I couldn't resist a grin. His lips said no but the rest of him agreed with my point of view. Pun intended.

"Tell me why we can't," I whispered.

He groaned and closed his eyes. He was losing this battle and he knew it. Strong hands gripped my waist, but instead of pushing me away, he tugged me closer.

"You heard the doc. There's no reason we can't," I whispered. "Just no biting."

His eyes opened a fraction, neon giving the planes of his face an odd greenish cast. "You do not trust me."

"It's not about trust." Reaching up, I threaded my fingers through his dark, silky waves. "We don't know what my blood could do to you."

The briefest of smiles tilted his lips. "A sensible precaution."

Our lips brushed, melded, explored. He pulled me tight against his chest, the pressure delightful. The kiss deepened, electrified, sent waves of sensation slamming through my body. The rub of my nipples against thin cotton amplified my reaction.

He drew back slightly, and I nibbled my way across his jaw line to his ear. He moaned as I swirled my tongue around the curve.

"Even so, we should not do this." He made absolutely no effort to get up, so I pressed the advantage. So to speak.

"Why?" I asked once again. "We're two consenting adults in the twenty-first century." Leaning back, I tugged off my t-shirt, the movements rocking my hips against his erection. I threw my shirt on top of his computer and grinned at him. "Though I guess there is that pesky law concerning necrophilia."

"Samantha?"

"Hmmm?" That was all I could manage as he palmed my breasts. The pads of his thumbs stroked the tips. Shivers ran across my skin.

"You talk too much."

Then he seized a nipple in his mouth, and any thoughts flew out of my head, leaving pure want in their wake. His tongue traced circles around the tip, leaving me breathless. He turned his attention to the other, lavishing the same careful attention.

My breath hissed and tension thrummed when his teeth caught the areola. The extra-sharp canines brought both pain and pleasure, but he was oh-so-careful not to break the delicate skin. Muscles relaxed, wallowing in the desire. Another nip, not so threatening this time, the pleasure turning to raw agony.

He cupped my head, pulled me closer for another tangling of tongues and lips. A long, slow exploration that nearly made me come right there. God, the man could kiss. Broad hands caressed my back, moved down to my ass and scooted me closer. If that were possible.

When he ended the kiss, I mumbled a protest and opened my eyes. His eyes definitely glowed neon green. A knowing smirk played along his lips. Somehow the tables had turned.

I didn't really care at that point. Need had replaced want. Need for him, need to touch him.

I fumbled for the hem of his sweater, but he swept it off in one smooth motion.

And there on his totally masculine chest was a totally feminine gold locket.

My breath caught, and I brushed a finger across the shiny surface. Why would he be wearing something like that? "Is there something you're not telling me?"

Amusement sparked in his eyes. "Why? Jealous?" Underneath his playful tone swam a painful ache.

Without any stupid telepathy, I knew. "Margaret's."

His sad nod left a shadow over the original mood, one I needed to drive away.

My gentle kisses brushed his forehead, his eyelids, his lips. Soft nips reignited the fire. Hands splayed of their own accord across his chest. I ran my fingers through crisp, dark hair, following the trail to the button of his jeans.

Jeans?

Hormones, the séance and our argument had addled my head so bad I hadn't even noticed Mr.-I-don't-wear-anything-but-slacks wore denim tonight. Somehow the change made him even more enticing. I unsnapped and unzipped.

Oh yeah, I knew he had to be a boxers kind of guy.

His erection strained against the emerald silk. I ran my fingers along the covered shaft, eliciting another groan from his throat. My thumb stroked the tip before repeating the same action. His eyes watched me, the desire unmistakable.

I found my feet long enough to skim the remaining clothes off both of us before settling back in his lap. Amazingly, Mr. Alpha Male didn't argue about me undressing him. He pressed against my core, and slickness followed. My body seemed to have a mind of its own when it came to Duncan St. James.

I rose again, this time I slid over him, the fit perfect, full, wonderfully tight. A sigh of delight escaped as he yanked my hips hard against his. All control was lost. Our bodies ground, capturing every inch of delicious friction.

Internal muscles squeezed around him, pulled him deeper, wanted all of him inside. Lips swallowed his answering moan, so his hands answered instead. Grasping, massaging, parting cheeks in an effort to get even closer. One hand on his chest to maintain my balance, I reached behind, fingers stroking his velvety sac. His mouth followed similar motions along my breasts. The bolder my touch, the more I was rewarded, sharp nips mingling in a pleasure/pain, sending me into a frenzy.

I matched him thrust for thrust until the world exploded into a million stars. He buried his face in my neck as his body stiffened from his own release. I gasped when the exquisite spasms of his cock launched another round of answering convulsions. I'd never come that hard, that fast, that many times.

Ever.

God, he was better than a ride at Disneyland.

He leaned back and chuckled as he eyed me. "You are not comparing me to 'It's a Small World,' are you?"

I blinked, trying to clear the mind-blowing orgasms. I didn't say the Disney ride thing aloud, did I?

One of his aristocratic eyebrows shot upward. *I delivered mind-blowing orgasms?* Male pride made his smirk even more irritating.

Then I realized his lips hadn't moved. *Can you hear me?*

He frowned. "You are very faint now."

Wonderful, just wonderful. Now he could read my mind.

I smacked his shoulder. "Think something to me."

I have half a mind to spank you for continually hitting me.

Really?

With a growl, he rose and threw me over his shoulder in one smooth motion. There's something to be said about men with superpowers.

I will give you a demonstration of superpowers, you little vixen.

He gave my ass a light slap, and I squealed. But I couldn't complain. My position gave me access to his backside as well. His gorgeous, taut, muscular . . .

Then I realized instead of heading for the couch, he was marching through the door.

"Duncan?"

He ignored my protest and continued up the stairs. I am normally not a prude, but traipsing through someone else's house in my birthday suit stretched even my natural lack of manners.

"Duncan! Someone will see us," I hissed.

And?

He was right. No one was anywhere close to us as he made a beeline for his bedroom. Though I had a sneaking suspicion the other vamps knew what we were up to.

Do not worry, Samantha. He nudged the door shut with his free shoulder before tossing me on his bed. He stopped my slide across the slippery navy and gold bedspread by pouncing on top of me. Tickles led to a languid kiss that heated things up again.

Except I realized we hadn't used protection, which is so not like me. Granted, Bebe had said I couldn't have kids, but what if she were wrong? What if Duncan and I couldn't make it as a couple? I'd certainly made a royal mess of things with Jake. And I didn't want to raise a kid alone. Hell, I had problems seeing me raise one at all.

A sudden desperation enveloped his touches and caresses, like he was afraid I would disappear. He stopped abruptly and gazed at me. A frown creased his forehead. "Do not do that."

"Do what?" A little confused and a lot frustrated, I wanted to yell at him to shut up and go back to what he was doing with that marvelous tongue of his. I wanted to tell my own insecurity to shut up as well.

"Do not shut me out," he whispered. He had this really weird look on his face, a mixture of sadness, anxiety, and something I couldn't quite put a finger on.

I blinked, now thoroughly confused. If I were a guy, I would have been deflating about now. I rose up on my elbows. "What the hell are you blathering about?"

"I could hear your thoughts, and then—" He shrugged and shook his head. "It was like you slammed a door in my face."

"I didn't mean to." I started to get a little peeved and a lot anxious. Why was I apologizing when he was the one who stopped the action? It wasn't lovemaking. I so wasn't going there. Just fun and games among the undead. Right? It was the only way I could deal with this.

I waggled my eyebrows. "Why don't you pick up where you left off and see if it clears up the reception?"

Rather than taking my suggestion, he took my face in his hands and started over from the beginning. He took his time, nothing like the frantic passion from downstairs.

But then I realized I couldn't hear him in my head either. Maybe that's what made sex in the library so exciting. I could feel his arousal in my mind as well as other places, and it turned me on even more.

Duncan seemed intent on driving me insane, bringing me to the edge, then backing off. Tears rimmed my eyes from frustration when his flesh teased the opening of mine. Teased, tantalized, tortured—

—you feel so wonderful, darling.

And suddenly I was in his head again, the sensations ping-ponging between us. There weren't enough adjectives in Webster's to describe . . . any of this. I wanted him deeper, and in response, he lifted my legs onto his shoulders, opening me even further. Slick, hot flesh plunging, caressing, contracting, releasing until I buried my head in his pillow to muffle my scream. With a groan and shudder, he collapsed on me, peppering my neck and shoulders with tiny kisses. His weight, a comforting blanket of solid muscle, felt oh-so-right.

How's that?

He rolled to his side and began kissing each of my fingers, sending aftershocks on top of the aftershocks. *Marvelous.*

I slapped his chest. *The reception, moron, not the sex.*

"What did I tell you about hitting me?" he growled. He flipped me on my tummy and pinned me down with one hand. I struggled, but it lasted only a few seconds. Talented fingers slid into me, hitting the spot of nerves that had my body shuddering under his ministrations. Apparently, there are some warnings that can't be delivered telepathically.

Chapter 25

I woke up with a start. Sunset. Damn. I had slept the day away.

It took another few seconds to realize I was alone in the huge bed. Then the shower spurted to life in the attached bath.

My lips curved as wicked thoughts raced. Sliding from the bed, I tiptoed into the bathroom. The intention was to watch him through the foggy glass.

I must not have been sneaky enough. Dark and wet, Duncan poked his head around the shower door and smiled. "Care to join me?"

I didn't dignify his stupid question with an answer. Steam billowed around me as I stepped into the double-sized shower.

An hour later, Duncan kissed the back of my neck because a towel covered the rest of my head while I rubbed the excess moisture out of the strands. "Meet you downstairs," he murmured before heading for the bathroom door. I flipped the ends of the towel out of my face to watch his backside as he left.

I hummed to myself and clicked on the hair dryer. A girl could get used to this kind of wake-up service. A few minutes later, I fished in one of the huge shopping bags sitting in the corner to retrieve my last pair of clean jeans. I wasn't sure when Duncan brought the bag to his room, but the thoughtful gesture wasn't lost on me.

Shifting through the bag didn't yield anything cleaner shirtwise, so I raided his drawer for a t-shirt. I winced before pulling one out. Black, of course. I needed to find out where Caesar and Bebe hid the washing machine in this place. I may not have the fresh-out-of-the-grave smell of George Romero's creatures, but I hadn't stopped sweating either.

Creature of the night odor was not exactly the way to impress the new boyfriend.

I rolled the word around my head.

Yeah. "Boyfriend" sounded about right. It was a hell of a lot better than "chauvinistic asshole". And the benefits were way better.

It's not like we declared undying love last night. I winced again. I had discovered through trial and error, okay through sex and recovery, we could only "hear" each other while doing the nasty. I would need to seriously edit my thoughts while he was feeling frisky. And Lord knew men feel frisky ninety-nine percent of the time.

Stomach grumbling once again, I jogged down the stairs.

And stumbled into another argument. These folks really loved to fight in their kitchens. To be fair, only Caesar and Duncan were yelling. Alex's head swung back and forth like he was watching Venus and Serena during their last set at Wimbledon. I, on the other hand, couldn't understand a damn word the boys were saying.

It's Latin, Alex thought, and he winged an apple my way.

"*Veni, vidi, vici*," I muttered before taking a nice big bite of my fruit.

You would have thought I dropped a dirty nuke in the middle of the Beverly Center the way the men stopped to stare at me.

I shrugged. "Sorry. It's all I remember from Latin 101."

"You're on your own in this one, kid," Alex whispered before slinking out the kitchen door.

"Do you have any idea of what you just said?" Duncan bit out. His eyes glowed neon. Definitely not a signal of impending nookie this time. Caesar's face was even scarier in its stillness, like a lion ready to pounce.

Sometimes the best defense is a good offense. Maybe I needed that phrase tattooed on my ass as a reminder not to put myself in defensive situations in the first place. No, the nanites would probably make a tattoo a total waste of money.

I took another bite and chewed before I answered. "'I came. I saw. I conquered.' It's the first line in Julius Caesar's account of his conquest of Gaul. Now known to the lowly Normals as France." I planted one fist on my hip and shook the apple in Duncan's direction. "I figured you'd like that part since you weren't exactly on friendly terms with them before your bloodsucking days."

"As for you—" I shot Caesar a dirty look. "I wouldn't be running around naming myself after his nephew if you have an objection to folks quoting him."

In the tense silence, I debated whether I could outrun two pissed-off vampires when Caesar dissolved into gales of laughter. Duncan didn't join in, but the unnatural glow in his eyes died out, though the outraged look remained plastered to his gorgeous jaw.

"Well said, well said," Caesar choked out as he wiped his eyes. "But I'd watch what I say around certain people without knowing them better, little zombie."

Curiosity welled, but a slight shake of Duncan's head deterred me from asking questions. It couldn't be what I suspected, could it? Was Augustine connected to the original Caesars somehow?

My stomach grumbled which sent Caesar into another laughing fit. "You cannot use your woman and not replenish her, my friend." He nudged Duncan in the ribs and gave me a knowing grin.

"Yeah," I said, putting the most pathetic look I could on my face. "At least Alex gave me an apple, and he didn't get any last night." I reached for the door. "I really should thank him properly."

Duncan yanked me into his arms and laid on a kiss so tender and so passionate it made me forget—well, everything. I don't normally go for PDAs, and I had forgotten Caesar was in the room until his not-so-discreet clearing of his throat caused Duncan to end the kiss.

"Now, where were you going?" he murmured.

"Don't remember." I grinned up at him. "But you still owe me breakfast for using me so thoroughly." I drifted from his arms and hopped up on one of the bar stools lining the island. "So whatcha going to cook for me?"

A slight look of discomfort crossed his features. "Cook for you?"

"Yeah. Cook for me." My stomach seconded the motion.

"Er," he fumbled and looked at Caesar, desperation in his eyes.

My suspected member of the ancient Roman Imperial family ignored

Duncan's silent plea for help. Instead, Caesar poured himself a cup of coffee and propped himself on the stool next to me, looking at Duncan expectantly.

I'm not a morning person even when the morning starts at sunset, but realization smacked me between the eyes. "Holy boiled eggs! Batman can't cook!"

Caesar hid his smile behind his mug.

"I am able to cook," came the stiff British protest.

I looked at Caesar, and he leaned closer to my ear. "Grilled cheese."

Lucky for me I had finished my apple. Otherwise I would have choked on it from the laughter.

"It is all Tiffany would eat when she was five!" Dark pink flared along Duncan's cheekbones.

I slapped the counter, laughing so hard I couldn't breathe. Finally, I wiped my eyes and composed myself. "Is there anything else besides driving and cooking you can't do?"

He ignored me, stalked across the kitchen and pulled cheese and butter from the fridge.

Fine. Two can play that game.

"So can you drive or cook, Mr. Augustine?"

"Yes, to both."

Duncan slammed the skillet onto the stove with a bang that probably raised the rest of the household, undead or not.

"So, did you first learn to drive in your daddy's chariot?"

Caesar smirked as he played along with my game. Duncan must have really pissed him off for the vampire prince to take my side. "My older brother's actually."

"Did you have a problem switching from live mustangs to mechanical ones?"

"No."

Butter sizzled and a wisp of smoke rose from the skillet. Duncan flipped the first sandwich. Wonderful. He was going to make me eat charcoal.

I ignored his tantrum and favored Caesar with a bright grin. "Cool. Did you have any other siblings?"

Caesar was silent for a moment before he said, "A younger brother and a twin sister."

Ouch. I'd stepped in the dog pile even though I'd been warned more than once. Caesar's sister was the only sticking point in his and Duncan's friendship.

The first sandwich landed with a clink on the plate. I didn't think my zombie stomach could handle a whole plateful of burnt toast and extra-hard cheese. Even Caesar winced in distaste when Duncan slammed the plate down in front of me.

I reached for it. The sandwich was as hard as it sounded. I took a tentative nibble, chewed forever and flashed Duncan a grin after I finally managed to swallow the mouthful. "Thanks, sweetie." The bits of charred bread I was sure were embedded in my teeth convinced him to fry the rest of my sandwiches properly.

I heard a muffled "No, Tiffany, don't go in there," from Alex a millisecond before the door swung open. My brother followed close on her stilettos. The rich, lush scent of fresh apples and full-bloom roses followed in their wake. Frowning at the scent, I searched my memory. Apples I could understand, but I hadn't spotted any flowers in Caesar's place yesterday. Maybe Tiffany was wearing perfume.

The first real smile I saw from the teen wonder appeared on her face when she spotted my stack. She turned pleading, puppy dog eyes on Duncan. "Make some for me?"

He grunted in assent and slathered more butter on slices of whole wheat.

Tiffany smiled up at Max. "You want some? Uncle Duncan grills the best."

The smile Max gave her in return nauseated my cast-iron zombie stomach more than the burnt bread. He nodded and gave me an affectionate nudge before he propped his elbows on the counter next to me. "Morning, sleepyhead." The fresh rose odor was even stronger coming from him. He must have grabbed the wrong shower gel and shampoo this morning.

"Back at-cha." I had consumed half my current grilled cheese before warning bells rang in my head. He hadn't followed up with any lewd comments about last night's sleeping arrangements. I swallowed my last bite. Okay, maybe he had common sense not to say anything in front of the vampire doing his sister. Or maybe I was luckier, and he really didn't know in whose room I slept.

Duncan placed full plates in front of Tiffany and Max. Then he peered rather too closely at Max's neck.

"Hey, there's blood in the fridge," Tiffany protested.

Duncan ignored her, grabbed the collar of Max's shirt and yanked him halfway across the granite countertop. "What the hell have you been doing to my niece!" he roared.

Alex dove through the door and into the chaos. It took all of us to loosen Duncan's grip from Max's throat.

"Cut it out! I'm an adult!" Tiffany's shriek should have broken every glass in the cupboards. She and I formed a barrier between the straining madman and my wheezing brother. I wasn't sure Alex and Caesar were going to keep their hold on Duncan. The commotion was enough to draw Bebe and Anne to the kitchen.

When the women distracted me from the pissed-off vampire, I spotted the enormous hickey that set off Duncan. No wonder Max kept his left side away from me. I railed on him. "What the hell were you thinking? She's too young for you!"

Tiffany jumped between me and my idiot brother. "I am not!"

"Just please tell me you two used a condom." Everyone turned to Bebe with various expressions of fury and amusement. A bemused smile curved the edges of her mouth.

"Doc!" Tiffany wailed.

"Well?" Duncan's lips twisted into a feral snarl. The green glow of his rage sent eerie shadows in counterpoint to the overhead fluorescents. Hands clenched and unclenched as if he wanted to continue his throttling of my brother.

Tears streamed down Tiffany's face, leaving black trails of mascara behind. Despite my own anger at Max, I felt sorry for the kid.

"We—" Max started.

"He proposed!" The stunned silence lasted a full minute in the wake of Tiffany's announcement. Apparently, the vampires had ignored them as thoroughly as they had Duncan and me last night.

Then the full implication of Max's words registered in my altered brain. "What!" My turn to scream. I grabbed Max by the throat and took up where Duncan left off. I couldn't believe my brother would use such a cheesy line to get into her pants. "You low-life son-of-a-bitch! How could you even think—"

Anne and Alex struggled to pull me off my asshole of a blood relation.

"I-it's true," Max choked out once the vamps pried my fingers from his trachea. He turned to look at Duncan. "Look, I'm sorry, St. James. This isn't how we wanted to tell you."

"I am sure it was not," Duncan said, his voice icy.

"As if you and Sam have acted in an exemplary manner conducting your relationship," Bebe said.

Alex bent over nearly double, hiding his expression in what was left of Anne's hair. Even Miss Serious Amish Vamp had a smile on her face.

"But—" Duncan started.

"There's less of an age difference between them than you and Sam. And your sandwiches are burning," Bebe finished primly a split second before the smoke alarm sounded.

He cursed, skirted around Caesar to snatch the skillet off the burner, and dumped the now flaming contents into the sink. Steam billowed as he ran the faucet over the ruined cheese and bread.

I grabbed Max's arm and dragged him out of the kitchen. I didn't stop until we reached the pool. Drowning him seemed a legitimate option.

I yanked him around to face me. "What the hell is your damage? These people are trying to save our lives, and you go around boffing their kids?"

"Unlike you, I don't boff and run." He was calm as he rubbed his bicep. Way too calm. Then his words hit me.

"What is that supposed to mean?"

"As soon as you're done with the novelty of vampire sex, you'll dump St. James faster than your garbage diving clothes."

I opened my mouth, but nothing came out so I closed it. I tried again with no success. Finally, I muttered, "He's not fresh out of high school."

Max shook his head, a sad, pained expression on his face. "You just don't get it, Sam. Tiffany's seen and done things you can't even comprehend. Intellectually she's way beyond her years. I can have a conversation with her that doesn't involve the latest Hollywood boy toy."

"I don't talk about Hollywood boy toys all the time." The pout formed on my lips of its own accord. "Besides, it's business related."

He rolled his eyes. "Why am I even surprised by you working for a tabloid? Your master's thesis was based on the historical equivalent of a celebrity slut."

My eyes narrowed. "You worked for the *Scoop* long before I did, and Cleopatra VII of Egypt is a valid historical personage."

Rose flared under pale stubble. "Then why do you waste that poli-sci/history/journalism triple major for no other reason than to get your rocks off pissing off Mom? You let her tell you you're a screw-up, and then you go out of your way to prove her right. You chase off any guy who shows the slightest interest in you just because Mom wants you to get hitched. Isn't that the real reason you dumped Jake?"

Red swam in my vision at his change in tactics. How dare he! "That was low, Snotface. Even for you."

He looked away for a second. "You're right. I'm sorry." His gaze met mine again, his expression no longer furious. "In case you hadn't noticed, St. James is crazy about you. As crazy as Jake was once. But I know you. The first sign of things getting serious, and you'll break the poor guy's heart."

I snorted. "Duncan St. James isn't a poor anything. And quit changing the subject. What do you think he's going to do to you for messing with his niece?"

"I'm well aware he could do anything to me at any time," he replied, his voice cool. "All the vampires are telepathic, so he knows I'm serious about Tiffany. This isn't about me, Sam." He jabbed a finger into my chest. "This is about your issues. You're too damn scared to take any chances in your life."

"I take plenty of chances." I wanted to take a swing at Max so bad I thrust my clenched fists into my pockets. The denim ripping would give him a two-second headstart if I lost control. "I've had so many close scrapes—"

"With your heart, Sam?" He had that damn sad, pitying look on his face again.

The scent of roses was stronger than ever. I glanced around, more to avoid Max's puppy dog eyes than to really take in the garden. Caesar didn't even have rose bushes back here.

And then all the scents assaulting me the last couple of days clicked into meaning. Under the base scents for each species, scents also changed based on the person's emotions. Tiffany and Max smelled the way they did because they really were in love.

I hated Max then, more than I had ever hated him. My nails bit into my palms. This had nothing to do with any childhood rivalry, and everything to do with a basic fact. He was alive. I wasn't. He could love someone, marry, have children, be normal. I couldn't. Things had changed too much. For both of us, and in more ways than I could count. I wanted to bitch-slap him.

But if I hit him now, I'd probably kill him.

"Look, Sam, I'm sorry." He held out a hand, but a latent fear shone in his eyes. Fear based on the awareness of what I had done to Mom's gun, what I could do to him now.

I hated that fear as much as I hated him.

"Max, you really need to shut up." It was difficult to force the words past my gritted teeth, but obviously, he understood me because he adopted his oh-so-delightful sanctimonious attitude.

"Why? Because you're mad I've taken the plunge you're to chicken-shit to take?"

"Go fuck yourself." Not one of my wittier responses.

He fumed for a second before he stalked back into the house, leaving me to gasp for air like a beached shark. I couldn't follow and nail him with one of my fabulous sarcastic comebacks because . . .

Because deep down, I knew he was right. Maybe not about Duncan. I wasn't really sure where our whole situation stood. But as for the rest, he was right.

Damn him. Damn Mom too for that matter. I didn't need to damn myself. I was already there.

A tear trickled down my cheek. I didn't need him to point out I was dead and pretty much had nothing to show for it. Hell, I probably didn't even have my job since I hadn't called Ralph in almost a week. The old man will put up with a lot of shit, but he won't tolerate one of his people not calling in. My death was irrelevant.

"Sam."

I sniffed and wiped my eyes on my sleeves before turning to face Caesar. "Yeah."

"We have twenty-four hours before Sierra's deadline. We need to talk."

I sniffed again and nodded.

My petty issues would have to wait. Time for the dead to go save the world.

<h1 style="text-align:center">Chapter 26</h1>

Duncan's eyes burned as bright as kryptonite crystals in the Chris Reeve movies. "She cannot go!"

The realization Duncan roared a lot sank into my head. No wonder Tiffany adopted the goth persona. It was sheer self-preservation. At least, I now knew for sure Duncan's argument with Caesar in the kitchen had been about me.

"Sierra's offer was to me. Not anyone else." I waved across the assemblage in Caesar's office. "I'm the perfect decoy."

Instead of continuing his pacing, Duncan planted his gorgeous body in front of the office door. "She will be expecting just such a move," Duncan snapped back.

It took all my willpower not to roll my eyes. The big lug meant well, but he wasn't thinking straight. I rather got the impression he didn't anytime his maker was involved. Maybe I wouldn't be either if I were confronting Tyrone Mallory. But his death took a certain subjectivity out of my emotional equation.

Instead of pointing out the obvious, which he'd only deny, I nonchalantly perched on the corner of Caesar's desk and tried my most convincing voice. The one I used to reason with Ralph when he's on the fence about running one of my stories. "Most likely. Think about it. The only reason Sierra let me go was to plant a bomb, me, in Caesar's place." Again, I waved a hand to include the group in Caesar's office. "So far, we're her only opposition. She's probably already triggered the self-destruct in the hopes of taking out you guys. If I walk in on my own, she'll assume I didn't know she's already tried to kill me—"

"Again," Duncan muttered.

I threw up my hands. "Okay, you were right. I shouldn't have brought her with us. Happy?"

Caesar's quiet voice broke through our argument. "There's no way we'll be able to break into the complex a third time. If her father hired rogues, I have no doubt Sierra's retained their services as well." Nice to know I wasn't the only one avoiding the Selene equation around Duncan.

Duncan ignored his boss's logic. "We could still bring additional support to Los Angeles—"

Caesar's high-planed cheeks pinked. "Not before Sierra comes here. She undoubtedly knows exactly where Sam is, and she's not about to lose her father's prototype."

I was on his side, but I didn't like being referred to as Mallory's science experiment. Next thing you know, my hair'll turn black and white with electricity fizzing through it.

I apologize, Sam.

Apology accepted, oh great and wise Prince.

Caesar shot me an irritated look before continuing. "John and Ziva have already volunteered some of their people to assist us."

Duncan scowled. "I do not like relying on outsiders."

Bebe laughed, a soft musical tinkle in the emotions clouding the room, and shook her head. "Sweet Goddess, you sound almost as conceited as an uppity little witch did two years ago."

I swear I heard enamel and bone crack when Duncan clenched his jaw.

An amused smile flitted across Caesar's face. "Yes, I seem to recall a lecture around that same time on taking action based on a well-reasoned decision."

My attention flicked between Bebe, Caesar and Duncan. I may not have understood the reason for the intimate teasing, but I could still thoroughly enjoy Duncan's squirming.

Breath left Duncan's pursed lips with a whoosh. His facial muscles relaxed enough for him to say, "Very well. I am listening."

Caesar's fingers steepled below his lips. "I found out through some of my business associates Mallory Investments is holding a party tomor-row night at the lab facility before the private shareholder meeting on Saturday. An alternative to Sam's theory, Sierra may simply want Sam with her when she announces the cure."

"Yeah, except the only thing they cured me of was life," I muttered.

Caesar ignored my whining. "That will be the perfect, and the only, opportunity to get in."

"Squirt here and I can give them their obvious break-in," Alex said, gesturing at himself and Anne. "Two tortured vamps wanting revenge? It'll be perfect."

I noticed Duncan didn't protest Alex's plan. I was flattered he con-sidered me more important than his best friend, but I resented he didn't believe I could take care of myself. Hell, even Tiffany was going on this little outing.

"No, she's not."

I jumped at Caesar's statement. Telepathy sucked the big one.

"Who's not what?" asked Tiffany.

"You're not going on this expedition," Duncan said.

"You left me out of the last one." Hands on hips, she glared at each of the vamps and Bebe in turn.

"And you'll be left out of this one as well. It's too dangerous," Duncan snapped.

I winced at the cliché. On the other hand, Tiffany hit her boiling point.

"I've held my own against Selene's best." Make that freezing point. She was eerily calm. Not the usual teen outburst I had come to expect. "As you've all pointed out, she's expecting us to try something. She won't be expecting me, and I won't be the helpless wimp left behind to be kid-napped for a trade by the bad guys."

"I think that's my job, honey," Max said.

From the look she gave him, he so wasn't getting any tonight.

"None of them should—" Duncan started.

"You're—" Caesar cut in.

"Enough!" I jumped to my feet at the same time I screamed. I couldn't handle the chest beating anymore. I just couldn't, not with my brother being a total wuss on top of everything. His girlfriend had more balls than he did.

"You—" I pointed to Max. "If you don't want to help, fine! Stay here and hide in the freakin' basement for all I care." Okay, so I was still pissed at him for the lecture by the pool.

"You!" I jabbed my index finger in Duncan's direction. "You were ready to slap the shit out of me for leaving Alex behind during my escape. Well, guess what? I'm not standing by while he risks his life to stop that psycho bitch. Caesar's come up with a viable plan. If you can't come up with something better, then shut the fuck up!"

"You are right."

I blinked in surprise. He couldn't have possibly just said what I thought I heard. "Excuse me?"

"You heard me the first time," he said, irritation plain in his tone. "I will not repeat myself." He crossed his arms over his chest.

Let it go, Sam. Just let it go.

Maybe I was too depressed from my argument with Max earlier, but I listened to Alex and returned to my perch on the desk.

Caesar summarized the whole plan. I was the first decoy. Basically I march up to the front door and ask my fellow zombie to come out and play. Alex and Anne play the second decoy at the back gate, and the rest would go through a different section of wall using one of Bebe's spells.

Was it only a week ago? God, I haven't been dead a week, and I'm out to save the world from the insane zombie queen. It was enough to make me crazy.

I tried to focus on what Caesar was saying, but all I could think about was how my stupidity put these people in danger. If I hadn't chased Duncan, would any of this be happening? Sierra would still be undergoing chemo, waiting for her daddy to save her. Duncan would have rescued his friends, and Caesar would have made some kind of ultra-rich gentleman's agreement with Tyrone Mallory to keep everything quiet. Life would have gone on for all of us.

When Caesar dismissed us, I wandered back out to the pool and sat on the edge, swirling my toes in the warm crystal water. I needed to do something to fix this mess. Normally, I do my best thinking at a coffee shop, but any private excursions were out of the question. And I was so tired of feeling like a prisoner.

Then there was the issue of Miss Zombie Queen. Not that I wanted to be the only one, but she presented a danger to the whole freakin' world. Everyone here had bent over backwards to save me—a total stranger. They didn't deserve to die because of me, trying to stop Sierra.

Fred had said I held the key to stopping little Miss Psycho Heiress. I just wish I knew what the hell he meant. Even if I couldn't figure out his cryptic statement, I had to face the bitch on my terms, not as a snatch-and-grab by her goon squad. Would Caesar's sister be with her? Doubtful, since she'd been doing her best to stay off the vampire prince's radar. The slender threads of an alternate plan started to weave together in my warped dead brain.

"May I join you?"

I jumped at Duncan's voice behind me. Plastering my fake smile on, the one I use for press agents I really hate, I twisted to look up at him. "Sure. What's up?"

Under the glow from the pool lights, a frown creased his forehead. "You have been unnaturally quiet since your outburst earlier."

I toed a floating leaf that had escaped the maniacal gardener who tended Caesar's place. He put the guys at Disneyland to shame.

"Sam?" Duncan knelt and took my hand in his, the pad of his thumb rubbing my palm. I tried to clamp down on the shivers of desire welling in my blood. That's the problem when someone can read your mind during sex. He knows what buttons to push.

"You did say I talked too much."

"Somehow, I do not think you were that offended by my teasing to take it to heart." Oh, he was so trying to play kiss and make up. And I wanted to play too, but I couldn't. Not tonight. He'd know what I was planning, and I would have a hard enough time hiding it from the other vamps.

"No." I choked on the next words but forced them out anyway. "I would have to care what you think to be offended."

He pulled back and his frown deepened. "Pardon me?"

God, this hurt. I knew then what I really felt for him. And I was about to crush any chance I had with him because if he knew what I planned to do in the morning, he'd find a way to stop me.

I inhaled deeply, trying to ease the ache in my chest. "Max is right." I turned to face him. "As much as I hate to admit it, he's right. I'm just using you. You're a novelty, something new and fun."

Pain clouded his eyes, and I couldn't look at him anymore. I gazed at the waves lapping the sides of the pool. "It's not fair to you. We need to end this now before someone really gets hurt."

"Do you love me?"

I froze at his question. My heart screamed to answer him. "What does that have to do with anything?"

"It is a simple question, Samantha. Yes or no?"

"No," I whispered.

I felt him rise and take a step away.

"You are lying," he said. "I do not know why when you were the one telling me to take a chance last night."

Ironic how I could dish out that little bit of advice. And now that I wanted to follow it myself, I couldn't. Not without getting the man I cared about permanently dead.

I dragged my eyes up to meet his. "I haven't lied to you since I met you, St. James. Last night was a mistake, and I'm sorry I hurt you." *Oh God, please make him leave before I start crying.*

"I see." His voice was as cold as his expression. "I am sorry too, Miss Ridgeway." I turned back to the pool and listened to the click of his boots as he strode back into the house.

The tears slid down my face as my heart shattered. My emotional bullshit would be enough to cover my thoughts from the other vamps, so for once in my life I let myself feel. Max was right. The few times my breakups weren't mutual, I initiated them to protect myself from falling for the guy.

Except Jake. He had been the one exception, and I deliberately fucked that one up too.

Yep, I deserved to be alone.

Surprisingly, no one came out to check on me. For once, the entire household left me alone. I wasn't sure if this was a good thing or not, but I didn't have to guard my thoughts for much longer. Close to dawn, the lights went out in the upstairs bedrooms one by one as everyone headed for bed. Except the kitchen light. They left it on, probably for me.

Voices speaking what sounded like Japanese filtered up from the guard house. The security detail's shift change. Good. The two Normal women who comprised the day guard wouldn't be a problem.

Fingers of pale blue light spread across the sky, followed by purple and pink. I couldn't remember the last time I had watched a sunrise. High school graduation maybe? The import struck me. If my plan didn't work, this could be my last.

I rose and went inside. The stillness was eerie in the early morning. Most people would be getting up and ready for work.

I crept up to Duncan's room and eased the door open. The sliver of light from the hall illuminated his broad chest and his right arm thrown over his eyes. The navy sheet covered him to the waist. Well, it did in theory. Certain parts were thrown into relief by the hall light. I sighed. His package was impressive at rest. And downright spectacular when he used it. Oh, he did know how to use it too.

His chest rose and fell in a steady rhythm from sleep. I eased the door closed and tiptoed to the bed. He deserved so much more than what I could give him, but I couldn't resist saying good-bye. I bent and placed a light kiss on his lips.

I never saw him move. I landed with a thump on the bed, pinned in place by his very powerful limbs. Okay, something new to add to my list of stupid things not to repeat—don't kiss a sleeping vampire.

Who was now a very wide-awake and irritated vampire. I squirmed, trying to get loose. Make that a wide-awake, irritated, and aroused vampire. And the pressure of his growing erection pushed my own thoughts south.

"What the bloody hell are you doing in my room?"

"Ummm . . ." I couldn't think with him touching me. All I wanted was to rip my own clothes off and join in the nakedness. And, lordy, the damn sheet wasn't covering anything anymore.

"Samantha." The evident warning in his tone didn't help.

"I don't know." I struggled some more, but with my hands trapped above my head, the only thing I did was rearrange my t-shirt. And not in a good way if I wanted to avoid sex.

He frowned at me, his eyes gleaming neon green in the darkness, also not a good sign. "What do you mean, you do not know?"

"I said I don't know," I snapped. "Now get off me!"

His frown switched to a sly grin. "In my day, there was only one purpose for a woman to be in a gentleman's bed chambers." One hand reached down to stroke the skin bared by my skewed shirt.

"So where's the chamber pot for me to empty?" I ripped back. My body betrayed my voice. His touch sent tremors through me, ignited my own desires. I was in serious danger, in more ways than one. I yanked my hands, but his one-handed hold was like steel cuffs.

Handcuffs are an excellent idea, darling.

His canines were white against his grinning lips. My breath harshened, and not from my fight to get free.

I licked my lips and tried to calm my racing heart. "Why are handcuffs an excellent idea?"

"All the better to keep you with," he murmured. His hand slid underneath my shirt, palmed my breast and thumbed my erect nipple through the lace bra.

I really should have bought the cotton granny underwear. The flimsy lace did nothing to restrict his access. If anything, the rasp of the material added its own sensual counterpoint to his strokes.

Keeping my mental shields intact under his sexual onslaught became impossible. A rush of desire flooded through me. I wasn't sure where his feelings ended and mine began.

His mouth found my other breast, his tongue keeping time with his thumb through the flimsy material until I squirmed and bucked. I wanted to touch him, but he kept me firmly pinned between his body and the bed.

He raised his head to blow lightly across the damp lace. The sensation sent ripples through my abdomen. Muscles clenched, demanding release and not from his imprisoning hold. A low moan started at the back of my throat.

No, I couldn't do this. I couldn't endure losing him. A strange pushing sensation rippled through my head, and Duncan jerked back as if I had slapped him.

"Do not shut me out." His voice half pleaded and half growled his words. "Samantha?"

"I can't do this, Duncan." I didn't realize I was crying until my voice sobbed out the words.

He released my hands and sat up. Pulling me into his lap, he cradled and rocked me against his chest. Incoherent murmurs whispered in my ear while I cried. The remaining tears I hadn't shed while sitting in the garden poured out.

After a while, the sobs petered out. I wanted to stay like this, just him and me. None of this other undead bullshit. Why couldn't I be a normal girl and he be a normal guy and we go on normal dates like the evening at the street carnival? I clutched my shoulders at the frustration.

He stroked damp strands of hair away from my face for a long time before he spoke, his touch comforting instead of arousing. "Are you going to tell me what tonight was about?"

I shook my head, not trusting myself to keep my plan secret.

His deep sigh ruffled the dry hairs on top of my head. "I am sorry if I frightened you."

I couldn't stop the smirk on my face. "Yeah, right. Like you ever scared me when I was alive."

He chuckled. "Forgive me for my assumptions."

I sat up to look him in the eye. "I'm sorry about earlier. I'm just not sure—" The unfamiliar emotions made me fumble for words. Until I discovered Duncan St. James, I had never had this problem in my life.

Desire rose, and I beat it back. Sex was too fucking risky no matter how much I wanted it. Hurting him again was not an option. I shouldn't have done it earlier.

A deep breath, and I tried again. "You're taking this way too fast. I died less than a week ago, and you're talking major commitment. The 'L' word." I grinned, hoping to ease the sting of my words. "Which in our case, literally means forever. I need some space and we'll see what happens."

His fingertips traced my temple and cheekbones as I held my breath. After a long, slow exhale, he nodded. "Would you stay?"

My eyes must have crossed in confusion because he added, "In my room." He smiled. "Just sleep."

"Put some pants on."

A bemused expression passed over his face, and he cocked an eyebrow. "Would that really stop us?"

"Please."

My tone convinced him to rise and scrounge a pair of silk pajama bottoms. Once we settled in his bed, he resumed stroking my hair.

Okay, stroking good, mind-reading not good. My muscles relaxed when I realized he was serious. He didn't push, didn't even try to cop an "accidental" feel. I don't think I ever had done the platonic in bed with a guy before.

It was . . . nice.

I snuggled closer and burrowed my head in the crook of his shoulder. The fresh scent of soap mingled with sandalwood and his own special maleness. My plan could wait a little while I indulged in some cuddle-time.

His caresses slowed then stopped as sleep claimed him. A half hour flew by as his soft snores filled the room. I didn't want to leave.

I couldn't see the man I loved get turned to meat slush either.

I eased from under the covers, but his eyes popped open the instant my feet hit the floor. "Where are you going?"

Thank God, my stomach decided to rumble before he finished his question. I flipped him a grin, and said, "You have to ask?" I bent to plant a quick smooch on his cheek, but he shifted his head at the last instant and grasped the back of my neck. His lips demanded mine open. His tongue lavished me in such a way I almost crawled back into bed.

Almost.

"Hold that thought until after I eat." I climbed back to my feet from my precarious perch on the side of the bed.

"I'll come with you." He flipped the covers back and started to swing his legs over. Oh mama, the p.j.'s were worse than just the sheets.

I waved him back. "No, get some sleep. Tonight's going to be insane enough." I leaned over and, this time, managed to peck him on the forehead. "I'll be back as soon as I clean out the fridge."

I'm such a liar.

The quizzical look he shot me made wonder if he actually heard my thought. Instead of confronting me, he nodded and lay back down.

Even with the UV film, the morning sun blinded me as I stumbled into the kitchen.

"Morning." Tiffany's cheery greeting made me jam my elbow into a cabinet. I really needed to remember to use my brand spankin' new zombie radar.

"Mornin'," I mumbled back. I snatched a mug out of the cupboard and poured the coffee Tiffany had already brewed.

"I didn't know if you wanted pancakes or waffles, so I made both."

Her appearance finally impacted the brain cells still obsessing over Duncan. Plain black tee, leggings, and sneakers. No fishnet, no hardware installed in or draped over various body parts, no make-up. The happy talk clinched my suspicions.

"You're pregnant, aren't you?"

Tiffany responded by flipping me off before flipping the over-easy eggs she had been frying onto a plate and shoving said plate into my free hand.

The jerk of the universe righting itself knocked me and my breakfast into a waiting chair.

"I figured we both needed a good meal before we head over to Mallory's." She plunked down in the chair across from me and proceeded to douse her own plate of eggs in a thick layer of ketchup.

"You know, Max hates ketchup on anything. And we have several hours before going to Mallory's." I frowned. "And you're not going, re-member?"

She shoveled a forkful of the red and yellow mess into her mouth. "Max'll just have to deal. And I'm going with you."

"Your uncle said you weren't going. If my uncle was a vampire, I wouldn't be pissing him off." My eggs devoured, I forked a couple of waf-fles onto my plate.

"At least my uncle's not Satan spawn." She speared some sausages.

"Hey, that's your future mother-in-law you're talking about. And I'm the only one who's allowed to call her Satan spawn." I snagged a couple more waffles then slathered a quarter-pound of margarine over them. I frowned at her while I reached for the bottle of Aunt Jemima. "Where'd you hear her called Satan spawn anyway?"

"Max. And I didn't say I was going with the group. I'm going early with you when you drive over this morning."

Her statement startled me so much I didn't notice I was still pouring syrup until it ran over my plate and into my lap.

"Shit!" I slammed the bottle down, which sent a spray of sticky drop-lets over the rest of the table. "What the hell are you blathering about?"

She jumped up, snatched the roll of paper towels off the counter and tossed them to me. "You're going over early to confront the bitch queen." She shrugged, undaunted by my glare of death. "You'll need backup."

I dabbed up the syrup running off the table and onto my jeans. "It's too dangerous."

She ran a dish towel under the faucet. "I had five kills before I hit high school. You've only staked one person, and she wasn't even a vamp."

I knew Duncan would hate me for sure if I got his niece killed. "What makes you think I'll take you?"

"I'll wake up Duncan if you don't."

I sighed. Goth Girl had a point. I guess I was breaking in a partner.

Chapter 27

After an hour, I decided maybe the teen terror would be an asset after all. We had gone out to the guesthouse where Caesar had created an exercise room. It wasn't the typical Brentwood aerobics and weight room. Swords from various eras hung on one wall, their appearance hardly decorative. He collected everything from Roman pikes and Mongolian cavalry bows to the latest in Glocks.

Tiffany demonstrated a few moves and a few weapons. She outlined the best method to get past Caesar's day guards. It sounded like she had plenty of experience in that department.

I filled her in on my plans.

"Kill Sierra and blow up the lab?" Tiffany's incredulous look didn't reinforce my confidence. "That's it?"

I crossed my arms and gave her the evil eye. "You've got a better plan? Then let's hear it."

She sighed and shook her head. "We'll need some C-4." She pulled open another cabinet door, removed a lid from a plastic container and pulled out what looked like a handful of talcum powder. She started playing with it, and in seconds, she had a wad of what looked like white Play-Doh in her palm.

"No." I held up a hand. From the little lesson Jake gave me when he was planning stunts for a Jackie Chan movie, C-4 was a very stable explosive. The knowledge didn't stop the nervous twitch in my gut when Tiffany started tossing the fist-sized mass into the air and catching it.

"No?"

I pointed at her R-rated toy. "Someone told me once the manufacturers put some kind of chemical marker in that stuff. Do you want to take the chance of it being traced back to Caesar?"

She looked at me, at the wad, and back at me. "Fine." She laid the C-4 in the canister and sealed it before closing the door. "What did you have in mind?"

Tiffany had the nonchalance I'd imagined in a Navy SEAL. Not that I was going to live long enough to meet a real live SEAL. Damn. And I'd always wanted to interview the ex-Governor of Minnesota.

"You have so gotta stop thinking terminally." Tiffany pulled her head out of the second storage closet. She rolled her eyes as she handed me a large messenger bag and a crossbow. "You're going to get us both killed."

"Would you stop reading my mind? It's creepy enough when the vamps do it."

A sour expression twisted her lipstick-free mouth. "I can't."

Not again. Anger at my own ineptitude with my new abilities flared.

"Would you freakin' stop screaming 'oh shit' in my head?" Tiffany slapped her hands over her ears.

Yeah, right. Like that would shield her from my mental shrieking. I had been so worried about keeping the vamps out I forgot my little nanite pals could transmit to everyone else as well.

"I remember what happened in the townhouse kitchen Sunday night." She reached up and smacked the side of my head. "Now, practice blocking or someone in the mansion is going to *hear* you."

I was getting very, very tired of everyone bitching at me about abilities I didn't want, much less could control. The same blackness welling deep inside I had felt earlier with Duncan snapped into place. Tiffany jerked and staggered back a couple of steps as if I had physically struck her.

Her eyes didn't just bulge. If she were a Looney Tunes character, they'd be out of their sockets and rolling on the floor now. "How the hell did you do that?" she whispered.

"I don't know." Guilt assailed me. I grabbed her arm to steady her. "Are you okay? I'm so sorry."

"Little bit of a headache." She studied me, more curious than fearful. "Your little talent may come in handy. Almost felt like a witch's psy-slap." She grinned. "The zombie equivalent of one anyway. Have you tried that stunt on anyone else?"

I grinned back, reassured I hadn't given her a brain aneurysm by accident. "Your uncle."

She laughed outright before she slid some silver knives into her bag. "He probably deserved it. So what did you have in mind for the lab?"

My grin widened. "Don't most laboratories have volatile chemicals?"

A matching smile spread across Tiffany's face and she nodded. "Make it look like an accident." She hefted the canvas strap over her arm. "Ready to go kick some zombie ass?"

I shouldered my weapons bag and gestured towards the garage. "Lead the way, Goth Girl."

She whipped around, fixing me with a stare more pointed than the dagger strapped to her ankle. "What did you call me?"

Oops.

We were three miles away from Mallory Labs before Tiffany let my slipup go.

Sort of.

"So what the hell do you call my uncle behind his back?" she snarled. How she could sound so evil around the wad of bubblegum in her mouth was beyond me.

But I was so not going there. Besides Duncan would need a new category. Super Stud? Rod of Steel? Just thinking about him gave me warm, gushy feelings, totally inappropriate for the maiming, killing, and general destruction I planned to do in the next few hours.

"Well . . ." Tiffany's acid tongue brought my attention back to her. And the road. I stomped on the brakes to keep from mowing down the jogger who darted across the road. I returned his friendly middle-finger wave before answering her.

"Look, how many times do I have to say 'I'm sorry'?" I shot her a grin. "Besides, you're way cooler than Chris O'Donnell in *Batman Forever*."

She made a gagging noise. "The Olsen twins are way cooler than him. Unless you count *The Three Musketeers*. He was cute with long hair."

Whipping Caesar's Hummer around a corner, I snorted in amusement. "I can't see Duncan letting you watch any movie having to do with a French theme."

"It's the Disney version, so he cut me some slack." She laughed. "You're right though. In his book, the only thing worse than a French story is *Buffy* and *Angel*."

Our conversation halted at the same time I braked at the main gate. I couldn't see the point of driving into the employee spill-over lot Duncan and Tiffany had used for their surveillance missions. Besides it wasn't like we were bothering to sneak into the damn place.

The goon who checked our IDs wasn't one I had assaulted, mangled, or otherwise encountered in my two previous trips inside the labs. His intense scrutiny still made me nervous. Tiffany's gum made a loud *pop*, and I jumped.

I glared at her while the goon circled the Hummer. "Would you stop chewing that?"

"No." Snap, snap. "It keeps me focused."

The soft hissing of air followed her words. I swallowed the urge to prick the huge pink bubble.

"Ms. Mallory is expecting you, Ms. Ridgeway. Your escort will meet you in the visitor's parking lot."

I nodded as he handed back my ID and gave me directions before he waved us forward.

"See? No problem." *Pop, snap, snap.*

"Spit out the damn gum," I growled.

"It was your idea to waltz through the front door," Tiffany muttered, but she must have been afraid I'd brain-fry her for real. She fished out a scrap of paper and wadded up the mess.

Ignoring the butterflies chased by electric eels in my stomach, I guided the humongous vehicle into a spot and cut the engine. On the sidewalk, Kane rocked on his heels as he and a couple of more goons waited for us to join them. These two wore the standard rent-a-cop uniforms, but you could tell from their stance, they were anything but. And I could smell that they weren't vamps either, even if the early afternoon sun wasn't a dead giveaway.

Damn, this whole sixth sense thing came in handy.

"Weebles wobble but they don't fall down," Tiffany sang under her breath. She was right. Kane's pear-shape looked like it would pop right back up if knocked over, but I knew better.

"This one does if you hit him hard enough," I whispered back. We stepped onto the sidewalk, and both goons took a half step back. Then I caught the sharp, ashy scent emanating from them. Fear. I didn't understand why the odor would be a turn-on to vamps when the scent was more akin to a dirty grill. It made the eels and butterflies nauseous. Maybe my perception was due to my lack of bloodlust. But it was still good to know I made them half as nervous as they made me.

"I beg your pardon, Miss Ridgeway?" Kane smiled, but sweat beaded along the edge of his Adolph moustache.

Crossing my arms, I smiled back. "I was just telling the Girl Wonder here I'm surprised Tyrone didn't feed you to the werewolves for letting me escape."

If possible, Kane's skin transformed to a new, lighter shade of paste. His smile disappeared at the sniggers of the goons behind him. "Take their bags," he snapped before he spun on his heel and waddled for the door.

We handed over the totes to Goon No. 1 with the most token of protests. He unzipped and peered into each before giving a long low whistle. "Dr. Kane?"

Kane halted and peered over his shoulder. Goon No. 1 crossed the few yards and whispered to him, "These chicks are carrying some serious shit."

Have I said how much I love my new abilities?

Kane sneered. "Don't give it back to them, idiot." He continued his waddling.

Tiffany looked up at me and shrugged. Sierra's people would now relax, thinking they had disarmed us. We were fine as long as no one insisted on a strip search. And I seriously doubted Goon No. 2's interest in Tiffany's enhanced cleavage had anything to do with the weapons stuffed in her bra. The goons marched behind us while we followed Kane into the building.

As we crossed the lobby, I glanced up. Definitely a different view from the first floor, especially since I was conscious this time. I had to give a hand to their maintenance department. They'd patched up all the bullet holes from Sunday and repainted the walls.

Of course, Mallory's employee incentive program probably included the pit.

A nagging feeling of wrongness picked at me that had nothing to do with my own nerves. I peeked behind me as we followed Kane to a private elevator. More fear drifted from our escort. Heck, any werewolf or vamp would say I reeked of it too. But intermixed with the fear was something else, a tangy citrus coming from Tiffany.

I tried not to gulp when Kane pressed "1" after we boarded. I so didn't want to go back down there. I didn't have a choice now. The goons would shoot Tiffany and me in an instant. Tears threatened to spill from my anger at my own weakness. Fingernails dug into my palms as I fought for control. Lucky for me the nanites repaired my skin as fast as I shredded it.

To distract myself, I puzzled out the odd odor coming from Tiffany. Her lack of fear didn't make sense, but I was certain it wasn't exactly confidence either. Granted, she wasn't as fatalistic about our little expedition as I was. It was almost like . . . anticipation. But of what? She didn't have a personal grudge against Sierra. At least none I knew of.

I should be more concerned about why I know what a human emotion smells like.

For cryin' out loud! Quit wondering what I smell like. That is so sick, you perv!

Tiffany tried to glare at me without being obvious. I glanced at the men in the elevator. No one looked my way. Okay, good. I wasn't transmitting to everyone. A good thing Duncan wasn't with us. Then Kane and the guards would have a front seat to my X-rated fantasies.

Oh, gag me! I didn't need those thoughts in my head.

A loud groan filled the elevator at the same time as Tiffany's mental comment. The drama queen clutched her stomach and bent over. Everyone looked at her.

Kane eased away as far away as he could in the enclosed space. "What's wrong with her?"

"Motion sickness," I answered. I grabbed the kid to keep her upright. Instead of flinching, she quivered in my grasp. "And if she doesn't get a grip, I'm going to eat her." My stomach growled its agreement.

The goons plastered themselves in the back corners of the elevator, guns braced in front of them, but Tiffany stopped her silent giggles.

The elevator halted and Kane couldn't dive out fast enough. I released Tiffany, and she managed to keep her face straight when she rose. We followed Kane down the hallway with our guards several steps behind.

He escorted us into a large room, one that could have been something from an '80's video. Purple velvet hung from the walls, gold trimmed everything, and the furniture consisted of matching pillows surrounding low ebony tables.

Sierra reclined on one elbow in the middle of the room, giggling with a dark-haired woman. A woman who reeked of sandalwood. The frankly bullshit act on both their parts rubbed since I knew damn well they could smell us long before they saw us. Hell, Sierra's metallic odor nearly overpowered the vampire's signature sandalwood. When she glanced up us, she graced me with a seductive smile. That smile would have scared the bejeezus out of me even if I swung in the non-guy direction. The other woman sat up as well and slowly turned to face us.

I nearly had a heart attack when I got a good look at the second woman. The Elvira impersonator I thought had been a drug-induced nightmare smiled at me too, the tips of her fangs gleaming red in the subdued lighting.

She raised her goblet of blood towards us. "So glad you ladies could join us."

"Selene," Tiffany breathed.

I looked down at her in shock, but before I could ask anything, Goth Girl charged.

Chapter 28

Tiffany never stood a chance. The vampire was on her feet, holding the kid by the throat a foot off the ground before I could blink.

"Such a delightful gift, my dear. How did you know she was something I've always wanted?" The vampire's kohl-lined eyes narrowed, examining Tiffany with a mix of distaste and excitement.

"Let her go." My heart hammered triple time. I didn't know what to do. If I dared to touch her, she could break Tiffany's neck with a flick of her wrist. If the impression I'd received from Duncan and Alex was right, she wouldn't need much of an excuse.

The vampire looked at me, amusement flitting across her features. Tiffany's feet flailed, and her face shifted to an ugly bluish-purple color.

I'd gotten stories from sheer attitude and prayed my bluff would work this time. "Let. Her. Go." I stepped forward with each word. "If you want me on your side, Sierra, tell her to release the kid."

"Really, Selene. We don't want to upset poor Samantha by eating her little friend." Sierra had risen to stand beside her partner? Friend? She laid a hand on Selene's arm, the gesture weirdly intimate.

"She's a St. James. Worthless." Selene sneered, then she shrugged and tossed Tiffany to the side. Thank God, there were so many pillows. The kid bounced and rolled twice before coming to a stop against the wall. She lay there as she fought for oxygen, the continued racking sounds doing nothing to slow my heart.

"You okay?" I asked. I didn't dare move towards her and settled for keeping an eye on the bad girls. My gut clenched at the knowledge I wouldn't be able to stop both a zombie and a vamp from getting to the kid if they decided to kill her.

"Yeah." She coughed a few more times before sitting up.

Selene eyed me, curiosity evident. "She's not my offering?"

"Beg pardon?"

"My offering. To show your loyalty to me." She stepped towards me, giving me the rich bitch Rodeo Drive up-and-down.

Like I cared. Hell, I endured such torture every time I met a friend of Mom's. I checked her out in return. I had expected Duncan's maker to be some drop-dead platinum babe with a rack that wouldn't quit. She wasn't beautiful, not in any usual L.A. sense. More ethnic pretty like Nia Vardalos from *My Big Fat Greek Wedding*.

Then her words hit me, and I tried to paste an appropriately simpering smile on my mug. "Sorry, ma'am. I forgot the hostess gift. My mom'll tell you my manners are simply atrocious."

"What's she doing here?" Sierra nodded towards Tiffany.

I flicked my gaze between Sierra and Tiffany but addressed my remarks to the vamp. Even without Alex's warning about Duncan's maker, trust wasn't a word I'd associate with this woman. I'd have to play this very carefully. The struggle to act nonchalant frayed the few undead nerves I had left. I hadn't counted on dealing with a vampire queen in addition to Sierra.

"She got tired of her uncle bullying her around. When she figured out I was joining you, she asked if she could come."

Selene flicked an eyebrow upwards. "And you expect me to believe such an asinine story?"

A whisper touched the edge of my consciousness. Then a pressure, steadily increasing, a finger trying to drill through the middle of my forehead. I couldn't afford to give in to Selene's attempt to read my mind. They'd kill us both. Well, Tiffany would end up dead. Selene and Sierra would have to get extra creative for me.

Either way would be ugly.

"No, I don't," I replied, struggling not to show my effort. "But Augustine and his little group won't take the chance with an innocent kid's life and do something stupid, will they?" My lips curled into what I hoped was an appropriate evil grin. "I figured she'd be a useful hostage."

"You bitch." Tiffany's words devolved into another round of coughing. I couldn't warn her without tipping off the bad girls, so I crossed my toes she'd get a clue I was faking.

The mental pressure disappeared so suddenly I almost fell. Something very strange showed on the vampire's face at the mention of Caesar's name, a mixture of fury and regret. The Los Angeles vampires certainly had nothing on Peyton Place. If she was nuts enough to slaughter Duncan's family when he rejected her, I hated to think of what lay between Caesar and Selene.

"Then she's your responsibility." The vampire's soft voice raised gooseflesh on my arms. She edged closer until our noses were millimeters apart, Sierra sidling along beside her. "If she performs any inappropriate act, you both will pay."

I couldn't nod without head-butting her. I settled for muttering, "Fine," from between my clenched teeth.

"Sam will make sure the girl behaves," Sierra said, her tone a verbal stroke to match her free fingers running through my hair.

And I thought the vampire gave me the willies.

Sierra released Selene's arm and glided toward the door, executing little ballet twirls as she went. The switch between seductress and little girl so sudden I jerked when she paused at the doorway and spoke. "Cocktails begin at five. We need to find you both something suitable to wear, not to mention make-up and hair." She gave me a smile, one more predatory than seductive or innocent. "I can't wait to introduce you to everybody."

Selene followed the heiress, but shot me a look far colder and more calculating than Sierra's. She wouldn't hesitate to kill anyone who got in her way, including her so-called allies. I wondered if Sierra knew what she was getting into, not that it would matter to the psychotic bitch.

"Oh, Sam?" Sierra poked her head back in the room. "I'm glad you're here, but Kane told me something very disturbing." She clucked her tongue. "You really shouldn't have brought weapons, so I'll just have the boys put them in a safe place for you. Someone will collect you around four-forty-five. Can't have my new best friend late." She disappeared from sight, but I only heard the women's footsteps retreat down the hall.

Great. I rolled my neck, attempting to stretch the kinks out as Tiffany staggered to her feet. I had five hours to figure out how to kill Sierra, destroy the secret lab and get Tiffany out of here intact before the posse showed up and a lot of people died. My death was just getting better and better.

I can't believe neither of them even questioned why we had guns with us. It's not like regular bullets would stop either one of them, and we didn't have any vampire-specific ammo in those bags. Tiffany paused to examine her reflection in the full-length mirror before glaring at me over her shoulder. *Selene knows better.* Her nose wrinkled as she tugged at the gauzy neckline, her attitude more to do with the frilly LBD Sierra had selected for her.

Well, I did have that crossbow, and I don't think a vampire can recover from a full clip from a semi-automatic that fast.

She wrestled with where to hide the pencils she had been carrying, but the dress didn't leave a whole lot of options. *You'd be surprised, but still the whole thing was too easy.*

I'll remember that the next time a vamp plays softball with your skull. I'm amazed they didn't question my intentions further. I wasn't about to say anything aloud. Finally, I was starting to get the hang of this telepathy thing. The sending anyway. We hadn't found any cameras, but the bugs had been pretty obvious even to a neophyte like me, so we were trying to be careful. *Hearing* Tiffany had as much to do with her familiarity with the process than any talent on my part. It sure as hell wasn't as easy as Charlaine Harris made it out to be in her books. Though now, I began to wonder how much of her stories were true.

Tiffany raised her eyebrow as she watched me in the mirror. *Did Selene or Sierra try to read your mind?*

I hadn't figured out how to *read* other people on purpose who weren't intentionally sending their thoughts to me. But heck, it'd been less than a week since I died, and I had figured out the particular tickle signifying someone trying to poke her nose in my brain.

I nodded. *Selene tried. I don't think she got through. Otherwise, we wouldn't be having this discussion. Sierra couldn't find her own mind right now with both hands and a searchlight.*

Tiffany rolled her eyes in response before she continued her examination of potential hiding places in her dress.

After our little interview with the queens of the undead, the goon squad had escorted us to a good-sized bedroom with two double beds and a private bath. From the utilitarian look, it was probably a spare for when the staff spent the night.

Sierra had waltzed in a few minutes later with her personal dresser and a rack of frocks in tow. I never liked someone else picking out my clothes. The intense annoyance stemmed from Mom trying to dress me as her little princess. The stuff she had selected for me was worse than the number Tiffany currently wore. I started to rebel but then chewed a hole through my tongue to keep from making any flip comments to Psycho Zombie. Tiffany started to—once. A quick stomp on her instep changed her mind. It beat Sierra eating the kid's brains.

At least Sierra's armed escort hadn't followed Tiffany and me into the bathroom as we tried on each outfit. The fact Sierra picked out undies and a garter to match the royal blue sheath I wore was bad enough.

To top it off, Sierra had sent a make-up artist, manicurist and hair stylist in, so we never had a chance to ditch the guards, retrieve our bags, and blow up the joint.

Which meant we'd have to be creative with what little we had.

Tiffany settled on sticking the pencils in the built-in shelf bra of her dress. The goon squad missed them during the second pat down. *We'll have a better chance in the confusion of the party.* She gave a little wiggle to make sure nothing fell out.

I sighed and tugged at the too tight silk. *I don't want to be responsible for any more innocents dying.*

She pivoted to face me, her elfin face hard. *Buy a clue. Selene plays for keeps.* Eyelids pinched shut, but I already glimpsed the tears gathering. *She killed Ptolemy, her own brother.*

Bile gathered at the back of my throat. No wonder Caesar had thrown out his sister. Something else was in Tiffany's voice. Grief. She must have known this Ptolemy. If all of Duncan's friends had helped raise her . . .

Shit. I really didn't know how Tiffany kept it together. If I faced someone who'd taken everything important in my life from me, I'd be a basket-case right now.

Brown eyes snapped open, eyes that had seen too much ugliness in such a short lifetime. Tiffany sucked in a deep breath and focused with an obvious effort. *Anyone joining her won't hesitate to kill us either. Or have you forgotten what Sierra did to her own father?*

I shook my head. Only the crunch of Charlie and Nurse Ratchett's broken skulls beat the crack of Tyrone Mallory's neck in my memory. Psychiatrists would make a fortune off my nightmares for the next million years.

Tiffany examined the pointed heel of the stiletto Sierra chose for her. *Remember what I said about killing vamps?*

I nodded. Contrary to all the stories and movies from my childhood, Tiffany had explained there were only two sure ways to kill a vampire— anything through the heart or decapitation. Unless delivered in a concentrated, liquefied form into the blood stream, silver or garlic were unpredictable, just like some folks were highly allergic to bees while a sting was a mild irritant to others. Holy water and religious paraphernalia were all Hollywood inventions. She swore a No. 2 in the right spot worked a hell of a lot better than a stake. It didn't reassure me about our chances. Especially since neither of us had a clue whether the nanites conformed Sierra and me to the same headless limitations as the vampires. I'd already found out the hard way staking didn't work.

The thought of shoving something through someone's heart made me want to puke. More visions of Nurse Ratchett and Charlie swam in front of my eyes, taunting me. What was I thinking by coming here? I sank down on one of the beds and laid my head in my hands.

A scrawny arm wrapped around my shoulder. *You didn't have a choice. She would have chased you down once she realized the self-destruct failed if you hadn't come.*

I raised my head to look at her. A haunted kid returned my gaze. A groan issued from my mouth. She had seen everything I had just remembered. I really needed to watch my transmissions. "I'm sorry. You shouldn't have to deal with my shit. Not on top of yours anyway."

She tossed a quick one-shoulder shrug. "It's not easy killing anyone. I killed my first vamp when I was twelve."

It was hard to remember she was barely out of high school. And why was she talking out loud now?

So whoever's listening in on us knows we won't be easy snacks.

I grinned at her comment and played along. "What happened?"

A sad, ironic smile twisted her lips. "I skipped school and didn't make it home before dark. One of Selene's people caught me. And I staked him with the handiest available wood." She patted her chest where she had hidden her ammo. *Now, you know why I rely on these.*

A new sickness spread through my stomach. I saw all too often what happened to the regular kids on Hollywood Boulevard. Now that I knew what else could be preying on them, nausea wrapped a fist around my gut and squeezed.

"So how long were you grounded?"

She laughed at my obvious attempt to lighten the mood. "Two months of no phone or T.V. and another six months without my game system. Phillippa escorted me to and from school for the rest of the year. Do you have any idea how embarrassing that is?"

"I can imagine." Mom had done something similar when I was fourteen though it wasn't like I had Wonder Woman and the vamps looking over my shoulder like Tiffany did. I never figured out how I always got caught and Max never did. Maybe Anne put the whammy on Mom for him.

A sharp rap on the door jerked us both out of our nostalgic, morbid reverie. "Show time," I muttered.

The human goons escorted us back to the elevator and up to the main lobby. When we stepped out, polite chit-chat rumbled through my eardrums. A tsunami of scent assaulted my nose. Once the sensory overload washed past me, I took a good look around.

Strands of tiny white bulbs wound their way around indoor palms. A dais perched to the left of the main staircase, a huge LED screen showing the Mallory logo behind it. Men in penguin suits and glittering women milled around, performing the Los Angeles meet-n-greet, also known as bone crushing handshakes and air kisses. In other words, the reception area looked like any other ritzy corporate party.

A tentative sniff told me the mix of folks in the room was not the usual for corporate America. Over the last few days, I had started to distinguish which scents belonged to which species. The sheer quantity of sandalwood in the air indicated a large number were vamps despite the early evening sunlight streaming through the three-story high windows. I hated to think of how much the ton of bullet-proof, polarized glass cost. Apple indicated Normals. What I'd mistaken for a certain brand of lotion on Bebe had been a witch's ginger signature with her own unique smell. I glanced around but couldn't place who or what gave off a honey odor.

The intermingling of odors definitely made me wonder just who all really held stock in Mallory Labs. That and considering the sheer amount of muscle-for-hire decorating each possible entrance.

Buffet tables framed the room, piled high with shrimp, egg rolls and the typical hors d'oeuvres. We joined the line of people snaking around the food. Our tuxedo-clad escort hung back at the edge of the crowd, close enough to keep an eye on us, but not close enough for an accusation of eating on the boss's time.

Okay, maybe Sierra didn't serve typical hors d'oeuvres. The red stuff spilling out of the centerpiece fountain definitely wasn't cold champagne.

The coppery smell of blood overwhelmed me for an instant. I fought the urge to retch in front of the crowd. Even Tiffany wrinkled her nose in distaste at the bloody prime rib a caterer slapped on a plate of someone ahead of us.

Of course, my stomach chose that moment to growl so loudly the couple in front of us turned to stare. They both carried the musky scent I was learning to associate with weres. The man had a couple of inches on me, filled out his suit in the broad, muscular sense, and sported a ten o'clock shadow at five in the afternoon. I wanted to tell him his purple paisley tie had gone out with Prince, when he was the artist known as Prince the first time around.

The were gave me an appraising look before he smiled the predatory type of toothy grin men had been giving women for millennia. "I like a woman with a good appetite."

Before I could phrase a comeback, his face twisted in a spasm of pain. A quick check showed his companion's left hand gripping his package. She was barely taller than Tiffany, but she left no doubt of who was in charge.

"Apologize to the nice—" The brunette stopped to give me a delicate sniff. "I'm sorry, Miss, but what the hell are you?"

I wasn't sure how to answer her question. Not the weirdly rude politeness of the were, but I wasn't sure what to call myself.

Tiffany was. "She's a zombie, Pack Mistress."

I glanced at her. She had her neck at an odd angle, and she kept her eyes on the floor. All those articles I'd read about dealing with threatening dogs must apply to werewolves.

"Glad to see your pup has some manners unlike some people." She squeezed, and the male were whimpered softly. "What's your name, sweetie?"

"Sam. Sam Ridgeway." I started to hold out my hand and stopped. *What the hell is proper protocol when meeting a were, especially when she's holding her guy's balls in public?*

The lady were grinned at me. "Handshake's fine." She reached over to grab my hand with her free one, still not letting go of her mate.

My thought had been aimed at Tiffany. I prayed I hadn't just accidentally transmitted it to the weres.

"I'm Emily. This here son-of-a-bitch is my husband, George."

She finally released the male, and he edged back a hair. "I apologize, Miss." His voice carried the same Texas twang as his wife's.

My stomach took the awkward break in the conversation to growl even louder.

Emily slapped me on the back. "Let's get you some food, Sam."

Once our plates were loaded, the lady were led us to the tables surrounding the dais. Her husband kept his silence but regarded me with a speculative eye. He wasn't stupid enough for another obvious sexual leer. More like a puzzle piece he had been considering had fallen into place.

The human goons trailed behind us but didn't interfere.

"So, are you what Selene's big announcement is all about?" Emily asked once we sat and spread napkins.

My mouth was crammed full of crab cake so Tiffany responded. "I'm afraid we cannot answer your inquiry at this time, Pack Mistress." She kept her eyes fixed on her plate.

Wow, who'd've thought Goth Girl had a political bent.

"So how'd you become a zombie, Sam?" Emily wasn't about to let the subject go.

I swallowed and nearly choked on the cake. "That's a long story, Miss Emily." I frowned at my faux pas. "I'm sorry. Pack Mistress."

She laughed and laid a hand on my arm. The nails were manicured but short with no polish. I suppose hot pink lacquer wouldn't translate well on a wolf's claws. Probably why she had a short, stylish cut instead of the usual Lone Star bouffant.

"Emily, sweetie. Call me Emily. You'd be an Alpha if you were one of us. I can tell."

"Thank you." At least it seemed like a compliment. A strange gurgle came from Tiffany's bent head. I suppressed the urge to smack her.

A group of tall Scandinavian-looking folks started to sit at the table next to us. The men were as impossibly attractive as the women, and everyone's hair was an equally impossible shade of platinum blond. As one, they all turned to stare at me. Then they rose and glided to another table much further away.

"I thought zombies were a figment of Voudon imagination," George said. He didn't seem to notice the statuesque blond folks' strange behavior. His assessing look was starting to make me nervous.

"As far as I know, we're a pretty rare breed." I plastered a fake smile on my mug, but it didn't fool the weres.

"Rumor is Selene's latest girlfriend has come up with a vaccine to the V-Virus. Are you a byproduct?" George said.

This whole conversation verged on the edge of ugly. Not that I was offended, but I wasn't sure how much to tell the couple. They seemed nice enough, but who knew how much of their act was just an act. It had taken our little cadre a few days to put everything together. And if the weres were shareholders in the Mallory holding company, lord only knew how deep they were in this shit.

"I'm sorry, but I don't know anything about a vaccine."

George shrugged and dropped his question. "Doesn't matter. It's not like we can catch it. There's another rumor going around the younger witches can't catch it either."

The were's little tidbit was certainly food for thought. Is that how Bebe lived with Caesar without becoming infected? I didn't know for sure, but the witch doctor didn't appear to be much older than me.

And Duncan assumed Sierra was holding a potential cure over the vamps' heads, but Selene didn't strike me as so stupid that Sierra could pull that kind of blackmail on her. So what exactly were the two of them up to?

"My goodness, child! You sure can pack away the food." Emily held her hand to her chest. "You sure you aren't part were, Sam?"

I looked down. My plate was bare, and I couldn't remember eating a damn thing besides the crab cake. My stomach warbled its desire for more food.

"George, why don't you get Sam another plate?" It wasn't a request.

Once he was gone, Emily smiled at me but not the friendly Southern grin from earlier. "Now, dear, tell me how you came about?"

I felt her hand in my thigh and not in the friendly I'm-tired-of-pretending-I'm-straight touch. Several sharp somethings dug into my skin just above the edge of my stocking. I bit my lip to keep from yelping and glanced down to see a fur covered paw with very long claws piercing my skin.

"You can answer my questions, or I'll gut you and St. James' pup before you can scream." Golden wolf eyes replaced Emily's hazel human ones.

Tiffany jerked in response, but I didn't dare look at her.

"Yes, dear," Emily said. "I recognize you from the I.C. I don't forget a scent."

The I.C.? Was this Caesar's mysterious Council?

She returned her attention to me. "And I wouldn't count on your pathetic human escort to rescue you." My gaze flicked to our totally oblivious goons holding up the wall a short distance away.

A chilly, thin smile twisted Emily's face. "Considering the animosity between the Antonius twins for the last two years, I was suspicious the moment I saw your little friend. Now, Sam, who created you and why?"

Who the hell were these Antonius people she was talking about? Was a chasm I couldn't see opening under my feet, or could Emily and George possibly be potential allies? Time was running out on my options. Deciding Tiffany's intestines were worth saving, I gave the pack mistress an edited version of recent events.

After a minute, she released my leg. I blessed my speed healing and the blood fountain. Without both, I would have attracted every vamp in the place. As it was, the rents and tiny blood spots ruined the silk dress.

"That's why you and the Mallory girl smell like steel." She said it more to herself than to us. She smiled at me, the wide toothy grin far more feral than her eyes had been. "No wonder the sidhe have been giving you such a wide berth."

"The 'she'?" I had the distinct feeling of sinking even deeper into supernatural political quicksand.

She nodded towards the Swedish Bikini Team on the other side of the room, who had refused to sit next to us and kept giving me strange looks. I still must have had a stupid look on my face. Emily snorted in exasperation and rolled her eyes. "Fairies, dear."

Now, my attention was riveted on the group. They were all in the six-foot range, the women a couple inches shorter maybe. White-blond hair covered everyone's ears so I couldn't tell if they were pointed. "I thought they were smaller."

Emily shrugged. "That table's all Unseelie elves. They and the Seelie are the largest of the sidhe."

Fairies were nature spirits, and considering what bees did with nectar . . .

I shot Emily a curious look. "Is that why they smell like honey?"

She slapped her hand on the table and roared with laughter. "No doubt your nose works just fine, girl."

The organ in question twitched when George plunked a dish full of shrimp, apple wedges and brie in front of me. I crammed a piece of cheese-smeared fruit in my mouth, but not before I noticed a subtle look between the two weres and a slight shake of the head from Emily. At the same time, a couple of vamps across the room spotted us.

I swallowed hard. Time to take a chance. "What ever you want, ask fast. We're about to have company."

The words came out of Emily in a near-silent, breathless rush. "We're looking for our son, Logan, who disappeared four months ago. He's friends with an Augustine vampire named Stanton."

Holy crap! Somehow I could tell without telepathic contact she wasn't lying. Things were starting to look up in my little plan. "He was here. He's fine now, and he's escorting a witch family to safety." Apparently, the dumbass were hadn't called anyone before cutting out of Caesar's place. My words were so quiet I could barely hear them, but Emily's eyes closed in relief as the uglier of the two vamps clasped my shoulder.

"Her majesty wants to see you."

Wow, I didn't realize how full of herself Sierra had become. Or he could be referring to Selene. I nipped a shrimp to the tail, trying to ignore him and the smell of rotten lemons surrounding him. Someone was in a pissy mood.

"Now," he muttered and jerked me up. Last week, my shoulder would have been dislocated from the force.

Selene and Sierra must be done playing nice, or they decided they didn't want me talking to the Texas weres. It was beginning to look like the bad guys hadn't been snatching supernatural folks randomly after all.

"You forgot to say 'please,' asshole." George's words came out in a growl, and he rose from the table. The air sizzled from Emily's tension beside me as she jumped to her feet as well.

"It's all right, Pack Master." I gave him a demure smile before I turned to the vampire. "I'm sure Selene's friend here didn't mean to be so rude." I leaned as forward as I could with the vise clamp on my upper arm and mock whispered, "I've noticed it's a failing common with male vampires."

Emily chuckled, and George's shoulders eased though the menacing scowl on his face didn't. Tall, Dark and Ugly didn't look one bit amused.

I nodded to the lady were. "It's been a pleasure, Pack Mistress. We must talk more later. Come along, Tiffany."

I spun on the ridiculously high heels so fast the vamp lost his grip on me. I amazed myself by not losing my balance and stalked off through the crowd. I felt Tiffany trotting behind me and the two vamps trailing her.

So intent on the fairies and weres, I didn't realize full dark had fallen until the lights dimmed as we approached the dais. The crowd quieted at the signal. When Selene stepped from a curtain draped across the entry to the private areas, the buzz of excited conversation echoed through the reception area.

The bodyguards flanking her sent cold slime down my spine. They looked like typical muscle, but a wrongness surrounded them. It wasn't just the scary predator stuff. I breathed deeply, trying to get a handle on our escort. It was more like . . .

Yes. I bit my tongue to keep from saying my thought out loud. A sharp, putrid lemony scent, mixed with ginger, ozone, and blood, began to fill the room. Selene's vamps had been amped somehow through magick, their anticipation and intentions somehow corrupting their normal odors. The bitches had one or more witches on the payroll as well as the rogue vamps.

Or the witches were more captives those two had threatened or out-

and-out blackmailed. Either way, the end result didn't bode well for the folks in the room.

More vampires covered the exits, effectively imprisoning everyone in the reception area. Everyone was so intent on Selene approaching the microphone I don't think they noticed. I had little doubt to whom the guards owed their allegiance. Funny though, none of the human members of the Mallory goon squad were anywhere in the room now. Even our original Normal escort had disappeared. Did Sierra know her soiree had been co-opted?

"A bright new day dawns for all of us," Selene began. She really needed a new speech writer.

Tiffany slid her tiny hand into mine and squeezed. *Can you hear me?*

I nearly jumped out of my skin at her voice in my head. *Yeah.* I squeezed back in case I wasn't transmitting to her.

"You've all heard the rumors about a cure for the V-virus. Let me say they are partly true." A murmur ran through the assemblage. "What if you could retain all you've become and walk in the daylight?" Selene asked the crowd.

We're not going to make it out of here. Tiffany's voice in my head was firm and commanding, not the voice of a terrified teenager. Why wasn't she scared? I, on the other hand, was about to piss my designer panties.

"What if you could wear your silver jewelry again, ladies?" Her words brought a few sprinkles of feminine laughter from the crowd.

I tried not to be obvious as I scanned the room. *No shit. I need to get you out of here. Maybe I could leverage a favor out of George and Emily.*

"What if you could eat again? Even—" Selene paused for a breathless instant, "—chocolate?" Laughter rang through the room. I had to give the ancient vamp credit; she could work a room.

Tiffany ignored me. *You need to keep the bodyguards off me long enough for me to take out Selene.*

You're nuts! This isn't going to work. I don't know what I was thinking.

But I did know. I wasn't thinking. Just like I didn't think during the South Central riots. Just like I didn't when Ralph told me to lay off Duncan. Just like I didn't after Fred was killed. I was so damn intent on my goal I didn't stop and think of the consequences. Oh god, if anything happened to Tiffany, Duncan would never forgive me.

"I'd like you to meet the newest member of my family, Sierra Mallory." Polite applause accompanied Sierra to the podium. She could have been Selene's photo negative. Diamonds and black velvet covered her compared Selene's onyx jewelry and white satin gown. The dress cuts were exactly the same with the same upswept 'do.

Sierra didn't wince at Selene's claim on her either. Had the vamp mindfucked her? Was that the cause of the heiress's psychosis?

Sierra favored the crowd with a confident smile. "Ladies and gentlemen, thank you for coming tonight. For all of Her Majesty's theatrics, our product is simple."

"Her Majesty" was Selene. Fuck. Why didn't anyone tell me Duncan's maker was literally a vampire queen?

"My company has developed a solution to your problems." Sierra smiled at the crowd. On the LED screen, an image of a spidery-looking robot hovered over the heads of the two women. "This is a nanite." The spider began a slow rotation. "A microscopic machine that can rewrite any entity's genetic code. It can literally fix the defects in the V-virus, allowing a vampire to live in the daylight and eat without losing any of the benefits, such as superior strength and eternal youth."

Tiffany and I shared wide-eyed looks. I swallowed hard.

What'll happen when the vamps find out she's lying?

I don't want to be here when they do. Her grim look underscored her thought.

"I'm sure the rest of our guests are asking what's in it for you." Sierra's gaze swept the crowd before locking eyes with me. "Anything you want." Her attention returned to the crowd. "I was a Normal. Last Friday I was in the final stages of leukemia. The doctors said I wouldn't make it through this week."

She stepped back from the mike and twirled, the long velvet skirt of her dress flaring at the motion. "Thanks to nanites developed by Mallory Labs, I'm standing before you healthy." Her eyes glittered. "Strong. Alive."

There was a *whoosh* and a *thunk.* Scarlet feathers blossomed in the middle of Sierra's chest. Eyes wide in shock, she stared up at the balcony to her right.

"Sorry, Miss Mallory." Duncan's voice rang through the darkened reception hall. "I am fresh out of spoons."

Chapter 29

Chaos erupted. The bodyguards dived for the stage, their attempt to protect Selene thwarted when she shoved them aside. The guests charged the exits, some changing shape as they ran. Sierra still stood on the stage, staring at the crossbow bolt sticking out of her chest.

I whirled and smacked Ugly in the nose with the base of my palm. Dark blood spurted as Ugly howled in pain. Thank God, I remembered something from the Y's self-defense class Mom made me take in high school.

Tiffany had already pulled a pencil out of her dress and put it to good use. Meat mush that used to be Ugly's partner spread all over the marble tile. I grabbed her arm and headed for the nearest exit. With any luck, Duncan would meet us at the Hummer.

So much for my idiotic plan to deal with Sierra.

A hard jerk ripped Tiffany's hand out of my mine. I whipped around to see Selene in full vamp-out mode, Tiffany squirming in her arms. She opened her mouth wide to chomp on the kid when a gigantic ball of fur flew through the air and collided with the vampire's face.

She dropped Tiffany as she crashed down on the marble hard enough to crack the tile with her elbow. Both she and the furball came up clawing and biting. The furball resolved itself into a huge timber wolf. A timber wolf wearing a purple paisley tie. George hadn't bothered to fully undress before he shifted.

Another wolf clamped jaws on Tiffany's arm and started dragging her away. The kid must have landed on her head because she wasn't putting up any struggle.

"No!" I doubted anyone heard my scream in the surrounding bedlam.

I dived for them only to slide into the pair. Blood and meat mush coated the floor and now the front of my dress.

The wolf let go of Tiffany and bared its teeth at me. It's pretty bad when Emily's wicked-ass grin looks the same whether she's wolf or human.

Her attention switched from me to the fight behind us. A whimper rose from her throat, and I turned in time to see Selene boot George ten feet into the air. He landed on the staircase and rolled down, his fuzzy form way too still.

With a growl, Emily launched herself at the vampire.

A whistle that would have been inaudible if I were still human was the only warning I had. I stumbled back, falling over Tiffany's prone form, as a silver sword whipped through the space where my neck had been.

A wild-eyed Sierra stood above me, feathered bolt still sticking out of her chest. Either Duncan had missed her heart or she was getting used to wooden shafts protruding from her body. Instead of passing out like she had in Phil's kitchen, she raised the sword over her head for another strike. I aimed a kick for her knee.

The bones shattered. Sierra screamed and collapsed to the marble. Rocking on the floor, she clutched the injured leg. I didn't have long to get lost before her nanites knitted her back together.

I gathered up the still unconscious Tiffany and stood. I tripped over a round thing, almost losing my bundle in the damned heels. Eyes from the disembodied head stared up at me. Now I knew elves did have pointed ears. I also had a pretty good idea of where Sierra liberated the sword. The poor elf's head had been ripped off.

A vicious battle raged around us. No rhyme or reason orchestrated the fight. Not all of the guest vamps were siding with Selene's contingent, which was good for the rest of us. Another set of wolves snarled and snapped from a defensive stand at the receptionist's desk. Emily and George had disappeared amidst the frenzy of bodies. My priority was to get the unconscious Tiffany to safety, but I doubted my ability to get us both out intact. Where the hell was Duncan?

I tried hard to ignore the bodily fluids and entrails littering the marble floor as I started for the main doors. Despite my sped-up metabolism, the shrimp I ate would be making an encore if I didn't get out of here soon. I swallowed the bile at the back of my throat and kicked off the heels for better footing. If I ever got the kid out of this damn war zone, I would have to bathe for a week to get the stench of death out of my toenails. Sliding and slipping my way across the tiles, I ducked and wove around combatants.

Something very large and doggy-smelling whammed into my back. Tiffany popped out of my arms, and I landed face-first in a melting vamp.

I didn't have a chance to throw-up before someone yanked me up by the back of my dress. Nails dug into my throat, pulling me to my feet. My hands reached for a solid purchase on something, anything.

"I'm going to rip out your guts, child. Did you think I couldn't smell *him* on you?" The jealousy in Selene's voice cut through me like the iceberg through the Titanic and just as frigid. No question the "him" she referred to was Duncan.

When she turned me to face her, I did puke. Thanks to George and Emily, her nose and lips had been chewed off and one eye was missing. And that was the least of the damage. The wolves had turned her into a living, bleeding exhibit from Body Worlds.

She squeezed harder. "How'd you disable the self-destruct? You and my brother should be dead."

Like I could answer while she choked me. Selene may have been shorter than me, but vampire strength hoisted me a couple of inches off the floor. Legs flailed, seeking a purchase on something, anything, to relieve the godawful pressure on my windpipe.

All seven of George Carlin's words ripped through my brain while I tried to wedge granite fingers from my throat. Selene's hands clenched tighter, and then I was drowning in my own vomit. Burning filled my lungs as stomach acid and lack of oxygen killed delicate tissues. Spots swam before me as I struggled to breathe. My fists beat at the talons crushing my airway. I could have been hitting Mount Rushmore for all the good it did.

Oh God, I'm going to die again. Why does dying have to hurt like this? The blows I landed barely registered in my oxygen-deprived brain. My toes were numb. The insanity of the battle blurred to dark gray, a prelude to the final black.

Something poked me in the ribs and then I fell, landing with a loud *splooch* on my ass. I bent over and coughed the rest of the crap out of my throat before I could suck in huge lungfuls of sweet, sweet oxygen. My throat hurt like hell, my chest worse, but cells and nanites alike rejoiced in the air. The scene snapped back into focus.

In slow motion, Selene collapsed to her knees beside me. Only when it was eye-level did I notice the tip of a crossbow bolt sticking out of her dress. Right where her heart should be. The golden glow faded from her remaining eye, and the bits of skin left began sliding off her skull. Her torso teetered for a moment before falling across my legs.

"Are you all right, darling?" Duncan knelt beside me, one arm wrapped around me, the other holding the crossbow. A crossbow I recognized. It had been the one I packed in my bag this morning. The one Kane and his boys had confiscated. I could only stare at him, totally dumbfounded.

"Samantha?"

I tried to talk, but nothing came out.

"Answer me, Samantha! Are you all right?" He shook me to emphasize the point.

So I smacked him in the chest and pointed to my neck.

"Oh." A delightfully sheepish smile spread across his face. "Sorry."

It was good to know the bastard had other expressions besides a scowl and a mocking grin. I tried to pull my feet out from under the melting and oozing vampire, but the gunk clung to my stockings. I really needed a shower.

"I guess that's what you'd call closure, huh?" Tiffany, bearing an awful resemblance to Sissy Spacek at the end of *Carrie,* stood on wobbly legs next to us. "Caesar isn't going to be happy you killed the bitch." An evil grin lit up her face. "But I'm pretty damned ecstatic right now."

Duncan looked up, a wry tilt to his eyebrow. "Are you all right?"

She started to nod but thought better of it. "Probably a concussion. Otherwise, I'm just fucking peachy."

"Watch your language," he said, but there was no bite in his tone.

I glanced away from their banter, and finally I noticed the fighting was pretty much over. Folks limped through the debris, searching for friends, relatives, and their own body parts.

"Where's Sierra? Better yet, where's George and Emily?" My words weren't much more than a croak. I didn't realize how much I missed the sound of my own voice.

"Who?"

"The Polks," Tiffany explained. At his confused expression, she added, "You know, the San Antonio Pack leaders?"

"Logan's parents are here?" Duncan rose. "Keep an eye on Sam. I'll find—" The rest of what he was about to say was swallowed by a hoarse cry as a silver swordpoint popped out of his shoulder. He crashed to the floor, his body racked by convulsions. Tiffany screamed.

Standing over Duncan, Sierra smiled at me. "You're next, bitch."

Chapter 30

I stared in disbelief. Why couldn't Psycho Zombie curl up in a corner and die like everyone else?

Time slowed to a crawl. Tiffany, crying, knelt next to Duncan and cradled his head in her lap. The survivors turned their heads in our direction. I stood up, each breath still torture from my partially crushed windpipe and vomit-filled lungs.

Duncan lay so still. His skin melded to the bones, anticipating the final disconnect before it began its slide to the floor. With every beat, I waited for my heart to explode out of my chest. *He can't be dead.* I gritted my teeth. *He just can't.*

Tears dripped down my face. The agony inside me, the inability to draw a breath without racking pain, had nothing to do with the damage Selene had inflicted.

My eyes met Sierra's mad ones.

Then everything whipped into fast forward. Sierra jerked the sword out of Duncan's body. She swung at Tiffany's bent head. I rammed her before the silver touched the kid. Sierra skidded through the debris.

"Don't you ever touch my boyfriend again!" I shouted. Or tried to. It came out more of a hoarse bark than a shout, but the nanites were doing their job.

The bitch scrambled to her feet and ran toward me, swinging wildly with the sword.

Well, she tried to run. The body parts and fluids made footing treacherous even without the heels she wore. I backpedaled. She slipped in what was at one time Selene's liver and went down hard on her backside. She was way too close to Duncan and Tiffany for my comfort.

"Aw, come on, Sierra" I taunted, sidling away from the vulnerable pair. "Is that the best you can do?"

Good plan, Sam. Piss off the maniacal, sword-wielding, bionic zombie. I told the logical portion of my brain to shut up and circled further away from Duncan and Tiffany.

My attitude had the desired effect. She ignored the people I cared about in order to behead me. Silver handle tight in her manicured hand, she kicked herself free of the remains of her former partner.

An even more disturbing thought occurred as Sierra stalked after me. What if I didn't die if she beheaded me?

She is going to behead you if you insist on such self-defeating thoughts. Duncan!

I risked a glance in his direction. He was barely conscious but alive. A human-shaped Emily, battered, bloody and naked, crouched next to him, helping Tiffany staunch his wound. Goth Girl stood, but Emily yanked her back. None of the other survivors ringing the room moved to interfere in this fight.

I ducked a wild swipe by Sierra and threw a chair at her head. She evaded my clumsy projectile. I dodged around a table, trying to keep out of reach of her sword. She leapt up on the plywood top.

I lashed out at the aluminum leg. It broke, but the jagged edge snagged my ultra run-resistant hose. She half fell, half jumped at me as the table collapsed. Sierra, the table, and I landed in a big tangled heap.

Except it wasn't the table that shot an elbow to my chin. My vision swam and the sharp, metallic taste of blood filled my mouth where I had bitten my tongue. A knee to my groin followed the elbow shot. For the record, it hurts pretty damn bad for girls, too.

I resisted the urge to cup myself. Instead, I shook my leg free of the table to gain some maneuverability, a nasty cut across my calf my reward for the effort. Before I could formulate a new plan, Sierra jumped behind me. With a yank on my hairspray-coated locks, she twisted my head back until it felt like a vertebra would snap.

An ugly smile filled my vision. "Let's find out just what you taste like." Beverly Hills-white teeth clamped onto my neck.

There's something intensely primal and terrifying when someone or something chomps a hunk of flesh out of you. I was sure Evander Holyfield would agree. My problem was I didn't have a referee and trainers to pull Psycho Bitch off me.

I thrashed and hit with everything left in me. A thick, dark heaviness gathered at the base of my skull. The pressure rose, gathering every thought, every breath. When it reached an unbearable level, I screamed.

Suddenly I was freefalling. The landing knocked the little air I had left right out of my lungs. Automatically, I slapped a hand to my neck for pressure and tried not think about the missing palm-sized section of muscle, ligaments and arteries.

Panicked, I felt around for a weapon, any weapon, with my free hand. My fingers closed around slick metal. I held the broken table leg between me and Sierra, who lay several feet away.

She sprawled across the disgusting marble, a sick grin spread across her face. My blood dripped from her chin and disappeared into the black material of her dress. She ran the back of her hand across her mouth. Red smeared across her cheek.

"I want some more," she whispered.

The aluminum makeshift stake wavered in front of me. I wasn't fooling myself about it killing her, but maybe if I stabbed her multiple times, she'd pass out long enough for us to chain her.

Yeah, right. And I'd suddenly develop J. Lo's figure.

Sierra rose to her hands and knees, the image unmistakably one of a jungle cat ready to pounce. Her muscles tensed, then confusion crossed her face. She rocked back, and her skin seemed to shimmer in the low light.

A raw scream of pain erupted from her throat. She rose to her knees, fingers scratching desperately at her face. Blood, a funky metallic scarlet color, dripped from the wounds. She started ripping at her clothing. No, not her clothing. Her abdomen. Skin hung in tattered shreds as she continued to tear at her own flesh. But when she clawed at her arms, instead of blood, metallic silver liquid oozed from her scratches.

What the hell? The table leg clattered to the floor. I dropped to my hands and crab-crawled away from her. Her agonized screaming rose in pitch. Sierra stood and continued to rip at her hair and skin. Skin which was no longer bleeding red or silver. Silver powder flaked from her body and drifted to the gore-coated marble.

With one last, horrific screech, Sierra Mallory exploded into a cloud of sparkling dust.

Chapter 31

Bebe tapped her pen against the clipboard she held. "Near as I can understand, your nanites thought they were still in your body."

"Thought? What do you mean 'thought'? They're robots. They can't think." I rubbed my damp hair with a towel.

She didn't answer and bent over the microscope once again.

Six hours ago, Caesar's search-and-destroy team had arrived at Mallory Labs and turned into a clean-up squad. Bob, the head of Mallory's security, hadn't argued over Augustine Research's "takeover" of the late Mallorys' assets. In fact, he seemed quite relieved. Additional "special" assistance arrived for the surviving guests. Tonight's chaos sure as hell wasn't going to be reported to the LAPD.

Bebe and a couple of paramedic weres had bundled me into an ambulance and drove me to Good Samaritan. I found out on the way that Caesar's generous donations paid for a special wing there. The board of directors believed Bebe headed up a cancer research program, but in reality, the folks working in the alleged program specialized in supernatural medicine.

While everyone else treated at the hospital had the luxury of a shower, or at least a sponge bath, the weres had wheeled me to Bebe's personal lab for an examination. A detailed examination. It royally sucked.

Didn't she have a clue of what decaying vampire smells like? After five hours of olfactory torture, she finally let me take a damn shower.

Bebe looked up from her microscope and rubbed her eyes. "Okay, bad choice of words. The nanites' program shuts them down when their sensors show they have left your body in minute quantities, such as in tears, saliva, or blood."

I tossed the towel on an empty stool and finger-combed my hair. I felt human again with the clean skin, clean hair and clean clothes.

My stomach grumbled.

No, I was never going to feel truly human again.

Bebe shrugged before she continued. "Before the shutdown engaged, Sierra's nanites attacked them as an outside threat or infection. That in turn triggered your nanites' self-defense and repair programs, which overrode the shutdown. It may also have to do with the size of the chunk she bit out of you."

I whistled. "Killed by a robot war inside her own body." Leaning against the lab table, I rubbed at the healed bite. No one could tell six hours ago I had a fist-sized hole in my neck. No redness, no scarring, nothing. Like the gunshot wound to my chest. The whole thing was so damn bizarre. "So Fred was right. My nanites were the answer to taking out Sierra."

Bebe nodded. Even without telepathy, I could tell from the twist of her lips that she was thinking the same thing I was. Why couldn't have Fred just told us that during the séance?

An open jar full of silvery flakes sat on the table next to Bebe's microscope, all that was left of the only other human zombie created by Tyrone Mallory. I reached over to poke at the "Sierra dust".

Bebe slapped my hand away. "Don't touch until I'm sure they're turned off for good."

I shook my head. "I had to have breathed in some of her nanites when she—" I stopped, not sure what to say. It's one thing to see someone go poof on TV, another in real life.

"That's why I want to see you in an hour for more tests."

I saluted her and barked, "Aye, Captain." As I closed the door behind me, the good doctor was shaking her head and muttering to herself about zombies and insanity.

Duncan waited for me in the hallway, his broad shoulders holding up the wall. Like me, the holes in his luscious body had healed hours ago, but his skin was paler than normal, even for him. He favored me with a quick peck on the lips before his face turned grim. "Caesar wants to talk to us."

Right. My guess was the vampire prince would take another chunk of flesh from my ass for taking matters into my own hands and getting a lot of people killed. The very thing I'd been trying to avoid. But I nodded and fell in step with him as we headed down the hall toward Bebe's office.

I couldn't read Duncan's mind, but I also couldn't blame him for his dour mood. Ralph wouldn't be happy if I waltzed into his office, saying I had just shot and killed one of his siblings.

Ralph. Damn, I needed to call my own boss. My heart sank. The chance for the assistant editor position had poofed faster than Sierra Mallory. Hell, I probably didn't even have a job at the *Scoop* anymore, but I owed him the notice I was still alive and kicking. Sort of.

Duncan's knock on the office door was followed by a soft "Come in."

Caesar sat behind Bebe's desk, elbows propped on the surface and fingers steepled. After Duncan and I each detailed our versions of the night's events, ending with Selene and Sierra's deaths, the older vampire stood, turned and stared out the window for a long time. His fist raised and clenched against the glass. Duncan stood so still, as if waiting for recrimination. I held my breath, not sure if I could stop Caesar if he did try anything.

Hours seemed to pass before he whispered, "So I'm the last Ptolemy."

I couldn't have been more surprised if he had whipped around and kicked me in the gut. He couldn't be who I thought.

Could he?

Bits and pieces spun through my brain as everything slipped into place. His age. His mention of his siblings. Emily's comment about the Antonius twins.

Alexander Helios Antonius of Egypt, the oldest son of Cleopatra VII and Mark Antony.

All the sudden I couldn't breathe.

One thing didn't make sense.

He straightened and turned back to us. His hands slid into his pockets, and he regarded me with a sad half-smile. "You simply cannot stop asking questions, can you, Samantha?"

"With all due respect, Your Highness…" I stopped, not sure of the proper form of address for an Egyptian prince, but he nodded for me to continue.

"Why the hell would you use the name of the man responsible for the deaths of half your family?" I blurted.

Duncan jerked, probably pissed at my disrespect. I was too stunned to word my question more carefully. I had written my history masters' thesis on Cleopatra VII. If I'd had an inkling two of her kids were still alive …

Caesar seemed to find the question hysterical. He roared with laughter for a full minute before wiping the red-tinged tears from his face. "I get that question a lot." He exhaled and shook his head. "Selene and Ptolemy did not understand either." He grinned at me. "I think you, of all people, would."

I couldn't help smiling back. It was as much a screw-you to his parents' nemesis, the first emperor of Rome, as it was a tribute to his beloved older brother, who just happened to be Cleopatra's by Julius Caesar. Yeah. I could definitely understand.

"Master—" Duncan stepped forward but his words seemed to catch in his throat.

Caesar shook his head. "It's over. I would like to be alone now." He turned back to the window.

But Tiffany had mentioned Ptolemy as if she knew him. Had Caesar's youngest brother been Turned as well as his twin sister? It made sense considering the two boys had disappeared from the history books shortly after the Battle of Actium.

My millions of questions would have to wait until another time. Sympathy overrode my curiosity. As much as Max pissed me off at times, I didn't know what I would do without him. Duncan and I left Caesar to grieve.

George and Emily met us in the hospital lobby as we exited the elevator. George held out his hand to Duncan.

"Thanks for the use of the phone and the clothes, son," the were said. The men gave each other that emotional, masculine handshake they give when they really want to hug but are afraid it'll ruin their images.

Luckily, Emily's tight hug helped smother my grin at George calling Duncan "son". "Thanks for letting us know Logan's all right." She released me before my ribs actually broke from her strength. "You come and visit us sometime, girl."

Not ones for extended good-byes, the weres strode through the main doors and climbed into a waiting cab. Once they departed, I turned the evil eye on Duncan.

"I thought Logan was a lone werewolf."

"Technically, he is. The oldest sons are turned out by the pack once they reach adulthood to start their own pack. Logan came out to Los Angeles to find a mate."

"Here? In La-La land?"

"Yes."

"Oh." I was so tired I couldn't think of much else to say.

He smirked at me. "What? The great Samantha Ridgeway has finally run out of questions?"

I glared at him some more. "Have you checked on Tiffany? And where's Max? There. That's two questions."

Duncan shook his head, but the amused glint remained in his eyes. He took me by the hand and led me down a side hallway, which seemed to contain only private conference rooms. Angry words wafted down the corridor from the only one with a closed door. We looked at each other.

"—just one day. Quit making a BFD about it, Max." Tiffany's voice snapped with tension.

Uh-oh. Trouble in paradise, already?

Duncan rapped on the door. He was greeted by silence. He knocked again.

"Either come in or go away!"

He eased the door open at Tiffany's sharp voice. "I just wanted to see how you were feeling."

She stood at the edge of the table, not bothering to look at us. Instead, she glared at my brother, who leaned back on the couch and matched her expression with a determined one of his own. She was back in her Goth Girl gear, ripped black t-shirt and black leather mini-skirt.

"My brains are still intact," she snarled.

She was definitely back to her original attitude problem.

My stomach rumbled again, and she shot me a nasty look. "Unless your girlfriend plans on eating them."

Max rose from the couch. "Just because you're pissed at me doesn't mean you can take it out on Sam."

Tiffany turned her glare back to Max. "For the record, I am breaking up with you."

My heart leapt at the same time I felt a pulse of excitement from Duncan. Could it be?

"You can't. We're engaged." Max crossed his arms over his chest.

Guess not. I recognized his stance.

Tiffany stamped her foot. "You can't make me, asshole."

Max unfolded his arms and took a step toward her, more determined than threatening. "If you think I'm going to let my child be born a bastard, you've got another think coming," he said with surety.

I don't know what shocked me more—Max's news or his caveman attitude.

"You two have only known each other five fucking days! How the bloody hell did this happen?" Duncan roared.

Tiffany rolled her eyes at him. "It's called sex, Duncan."

"Then you are damn well going to marry the idiot!"

"Hey!" Max and I protested at the same time.

Pounding footsteps announced Alex and Anne's arrival.

"What's all the shouting about?"

I knew Alex's question was rhetorical. He and Anne would have had their heads encased in cement and buried two miles below ground not to have heard the commotion.

I answered anyway. "My genius brother knocked up the kid."

"We don't know for sure I'm pregnant." Her voice shook, the reality starting to sink in.

"Yes, you are," the vamps and I answered in unison.

Then I knew the source of Tiffany's citrus-y smell from earlier in the evening. Well, technically yesterday. The hormonal changes had already started, and deep down, she knew Selene had to die for her baby to be safe.

"We'll get out of here. You two need to talk," I said before walking over and giving each of them a hug. I shooed the vamps out and shut the door behind me.

Jealousy and excitement battled for supremacy. It stung I would never know the feeling of my tummy swelling or the kick of a tiny life inside of me.

Excitement won, with a smidgen of revenge assisting it. I would be able to spoil my niece or nephew rotten. The thought of hyping the tot on sugar and caffeine before sending him or her home to Max made me rub my hands in delight. My stomach chose that moment for a more insistent growl.

"I hope you're not planning on eating the baby." Duncan had a slightly horrified look on his handsome but still gaunt face.

"No," I said, smiling back at him. "But we'd better get down to the cafeteria before I change my mind."

Alex and Anne didn't follow us since they were still on security duty. The private cafeteria was an experience. Duncan snagged a bottle of blood from a cooler. While he set it in the microwave and punched the buttons to warm it, I pulled or requested one of everything from the counter.

Once we sat, Duncan kept his gaze fixed on the bottle. I tapped my foot, waiting for him to say something since I was busy inhaling a bowl of chicken noodle soup along with half of a basket of Zestas. After tonight, I had to wonder if the crackers really were made by elves.

Without a word, he drained and discarded the first bottle before he rose and retrieved another out of the cooler. While I was relieved to see color and tone liven his skin, the silent treatment sucked.

When he sat for the second time, I snatched the bottle out of his hand.

"Samantha." He swiped at the bottle I held out of reach.

"You'll get it back after we're done, buster." I glared at him.

"Sam—"

I reached across the table and touched his lips. "No, let me finish. I'm the last woman on earth who wants to have 'the talk.' I'm also not looking for a commitment."

"No, you should be committed," he mumbled against my fingers. His lips were sending signals to a part of my anatomy I sure as hell shouldn't be listening to. Duncan's eyes flared neon, and he nibbled on my fingers.

"Stop that!" I jerked my hand away. My fingers wanted his tongue back. Parts further south agreed. "And while you're at it, shut the fuck up and let me finish."

"We should get married."

Brain-freeze. So not what I was expecting.

Vampire speed caught the bottle plummeting towards the floor tile. He set it on the table before he scooted my chair closer to him and wrapped his arms around me. His chest rumbled with his chuckle as he hugged me.

"Had I but known what it would take to silence you, I would have proposed much earlier this week."

"No."

He cupped my chin and tilted my head to stare into my eyes. The cute little frown of his creased his forehead. "'No'? What do you mean 'no'?"

"First of all, that wasn't a proposal. It was a suggestion. Second, we haven't even been on a first date yet. And third—" Oh, God, I was channeling Max, but I couldn't stop myself. "You haven't even told me you love me."

"What are you saying? You want to court before we marry?"

I bit my bottom lip to keep from breaking into hysterics at his incredulous look. "Well. Duh." I rolled my eyes. If men didn't get a better clue with age, then the human race truly was doomed.

Hooking my upper arms, he set me back in my chair. He rose, grabbed his blood and sauntered toward the cafeteria door.

"Where the hell are you going?"

Duncan shot a wicked look over his shoulder. "Home."

"Without me?" I squeaked.

"Yes." The glowing eyes belied his stern look.

"But, but, but—"

"I do love you, heaven help me, but no more lovemaking until we are properly wed." His head disappeared. Sharp bootsteps retreated down the hallway.

That bastard!

I charged out of the cafeteria and caught up with him as he passed an empty patient room. A rough shove propelled him through the door. From the antiseptic odor, no one was currently staying in the room.

Once he caught his balance, Duncan cocked an eyebrow at me. "Excuse me?"

"What the fuck do you think you're playing at?" I growled.

The amused look was back in his eyes. "I am not playing at anything, darling. I simply refuse to go to bed with a woman who cannot do me the courtesy of replying when I tell her I love her."

"And what do I get if I tell you I love you?" I snapped.

He set his bottle on the patient tray before he lowered himself to the hospital bed and patted the blanket. "Come over here and I will show you."

Rational thought followed Elvis out of the building. Wary, I eased closer and sat next to him.

He reached for my hand and picked up nibbling where he left off in the cafeteria. I sighed and sank down into the nubby blanket, relishing the rough texture of his tongue snaking across my palm. Our clothes disappeared before I realized it.

Nerves ignited faster than a canyon wildfire. I bucked and moaned, but his fingers and mouth withdrew every time I closed in on an orgasm.

Within seconds, I begged him to enter me. He paused, his arms braced on each side of me. "Not until you say it."

"I already did."

"No, you asked what I would do if you said it. I've made a good faith demonstration. Now, I want to hear it."

"Duncan." It was a feeble protest even by my standards.

"Say it," he demanded.

"Duncan," I wailed. "You're not fighting fair!"

A wicked grin spread across his face. "I know." He teased his tip against my clit.

"Dammit, all right all ready. I love you."

I know. I love you too, darling.

He plunged into me, and my world shattered in an explosion rivaling Krakatoa.

Cool air replaced his warmth when he collapsed next to me. He snatched the extra blanket from the foot of the bed and spread it over my goose bumps before snugging me tight against his chest.

"See, was that so terrible?"

Ignoring his asinine question, I rolled to my side, an interesting maneuver considering the size of the standard hospital bed. Propping my head on my hand, I regarded him. "How did you hear me tonight at the lab? I thought the only time you could read my mind was . . ." I waved at the bed.

He stroked my waist and hip. I could almost see the little cogs whirring in his head. After I was sure he would ignore my question in favor of more sex, he answered. "Physical intimacy is not the trigger."

"Then what?"

"You have a very difficult time displaying your true feelings, especially where I am concerned. Tonight you were so afraid you would lose me you dropped your mental barriers."

"So you're the psychic equivalent of a Klingon battle cruiser? I get anywhere near you and I raise shields?"

His small smile indicated he was laughing with me for once.

"Something like that," he admitted.

"Okay," I drawled. "I'll buy your theory. Now, how the hell did you get to Mallory Labs by yourself in the daylight, Mr. I-Can't-Drive?"

"Caesar is correct. You simply cannot stop asking questions."

"Come on, give." I socked him in the shoulder, gently though since I didn't want to take the chance he wasn't completely healed.

"Obviously, you were not paying attention to Alex's story of how he and I first met." Now, he did smirk.

"Oh, shit!" I flopped over on my back at my own stupidity. Of course, the supply compartment under the back floor of the Hummer.

I peered at him with suspicion through slitted eyelids. "If you couldn't read my mind—"

He rose up on his elbow and cocked an eyebrow.

"I'm so going to kill Tiffany."

He chuckled. "As you would say, cut the kid a break. She did not leak her thoughts on purpose. You caught her by surprise with your psychic talent." He lifted my hand and nuzzled the palm. I floated on the erotic sensation when his next words registered. "However I suspected you would attempt some idiotic stunt."

I jerked out of his grasp, but he pinned me before I could slide off the bed.

"I was not about to let harm come to the woman I love."

Unfamiliar warmth curled inside of me, but I wasn't about to give in so easily. "Don't you ever fuck with me again, asshole."

"Are you sure?" He ducked to nibble my left breast. Soft laughter echoed through my head. That boy was going to find out just how nasty I could be. My toes curled as he paid extra attention to my other breast. Then he bent his head, his hair tickling my tummy as he laved my very sensitive flesh.

Paybacks could wait until tomorrow.

Chapter 32

Ralph was usually at the office on Saturday mornings, and he didn't disappoint me when I arrived the next day.

"Dammit, Ridgeway, you scared the shit out of me, disappearing like that. You're sure you're all right?" His gruff voice almost sounded emotional.

"I'm fine." I hesitated and glanced around the bullpen. Everyone's eyes immediately fell back to their tasks. Everyone except Bill Morton's. A salacious smile jeered back at me.

I couldn't blame Ralph for giving Bill the position since I was the one who fell off the face of the earth for the last week. I faced my waiting editor. "Can we talk privately?"

Ralph nodded. He hadn't missed the exchange. Once the door closed behind him, and he waved at the guest chair, he said, "I'm sorry, Sam."

I flopped in the seat. Emerson peered around the corner of the desk, and I held out my hand. He whined and ducked back behind the scarred furniture. It figured that the dog would freak over my new smell. Ralph eased into his chair, one arm moving rhythmically as he comforted the distressed bulldog.

Not sure how to start, I tapped the armrest. I mean, how exactly do you call in dead to your boss?

Ralph broke the silence first. "You should have listened when I told you to lay off St. James. And you got my offices trashed."

I couldn't help grinning at Ralph's pissed off tone. "You can blame the trashing on a story Max was working on. The bad guys thought you and I were hiding shit for my dumbass brother."

"Doesn't make you any less dead, does it?"

My jaw dropped. It took a couple of tries to close it. Finally, I stammered, "How do you know?"

"How do you think the covens and packs keep an eye on unusual happenings?"

This thing went far deeper than I realized. "The supernaturals own United Media?"

He nodded. "Augustine has controlling interest in our parent company." A sad smile followed. "You're not the first stray he's taken in, Sam."

I breathed deeply, trying to ground the raging turmoil in my head. Ralph knew he worked for a vampire. He fed unusual street information to Caesar.

And underneath the smell of paper and dog and cigarettes lay the faint musk of were.

"Where's your pack?"

He shrugged. "They tossed me and my brothers out years ago." A confirming bark echoed under the desk.

No fucking way. I shook my head, but before I could ask, Ralph handed me the answer.

"Emerson and I can't shift, Sam." He shrugged. "Waldo can, but he chose to stay with us, protect us." Ralph rarely mentioned his twin brother, a security consultant up in Seattle. Okay, litter mate.

Before I could formulate an answer to Ralph's bombshell, he leaned forward, resting beefy arms on top of someone's redlined story. Sharp, blue eyes bored into mine. "Are you going to accept Augustine's protection?"

Duncan had mentioned joining the vampire coven to me before I left for the *Scoop*. "I meet with Caesar in a couple of hours." I swallowed hard, slightly embarrassed. "He's still cleaning up some problems from last night."

"For what it's worth, Sam, I think you should take him up on it. The word about you is out thanks to last night's fiasco. You're going to need all the help you can get."

"About my job—"

"Talk to Augustine first."

I didn't like the finality in his voice, but for once, I listened. I'd screwed up enough to last a lifetime. Okay, a deathtime.

I rose and headed for the door.

"Sam?"

My hand on the knob, I looked at Ralph.

"Tell Max I passed his notes to the authorities like he asked."

"You had them all along?" I couldn't keep the disbelief from my voice. If the police had Max's notes, it could blow the lid off the whole supernatural world. How could Ralph do such a thing when he was one of them? Caesar was not going to be pleased. Nope, not at all.

"Yeah." Ralph smiled and reached for the pack of cigarettes lying on a pile of paperwork. "Now get the hell out of my office. I've got work to do." He made shoo-ing motions with the hand not busy pulling out a smoke.

The incidents of the last week chased each other around my head on the drive back to Brentwood. Some questions had been answered, but not all. Like what the hell the damn nanites were doing to me? I was still hungry all the time. All Bebe could say was they were still rewriting my DNA. But until they were done, we all agreed "zombie" was the best description for what I was.

The more I thought though, the angrier I became at Caesar for interfering with my employment. Unlike him, I wasn't independently wealthy. Dammit, I needed my job to pay for my ravenous appetite.

I wheeled my retrieved Honda into Caesar's drive and waved at Miko, one of the day guards. She waved back and the gates slid open. After I parked, I put my zombie radar to good use. Only three people in the house, two male vamps and one male human, all of them in Caesar's study. Good. I needed to bitch out my brother too.

I didn't bother knocking on the study door. In the split second I burst into the room, I realized the human sitting in the chair facing away from me had a full head of sun-bleached hair. He turned and shot out of his chair, piercing blue eyes wide with shock.

Then he lunged for me, and Duncan's firm grip on his arm prevented Brent Poole from tackling me.

"What the fuck is she doing here?" Poole tried to lunge again. "Let me go!" He struggled against Duncan's hold.

Damn. Attempted assault and me without my camera.

"Control yourself, Brent." Amusement and annoyance chased each other across Caesar's features. "I won't have you assaulting my guest."

"Guest?" Poole spat. "Uncle Caesar, you cannot be serious?"

Uncle? Caesar? Alton's soap star father was a distant cousin of the deposed Greek royal family. Was Poole and Alton's relationship a freakin' arranged royal marriage?

I clenched my fists. The story of a freakin' lifetime and I couldn't write it. Not without destroying people I'd begun to care about in the process. Death was so unfair.

At least Poole smelled like apples, which meant he was human. And I really wanted to put my new nose to work to find which stars were human and which weren't because I had some serious suspicions about Rebecca Romjin being elven.

"Duncan?" Poole looked at my man, trying to find an ally. "You know everything she's—" He pointed at me. "—done to me and Jess. Why would you let her in Uncle Caesar's house?"

"She's my fiancée," Duncan said.

"What?" Poole and I spluttered at the same time.

"I am not!" I yelled.

"She can't be!" Horror engulfed Poole's classic cinema features. He gazed at Duncan like a little boy who's realized his hero has feet of clay. He pointed at me again. "She's a tabloid reporter. She's using you to get to me."

Red hazed my vision. After the week I had, I didn't need his shit. "You have a really high opinion of yourself, don't you, jerkwad? Has it occurred to you the only reason I'm here in a vampire's house is because I died last weekend?"

"Oh my God." Poole rolled his eyes in disgust. He turned to Duncan. "You were my Qui-Gon, man." He whipped to face Caesar. "And you're family for chrissakes! How the fuck could you two Turn someone like her?" He grabbed his designer jean jacket and gave me one last ugly glare before storming out of Caesar's study. A resounding boom of the front door slamming echoed through the house.

I looked up at Duncan. "Qui-Gon?"

He shrugged. "I gave Brent pointers when he was preparing for *Conversation with a Bloodsucker*."

As much as I wanted to snicker at the thought of Poole using Duncan St. James as a model, I couldn't forget the reason I came in and turned to Caesar. "I have a bone to pick with you, Your Highness."

"Yes?" Caesar knew, he was going to make me say it out loud, and he didn't even bother to look apologetic.

I crossed my arms and gave him my best Siamese cat stare-down. "Where do you get off telling my boss—"

"Technically, I am your employer."

"So what are you saying? I'm fired? Don't you think I can take care of myself?" I snapped. "I took care of Sierra, didn't I? I could have handled Ralph too."

"I have no doubt you could have, Samantha." Uh-oh. Warning bells began dinging in my head at my full name. "But you are part of a whole other world now, the supernatural world."

"Gee, thanks, Caesar," I sneered. "Like I need the reminder."

"Maybe you do, Samantha. What are you going to do when someone notices you're not aging? What about when you move too fast or lift something a normal human woman shouldn't be able to lift?" Caesar steepled his index fingers and gazed at me, his expression reminiscent of the warning look he had given me once before in his safe house. God, that seemed a lifetime ago.

I took a deep breath to calm my nerves. "Look, Caesar, I have no intention of betraying any of you or your secrets, and I do appreciate all your help, but I need my own life. I need to feel as normal as possible."

My stomach decided to gurgle at that instant. Duncan chuckled, and I elbowed him in the ribs, none too gently. He rewarded me with a startled *oof*.

Amusement danced in Caesar's eyes even though his expression never wavered. "Samantha, you are newly made and still very vulnerable. If you were a recently Turned vampire, you'd have two options. You could tell your immediate family the truth."

I opened my mouth, but a cautionary look from Caesar made me hesitate.

"If you can't trust your parents with the truth, we will arrange for a new identity in a location far from Los Angeles with adequate resources to carve a new life."

"Like a Witness Protection Program?"

He gave me an approving smile. "Similar, yes. However, if you don't accept my protection, it not only will put you at risk for those seeking to capitalize on Mallory's research, your family could be in jeopardy as well.

Oh, fuck. I collapsed on the chair Poole had vacated. Black spots swam in my vision. This was not what I was expecting. Expecting . . .

A slim hope occurred. I glanced up at Caesar. "But wouldn't Max be part of your Family?" I swallowed hard. "Now he and Tiffany are engaged?"

The vampire nodded. "But not your parents. Protection only extends so far."

"Don't I have any time to decide?" I hated the whine in my voice.

"Ideally, a new vampire would have already finalized these affairs before being Turned, but vampire laws allow a coven master certain discretion in unusual situations." He looked up at Duncan. "Have Max and Tiffany set a date yet?"

My man's face carried a certain distaste though his posture remained at parade rest. "I believe they are looking at the first weekend in April."

Damn, that was fast. My attention swung back to Caesar, who gave a sharp nod.

"Seven weeks is well within the legal extension. You'll have until the day after the wedding to make your decision. Very well, then." His golden brown eyes swept over me. "I have a special project for you." He held up a hand to forestall my attempted protest. "You can work on this in your spare time when you're not on a *Scoop* assignment, and you will be paid accordingly."

I nearly choked on the figure he named.

"I believe that should be sufficient to cover the change in your grocery bill," he added.

I immediately became suspicious. "What do I have to do?"

"I want you to become our chronicler. With your history degree, your talent for the written word, and your—" He blinked as he chose his words. "—refreshing honesty, I believe you would do an excellent job."

Okaaaaaaay. Not what I was expecting. "I figured you'd want me to inform you if anything suspicious came across at the *Scoop*."

Caesar smiled, a very dangerous smile. "I already have Ralph O'Malley covering that angle." He tossed a folder on his desk, clearly labeled Tyrone Mallory in Max's neat handwriting.

Holy crap! My mouth fell open. It took a couple of tries before I could speak. "Ralph said he gave it to the authorities."

"He did. At least, the proper authorities for him." A sly smile spread across Caesar's face. "Since you haven't answered, I will assume it is a 'yes'. Speaking of exposure, Duncan—" Caesar's smile disappeared. "Your work has been incredibly sloppy to allow a mortal to discover our world. As your punishment, you will be required to educate your fiancée—"

"I am not his fiancée!" I blurted.

Caesar ignored me. "—concerning our ways so we don't have any more accidental discoveries by the Normals."

"Yes, sir," Duncan muttered through gritted teeth.

"Dismissed." Caesar examined something on his desk, like we no longer existed.

"B-b-but—" My protest was cut short when Duncan dragged me out of the study and closed the door behind us.

"Wait a minute!" I yanked my arm out of his grip and jabbed a thumb at the door. "Where does he get off ordering us around?"

Green eyes bore into me. "He's my coven master and your employer."

Damn, I hated when he was right. And Caesar might be my coven master too, if I accepted his offer of protection.

I blew out an exasperated breath. Oh, who the hell was I kidding?

I didn't really have a choice in the matter unless I wanted to become someone else's science experiment.

Duncan stepped forward, pressing me against the wall with his sheer presence. "Or do you really want to end up in a government lab?"

"No," I mumbled. "And stop reading my mind." It was really, really hard to think with one of his hands sliding underneath my t-shirt and the other stroking my cheek, the rough texture of his fingertips sending trills of sensation across my skin. "It still would have been polite to ask nicely."

"All right, would you care to accompany me to dinner this evening?" he whispered, his breath tickling my ear. The bastard was destroying all my attempts at pouting.

I know. Duncan's thoughts were as hot as the wayward hand fondling my bra.

Could you two please not have sex right outside my office?

Duncan and I jumped apart at Caesar's annoyed thought.

I eyed Duncan. "Your place or mine?"

He snorted. "Until we get your apartment modified for daylight use—"

"Your place it is." For once, I grabbed his hand and dragged him into the garage. "By the way, this does not qualify as an official date, nor does it mean we're engaged."

"Of course, darling," he said, his eyes gleaming neon green in the darkness.

We never made it out of Caesar's garage before sundown.

Turn the page for a sneak peek of the next Bloodlines novel,
Zombie Wedding.

Zombie Wedding

Chapter 1

My future sister-in-law leaned close and whispered, "Sam, get your mother out of my face, or I'm going to stake her."

My sympathy for Tiffany Stephens didn't extend far while we waited for Mom and Antoine to come back with a load of designer bridal gowns. I knew Mom would start on my bridesmaid dress once Tiffany's wedding wear satisfied her Beverly Hills sensibility. Mom had already complained all the way to the boutique about buying off the rack, but with the wedding a week from Saturday, there wasn't much choice.

I cast a surreptitious look at my brother's homicidal fiancée. With all the mascara and eyeliner, her squinted eyes were little more than black slashes on her nearly white face. A quick glance around the Rodeo boutique reassured me that everyone else was out of hearing range. Normal hearing range anyway.

I leaned closer to her and whispered back, "Killing her would be the perfect Christmas gift for me."

She snorted at my teasing and pursed her purple-black lips. Her size two combat boot tapped an irritated rhythm. As one of the three human Enforcers of the Augustine Vampire Coven, she could hold her own against any supernatural menace.

Standing up to my mother was another story. Not that Tiffany didn't do a superb job, but resistance didn't register in Mom's self-centered, materialistic universe.

The subject of our discussion charged back toward the dressing area where she had planted the two of us. Antoine, Mom's personal image consultant, floated in her wake, loaded to the gills with fluffy white material.

I wasn't precognitive—at least not yet—but I could see what was about to happen. Hell, the blind guy who panhandled outside of my apartment complex could have seen what was about to happen.

Mom shoved her purse in my arms. Mr. Cuddles, her toy poodle, poked his head out and growled. I wished it were because he detected my "change" from two months ago. Unfortunately, his attitude toward me had more to do with his owner's and had existed from the moment Mom brought him home from the breeder. I set the purse on the floor, and Mr. Cuddles hopped out and trotted over to sit primly at Mom's feet.

She held up the first filmy concoction.

"No fuckin' way." Tiffany glared at her.

"Now, Tiffany, darling, since you don't have any family to assist you with planning your wedding, you really need me."

Smooth move, Mom. Remind the psychotic future daughter-in-law that her parents are pushing up daisies. I bit my tongue to keep from saying those thoughts aloud.

"I have my uncle, and I already told you I have a dress."

I could barely understand Tiffany through her gritted teeth.

Mom sniffed. "Really, dear, fishnet is inappropriate in a society wedding." Tossing the first gown aside, she snatched the next one in the pile.

Picking up the hanger, I straightened to find a perfectly coifed woman. With a fake smile surgically grafted to her skin, the owner took the dress from my outstretched hand.

"Sorry," I mouthed.

Her eyes flicked from me to Mom and back, the pleading evident. Like I could stop the rampage.

"No, no, this one won't do, either." The bundle of satin flew in my general direction.

Tiffany planted silver-decked fists on her non-existent hips. "I don't need—"

Mom just tutted and reached for the next dress in Antoine's arms. She held the blinding whiteness in front of the seething enforcer. "What do you think, Antoine?"

He shook his head. "I really would suggest off-white or pale rose with

Ms. Stephens's coloring," Antoine simpered. "Nothing fitted with her—" His cough barely registered as semi-discreet. "—delicate condition," he finished sotto voce.

Mom shot him a nasty look. I switched to gnawing on my lower lip and stared at the ceiling to keep from breaking out in hysterics. Tiffany's pre-marital pregnancy was a touchy subject for everyone, except Max since it proved my brother's manhood. But she was a little over seven weeks along so it wasn't like the baby would be showing on her petite frame at the wedding.

"I'll give him delicate," Tiffany muttered. I held my breath, but she didn't reach for the silver dagger tucked in her right boot.

A gusty sigh blew from Antoine's artificially puffed lips. "Not much we can do about the hair."

Red flared across Tiffany's pale cheeks. I released the pent-up breath when she didn't reach for the dart gun in her messenger bag either. The silver iodide and concentrated garlic solution may not be lethal to a human, but it stung like hell.

Antoine's shook his head. "And that atrocious make-up she has on simply won't do—"

Tiffany leapt, black-nailed hands reaching for Antoine's throat.

Okay, I didn't foresee that one. Mr. Cuddles yipped and dove back into Mom's purse.

Honestly, I could have stopped Tiffany, but it was more fun to watch the nineteen-year-old goth try to strangle Mom's snobby image consultant. That is, if she could find his pencil neck amid all the taffeta.

"Samantha! Do something!" Mom's shriek had more to do with mortification at the scene Tiffany made than concern over harm to Antoine. Especially now that everyone in the boutique, not just the owner, watched Tiffany pound Antoine's head against the floor. Lucky for him, it was plush carpet instead of something harder.

I sighed and rolled my eyes. "Tiff?"

She was too far gone, screaming insults at Antoine that definitely wouldn't win her brownie points with the Gay and Lesbian Alliance. I scooped her up under my left arm, but she still had a firm grasp on Antoine's emerald collarless silk shirt. I shook her, as if she were Mr. Cuddles and I'd caught him humping one of my stuffed animals. Unlike Mr. Cuddles, Tiffany ignored me and continued her assault.

I shook Tiffany again. Antoine's head bobbed, but she still wouldn't let go. On the third shake, it registered in her pea-brain that I had her hoisted on my hip. She dropped Antoine, whose skull hit the carpet with a dense *thud.*

"Put me the fuck down, bitch!" She began fighting me in earnest. Not that it had much effect in her awkward position or with my new gifts.

"Let me go, you freak! So help me, I'm going to whip your z—"

I slapped my free hand over her mouth. Tiffany bit me. Hard. I discovered how difficult it was to keep a smile planted on my face while Goth Girl gnawed on my palm.

"We're just going to step outside and have a little girl-to-girl chat. Be right back, Mom." I hauled the still struggling Tiffany out the boutique door and into the hot afternoon California sun. Mom said nothing behind me. I guess she wasn't too worried about Tiffany's "delicate condition".

Once outside of the boutique, I set Tiffany upright. She stomped back a couple of paces on the sidewalk, her breathing heavy. She glared at me, fingers flexing, but she didn't reach for either the silver dagger, the gun or the pencils in the pockets of her camouflage pants. She was the only enforcer I had met whose favorite weapon against rogue vampires was a yellow No. 2.

Eyeing her just as warily, I shook my right hand to get some feeling back into it. A quick glance showed that she had nearly severed off a large chunk of flesh. I may heal fast, but a wound like that still hurts like a sonuvabitch for the few seconds it existed. After a minute, not even a bruise showed, but I had to fish in my shoulder bag for a tissue to wipe off the excess blood.

"You still haven't told your folks, have you?" Tiffany's expression wasn't friendly, but it no longer had that endearing maniacal quality.

"No, I haven't." I shoved the nasty-looking tissue back in a Ziploc I kept in my bag for these types of occasions, crossed my arms and glared back at her. I didn't like the reminder of the ticking clock over my head. Jack Bauer didn't have this much pressure. "But you have no excuse for screaming the z-word in public. You know better."

She had the grace to look abashed and muttered, "Sorry." With a gusty exhalation, all the fight rushed out of her. She slumped against the boutique's brick wall. "You're right. I've never slipped up in front of Normals like that."

I believed her. Ignorance was bliss when it came to John and Jane Public. The less they knew about the supernatural world, the better off everyone was. And Tiffany had been living in the dual cultures far longer than my measly two months.

The tears welling up in her big, brown eyes disturbed me on more levels than I cared to admit. Weepy was not a word anyone would use to describe Tiffany. I stepped forward and laid a hand on her shoulder. "It's probably the hormones talking, but—"

"I know, I know." She wiped the tears away on the hem of her black t-shirt, leaving streaks of blue-black mascara across her pale cheeks. "I'll be more careful."

I let my hand fall from her shoulder, reassured that Tiffany had regained control of her temper. Her touch on my sleeve stopped me as I turned back for the door. My initial tension released at her uneasy expression.

"Sam, it's not my business, but—" She paused as if searching for the right words. This had to be a first. I mean, Tiffany? Using tact?

She glanced around to make sure no one was near, but she still lowered her voice. "Maybe you should tell your parents the truth before they find out accidentally."

"Ri-i-ight." I glanced around myself, but few shoppers were on the sidewalk this time of day with the unusual spring heat. "The only thing Mom and Dad are going to love more than Max knocking you up is finding out I'm a zombie."

⤜⚬⤛

Zombie Wedding is available at your favorite online retailer.

Acknowledgements

So many people to thank and I pray I don't forget them all:

Love and thanks to DH for encouraging me to follow the dream and GK for shoving the laptop case in my hand and telling me to go to the coffee shop so I wouldn't be grumpy.

To Will Graham and Nina Cordoba for having the courage to read the original story.

Many thanks to my critique group, the Panera Pals: Nancy Bowden, Christie Craig, Jody Payne and Teri Thackston.

To my original cover artist Sierra Acy who gave me the perfect cover that I needed at the time.

And a special thank you to my mentor, the marvelous Colleen Thompson, who told me I had a great title and to fight for it if some publisher wanted to change it. I'm lucky the head of Angry Sheep Publishing is such a smart lady and agreed with Colleen.

SUZAN HARDEN transitioned from writing information technology manuals for companies and legal articles for a law enforcement magazine to her first love, fantasy and science fiction in all their forms. She's the author of the Millersburg Magick Mysteries, the Soccer Moms of the Apocalypse series, and the Books of Apep series.

Contact Suzan Harden

Facebook: Suzan Harden
Email: suzan@suzanharden.com
Website: www.suzanharden.com

Sign up for Suzan's mailing list

www.ingramcontent.com/pod-product-compliance
Lightning Source LLC
Chambersburg PA
CBHW072003180726
48291CB00002BA/556